The Singer
Behind
the Wire

BOOKS BY SHARI J. RYAN

The Bookseller of Dachau

The Doctor's Daughter

The Lieutenant's Girl

The Maid's Secret

The Stolen Twins

The Homemaker

The Glovemaker's Daughter

The Perfect Nanny

The Nurse Behind the Gates

My Husband's Past

The Family Behind the Walls

LAST WORDS

The Girl with the Diary

The Prison Child

The Soldier's Letters

The Singer Behind the Wire

SHARI J. RYAN

bookouture

Published by Bookouture in 2025

An imprint of Storyfire Ltd.
Carmelite House
50 Victoria Embankment
London EC4Y 0DZ

www.bookouture.com

The authorised representative in the EEA is Hachette Ireland
8 Castlecourt Centre
Dublin 15 D15 XTP3
Ireland
(email: info@hbgi.ie)

ISBN: 978-1-80550-015-5
eBook ISBN: 978-1-80550-014-8

To the ones who never forget.

PROLOGUE

ELLA

September 1943
Auschwitz, Poland

The winds shift, and the sharp stench of sweat and burned flesh chokes me. My stomach contracts into a hollow pit but still revolts. Jarring shouts from block-elders—the submissive servants to the SS officers—echo off the towering grid of red and brown brick buildings enclosing us. In the center of a long row of sickly, pale prisoners who look just like me, I stand in my tattered, blue-striped uniform, shivering and weak from malnutrition, trying to ignore the bitter taste coating my tongue.

I'm strong enough to remain upright. I must remain still, though the squelching mud pulls at my feet and the sea of swaying skeletal bodies presses close.

The numbers are endless, one for each of us, called out one by one until they're all claimed. My number rings out, followed by the next—muddled syllables. Names are just a memory, and the countless faces around me blur into one. I lift my arm at the sound of my number then let it fall like dead weight against my side.

A bruised lump protruding from the shaven head in front of me is my focal point as I block out the sound of other women collapsing nearby, their bony legs buckling beneath them as a surrender to the end. I can't watch it happen. *Don't look. Don't think. Keep your eyes forward.* Despite closing my eyes, I see the truth of what I live among. My ribs sweep against the terse fabric of my prison smock, and my fingers are numb from clenching them into fists for so long.

The last number is called, and we're dismissed by a piercing whistle that weaves through the air and slices my ears like a knife. I fall into another line and shuffle forward. With caution, I take each step, hoping not to trip along one of the muddy divots my clogs often catch on. *Don't fall. Please.*

I pass by two barrack blocks before reaching the one I've been assigned. Those of us on the second floor struggle with the narrow stairwell, each step creaking and bowing beneath our weight. The corroding wooden walls, sloping ceilings and three-tiered bunks greet me at the top where I search for my sleeping square shared by three women. There isn't a space unclaimed.

My listless body clambers into a narrow spot on the second-level tier and squeezes in between two others already lying limply on top of the thin, straw-filled mattress we share. With my coarse canvas blanket, I wrap myself up tightly, hoping it will protect me from bedbugs and lice. I can only try to convince myself it's clean and will keep me safe.

Our assigned block-elder, Francine, a tall, middle-aged woman with masculine shoulders, accentuated by the man's overcoat she wears as a shawl, prowls around with a permanent sneer that deforms the lower half of her face. Her heavy foot-steps as she walks with a sense of vengeance boom louder than anything else.

"What is this?" Francine growls, tone demanding. She should have already left for the privileged living quarters within the block-elder's building, but it's clear she's still here looking for someone's mistake—an oversight she can report. Every infraction she writes up boosts her appearance of loyalty to the SS. Her wooden clogs thud with each step, and my muscles tense, terrified of what she's referring to. "A black and red floral scarf, left on the ground." She clucks her tongue and taps her fingers against her coat sleeve. "This is a cherished item, isn't it?" she teases with glee. "Probably just a silly reminder of home, I assume?" I breathe a silent sigh of relief—it isn't mine— but the tension returns as I await what comes next...

"It's mine, it belongs to me," a woman cries out. "I didn't mean to—"

"What a shame," Francine says, releasing an exaggerated breath before slowly, meticulously, tearing the fabric in half.

I jam my fists against my ears, trying to drown out the sound of her looming punishment. With my eyes squeezed shut, I will myself to believe I'm somewhere else, not listening to my barrack-mate's cries of pain.

The floor shudders beneath me as Francine makes her way out the door, signaling that the punishment is over...for now.

Timely as ever, the second gong rattles the walls, a warning for the lights to go out, bringing me to the moment I fear all day: the darkness between the sweeping spotlights and the long shadows of barbed-wire fences on the chipped, white-washed barrack walls is unlike anything I knew before Auschwitz.

A black canvas sprawls through my head as a flood of memories from the day and all prior days here return in full color, vivid and fresh to loop along an endless reel of film.

The definition of silence here is the moans of prisoners, the creaking wooden bunks, and the steady patter of rain on the old roof—a symphony of suffering.

With a shaky breath, I drop my fists and roll onto my side, clutching the rough canvas sheet to my chin. Outside, the wind whistles, and then the rain ends, a hum of silent static filling the air.

My heart hammers in my chest as I lie motionless, confined to this one spot for the long hours of the night. But then—there's a sound in the silence.

A prisoner, forced to sing.

The song kindles faintly, like the first glimmer of sun cresting over the horizon in pursuit of the endless night—a velvety hum slips through the cracks of the windows, wrapping me in its embrace. I draw in a breath, straining to catch every note until the song grows clearer, the gentle melody a caress against my fractured heart.

It's my Luka.

His voice is the one thing I live for now. He's close enough to hear, but unreachable with the barbed-wire fences separating us in the pit of Auschwitz. *He's still alive. That's what matters. We've made it another night here.*

Despite the torture we all face here, Luka's voice still somehow defies the despair surrounding us, carrying a sense of comfort and hope, even with the growing damage to his singing voice. It's as if his life depends on each word...

> *The sky is dark and gray*
> *but behind the clouds, it's blue.*
> *Lovely days will come*
> *soon for me and you.*

If his voice were a record, I might think it was scratched—the struggle in the lyrics, the gravel lining every other word... something's wrong.

> *Keep me in your dreams,*
> *and I'll co—*

A blunt crack slices through the air. The song halts mid-word, choked by Luka's sudden gut-wrenching howl of pain. Then there is only silence...

I can't blink, breathe, or move. My body stiffens like ice as I wait for what comes next. Or is this...

The end?

ONE

ELLA

May 1940
Warsaw, Poland

My fingers tighten around the handlebars of my bicycle as I pass through the quiet, narrow and winding roads along the desolate outskirts of Leszno Street in Warsaw's Jewish quarter. The vacant shops, shattered windows, and scattered rubbish cry of an abandoned district, but that isn't the case. German soldiers lurk everywhere in Poland now, and have done since last September when the Wehrmacht, Germany's unified armed forces invaded our country. However, their presence is much greater in the Jewish districts as their demand for relentless control grows by the day.

It's hard to tell if the residents are locked inside, hiding, or if they've left Warsaw altogether. I try not to fear the soldiers, but they lurk in inconspicuous places just to stir up paranoia, then emerge like dark creatures from a nightmare to demand proof of identification.

Being nineteen and the daughter of a Polish Catholic grocer, I spend most of my time working at our family store.

The little free time I have hasn't allowed me to visit this district since segregation laws, ration cuts, and curfews closed in on our city. However, working in the grocery as endless lines of customers come and go, I overhear whispered accounts of life there...the public beatings and arrests for something as minor as questioning a German soldier. Still, nothing compares to seeing it up close. These streets were once bustling with life—horse-drawn wagons, bookshops, and street vendors selling newspapers and fresh produce. Now, the streets are nearly vacant.

Even the air is stale, not a hint of baked goods or fresh flowers, scents that once cloaked the district with a friendly warm welcoming. It's a different city within our city. *These people—they are us*. We're all Poles. Yet, in the eyes of the Wehrmacht, it's the Jewish people they despise most of all.

I came down here at my father's request, delivering a wrapped bundle of bread to a Jewish woman—a former neighbor and friend of my parents. He said she's been unwell, but when she opened the door, her gaunt figure and drooping eyes spoke more of hunger than illness. All of Warsaw is suffering from food shortages, but the Jewish population survives on half of the rations we do.

The surrounding desolation yanks at my heart as I veer toward the main road, but a nearby spark of commotion distracts me from my direction. I clutch the handbrake of my bicycle and lower my feet to the ground, listening for where the noise is coming from.

A melody floats around the corner, carried by a soulful voice singing an uplifting tune. I haven't heard anyone singing on the streets anywhere in Warsaw in a very long time. Curiosity gets the best of me as I take a turn down a side street, the squeaky gears of my bicycle echoing between building walls. I peek around the corner before entering the square, finding a gathering of people.

"Please, do you have any food to spare?" The question

breaks through the music, startling me. I hadn't noticed the old woman before, her black scarf draped over her head and knotted beneath her chin. She's sitting on the ground with her back against the building, studying me carefully. Her eyes beg louder than her words, and my heart breaks when I realize I have nothing left to give her.

"I'm so sorry," I utter, my throat tightening as I continue forward into the square. *I should do something. There must be something.* The swift change between the sight of what must be someone's starving grandmother, and a slew of whistles zinging through the air makes me dizzy.

I move toward the crowd of people and settle within a nook alongside a building. An elderly couple pass, the husband in something of a tizzy. "That boy is asking for trouble. All the folks listening, too. The last thing we need around here is a gathering."

"It's just a song," the wife argues.

"Well, it won't be long before we'll be forbidden from singing, too," the husband states, ending the argument.

I haven't heard of public gatherings being a crime, but the rules are different in the Jewish district.

For a short moment, a flicker of disappointment sets in, assuming I've missed the beautiful performance, but when the cheers fade into silence, a beautiful harmony ascends and spirals around me, sending a chill down my spine.

> *How can I not start to sigh?*
> *I'm wondering, wondering why*
> *the world is feeling unkind.*
> *but soon I know we will find*
>
> *Our way back to smiles and love.*
> *The sun will shine brightly above.*

And once again we will be,
who we once were, we'll be free.

His voice—so pure, smooth, and flawless. It's as if he's singing from his soul. His voice pulses through me like flickering sparks, drawing a smile along my lips, and tears from my eyes. The crowd shifts, offering a peephole view of the man they're surrounding. He's young, younger than the sound of his voice, but maybe older than me. He's smiling, too—it's contagious. No one smiles anymore, but here...they are.

"Look at them," a man mutters in German, nudging his counterpart.

The second man lets out a snort. "These people can't figure out when to be quiet."

"We should remind him," the first man says, tapping his fingers against his holster.

I peer to my left at the two, watching the evil glimmer in the soldiers' eyes.

They both laugh as if killing innocent people is a joke. Still watching them in disbelief, I notice one reach for the whistle dangling from his neck. My heart pounds and heat writhes through me as I rebalance my weight on my bike and push forward to leave the nook. I head straight for the crowd. "Pardon me," I say again and again, warning people I'm coming through.

Shrill whistles cut through the air as German commands ring loudly in the square. The cobblestones scrape beneath my bicycle tires as I skid my feet against the rubble, stopping my bike from rolling into the man who was performing and his flattop hat sitting by his feet, filled with one-cent coins. Fist fights are breaking out behind me and to the sides, everyone stumbling to escape but caught between too many others as the German soldiers move in closer, enforcing terror.

"All Jews, stay where you are!" a soldier hollers.

The singer wears a black overcoat, unbuttoned over a white dress shirt, dark pants, and worn black boots. His white armband donning the Star of David, stands in stark contrast against the dark fabric. They're all branded this way. My heart pounds as I glance around, caught between fear and instinct. *I shouldn't even be considering what I can do to help...* I don't have anything to offer anyone. But his voice—the raw hope it carries, compels me. Before I can stop myself, I drop my bike and hop to the side.

Why am I doing this? The thought echoes through me as I run toward the singer. "Run," I whisper. He hesitates for a split-second, and in that second, our gazes meet. His hooded eyes, hazel, flecked with a hint of blue, and fringed with dark lashes, steal my ragged breath. Our shared look, fierce with disbelief, speaks through our silent exchange. "Did you hear me?" My words come out in a hiss as I grab his armband, tear it from his sleeve, snatch up his hat full of coins and shove both against his chest. "Go!"

I whip my head around, searching in every direction for who might have witnessed my defiant act, but with everyone scampering away, I don't think anyone was focused on us. *Us? What has gotten into me?* Our eyes meet for one more fleeting moment, carrying an inexplicable draw to him, and a need to prove humanity still exists among us. Finally, he takes off running, weaving through the others.

The whistles grow louder, and I grab my bike's handlebars and jump back on, turning in a circle along the stone to leave the inlet.

"You there, halt!" a soldier shouts, pointing at the singer.

Keep running, I want to shout out to him.

I pick up speed on my bike and ride through the dispersing commotion, wondering why anyone would stay and do as they were commanded while others have fled to hide. The whistles blow again, louder and piercing. "Jews, line up!"

Are they really going to punish these people for simply standing together in the square?

Both soldiers have assault rifles clutched in their grips and my veins flood with cold as my heart races with anger. As I approach the space between the soldiers and the group of quivering Jewish people, I deliberately let my front tire catch on a cobblestone divot and tumble off my bike. The action is jarring, but it works. I crash hard onto the street. Pain fires through my ankle, sharp and stinging, but I don't let myself stop to think about it.

My purse spills out of the basket, scattering its contents across the ground. I cry out and clutch my ankle, the pitch of my voice drawing the attention of the German soldiers who walk toward me, their faces expressionless.

With a sideways glance, I spot the Jewish people slipping away, their desperate movements hidden by the growing commotion. Relief consumes me, but it's quickly replaced by the weight of what I've just done. I'm shaking, not from the pain, but from realizing I've just acted out in a form of resistance.

"You shouldn't be here," one of the soldiers says to me, his voice gruff as he hauls me to my feet.

I don't wear a white armband with the Star of David because I'm not Jewish, and my blonde hair and blue eyes make it easy for others to mistake my Polish heritage. At times, it seems I can move along more freely than most, but there's no mistaking the vitriol these German soldiers have for all Poles.

Everything inside of me wants to fight back, to tell them they're nothing but scoundrels with weapons. I should have the right to be wherever I choose. So should the Jewish people of this city. This is *our* home.

"I—I got lost," I stutter and reach for my hurt ankle, trying to sound more pitiful. "All that whistling—well, it startled me."

"Is that right? You're lost?" one of them asks as the others share a laugh.

My heart hammers against my ribs as I question whether they'll accept my lie. And what will happen if they don't...

TWO

ELLA

I peer up through my lashes at the German soldiers, ashamed of my fake damsel-like behavior. "Here, let me help you, miss." One of them helps me to my feet and the other scoops up my belongings from my purse, drops them back inside and lifts my bicycle back upright.

"Do you need a doctor?"

"Oh, bother. No, I'm all right. Please, I need to get home. My father is expecting me," I say, brushing my hands off on my dress before taking the handlebars into my grip.

"How about I help you get home," one of them offers.

Dear God. Would anyone agree to this offer? He must be out of his mind. The thought of a German soldier taking me home...it's unthinkable. I shake my head and smooth my hair down behind my ears. "My father is waiting for me and I'm late. I'll be fine finding my way home." With a shove forward against the handlebars on my bicycle, I walk alongside it, making sure to accentuate my limp as I do.

The Jewish people have all made it out of the square. *Thank goodness*. I breathe a sigh of relief, knowing all those people made it away from the soldiers safely. I turn down the main road to go home, my heart hammering against my chest as I realize what I just did. What I risked for a stranger.

This isn't the first time I've thought about defying German laws, but it's the first time something has pushed me to this point. Before today, I've tried to mind my own business aside from delivering a few "packages" to friends of my parents, but not in the Jewish district. Of course, I've shared my feelings of helplessness in the face of so much persecution happening all around us here, only to be met with the stern warning of danger by my parents.

Complacency isn't an option when so many are suffering, and I'm not the only one who feels this way, especially seeing as we avoid discussions about my father and brother sneaking off every night to "help" our fellow citizens. I've asked to join many times, but I'm a "proper young woman and should follow the laws," as they tell me. Yet, here I am, forming a distraction that could cost me the freedom I have left. *I would do it again if I had to.* Maybe I'm tired of being a "proper young woman."

Now that I'm out of sight and far enough away from the square, I stop and curl over the front of my bike, clutching my chest to catch my breath before I continue. Those soldiers take far too much pride in walking around, torturing innocent people. It's obvious their intent was to steal the one inkling of happiness some of the Jewish people found tonight while listening to the beautiful music.

Thugs. They're all thugs who want to steal every bit of our bravery.

I continue home as a fleeting memory of the singer flashes through my mind. His talent and charm, unmatched with anything I've seen before. But everything beautiful about him was overshadowed by the fear in his eyes as the soldiers shouted their threats.

I made a hasty decision trying to help him, but it was because he was bringing other people happiness—something so rare to find these days. My erratic reaction was a split-second decision and came without a thought of consequence. The soldiers could have arrested me. *But they didn't.*

"Miss?" A whisper pulls my attention back down the street, finding someone standing in a sharp angular shadow of the building.

I move faster.

"Wait, please, wait." His voice...the sound. He speaks the way he sings. "Why did you save me?" He sounds perplexed, concerned even.

I falter, glancing behind me, finding the singer with his hand on his heart and the other clenched around his hat. After searching in each direction to make sure there isn't a soldier within sight, I roll my bike down the dark street toward the man. "You're the singer," I say in awe.

I step in closer, joining him in the shadow where I can catch a better glimpse of him. He's tall and slender, his dark loose curls framing the corners of his eyes. He's...quite breathtaking. "I—I'm just a girl who foolishly fell off her bike," I argue.

"'Foolishly,'" he repeats. "Is that right?" He smirks and raises an eyebrow. "Are you hurt?"

I stare as a shimmer of light cuts across his eyes, revealing his soul. This man is a stranger and I shouldn't be standing on an empty street with someone I've never met before.

"Ah—oh dear, no, I'm well," I tell him.

"That was a pretty hard fall," he says. I must have played the part well. My body certainly thinks so.

"Truly, I'll be all right, but thank you for checking on me." Is that all he was doing? Checking on me? I sound like a young, lovesick girl in the face of a stranger.

"How can I thank you?"

"There's no need, I assure you."

"Don't be so humble," he says, his words sharp and unexpected. "No one does anything for nothing these days."

"Humble?" I quip. "Is it a crime to help a person?"

"When your ankle is bleeding through your sock, it might be."

I look down at my feet, finding my white ankle sock soaked in blood. He crouches down on his knee, places his hat down and rolls my sock below my ankle. His tousled dark hair blows in the breeze as he peers up at me. "That's a good one. We should get you bandaged up."

"I don't have anything—"

"You must have something in your purse," he says, standing back up. He takes the bike from my hands and leans it up against the brick wall behind him, then takes my purse out of the front basket. "I've heard women can keep an entire pharmacy stored in one small bag."

He pulls open my purse and I'm taken aback by his forwardness—and a bit amused.

He shakes his head. "See here...a handkerchief and two bobby pins." He pulls them out of my purse, then hands me my bag and drops back down to his knee before tending to my ankle. My chest tightens as he carefully wraps the fabric over the wound. His hands are steady, despite everything that's just happened.

"I'm more than capable of taking care of myself—" I say, my words hesitant.

"I can see that," he replies, ignoring my statement as he secures the handkerchief with the two bobby pins and pulls my sock back up. The kind gesture jolts my nerves in an unfamiliar way—a pleasant way. "There. Good as new." He brushes himself off as he stands.

I can't stop myself from grinning as a warm blush fills my cheeks. "Well, it seems I have a reason to repay you for *your* kindness?"

"There's no need," he says, his dimples deepening.

"Oh, don't be so humble," I retort, throwing his words back at him.

His smile wanes as he fiddles with the loose braid dangling over my shoulder. "Could I at least walk you home?"

"What if I live across the city? You'd be walking all night."

"It doesn't matter, because I'd be sure you got home safely," he says. Except the Jewish people have a curfew that begins at seven o'clock—in less than an hour. Even without the armband, his identification stamped with the letter "J" would betray him. If the soldiers caught him out after curfew, they'd arrest him on the spot.

"I don't live too far from here." I don't accept his offer, but don't reject it either.

He takes my bicycle from the brick wall and begins walking with it on his right side, me to his left.

"Your voice—I've never heard anything like it. It—well, it reminds me of Fred Astaire. Have you been singing your whole life?"

He takes in a deep breath and holds it for a long second before exhaling. "Well, to avoid being too humble for this conversation, I thank you for your kind words, and yes, I have been singing my entire life, but only in my bedroom for the most part. When my father and grandfather lost their jobs, I had to help. I didn't think performing on the street would be my work for too long, but until the others tire of me, I'll keep showing up."

We walk in silence as my mind races with hundreds of questions, my pulse racing with every aching step forward.

"My turn to ask you a question now. Why did you save me?" he asks.

I hesitate, because it all happened so fast. "Those German soldiers... I overheard them talking, they were saying terrible things and making jokes about lining all the Jewish people up and—they wanted to terrorize everyone. It was the right thing to do," I say with a shrug.

He stops walking, so I do, too, finding him gazing at me with wonder. "A few weeks ago, the Reich imposed new laws prohibiting large public gatherings in Jewish communities. I wouldn't classify the size of the crowd in the square today as being large, nor have they caused a commotion before today, but I don't make those rules."

"Will you have to stop singing now?" I ask, staring up at him, finding despair filling his eyes.

He shakes his head and straightens his shoulders. "No, no. I should be more mindful of the crowd, I suppose."

"They all want to hear you sing," I utter. "Who can blame them?"

His cheeks burn as he fights a small smile, but the smile fades just as fast when his eyebrows knit together. "You could have gotten yourself in trouble with those soldiers today. What if they went after you?"

I drop my gaze and press my hand to my chest. "They didn't."

A sigh floats over my head. "They might not let you go next time."

Before I can respond, a throaty voice cuts through the air: "You two! Stop and retrieve your papers."

I gasp and twist around, finding two soldiers cruising toward us on a motorcycle with a sidecar. For a split second, I can't move, my mind racing over every option for escape—but there's no time. I grab my bike from his hands. "Get on," I whisper, my voice shaky. *Are they after us?* He swings his leg over the seat as I clamber onto the metal basket in front. His hands wrap around my hips as he helps me balance my weight. The heat from his touch radiates through me, adding another layer of shock to the frenzy. "Now, go!" I shout through a breath. The wind stings against my face and my pulse thrums between my ears as we lurch forward.

I clench my grip on the basket, my heart bouncing around in the same rhythmic speed and pattern as the hop on every cobblestone. I haven't acted so recklessly since I was a curious young girl searching for the tallest trees to climb with the hope of someday touching a cloud. Now, fleeing for safety and protection—escaping the enemy—it's as if I'm reaching for the clouds again.

The street twists and turns into sharp bends, and the bike wobbles below us. "Hold on tight," he rasps through a labored breath. For a fleeting second, I believe we might escape.

Then, a guttural rumble whomps through the air, bouncing between the buildings. They're following us.

"Stop now, or we shoot!" a soldier shouts over a sputtering engine.

I glance over my shoulder, finding the motorcycle gaining on us, and the soldier in the sidecar is armed with a pistol, pointing it directly at us. I face forward and clench my eyes as a sharp crack fires from the pistol. Something whizzes past my ear.

The singer swerves, the bike skidding as the front wheel scrapes against the cobblestone.

Too close. Far too close.

A metallic shatter screams through the air. A bullet hit the frame and the handlebars jerk. He's barely keeping control. I clench my teeth and grip the basket so hard the metal is biting into my flesh.

"We'll find you, girl! We don't forget a face!" they shout.

My limbs grow cold, knowing they saw me, but that might not matter since they're closing in on us. What we do next could determine whether we're still breathing tomorrow…

THREE

LUKA

I should be counting my blessings, escaping from prowling soldiers and gestapo twice in one night. On my savior's bike, with her perched precariously on the basket, we managed to lose the German soldiers, taking a sharp turn down a dark narrow inlet of an alley. We've been standing here, barely breathing, for long minutes now, our backs pinned to the gritty edifice of the building behind us. I've come to notice our height difference—she's a head shorter than me, petite, almost delicate-looking with her long blonde braid and light-colored freckles flecked across her cheeks and nose. But there's a bold, fiery spirit within her actions that defies societal norms. Her impish edge radiates with real spirit. Yet, despite her show of revolt, she exudes natural beauty and sweetness—breathtaking femininity. One could easily confuse her for a timid, dainty woman at first glance. And they would be quite wrong.

A sudden roll of laughter spills out of her like a deflating balloon. "Dear me...I thought we were done for," she says, pressing her hand to her white button-down blouse as her olive green and gray plaid skirt sweeps against my hand with a passing gust of wind. "You've escaped a soldier or two in the past, haven't you?"

"Running from a soldier isn't one of my favorite skills, but a necessary one, unfortunately," I tell her.

"Well, it's clear skill and talent runs deep in your veins," she says. "By the way, I'm sorry for tearing your badge, but—"

"It was—it was my favorite. It fit just right," I say with a huff, keeping a straight face.

"Oh, dear! I'm—I didn't want them to come after you for singing in the square."

The laughter rolls out of me. I'm not sure when the last time I've even let out a laugh was, it's like stretching a muscle that's been restrained for far too long. "I was making a joke."

She breathes a sigh of relief. "Thank goodness."

"I'm sorry, I couldn't stop myself. But truly, the day I don't have to wear a badge to walk down the street will be quite liberating. You did me a favor, and I'm grateful."

A blush sweeps over her pink cheeks as she drops her stormy-blue, doe-like gaze. "I'm glad I could help."

My heart is tumbling in my chest, and my clammy palms tell me I'm a fool for allowing myself to notice so many details about this woman, who I'll likely never have the privilege of meeting again. A Jewish man and a non-Jewish woman, conversing in this way—it's trouble in the making per German law.

"Let's get you home," I tell her, grabbing the bicycle handles to pull it upright away from the wall.

"You already did," she says with a quiet laugh. "I live in this building here. The door is right around the corner. What about you? How long will it take you to get home?" she asks, breathlessly. "Curfew is in ten minutes for you." Panic laces her words.

Curfew. I gaze up at the darkening sky as if I need proof of nightfall. The heaviness of time weighs on my chest. "My apartment is less than a dozen blocks from here." If I walk quickly and take a direct route, which will surely be guarded by gestapo, I could make it in time. But those aren't the safest roads to take home. The alternate route will take longer than ten minutes...

"Take my bicycle so you can get home quickly," she offers.

"No, no. I can't—we're not allowed—I'll be fine, I assure you," I say, my heart pounding with a mixture of anger and disappointment. I want to stay here and talk to her. I've never met this girl before, but there's a sense of familiarity about her, like a distant memory whispering to me. I clasp my hand around the back of my neck, searching for something more to say, biding time I don't have.

"Will I see you again?" My question blurts out before I've had a chance to think it through.

Her gaze flickers toward the main road before staring back up at me. "You shouldn't be asking such things," she says with a coy smile.

"Yes, I'm aware. But I am," I respond softly.

She straightens her skirt then curls the wild blonde strands of hair flying free from her braid behind her ears. Again, my heart gallops in my chest—all I can do is stare at her, wondering where she came from tonight and why she chose to help me, of all people. If I believed in angels, I might consider the thought. She's as beautiful as one.

A hollering in the distance breaks our stare and she grasps the handles of her bicycle. "Please be careful," she says. "Hurry home. Don't let them find you."

I take a step backward and drop my hands into my pockets, but she doesn't turn away. We're captured in the moment with a longing stare I wish could last all night, until I force myself to break away. "Right—well, good—good night now," I say, my words rattling against each other as I turn and jog off in the opposite direction.

"Good night," she replies, her voice falling off in the distance.

I stare straight ahead at the darkening roads, wondering if I'll ever catch another glimpse of her. "Wait!" I stop and turn around, as if she'd still be standing at the corner. But she's gone. It's too late. I never asked for her name...

FOUR

LUKA

The uneven pavement presses against the worn soles of my old shoes as I move along the darkening streets, keeping a stern eye out for any other meandering soldiers as I make it home right in time for curfew. I had been tempted to risk the time, if it had meant spending another few minutes with the girl whose name I might never know.

I turn the last corner onto my street, the road too narrow for vehicles to drive through. A few neighbors are sitting outside on wooden crates. One is smoking, another is talking to himself, and a young boy is searching through a pile of rubbish with determination, as if he's lost something very important.

"What are you looking for, Jak? Did you lose something?" I ask him while passing by.

"No, no," he utters through a groan. "It's nothing."

"Well, it can't be nothing," I argue. "You're looking quite hard for—nothing, yes?"

Jak takes a step back from the rubbish and takes a few deep breaths, wheezing through them. "It was an old toy. I was going to give away, but it must have ended up in the rubbish pile."

"What is this toy?" I ask.

Jak takes a shuddered breath. "It was just a stupid old stuffed bear. No one would want it, anyway."

I've seen Jak with this bear. It's small and he's had it since he was very little. Though he's only nine or ten now. I want to tell him I understand why he's looking so hard for something that he's attached to. We all need items like that now.

"Jak, come inside at once," his mother shouts from the window above his head. "Have you seen the time?"

Jak kicks a box into the pile and scuffs his way into the side entrance. "Bye, Luka," he says.

"See you soon, kid."

I check my watch, finding I have a few minutes left before curfew, and dig through the pile, separating the larger items to one side so I can inspect what smaller items might have fallen to the bottom. One brown, stuffed arm sticks out from between some rusty tins.

I pluck the bear out and dust him off. "There you are."

On the way up the black and white checkered tile stairs, I take a hard look at the poor bear, noticing the years of love and squeezing it has endured. Poor kid. I stop at the floor below mine and squeeze the bear to fit between the doorknob and doorframe of Jak's apartment, knowing one of them will find it in the morning.

Amid the remainder of my hike up to the third floor, it's hard to block out the background noise of arguing couples, and cries of hungry children. It doesn't matter what part of our building we're in, it's all we hear lately. I fish out the key and unlock our apartment door, stepping inside to a flickering glow of candles on the wooden kitchen table beneath the double-pane window. Then I find Mother and Father hunched together on the sofa to my left. Mother never sits on the sofa. She can't seem to sit still long enough. Father, though, he has the newspaper spread out across the lace-covered coffee table as usual, but he's not reading it—he's staring through it as if it was glass.

Grandmother and Grandfather are seated in the two rocking armchairs at either side of the sofa, but aren't rocking. Grandmother is holding her knitting needles, yarn looped between the two, stretching from the basket of colorful skeins by her feet, but her hands are still. Strands of her silver hair have come loose from the black scarf she always wears around her head, claiming it's cold inside no matter what time of year it is. Grandfather's white eyebrows are wild and look as if he's ruffled them up with the heel of his palm too many times today. He has a pipe pinched between his lips, but there's no smoke pouring out. It's like a haunting still life.

I swallow hard as heat swells through my body. They've received news—my gut says so.

"Where have you been, Luka?" Mama scolds me, standing from her seat. "Do you have any idea how worried we've been?"

I'm twenty, old enough to take a walk without having to check in. Although, I suspect they might have gotten word about the disruption in the square.

"I took the long way home to avoid the soldiers. I didn't mean to worry you." I snatch my rolled-up hat out of my coat pocket and place it down on the coffee table, the coins clattering against each other.

"No more of this. I don't want you performing anymore—and where is your armband? Luka? Do you understand what would happen if you were caught?"

"Dear, let him take his coat off. He's all right, as we can all see." My father sighs.

"This time, he is," Mother argues.

"How about I go down to the square with you tomorrow and if any of those Germans give you a hard time, I'll handle it," Grandfather says, snickering. My grandfather has no tolerance for what the Wehrmacht is doing to our country, and we try to keep him away from any encounter that will get him into trouble. My grandmother, however, she's staring between my parents at the oil painting of a tulip field hanging on the wall. An escape, perhaps.

"I removed my armband when the soldiers showed up in the square. I thought I'd be safer making a run for it than sitting around waiting for them to ask me for my papers."

"Next time, you should tell them exactly what they can do with those papers," Grandfather mutters.

"Stop it, Foter," Mother argues. Grandfather doesn't go too long without cracking a joke or trying to make light of our dim situation. It's hard to hold back my laughter sometimes, but it's best not enrage my mother. For a woman who has always had full control over this family, she isn't faring well, ensuring each one of us follow every given law and rule imposed over us.

"I've paid dues for this country. I have more rights than those nudnicks, and I'll be damned if they think they can tell me what to do. They can kish mir en—"

"Dear, no one wants to kiss your behind. Quiet down," Grandmother hushes him.

I've always agreed with my grandfather's ideals and perspective on life, and he's been one to see life through my eyes a bit clearer than most, too. He's the reason I still sing, three years after my father wanted me to give it up...

"What will the boy do with himself if singing doesn't work out for him? You've spoiled him rotten with this singing shtick and now I'm not sure he can fend for himself, if need be," Father says to Mother. They told me to go to bed an hour ago, but the walls in our apartment are thin and their argument has kept me awake.

"You're meshuga—crazy, you know that?" Mother hisses at Father. "Your father, may he rest in peace, would be so ashamed

to listen to you speak this way," Mother says. "That wonderful man had the most beautiful voice and used it for the same good as Luka uses his. He made a living out of entertaining others. Why can't we allow Luka to do the same? It's obvious he inherited your father's talent."

Father responds right away, nearly interrupting Mother's final word. "I grew up poor, dear. Sure, my father entertained people, but he would work all week and get paid bubkes. We lived off my mother's baked goods, selling them at the square markets each weekend. I want to make sure Luka will be able to provide for a wife someday, as I've done for you."

I'm seventeen and not ready to think about marriage. Father thinks I'm useless and Mother loves to hear me sing because what mother wouldn't want to listen to her son sing? I'll find a trade, something else I can succeed at, so I don't let anyone down. I'll do it on my own and prove to them I can both sing and be useful. I don't want them to argue over me.

"You're supposed to be sleeping," Grandfather says from my doorway, stepping in quietly before taking a seat on the edge of my bed. "Luka, listen to your grandfather—the one without a nice singing voice—your father kvetches because he wants to make sure you can survive in this world, and your mother will always see you as a little boy, one with an abundance of talent. They both love you more than you'll ever understand, and that is why they argue over you." Grandfather uses his hands like yapping mouths shouting at each other to prove his point and I try not to laugh.

"Then what do I do?" I whisper.

"Oy, listen. Where do your lyrics come from, huh?" he asks.

My head leans to the side with confusion. Where else could they come from other than my head? "My brain?"

"Exactly," Grandfather says. "We live in Warsaw, a city booming with opportunities—especially within radio broadcasting. When you listen to the radio, what do you hear besides music and news updates?"

"Advertisements about household products and cigarettes?" I ask.

"Yes, son. Yes," he says, shuffling his hand through my hair. "Think about finding a job with a radio station that needs jingles for products they're advertising. Newspapers need writers who can capture a reader's attention with a headline and if words come to you the way they do, there are many more opportunities out there than singing. You can do both, yes?"

All along, I've been thinking every career would involve a skill in a physical trade. The thought of journalism or media never crossed my mind. "Of course I can," I say, excitement riveting through my response.

"Shh, shh. How about this little talk of ours is a secret. Tomorrow, why don't you share your plan with your parents. I think you'll find your father...singing a different tune." Grandfather utters a chuckle at his play on words and I follow.

"Thank you, Grandfather."

"You're a mensch—really, something special, son. Don't ever let anyone tell you differently.

* * *

Grandfather has always fought for happiness and that's the legacy he's given me. Mother and Father were thrilled with the idea of me using my skills for more than singing, and the radio hired me about six months after the talk Grandfather and I had that night. They had me working on creating jingles and sometimes even singing them over the radio. It was like a dream come true, until a year later when I was let go, just because I'm a Jew.

"I can't bear much more." Mother paces back and forth between the small living room and the kitchen table.

"Chana, dear," Father says, reaching for my mother's shoulders, his tone preempting words of reason. "We don't have a choice, and you three—you, your mother, and our son—are going to need whatever money Luka can bring in—more than ever now."

His statement makes my blood run cold. Something has happened while I've been gone. "What do you mean, 'you three'?" I ask, struggling to pull my coat off my shoulders.

The silence following my question should be enough of an answer, but with how much has changed over the past year, it's hard to predict what they're about to say.

"Your father and grandfather are being sent to Skarżysko-Kamienna for factory work next week. It's slave labor, unpaid. They're just being taken from us," Mother squawks, throwing her arms up in the air.

My heart pounds and sweat crawls up my spine as I try to digest this news. "Why them? What about me?" Why would they send my grandfather and not me?

"I—I'm not sure, Luka. Your name wasn't on the letter," Mother says, her voice tense. Her heavy brown eyes focus on the ground as she shifts her weight from foot to foot while fidgeting with her apron's fraying hem. "May—maybe perhaps —well, it could be because you've never worked in a factory before." A breath hitches in her throat. "We should just be grateful you were spared."

I turn away to hang my coat up on the hook by the door next to Father's tan overcoat, trying to make sense of it all.

I return to the living room where my grandparents are still seated and drop my gaze, letting out a heavy exhale as I form one of many questions barreling through my head. "This makes no sense. I'm capable of labor and, well, grandfather is in no such condition. He shouldn't be the one going. It should be me."

Grandfather holds up his arm and flexes, pointing to his thin biceps. "I will be just fine. You see that?" He squeezes his other hand around his flexed arm.

"Oy," Grandmother says. "Stop it. You're embarrassing yourself."

I hold my palms up, silently asking everyone to stop. "This is absurd. There must be a mistake, or an oversight."

"It doesn't matter. You're not going," Grandfather states with a hard stare. "Kapeesh?"

I nod, but I don't mean it. It's not right. "For how long? I mean, how long will you be gone?"

"The letter didn't say. We can hope it's temporary, right?" Father asks, smoothing his fingers through his thin, graying hair that he neatly slicks back every morning. He stares at mother and adjusts his round rimmed black glasses as if sending her a secret sign, but it's a nervous habit. His eyes say one thing—worry—and his words say another, and I'm at a loss for what I should be thinking.

I'm not sure how either of them will be able to work in a factory line all day. We've been living off scraps of food for nearly a year, and it shows in all of us.

Father moves over to the coffee table and lifts my hat, jingling the coins. "I'm baffled by how you're managing to get as much as you are when no one has anything left, but you must keep doing what you're doing. Whatever you can do to put food on this table for your mother and grandmother, I need you—"

"Abram, please—stop this nonsense. I don't want our son putting himself at risk every day. We will survive off our rations," Mama says, her words unsure, lacking confidence. The rations aren't enough—we're all well aware.

"He's the man of the house now, Chana, and he's capable of taking care of you," Father tells her, keeping his voice strong and dominant. He never speaks to her that way.

I choke back a hitched breath, understanding the responsibilities that have just been handed over to me. What if I'm not cut out to be the provider like Father has always been? Maybe Mother is thinking the same way I am, and that I'm not capable.

She's the one who has said singing and busking will only take me so far in life, but right now, it's all I have and all I can do. Jews aren't allowed common jobs here. It's been that way for quite a while.

Father places the hat back on the table and returns to Mother's side, stopping her mid-pace. He takes her hand and presses her knuckles to his lips. "I love you and we'll make it through this." He releases her in exchange for my shoulder, squeezing firmly. "You've become a fine young man, Luka. I'm proud of you, always. And I'm confident you can handle whatever comes our family's way."

"They'll probably be eating better than we will be," Grandfather utters. "Don't be afraid of the black market, my boy."

"Foter!" Mother hollers at him again. "No, absolutely not. No black market. Don't even utter those words in our home."

The room falls quiet, except for a faint swoosh from the floral drapes as a draft sneaks in through the cracked seals of the window. Then a sharp, urgent knock against the door shatters the silence.

FIVE

LUKA

Jak's mother was the person knocking on our door the other night, wanting to thank us for finding her son's stuffed bear. But these days, every knock we hear, letter we receive, and shout echoing from outside the window is a deadly threat. We can deny our fear, but it's been laced into our lives for so long that it's tainted the blood running through our veins. We had been sure there was a soldier waiting at our door with a rifle...

Now, the walls are closing in as we prepare to say goodbye to Father and Grandfather. I've been in something of a trance for the last few days, suffering with the turmoil of guilt and worry over them leaving us rather than me going with them. The letter says they're being sent to forced labor but in truth, that could mean anything.

My name was left off that letter, for a reason I still can't understand. Despite the number of times I've asked Mother if she has any other ideas as to why I was left off the list, she will not bat an eyelid, reciting the same excuse about factory experience. The soldiers don't care about former work experience when it comes to forced labor. They want working bodies, and my body works just fine. If I could go in place of one or both, I would without a second thought. I'm supposed to protect Mother and Grandmother here at home, but what about Father and Grandfather? Instead, I'm standing in the doorway of my bedroom, watching them gather their belongings, shoving what they can into battered brown suitcases with lock clasps that need repair and handles covered in torn leather and loose seams.

Mother stands between the kitchen and dining table, squeezing her hands together atop her apron with a handkerchief dangling from her pinched fingers. She hasn't said much in the last couple of days, but her quiet is a sign of grief and one that pains us all.

Grandmother is pacing back and forth from the bedroom she shares with Grandfather, bringing out additional belongings with each return. "You must take this—you need it more than me." She places her balled-up fist into his, concealing whatever it is she's giving him. But he isn't questioning a thing. The tears in his eyes say so.

"It's time," Father says, tapping his palm against his suitcase. He gives Mother a kiss and a tight embrace as I step toward them. I must be strong, for him, for Mother and Grandmother and Grandfather. It's up to me to be that person for them now.

"Father, I promise to watch over everything here. You have nothing to worry about while you're away," I say, my voice stern and deep to conceal the pain splintering through my heart.

He places his hand behind the back of my head and squeezes, staring me in the eyes with resolve and trust. "I know, son. I know." He kisses me on the forehead and pulls me in for a hug. "I'll miss you, my boy."

I swallow my response; afraid it won't come out in just words. I shake my head instead, knowing it's not a proper response. There's more to say. But I can't.

The goodbyes carry on, the distress growing as Mother and

Grandmother pull away and stand back by the dining table, both with their hands pressed to their hearts.

I follow Father and Grandfather out the door as they make their way down the stairs. I pause at the window in the corridor, waiting as they walk towards a truck surrounded by soldiers. One of the men tears the suitcases out of Father and Grandfather's hands. "Geh jetzt!" a soldier shouts, telling them to move faster. They duck their heads while climbing into the vehicle and the door closes. Their luggage is tossed into the back and—that's it. I can't move or do anything—I can only stare. My heart sinks, falling heavily into the pit of my stomach. *We're still breathing,* I remind myself. We have no choice but to be strong —stronger now than before.

* * *

The gathering of people in the square is larger than usual but more people are hesitating to stick around. I'm used to people coming and going, fear of our surroundings getting the best of them. We're all doing what we must to get by, and for me...this is surviving. "You don't want to be doing this—making a scene," says a man with two coiled curls hanging down the sides of his eyes. "They're everywhere. Get yourself home and be safe, young man."

I give him a nod out of respect and wait for him to leave the area before making it clear I'm choosing to continue. The real dread is noticing how few men I see walking around. They're all being taken. Any of these women might have had their husbands, brothers, or sons taken from them this morning, too. There are still some men here in the crowd but, like me, I'm sure their time will come when they disappear, too.

"Sing!" someone shouts, breaking through the blur of my thoughts.

"Sing!" another voice follows.

My heart aches too much to sing with this morning's good-byes still fresh in my mind. Mother's tears and Grandmother's attempt to show strength despite all she has already lived through, gnaws at my stomach. And Father's voice as he told me he'll miss me... Everything hurts and no matter how many last words we shared, none of them convey the immeasurable distance between us.

Despite it all, I take in the view of the sky and let the melody form deep within my throat, my voice trembling as I attempt to shut out the world around me.

> *The sky is dark and gray*
> *but behind the clouds, it's blue.*

When I return to the present moment following the chorus, my heart leaps into my throat as I spot her figure glowing in the murky light, her face a golden ray of light amid the gray flock of spectators. She isn't smiling, but her gaze draws me in, holding me still within this dreamlike moment where the notes of my song float through the air between us. My savior...

> *Lovely days will come*
> *soon for me and you.*

> *Keep me in your dreams,*
> *And I'll come to you each night.*
> *Hold me in your arms*
> *Until the morning light*

The words of the song fade away and I stumble forward, reaching to grasp her hand, my heart pounding in my chest. "What is your name?" I press with determination, making sure I don't miss the opportunity to ask again.

Her cheeks blush and she touches her fingers to them,

smiling shyly. "It was too late when I realized we didn't exchange—I'm Ella Bosko," she says, tucking a loose strand of hair behind her ear.

"I'm Luka Dulski, and—and I can't believe you're here."

She peers up at the sky for a short second then shakes her head. "Boy, you're really taking this humble act a little too far..." Her gaze floats back to mine with a look of intent. "I wanted to hear you sing again," she admits, her eyes falling to my watch. It's around the time when the German soldiers will be making their rounds.

"Sing," she whispers.

"You just took my breath away... Now, I can't sing."

"Oh, but you must. Please, do sing!" a gruff voice thunders over mine. "Entertain us, Jewish singer!" A soldier—he must have been standing here this whole time.

"I—I think I'm done," I say, pulling Ella in behind me.

"No, don't stop on account of me. Everyone wants to hear you. It's clear, yes? You've even captured the attention of a non-Jewish woman." He tsks his tongue at me. "We can't have that here. Shame, shame."

"She's a friend," I argue, nearly choking on my words as this soldier stares at me like I'm his next meal.

"You shouldn't be hanging around these dirty Jews...friend," he says to Ella.

I reach down and grab my cap full of coins as the gathering disperses behind the soldier who's holding his hard stare over me.

"They aren't—" Ella replies.

But I cut her off, speaking over her. "Good night to you," I say, leading us away from the soldier. My pulse races and my breaths are short the faster I walk and pull Ella alongside.

The soldier laughs from behind us. "Good night to you," he says, mocking me in a feminine tone.

"I'm so sorry. It's not safe for you here, clearly."

"It's not safe anywhere in this city," she says. "But at least I have a good reason for being here."

"I'm not sure I'm much of a good reason." I peer over my shoulder, making sure we're not being followed. He's out of sight, thankfully.

"I came to see if you were singing last night and the night before," she says, making her statement sound more like an embarrassing confession. "I got to thinking you'll probably become famous someday and I'd have to wait until then to learn your name."

"That would be a very long time," I reply, trying not to let my own smile betray me.

"You never know," she adds. Her optimism makes me wonder if she's aware of the type of life we're living in the Jewish neighborhoods. It's become a stark contrast to any other district in Warsaw.

We pass by closed shops owned by Jewish people with propaganda posters depicting us as hideous creatures. Ella's pace slows and her face contorts with disgust as we move past each demoralizing display. As if she can't take much more, she comes to a sudden stop as we approach a storefront window with crude remarks etched in shaving cream. Ella's forehead crinkles and her bottom lip falls with what must be shock.

"It's a lot. Are you sure you want to be here?"

Her blonde eyebrows furrow over her small, freckled nose and she nods insistently. "Yes, I want to understand what you, all of you, are living through here. Everyone should be aware."

My heart swells with appreciation and sorrow. It's easy to avoid this reality, but this girl—this beautiful girl wants to understand more, despite the danger surrounding us.

With a stiff breath, I take her hand in mine. In a normal world that doesn't run out of free minutes, I wouldn't be so forward, but there's something about her that I need to hold on to.

"I'm not going to run off," she says, glancing down at our hands.

I let go, worried I've moved too fast too soon, but she reaches back for my hand. "I didn't mean you should let go. I meant I wouldn't run, in case that's why you were holding on."

"You're something else," I tell her, peering over at her confident smile.

"And you—you and your voice have brought the only semblance of beauty left in this desolate city...but—"

"But?" I echo.

"You sounded different tonight. It was like someone broke your heart, maybe." Her words spark a pain in my chest. I didn't realize my grief was so obvious. "I'm being far too nosy. I should —I should try harder to keep some thoughts to myself." She shakes her head and presses her hand to her lips.

"I'm impressed by your ability to hear emotions within music."

"I've never been able to before I don't think, not before listening to you."

I want to tell her I'm unsure how much longer I can keep this up—performing here—or anywhere. Any day now, I'll be told to pack my belongings and report to a factory for forced labor.

"That means the world to me," I say, peering down to catch a faint smile growing across her lips.

No sooner than the words slip off my tongue, the clomping of horses trotting in sync acts as a countdown for the seconds left before we need to be away from the square.

"The German soldiers," Ella says, glancing over her shoulder.

"I should get home. You should, too," I say, hating the thought of her walking home alone with soldiers on the prowl. My curfew ends three hours earlier than hers though, and I can't take any chances with Father and Grandfather being gone. "Will you be all right?"

"Of course," she says without hesitation.

"Be careful," I say as she begins to walk away. "I don't want you in danger because of me."

Ella turns around and steps back in toward me. "Well, I happen to humbly disagree." She takes a hold of my wrists, presses up on her toes and kisses my cheek. "I'll be back tomorrow, earlier so I can listen to you for longer," she says before disappearing into the growing darkness of the night.

"Papers!" a soldier shouts from the around the corner. *Please get home safely.*

SIX

ELLA

I rush through my apartment, the wooden framed family portraits rumbling against the hallway walls as I charge into my bedroom. I don't have much time to change out of my work clothes in exchange for a dress with a bit more color. The drawers of my bureau clap and swoosh over and over until I find what I'm looking for. Then it's the clomp of my work boots hitting the ground one at a time. I sweep my fingers over the disarray of cosmetic items sitting in the silver tray on my vanity table then add some rouge to my cheeks and a smudge of lipstick to my dry lips. It's enough to mask the look of exhaustion from the day. There are only a couple of hours before Luka's curfew, and I refuse to waste a minute of that time.

"Ella, where are you rushing off to again? This is the third time this week and it's almost supper time," Mama says, poking her head out of the kitchen, and wiping her hands on her buttercup yellow apron.

I need to find my handbag. I always manage to put the darn thing in a different spot whenever I walk through the door.

"Out for a bit with a couple of the girls from—" I almost say church but realize lying is already a sin. I don't need to add to it by using the church in my lie. "My book club."

"Your book club?" she questions with a raised brow. "Ella, you haven't finished a book in—so long, I've lost track of time. You borrow books from the library, read a chapter and put them down until they're due to be returned."

I make my way over to Mama and brush a dusting of flour from her cheek. "That's not true, Mama. The club decided to read *The Midas Touch* by Margaret Kennedy, and I was quite taken by the story."

"I haven't seen you pick up a book, Ella," she says, chiding with a nod of her head.

"I read at night before I go to bed."

"I see. Who is your favorite character in this book?" Mama has read so many books, she might have read them all. I shouldn't be tempting my fate by discussing a book with her, but I am at least familiar with this story.

"Mrs. Carter Blake, of course. That's a silly question, Mama," I say with laughter. I had to read the book last year for my final paper. "I'll be home before curfew." I spot my handbag on the floor next to the sofa, scoop it up and return to the kitchen once more to give Mama a kiss on the cheek.

"What about your supper? Your tata and Miko will be home in a few moments," she presses.

"Could you save me a plate, perhaps? If it's too much trouble, I'll fix myself something when I return."

"You are the cause of my wrinkles, Ella," she murmurs with a sigh. "But I love you."

"I love you too, Mama. And you're beautiful—not a wrinkle in sight."

The repeating tick-tocks from the miniature grandfather clock hanging on the wall add another layer of guilt and stress to my racing heart, knowing my father, and overprotective older brother—or a hound dog as I like to call him—will be coming up the stairs within minutes, ready with their interrogation of where I'm going if I haven't already left.

I make it out of the building, unlock my bicycle chain and flee the block without spotting Tata or Miko. I travel the narrow side streets through two small villages before crossing into the Jewish district, where I find the familiar narrow roads that led me to the square the night I was delivering the bundle of bread for Tata.

When I come to the corner block before the square, I spot the elderly woman who asked me for help, the one I couldn't do anything for. The sight of her despair has clung to me. She's only one person out of so many in the same position, but I need to do something. I roll my bicycle up to the side of where she's sitting and reach forward, slipping my hand into the metal basket. "I'm sorry I couldn't help you the last time you asked, but I'd like to offer you a little something." I retrieve the brown bag with bread and canned goods I brought and hand it to her.

"Oh, my dear," she says. "Oh. I'm—I'm not sure what to say." She peeks inside the bag and cups her trembling hand over her mouth. "Bless you, sweet girl."

"It's not much," I say. I had to sneak this loaf into a bag when Tata and Miko were out earlier. Food is scant, but so is compassion. The woman smiles, a strain that looks as if she's stretching unused muscles. A sense of peace warms me. It isn't much, but it's more than nothing.

"Are you giving this poor woman a hard time?" The question arises from behind me, followed by a soft laugh.

"Oh, you rascal, you," the woman replies. "This young lady is a gift from God, and don't you say anything otherwise."

An arm wraps around my shoulders, carrying the scent of spring air. "I was wondering if you would be coming here tonight," Luka says. "I was collecting my coat and hat when I spotted you over here."

"Are you aware that he writes all of the music himself?" the old lady says with a small smile. "He has more talent than this world will ever be lucky enough to hear."

"I was unaware of this additional talent," I reply, stunned.

"It's nothing but words," he says shooing away the topic with a blush tinting his cheeks. "Ella, Pan Monowitz lives in my apartment building."

"But I come down here every afternoon to listen to the beautiful music. For many of us, it's all we have left."

I stare to the side, finding Luka's cheeks burning from pink to red. "I'm sure that's not true, Pan Monowitz," he says with a heavy exhale. "After all, we're still breathing, and the sun is in the sky. We're resilient, yes?"

"With good people still left in this world, you are right, young man."

Luka releases his arm from my shoulders and takes hold of my bike's handlebars so I can slide off the seat. "Have a good night, Pan Monowitz," Luka says, dipping his head.

"Yes, have a nice night," I follow.

"Thank you, dear. For everything," she says.

"I'm sorry," Luka says as we turn the corner.

"For what?"

"She begs for help often. Everyone here is in the same situation. There's no sense in begging when we're all hungry."

More guilt filters through me. I'm sure I'm not as hungry as anyone in this district, and it's not fair.

"I brought you something, too," I offer.

"Ella," he says. "I don't want the difference in our ration sizes to define—"

"I didn't mean—"

"I—" he says. "I forget about the grim world around me when I see you. It's as if you're a clearing in a cloudy sky. All I want is to spend time with you, learn everything about you. You bring a smile to face and it's no easy feat these days." He huffs a laugh and drops his gaze to the ground while pushing my bike forward.

"Why do you think I've been coming back here since last week?" I ask.

Luka shrugs. "I'm not sure. I'm Jewish, have nothing to offer, and I've been told I try too hard to be funny."

I can't keep myself from laughing at what likely isn't meant to be a joke. "I don't care that you're Jewish, and I'm not looking for an offer."

"But I do try too hard to be funny?" he counters.

I sweep the fallen strands of hair from my loose braid behind my ear. "You make people smile, Luka. In times like these, it's a rare thing to find in someone. It's like—when the sun breaks through the clouds after a heavy storm, it's a reminder we're still here and still surviving. My heart races when you sing, and when you look at me, I forget how to take my next breath. I—I didn't think it was possible to find a shred of joy in times like these. I've never taken risks or acted on impulse. But now that I have, I want more. Is that strange?"

Luka shakes his head. "Not at all. Though I worry about the trouble I could cause you."

He's said that a couple of times now and I'm questioning if I'm the one putting him in possible danger. Anyone who sees us walking together can tell he's Jewish and I'm not, by the band around his arm.

"And what about the danger I'm putting you in? I don't want to be the reason you get caught."

"If trouble comes, it won't be because of you. I'm one of the only men my age here who hasn't been sent to forced labor and I'm still not sure why, but I assume sooner or later they'll come for me."

My heart sinks and my gaze falls, because I didn't stop to think he could be sent away at any given moment.

I sigh. "But—right now, in this moment...the sun is in the

sky, right? So, we shouldn't think about what could happen tomorrow."

He twists his head, pinches his lips tight and smiles. "Right."

We come up to a small park surrounded with towering oak trees, full of lush greenery. He places my bicycle up against a wooden bench and gestures for me to sit down. "Will we be safe here? I don't want to—"

"The ground will vibrate from the marching soldiers before they come into view—as long as I'm not singing, that is."

I lower myself onto the bench, smoothing the folds of my dress as he sits down beside me. He's close enough that our shoulders nearly touch, making my heart flutter. It's been so long since I've wanted to get to know someone. No one seems genuine anymore, or maybe it's that I can't figure out who is and who isn't. We all want the same thing—our freedom back, but it won't be easy or a fair battle, evenly fought by all. Of course, I could never compare my life to Luka's, not with the way the Jews are being treated and tormented.

"I've been thinking..."

"I'm not sure I like the sound of that," he says with a grin.

"Good. Because it likely won't come out the right way..." I take a breath before continuing, watching Luka's eyebrows furrow. "How can any of the Jewish people think much of us who aren't Jewish? My parents say we'll never be forgiven for not doing more. But when I ask what more we could do, no one has an answer."

Luka twists his body toward me, crossing his ankles and resting his elbow on the back of the bench. The last of the sunlight filters through the trees and sparkles against his hazel eyes. "We—or my family and me, don't think that way about anyone who isn't Jewish. The Germans have made it clear of their hatred toward us and they've done nothing but instill fear into everyone in Poland. Fear has a hold on all of us. It just looks different on some. These imposed laws are enforced with fear and punishment, but by giving in to them we're complying with their demands inside of our homes. They can force us to behave in a certain way, but they can't control the way we think."

I twist in my seat to face him straight on and rest my hand on his. "It's as if I've lost my way and you're the only source of light ahead," I utter.

"Then don't," he says without hesitation. "You've brought me happiness and I'm not willing to give that up because I'm not *supposed* to feel that way."

"Then don't," I repeat his words.

I lean into the spine of the bench and stare at Luka for a moment, taking him all in, his dimples, the faded freckles on his nose, the shimmer of auburn in his dark hair. He slides his arm across the bench, close to mine. My breath trembles on my lips as he twirls a strand of my hair around his finger before reaching in a little closer. A knot tightens in my stomach and my pulse stammers.

Yet, not as loud as the synchronous marching of boots and a whistle howling through the air...

"We should go," Luka says, taking my hand and promptly standing up from the bench.

"I want to stay here with you," I tell him, foolishly. If I stay here, I can be sure he hasn't been taken away.

"No, you don't. Trust me, please," he says.

"What about tomorrow?" I ask. How long do I have before I come to find him, and he's gone?

"What about for as long as possible?" he replies, squeezing my hand a little tighter. "It's against the law. You, not being Jewish and me, a Jew—it's not allowed. We could both face severe punishment, not only me. I need you to understand that."

"I'm well versed with the laws," I tell him, glancing away as rejection starts to prickle at my skin.

"But," he says, nudging my chin so I look up at him, "if I don't tell the soldiers about us, and you don't tell them..."

"We aren't letting them win," I finish his sentence, staring up into his eyes, knowing that whether they find out or not, our seconds are still running out. They're sending all the men away. Like he said, it's just a matter of when... One thing is certain, the Germans don't give up.

"So..." he says, swallowing hard, peering off into the distance between the tree branches. "I can call you mine?"

Despite the fear and the clomping boots growing louder, heat rushes through my face. I want to forget the threat hanging over our heads, even if only for a moment. One simple moment.

"For as long as we're breathing and the sun is in the sky," I say, repeating his words from earlier. We can enjoy this spark, racing hearts, flutters, and the strong desire to be together. Anything could happen tomorrow, so today is important.

I reach into the basket of my bike and take out the other brown paper bag. "Fresh bread and some fruit. And not because I'm sure you're hungry. It's payment for the songs of hope—your words that play on repeat in my head that have given me reason to believe there will always be a tomorrow."

I pray tomorrow will come. It's all any of us can do now.

SEVEN

LUKA

July 1940
Warsaw, Poland

Tomorrow. The day after that, and then a couple more dozen days after that, too—there she was, here she is—appearing in the crowd like the North Star. She's held true to her promise, one I would never hold her accountable to.

Today, I see her on her bicycle before I've even taken my hat off and set it beside me. There's no crowd, just us.

"What are you doing here so early today? Shouldn't you be at your family's store?"

"I told my father I had to leave. I had to come warn you. They're coming this way."

"What do you mean?" I ask, my heart racing, my breaths short.

"The Germans. There's a lot of them. It's hard to tell what's happening, but there's a convoy of trucks heading in this direction. They stopped a couple of streets down, but they'll be here soon, I'm sure."

"Trucks?" I understand what she's describing. There's no

reason for me to be asking. That's how the soldiers arrived when they came to take Father, Grandfather, and many other men away, too.

"I didn't receive a letter. It seems that's what they do before taking people away. They give them a short warning, but I still don't want to be here when they arrive." I glance around. "What direction were they coming from?"

Ella points south. "There's a place we can go. We'll make our way behind their convoy so we're not in their path. Come on."

Without another thought, I follow Ella through the square and down several side streets. She shoves her bike behind a row of metal rubbish bins and grabs my hand, continuing to lead me to wherever we're going.

We hobble over a short iron gate and into a small park with a cluster of sky-scraping oaks, then dart through the center of the trees, stopping halfway through. "Climb," she commands.

My eyes travel upward into the rich cluster of green leaves, hoping there are enough branches within reach. People are walking along the exterior paths, passing along as if nothing is out of the ordinary. I reach for the lowest limb and pull myself up, anchoring on a thick, sturdy branch, then reach down to help Ella up along with me. She's nimble and quick, making the act of climbing trees seem no more difficult than playing hopscotch.

I climb up to the thickest part of the tree and rest between the crook of the branch and the trunk. Ella situates herself across from me on a parallel branch, bringing us knee to knee.

"There, no one will find us up here," she whispers.

"You mean, me?" I remind her.

"I mean us," she says. "I'm by your side, Luka."

The synchronized march of boots grows in volume in the distance, clacking horseshoes, and motorized vehicles, just as she'd warned. I stare through a small window of leaves, out to the street to see if I can sneak a glance at what they're doing.

"Men are exiting their buildings with a suitcase in hand like Father and Grandfather." The thought of why I hadn't been pulled for labor keeps me up at night, fearing that the longer I go, the worse it will be when I am called. "They've come to take away more men..."

Ella understands my concern for where they've gone, how they are, if they are surviving, and the guilt I live with. I hate to remind her, but it's a reality I can't ignore. "It's still only a matter of time before they come for me."

Ella stares at me with grief swelling through her blue eyes. I don't want her to pity me. I don't want that to be the reason she wants to spend time with me. "But you haven't gotten a letter, so it's not today," she snaps, before taking in a shuddered breath. She tries to conceal her worry, but I see it.

Ella tugs at my arm, pulling my attention away from the awful sight in the distance. "Tell me how you find the energy to sing every night with what's happening around us? Your voice is always filled with such hope and happiness, contrasting the despair within everyone who watches you. You give them—us—so much more than you realize."

"When I sing, I forget about the pain and worry. I block out the suffering and hunger and imagine the world I paint in my dreams at night. It's hard to explain."

"You just did," she says. "That's what your songs do to me, too."

The marching soldiers are so close, the branches rattle around us. A shouting slew of insults rips through the air toward a Jewish person, following a demand to turn around. Hardly a second passes before a gunshot pierces the air.

Ella startles and clutches her chest, and fear appears in her eyes, one I haven't seen before. I take her hands and hold them in mine, both of us staring at one another as the freight train of evil passes us by. Her hands are warm and trembling. Mine might be, too. My heart's racing so hard it's stealing my breath.

Ella's branch crackles and makes her jump, releasing my hands to hold onto the tree trunk. I grab her arm and swing her over to my side, knowing the branch I'm on can hold us both. I wrap my arm around her and hold on tightly. She's breathing so hard as she presses her cheek to my chest. I close my eyes and sing softly into her ear:

> *Whenever you smile*
> *It's no real surprise*
> *I could stare for a while*
>
> *When souls collide*
> *Like yours and mine*
> *It's a sign, can't be denied*
>
> *I think this must be love*
> *What else could it be...*
> *Only the sky sings from above*
> *So, darling, the answer's clear to me*

The commotion has moved past us by the time I finish singing the short verses, but she's still holding on to me with all her might.

"Did you write that one?" she utters.

A rush of heat envelops my neck and crawls up my cheeks. "I did. You see...I'm quite taken with you."

She touches her fingers to her chest, and her glimmering eyes question if it's truly her I was singing to.

A thunder cloud rumbles above us and the air thickens with moisture seconds before rain trickles through the leaves. I yank my coat open around her to shield her from the rain, but she lifts her head above the collar, staring up into my eyes. My gaze is helplessly drawn to her lips, desperate to close the space between us.

I shouldn't pull her into my world. It's wrong. It's unfair to her.

My self-control fails me, and I slide my hand across her damp cheek. My heart quakes and my breath hitches as I gently lean in closer until our lips meet. Warmth consumes me as a frenzy of nerves flicker in my chest...she's a song, my favorite song, a song I might want to sing over and over just to feel like this.

She pulls back to take a breath, staring into my eyes helplessly before surging forward to kiss me again.

If only we could stay in this tree forever...

EIGHT

ELLA

September 1940
Warsaw, Poland

The city is being chipped away, little by little every day. It's been six weeks since Luka and I sat in that single most perfect tree, relishing the moments of joy between measures of fear as a Nazi demonstration unfolded in the street. Since then, there have been larger and more frequent demonstrations, escalating the destruction of our city.

The empty shelves in my family's store amplify the truth of how many people are going hungry. Amid every person who circles around our small grocery store, disappointment weighs on me. There must be something more I could be doing for them, but it would likely be against the law. We ran out of full loaves of bread hours ago, much earlier than we usually do, but some still come inside to see what's left.

"Do you think you'll have more flour tomorrow?" Madame Adamski asks. She's one of our most loyal customers who has been shopping in our store since before I stepped foot in this world. Her question bears weight on my heart and her forlorn eyes and hollow cheeks plead for a good answer when I can't give one. Sprigs of gray curls dangle by her ears beneath her maroon scarf that she clings to beneath her chin with a white-knuckled fist.

"I should hope so, but—"

"I understand, dear. No promises expected."

"I'm sorry," I tell her, reaching across the narrow wooden counter for her free hand. All I can offer is comfort.

"This isn't your fault," she says, taking my hand and giving it a quick squeeze. "Has your tata returned with tomorrow's inventory?"

I give a small shake of my head. "Not yet. I'll tell him you stopped by."

"Take care, dear," she says, her hand slipping out of mine. "Oh, and Ella..." her words become a whisper. "I saw you in the Jewish quarter just the other day. You were walking around with a young man—a Jewish man." She swallows hard and lifts her hand to her throat. "Dear, you should be more careful where you go and with whom you're seen."

"Thank you for your concern, madame."

I hold back the frustration rippling through my veins and take the clipboard from beneath the counter and a pencil from the tin can beside the register, then walk across the creaking wooden floor to the nearest shelves. I straighten the last of the jars of jam and pickled vegetables, counting the remnants to mark down on the inventory list. The baskets by the front counter have only a few potatoes, stalks of carrots, turnips, and beets. Most of them are already turning brown. The store rarely smells like fresh bread or fresh produce anymore.

A commotion from the storage room pulls me toward the back door, curious to see what Tata and my brother, Miko were able to collect while restocking supplies. I rest my ear against the door before walking into the back room, hearing them mid conversation about setting aside a stack of paper for their underground meeting tonight. Whenever I ask where they're going after supper, the answer is "nowhere." Except, I know where they're going. They just don't want me there because it's dangerous to be in the Polish resistance. It also feels dangerous to *not* be among the Polish resistance. I'd rather be a component of the solution than waiting for someone else to save us all.

I push the door open into the dimly-lit small space, finding Tata and Miko ushering in crates from the truck parked out back. The two of them are tall, broad-shouldered, with hands rougher than sandpaper from all the heavy lifting of daily inventory. The only difference between them is the stark bald circle on the center of Tata's head that he makes up for with his thick, wide, strawberry-blonde mustache, and Miko, no mustache, still has all his light hair, but keeps it short and cropped. I share the same eye color and hair color with them, but I look more like Mama. "Do you need help?" I ask Miko after he drops the load in his arms.

"No, of course not. I wouldn't want you to break a sweat," he says mocking my higher-pitched voice. I've never said such a thing about sweating. He just needs to entertain himself by being a pest to me. Miko wipes his arm against his sweat-covered forehead, then his arm against my sleeve.

I jerk away from him, disgusted by his behavior. "You're vile," I say, holding myself back from shoving him.

"Sweetheart, could you tally up the items left on the shelves for me?" Tata asks as he carries in a load of crates.

"I already have," I say, removing my apron. "I have some books to return to the library, so I was hoping I could leave when you returned."

"The library?" he repeats. He doesn't believe me. I can't say I blame him as my excuses for disappearing somewhere between here and home every day are becoming repetitive. However, since he and Miko aren't honest with me about where they go at night, I won't let the guilt get to me.

"Yes."

"Very well. Your brother and I will restock the shelves. Be home before curfew."

"Will *you* be home before curfew?" I reply with a raised brow.

"Ella, please. You're beginning to sound like your mother."

I take my satchel from the corner between the metal storage shelves and give Tata a kiss on the cheek before leaving.

* * *

Traveling the same route every day for the last few months has left me with nothing but questions as I witness the deterioration of our community grow at a rate that should be impossible.

The Germans have plans and secrets for Warsaw, and none of them are public knowledge. We're left to make assumptions and hope that we're wrong. It was easier to do when Jewish families weren't being evicted from their homes by other Jews. Luka said there's been a formation of a Jewish council, the Judenrat, leading the Jewish communities through the hardships, but lately their objectives have seemed amiss as more and more people are being forced to move closer to the center of the city.

The square where he used to sing is crowded with people trying to barter and sell belongings or trades. Even children are set up on the ground, displaying gemstones they're hoping to collect some coins for. There's no food, though. No one is selling food. Their grocery store has a line wrapped around the building and the door never seems to open.

A brick building three blocks away from the square has been closed, windows boarded up the sides. But on the side of the building where an alleyway no longer than the length of my body exists in the dark, is a door that leads down into a stone cellar.

I've stopped riding my bicycle down here after learning that Jewish people aren't allowed to have them anymore. It would be rude to ride through their quarter on mine. I knock gently on the wooden door, buried in the shadow of the building. The door opens a sliver, enough for someone to catch sight of my eyes. Then the door opens. I'm ushered in and closed inside just as quickly.

At the bottom of the stone stairs, round tables and chairs fill the space and, in the center, Luka stands like a centerpiece on an empty table, singing his heart out. His voice, honeyed and warm, fills the air. The people watching him are all smiling, something never seen on the streets now. His eyes are closed as they always are when he's composing lyrics that often formulate mid-song. I've never known anyone to think in rhymes woven with beautiful prose. Although, I've never known anyone who can sing like he can either.

I sit in the back, hoping not to disturb his focus, but between songs he scans the space until he spots me, knowing I show up every afternoon. Then, his eyes remain open as he stares directly at me through each song he has left to sing.

"It's time," a gentleman by the door announces. "Wrap it up."

Everyone scatters from their seats and hustles up the stairs to leave the building. Luka reaches out for my hand, and I follow him up and onto the street. "There's a place...with a good tree," I tell him, nudging my elbow into his. It's become one of our favorite places to go, and one of the only places we *can* go. If only we didn't have to climb down to get home before curfew, I could easily spend every night in the crook of his arm, telling him stories, listening to his, laughing, kissing, feeling my heart swell with an unfamiliar type of love. It's just us in our tree, avoiding the world around us.

Luka loops his arms around my waist and kisses my cheek. "Actually, I want to bring you home to meet my mother and grandmother. If you think you're up to it, of course."

The skin on my arm prickles despite the summer heat still floating through the air. I wasn't expecting him to suggest this.

"I'm afraid they won't like me, and where would that leave us?" We've had this conversation a few times before in the last month or so, which we've spent fervently making use of every free moment together. He wants to meet my family, too, but it's too dangerous. Jewish people are not allowed to have a relationship with non-Jewish people, and we knew that before we met and did nothing to stop what was happening between us. I still don't regret our decision, but I worry about disrespecting our parents.

"They will love you," he assures me. He's never said otherwise but has been worried about causing them more concern than they already have with everyone being kicked out of their homes or sent to forced labor.

"And if they don't?" I ask, folding my arms over my chest.

"It doesn't matter, Ella. I'm twenty. I'm a man of my own and I love you. No one can change that, not even the two women who try to control my life with their stabbing glares." He chuckles.

"Of course, I'd love to meet them."

"Do you remember everything I've told you about them?" he asks.

"Sure, I do."

We travel down the slim side streets until we reach his apartment building, all windows dark with curtains, no flowerbeds, and no children playing out front. It looks empty from the outside.

I clench my hand around my satchel as we make our way up the steps. He pulls a key from his pocket and unlocks one of the three doors on the fourth floor.

The aroma of lavender and vanilla wafts out into the hallway, pulling me in as if I was smelling a freshly baked pastry. The apartment is spotless and minimally furnished with what looks to be the bare necessities. Luka curls his arm around my back and guides me around a shallow corner where we find two women sitting on a sofa, knitting.

They both glance up at us in silence, wide-eyed, and their mouths identically parted. They look alike, but with a twenty-something age difference.

"Mother, Grandmother, I would like you to meet—"

"I was right. I told you, Ma, he has a girlfriend," the younger of the two women says, standing from the sofa. "When a boy smiles in a certain way, you can just see it, and I saw it, didn't I?"

"Mother," Luka interrupts her. "This is Ella."

"Oy, what a beauty you are," she says, coming toward me with her arms open wide. "Welcome, darling. Welcome to our home."

"Thank you so much. You're so kind, and I see where Luka gets his lovely smile from."

She pulls me in for a hug, squeezing quite tightly before she wraps her hands around my arms to take a step back. "Where's your armband, dear? It's against the law to leave the house without it on."

"Mother," Luka says, taking his mother by the arm and breathing deeply, "Ella isn't Jewish."

There's a pause, and then, "This is why you haven't brought her to meet me in all this time, is it?" she scolds Luka.

"Well, yes," he says, holding his hands behind his back, his posture stiff.

Luka's mother places her hands on her heart, peering between the two of us. "Why would you do this to yourselves? It's impossible to marry if that were to be your desire at some point."

The thought has crossed my mind but in a time of so much

ambiguity, it's hard to think ahead and worry about what might or might not happen. There's little happiness left for anyone and if there's an opportunity to escape the misery we're all living in, why wouldn't we grasp at what we can?

"I love her," Luka says, his face lined with despair as he stares at his mother. His response is so simple but defines the reason we're here together. We don't want to be apart.

"If you're caught—" She lifts her hand to her mouth.

"Lie," Luka's grandmother utters. "Just lie to the bastards, lie like they do about that godforsaken wall they're building downtown. They've already taken so much from us and they're about to take a whole lot more. But I'll tell you one thing they can't take away, is love. Marriage is nothing more than a binding piece of paper, and nowhere on it do the words speak to the true meaning of love."

I'm not sure if it's shock or enlightenment that has my pulse racing, but his grandmother has said what I haven't been able to put into words.

Luka's mother drops her head, quiet with the thoughts going through her head. After a moment, she shakes her head and straightens her shoulders then turns to face me. "Do you love my son?" she asks.

"Very much so," I answer. My simple words aren't proof, but I hope she realizes I wouldn't be here in her home if I didn't.

She opens her arms back up and steps toward me for another embrace. "I'm sorry for my reaction. If you love my son and he loves you, then I love you, as well. It's lovely to finally meet the person who has put a smile on my boy's face."

"I have something for you. I was going to give it to Luka before he told me he wanted to bring me here to meet you, but he mentioned you have a passion for horticulture."

"Oh, I do, very much. Though it's been close to impossible to grow much of anything with our windows covered and so few resources."

I lower my satchel from my shoulder and reach inside for the brown-paper wrapped package I prepared at the store earlier. "This is for you," I say. "They'll flourish without much light."

Luka's mother's eyes are wide, unblinking, as her trembling hands reach out to take the package from my hand and she unwraps the paper.

"Chamomile, mint, and calendula bulbs."

Her hands tremble as she stares at the roots. "How—how were you able to find—"

"Her family owns a grocery store," Luka says.

"No one would notice these were missing." *Because I keep track of the inventory.*

"How can I repay you?" she asks, holding the package back out to me.

"I already have more than I could ask for," I tell her. "I only wish I could do more."

"I'm going to plant this right away. Come," she says, placing her arm around my back. She guides me through their apartment into the narrow kitchen where she has empty ceramic pots of soil lined up on the darkened windowsill. Above the stovetop, she has a variety of decorative tea tins.

She gently digs through the soil to create space for the bulbs. The smile on her face wavers and I find myself wondering what she's thinking about. I would be terrified, living on the edge of not knowing what will happen next to this quarter. People keep leaving and not returning, and we can only wonder why.

As I continue to look around, I notice two small, rotting potatoes on an old cutting board next to two meager slices of bread.

"I should get home. I don't want to keep you from supper," I say.

"Oh, my dear, please, stay."

I look at the potatoes again, fearing that is all they have for dinner. Luka never complains about hunger, though I've noticed he's lost weight during the time we've known each other. Jewish people are given much less than non-Jewish when it comes to rations.

Luka steps into the kitchen, making it crowded with three of us. He peers over at the potatoes and slices of bread and his cheeks burn pink. "I was just telling your mother I should get home. I'm sure you're hungry for supper." I shouldn't have said that. I hope he's not hungry. There doesn't look to be enough to fill one person. "I—I didn't—"

"She should stay," Luka's mother says, still fumbling with the bulbs and soil.

Luka weaves his fingers through mine and leads me between the living room and kitchen. "Are you all right?" he asks.

"Is that all you have for supper?"

He shrugs. "Well, yes, just the same as everyone else."

I shake my head in refusal. "I didn't realize how much more I had until now. I'm going to help. May I help? I wouldn't want to offend you or your mother. I—I realize I shouldn't be taking from what little my family's store has, but I can't just stand by..." Tears fill my eyes and I'm ashamed of my irrational emotions when it isn't me who's going hungry to this extent. He wouldn't want me to feel sorry for him. It would make him uncomfortable, embarrassed.

Luka places his hands on my shoulders. "We'll be fine. I promise you don't have to worry about us. Don't take any more food from your family's store. Every store owner is being watched by the Germans with an eagle eye. You could get into more trouble than I want to think about."

I've been living in denial or lost in my head. Maybe I'm numb to the reality around me. My chest tightens as I stare into

Luka's eyes, realizing how many conversations we've avoided—or perhaps he's avoided. "I've been so ignorant."

"Mother, I'm going to walk Ella to the edge of the district before it gets too late. I'll be home shortly."

"Are you sure you can't stay a little longer, dear?"

"My parents will worry," I tell her.

"Well, of course. I wouldn't want that. Send them my best. Maybe we can all meet at some point."

My parents still don't know about Luka because they would be beside themselves with worry if they knew I was spending so much time in the Jewish district, a place where non-Jews should no longer be. Their concern would cause me guilt and take away the joy I've been lucky enough to experience in a time when it should be nearly impossible to find happiness. Though, it's been a while and it's time to be honest with them about where I've been spending so much of my time. I want them to meet Luka, somehow.

"It was so lovely to meet you both."

Luka hurries me out the door, down the stairs, and outside before he says another word.

"Don't ever talk about yourself like that again. You're far from ignorant," he says, pressing his hands to my shoulders to bring himself eye level with me.

"I just want to be with you, and sitting in that tree every day is giving me a false sense of reality. You're starving, Luka. You are far hungrier than me, and it tears me apart inside. I wanted to believe you weren't much worse off than people like me, but it's not the truth. How can you even stand to be near me?"

"Stop talking that way," he says before swallowing hard.

"I'm bringing you food. Don't tell me not to. My tata and brother are members of the—" I edge my lips to his ear to whisper what I must say—"underground resistance. There's an army of Polish fighters in the tunnels beneath the city. They take food to help others. Likely more than I can even imagine.

I'm desperate for them to meet you. They will adore you. You are also the perfect reminder of what they are fighting for alongside our freedom."

"You never mentioned..." he says, his breath tapering into the wind.

"I'm not supposed to... I overhear snippets."

The squeals and clomps from a horse and wagon serve as a caveat—incoming Germans. Other than a few rickshaws for Jews to transport Germans from place to place, there are no other modes of transportation in this district.

We both stare beyond the end of the road, but waiting won't do either of us much good. "I'm going to go. I'll be back tomorrow."

"Please, Ella, please... I don't want you to do anything dangerous. I beg of you."

"I will be fine," I tell him, enunciating each word.

His hands cup my face, and he presses his forehead to mine before reaching in to kiss me with a sharp inhale. My chest is pressing against his, two hearts pound at each other with an ache, fear, and endless desire as if we're fighting for something we can never truly win. Yet, it's a fight I'm willing to endure even knowing there may not be an end for us.

Just this beginning.

* * *

I burst into my apartment like I've been blown in by a heavy gust of wind, startling my parents and Miko. Mama is setting the dinner table, humming a soft tune as the loose strands from the knot in her hair wisp over her forehead as she spins around the kitchen, hurrying to set everything in place. Tata and Miko are huddled around the coffee table in what must have been a serious discussion based on the amount of cigarette smoke pluming above their heads.

"Is everything all right, Ella?" Mama asks, her emerald eyes piercing through me. I have a knack for running or speeding on my bicycle to wherever I'm going. Mama says I'm always in a race to get somewhere and never take the time to smell the tulips. It's true now, I suppose, since flowers are rare to find around the city.

"Yes, why?" I ask, stopping alongside the coffee table between Miko and Papa.

Mama shakes her head and returns to the kitchen.

In a whisper, I state: "I want to help you." I hold my stare on Tata, realizing my statement might not have been firm enough. "I'm going with you and Miko tonight."

"Quiet, Ella," Tata argues in a mirroring whisper. "You want your mother to hear you speaking like this?"

"You think she doesn't know where you two go every night?"

Tata pinches at his mustache and narrows his eyes at me.

"A better question is, how are you so sure about where we go every night?" Miko adds, taking a long drag of his cigarette, asking the obvious question Tata was debating whether to ask.

I hold my arms out to the side. The answer should be somewhat obvious. "I've followed you. How else?"

"Ella, you can't—this isn't a place for you, sweetheart," Tata says, reaching out for my hand. His warm hugs and gentle explanations for everything could easily persuade me out of everything I want to do, but the thoughts that follow when he releases me are too loud to ignore.

I pull away from him so I can speak my mind before I allow myself to become weak as Tata's little girl—the way he still sees me, even as a grown woman. "Why, because I'm a girl? Plenty of women are part of the resistance. I've seen them walking around with rifles."

"So, you want to walk around town with a rifle under your

arm now? You think that'll end well for you?" Tata says, frustration evident.

"I want to help the Jewish people who are starving to death in our own city, in front of our foggy vision. It may take years to push the Wehrmacht out of here, but the Jewish will all be dead by then."

"Where is this all coming from? How are you so sure?" Miko adds with a raised brow.

"I had to deliver bread to Madame Kaminsky, remember?" I remind them. Tata stares up at the ceiling and closes his eyes.

"Right, of course."

He can't act as if we don't know what the Jewish ration cards look like. We don't need to see the quarter they live in to realize the truth. Those who live nearby shop in our store, too, and we can only give them what they're allowed to collect, which is far less than what non-Jewish people receive. What if everyone in this city who isn't Jewish is just avoiding the truth—because we're all scared? Where will that leave us in the end?

I pause, and take a deep breath, steeling myself.

"I've been seeing a man. He's Jewish. His name is Luka Dulski. He's twenty years old, brilliant, incredibly talented, and simply wonderful. In fact, I love him. And I'm watching him starve to death along with his mother and grandmother. His father and grandfather were already sent away for forced labor to some German factory. They haven't returned home since. And that wall in the center of Warsaw...the one no one talks about—we all see it. We all feel something brewing in the air."

Tata shoves the heels of his hands against his temples so hard it looks as if his head might explode. "How long has this been going on? Why haven't you told me? You love this man and we're just now finding out? You've never even had a boyfriend for more than a few weeks."

"Shall I get a mirror so you can see the reason I've kept this to myself?"

"Ella, calm down. You're angry at the wrong person," Tata says.

"So are you."

"Luka Dulski, huh?" Miko says, leaning forward inquisitively.

"If I thought you'd remember his name five minutes from now, I'd be worried," I snap at him. "Stay out of this."

"What is going on out here?" Mama asks. She steps into the living room with a dish rag pinched between her hands.

"I need to tell you something," I say, holding my chin up with a show of strength. "There's a young man I've been seeing... He's Jewish."

Mama's bottom lip falls and her brows rise toward her hairline. "Why haven't you told us?" she echoes Tata.

"He's Jewish," Miko repeats. "I think that might be why."

"Do not speak like that in my home, son. We will not disrespect any Polish person, no matter what their faith," Mama snaps.

Miko drops back into his chair and rolls his eyes. "It wasn't an offensive statement, just a fact. We aren't supposed to be mingling with them."

"Them?" I demand.

"Everyone, calm down," Tata says.

"Bring him here for us to meet," Mama says before returning to the kitchen.

Papa drops his head to his tented fingers. "Yes, I agree with your mother. I want to meet this man you're willing to sacrifice your safety for."

"Thank you," I say.

"And while I agree that the Jewish people need our help, I do not want you joining the resistance. I'm sorry. I can't let you. You're my little girl."

"I'm nineteen. I'm not a little girl, I'm a woman. And I *will* help those affected most by the invasion of our city."

NINE

LUKA

September 1940
Warsaw, Poland

My hand trembles as I pull the curtain back from the window, peeking outside as I do each morning when I wake up. A flicker of dread stirs inside of me, fearing I might find myself in the world alone without another person in sight. That's what the German soldiers want us to feel. Today could be the day they come for me and send me to wherever they sent Father four months ago. We haven't heard a word from him or Grandfather since then, leaving my mind to conjure the worst possible thoughts when I'm alone or trying to fall asleep. I miss them terribly and would do anything to find out that they're all right, wherever they are.

The sight of people wandering aimlessly reassures me I'm not the only one left here, but their heads are bowed, hands clasped behind their backs, stares clinging to the pavement beneath their feet.

The act of waiting for them to pull the trigger takes every bit of control out of my life, but I must put on a brave face for

Mother and Grandmother. Mama, especially. Her mental state has been out of sorts, almost as if she's living in a child's state of mind sometimes.

My body tenses as I peer around outside. I search in every direction, but thankfully find others walking around as usual, conducting their daily business. All is fine for the moment, I suppose.

"Luka, someone is knocking on the door," Grandmother shouts.

I grab my table-side clock, curious who would be at the door before seven in the morning. Pulling on a pair of trousers and grabbing a shirt from my closet, I button it on the way to the door.

"Who is it?" I ask, unlocking the door and opening it enough to see out into the dimly lit corridor.

Those sparkling blue eyes, rosy cheeks, and long dark lashes are peering up at me again and my shoulders fall with relief to see her in one piece after the state of mind she left in last night.

I open the door wider and usher her inside. "I'm sorry for showing up unannounced," she says.

"Don't be. Never. Is everything all right?" She doesn't look worse for wear. In fact, her eyes are smiling.

She hands me her satchel. "Go on, look inside," she says, biting on her lip in mischief.

"Ella," I say, before opening the bag. "What have you done?" I separate the two canvas flaps, finding multiple paper-wrapped goods nearly piled up to the rim of the bag.

I turn toward the kitchen without taking my eyes off the wrapped goods, wondering what might be inside, while trying to avoid thinking about what she did to acquire everything within. I stop in front of the countertop and gently slide everything out of the bag. I smell baked bread. There's a round bundle I rest my hand on first, a warmth seeping through the paper.

"Why are you breathing so hard?" Ella asks.

"I'm not," I lie, swallowing back a breath.

"Ella, it's so nice to see you back," Mama says, pulling her robe taut. "What is it that I'm smelling? I can't quite put my finger on it."

"Good morning, Madame Dulski. I hope I'm not disturbing you," I greet Luka's mother.

I unwrap the bundle I believe to be bread, finding the most perfect loaf, lightly covered in flour.

"Is that fresh bread?" Mama utters in disbelief.

"I made it for you. Sawdust free. All natural."

Mama's chin quivers as I unwrap the next item, finding a slim block of cheese.

Ella reaches out for a square shaped bundle. "This one should be kept cold." I unwrap it—a stack of six hamburger patties. We haven't had meat in over a year. "And this one, too." She lifts another square shaped package. "It's margarine."

I open the last of the packages, finding a cloth bundle of legumes. My face fills with heat and my nose burns. Tears fill my eyes, and I tilt my head up toward the ceiling, embarrassed, grateful, joyful, and worried. I sniffle and take in a full breath then tighten my arms around Ella, pulling her in tightly.

"How did you manage this, sweetheart?" Madame Dulski asks.

"After I told my father about what was happening in your district, he broke into today's inventory before the Germans showed up at the front door this morning. He's going to do what he can to help here. We all are."

"Ella," I say through an exhale. "You've done more than enough."

"Well, I'll let you enjoy your breakfast. I should return to the store," she says.

I walk her to the door and step out of the apartment with her. "The words, thank you, aren't sufficient," I tell her.

"It's not necessary. I'd do anything for you."

I kiss her forehead then her button nose. "Someday, I'll be able to do something for you, I'll be able to give you the world. Someday, you'll see."

She reaches up to kiss me then takes my hand and presses it to her heart. "As long as I have you."

* * *

A feast of sliced warm bread with margarine on the side makes my mouth water before I've even taken a bite. Grandmother is reciting a brachot over the meal, thanking God for the nutrients.

I'm thanking God for Ella.

Before Grandmother says her *Amen*, a scream pierces through the windows, followed by several others. Shots are fired from weapons, and fists pound against doors, more screams commencing. Mama, Grandmother and I study each other in silent shock, wondering what's happening outside. None of us move to the covered window or from our seat. Papa would. He would want to know what's happening before it happens to protect us.

That's my job now. I push my chair away from the table, away from the warm bread my stomach is clawing for, and step in toward the window to peek outside.

"More people are leaving with suitcases in hand. They're in lines, being shoved," I say. "Grab your belongings. I'll retrieve the money and papers. They're already in the building. They're coming for us."

I look at the bread, passing by the table to get to the loose floorboard where we keep our valuables. I have a suitcase prepared. We all do, just in case. With my belongings in hand and on my back, I wrap all the food back up and shove it into my knapsack, carefully placing the bread on top. Mama rushes into the kitchen, stares at her plants for a long second then moves to the stove where she chooses a few tins to drop into her purse.

Please spare us. Just a little longer. God, please.

The pounding on doors is relentless, two or three at a time and we're holding our breath, staring at our door, the door that welcomed so much happiness just minutes ago.

My throat tightens, constricting my breath. Grandmother has a scowl drawn across her lips and Mama's eyes are filled with tears. She's shaking her head, silently praying they leave us be. It doesn't sound as if they're skipping any doors beneath us.

Despite expecting the clobbering against our door, I choke on a breath when it happens. "Aufgehen!"

I swallow hard and walk to the door, my last steps before I come to face to face with the German soldier who will tell us to join the others. I peer back at Mama and Grandmother, both squeezing their eyes shut. It all happens in slow motion: the spit flying from the soldier's mouth as he shouts at us to take our belongings, in no more than one suitcase, and leave.

"This is the Aryan side of Warsaw. No Jews!"

The wall. The one we've all been watching rise higher and higher in the center of Warsaw without knowing its purpose.

I walk first, hoping it's the right thing to do to protect Mother and Grandmother. Behind me, I hear Mother's sob catch in her throat as the soldier orders us to leave our home— the last place where Father and Grandfather were with us. This is the moment we lose more of our identity regardless of where we go. Ella won't find me.

We follow others down the stairs of our building and out into a bright sunny day, a cruel mirage above us when we're walking eastward toward the wall. The streets I've known my entire life are nearly unrecognizable, filled with lines of disheveled fellow Jews shuffling forward with emptiness in their eyes as they leave their lives behind.

Our line merges with others, forming a stream of despair

winding around the streets as we head east. I turn back to look over my shoulder at our apartment, needing one last glance. I find the front stoop where I kissed Ella just yesterday—in a different lifetime.

I can almost still see her standing in the same place.

Wait, no.

She *is* there.

Watching.

Holding her hand over her mouth, shaking her head.

She darts to the next building corner, toward me, and I cast a doubtful glance, knowing we can't control what's happening. She can't follow me where I'm going. She's crying, reaching her hand out to me. Her cheeks are so red, the color is sharp and clear from too many footsteps away. "I'm sorry," I mouth to her. "I love you."

My throat burns as I fight to take in air. Everything hurts.

Mothers are holding their children tightly, handkerchiefs balled up in their hands. Children are whimpering, squeezing a toy, just a single toy. Little Jak, who thinks he's too big for a stuffed bear, clings to his mother's arm, squeezing the bear in the other. He peers over his shoulder, looking behind him, catching me in his view. I force a small smile, showing him I'm here, too. He looks down at the stuffed bear then back up at me and smiles faintly before turning to face forward.

There aren't many men, and I still don't have answers as to why I'm here and others aren't. There's never a clear reason for anything that happens to us anymore.

With the one final corner behind us just minutes from our home, the sight of the brick wall looms ahead. The height of the incumbent wall casts shadows for as far as I can see, and the closer we come, a change of smell—of sweat and dust—fills the air.

"It was right in front of us all this time," Grandmother says.

"What was?" I ask.

"The wall." Grandmother shakes her head and wraps her hand around her throat. "This is why no one knew what purpose the wall was to serve. This must be how the soldiers will close us out of the city—confining us to live within the bordering wall like caged animals."

The circulating questions about why the wall was being built in the middle of Warsaw had never been answered, but it's been hard to avoid the idea that it's always had something to do with the Jewish population. As the lines slow, it takes some time before we're forced to march up the wooden bridge, leading over the train tracks. The bridge complains beneath our weight, the boards groaning with every step.

As we descend the ramp that leads beyond the wall, it becomes clear that we've walked into our own trap. It was so easy to capture us. It's as if none of us have any fight left within us, but that isn't the case. We just have nothing to fight *with*.

We're led straight into a building, a sign on the door stating:

Administration of the Jewish District of Warsaw
Reception Center

Everyone pauses for a split second to read the sign—it says so little, but it means too much. Each person is carrying their life within their hands or on their backs, and yet no one is prepared for what will happen next.

The line leads to a table where a fellow Jewish man cranes his neck over a logbook, a pen in hand, jotting down our names. Then we're sent to an overcrowded room where we're supposed to wait for further instructions. The people around me are quiet aside from a few exchanging words of gossip or guesses as to what's next for us. The rest sit in silence, staring into a void. That's all I can do. Stare at the blur of people holding themselves up with a relentless sense of doubt and fear we can't escape.

Eventually, we hear that Pawia, building eleven in the Muranów neighborhood, is where the Judenrat committee has assigned us to live. We're herded through the streets once again, except this time, the streets within the foreboding wall are all dark, covered in soot and construction debris, with people lining the roads with no sense of direction. Deeper into the enclosure, the surroundings swallow us up as we reach a tenement over-filled with residents who lived here prior to the merge, and people who have been forced in since. Ten other people live in our unit, a space large enough for only two or three to live comfortably. The windows are to be kept open for airflow, the toilets are across the hall, outside the unit, and there's no running water. The building reeks of sewage.

A baby is crying, his mother desperately trying to soothe him with a quiet hum as she curls him up in her arms in the corner of the room. I'm not sure who might have lived here first, or sure if it's appropriate to ask.

Mother, Grandmother, and I find a space amid the room and place our bags down. "They expect us all to live here?" Mama whispers in my ear.

"I suppose we're all family now," I speak out. "My sincerest apologies to whoever lived here first. I can't imagine having your home infiltrated like this. And to the rest, we stand beside you. I'm Luka, and this is my mother, Chana, and my grandmother, Golda."

A few speak up with their names, but most don't lift their heads from staring at the ground beneath us.

"It's nice to meet you," a man says, walking up to me with his hand outstretched. He might be around my age. "Apollo. I'm here with my mother and little sisters—the three over near the window."

"I might just call you my one and only friend now. Hope that's all right," I say, trying a dose of humor, something that should seem foreign now.

"Same, brother," he says. "These folks aren't doing well from what I can see, but as the only two younger men in the room, I suspect we'll be assigned to work soon enough. Hopefully, we can still help the others out."

"Did you just arrive, too?"

"Yesterday," he says. "I wandered around a bit but it's a grim scene."

"Is there any way out? Can we come and go from this entrapment—the ghetto?" I ask, praying he says this is only where we live now. I doubt he knows too much more than I do as nothing has been made public knowledge.

"It doesn't look like we can leave, but non-Jewish Poles seem to come and go...at least from what I saw yesterday."

My thoughts cycle around Ella. If she finds a way to enter, nothing will stop her—not even warnings of danger. Despite the effort, it would be a waste as it will be impossible to find me among the dense population.

TEN

ELLA

October 1940
Warsaw, Poland

I can't believe what I'm watching. The German soldiers are forcing all the Jewish citizens in through a set of gates between the rising wall they've been building for months. I watched as Luka walked inside, then disappeared among the crowd. I've had my hands gripped on the corner of a brick building for so long, watching, that I can't straighten my fingers. How can they do this? How many times can I ask this same question?

Every person walking through the gates has grim, matching looks of confusion painted across their faces, each clutching their valuables within a suitcase or knapsack. There isn't enough space within the confines for everyone. Even though the wall consumes around four-hundred streets made up of small city blocks, it merely makes up three percent of the populated living space in Warsaw. Yet they're forcing over a third of the population to live between the enclosure.

I don't know how I'll find Luka now.

The line is endless, people forcefully waiting for their

admission. With my heart heavy and my chest burning, I turn away and run to the shop. I can hardly breathe by the time I spot the line of customers waiting outside to be let in. Some of the locals call my name as I burst in through the door, dodging questions of "what's wrong?" I can't be the only one witnessing these atrocities. Are people just acting as if they don't see what I see?

"Ella, what's the matter?" Tata asks while counting change from the register.

"They're pushing all the Jewish people into the walls. They made Luka and his family leave their home. They all had suitcases and knapsacks. The soldiers were banging on every door, telling them all to leave."

Tata glances past me toward the shop window and I turn, too, finding many pairs of eyes staring at the silent scene. Tata takes my hand and pulls me to the back of the store. "How are you so well informed about this?" he asks.

"After I brought Luka the food and left, I stood behind a corner and watched the soldiers as they paraded into the Jewish quarter, storming through the buildings with rage. I watched them force Luka out. They took them to the walls where so many people are now in line, waiting to get inside, against their will. They're locking up the Jews, Tata."

"It wasn't supposed to happen this soon," he says.

"What does that mean?" I snap, throwing my hands in the air. "You knew this was happening?"

"I can only depend on the words I hear from others. There wasn't much logic to building a wall encircling part of the city if they didn't intend to use the space. The Germans have made it clear they want to segregate the Jewish people."

"I have to get to him before it's too late, Tata. I must."

"You can't go into that confinement, you may never make it back out," Tata argues. "He could be in any one of those buildings within the walls."

"There must be a method to reach him. Would the Judenrat deliver a message?"

"Ella, sweetheart, you are moving into a dangerous territory. No one knows what's allowed and what isn't. This isn't what you want to hear, but—"

"But, what? Should I give up on him? Forget that he's just been forced into a prison where he can't communicate with anyone beyond those walls?"

"No citizen of Poland wants this, darling. We want to see the Wehrmacht go, but nothing is going to happen overnight. People are trying. We are. We're doing all we can."

No, we aren't. Tata drops his head and makes his way into the back room, passing Miko on the way.

"What's the matter with you?" my brother asks. His question doesn't come out in his usual irritating older brother tone, but with concern instead.

"It's nothing you would worry about," I reply, knowing he hasn't shown much support for my feelings toward Luka. He never even got to meet him, which just makes him another Jewish person in this city.

Miko leans his head to the side and places down a sack of onions. "What is it?" he asks again, peering at me with a hard look.

I grit my teeth, knowing I'll likely regret telling him, but I can't keep it inside either. "Luka's family was forced out of their house this morning and sent to part of the city within the brick walls. I may never find him again."

Miko pulls in a heavy breath and peers up to the ceiling. "This is what I was worried about."

"I love him," I remind him. "That didn't happen overnight. I've been spending much of my free time with him since the end of April. He's the most wonderful—"

"All right, I don't need more details. I understand. It's unfortunate we didn't get a chance to meet him."

"Miko...is there a way I can have a message delivered to him? Is there anyone who can help me?"

He shakes his head before looking back over his shoulder toward the back door. "Are we allowed through the gates, or is it only Jewish people who are entering?"

"I'm not sure."

Miko places his hand down on my shoulder. "Let me see what I can find out from the others tonight during our meeting."

"I want to go with you," I tell him.

"Ella—the people in the resistance...they're not like you. They want our freedom back. They aren't trying to save just one person. This isn't meant to be an insult. I know you better than anyone else in the world, and I can't let you become mixed up with these people."

"Why are you mixed up with them then?"

"I want what they want, and Tata shouldn't be there alone." I get the sense it's more of the latter than the former reason. I don't think Miko would have joined if it hadn't been for our father. He prefers routine simplicities in life—work, sleep, food.

"I want what they want, too," I argue.

"Give me a day to find out if I can get a message sent to a connection within the enclosure, and don't follow us tonight, you hear me?"

I cross my fingers hard behind my back when I agree.

They're letting non-Jewish Poles inside the gates. I've watched day after day for almost three weeks now, still searching for a way to reach Luka. Miko had no connections to help me. He said there was a lot of black-market action—people trading goods through inconspicuous holes amid the walls, risking their lives with each pass. He also said that the SS troops were aware and killing people trying to bring goods into the confinement. Even children.

I tried my luck yesterday, the proper way, at the gates and with identification, stating my need to visit a friend. The guards told me if I had no business matters to conduct within the confinement, my visit wasn't necessary.

I haven't done much else but watch the square from outside the gate, hoping I could catch sight of Luka walking by, but the walls cover almost two dozen city blocks on each square side.

The sun has fallen beneath the horizon and darkness is beginning to cloak the city streets and, again, defeat falls over me, just as it has every other day I've stood here with any flicker of hope.

I walk along the exterior of the wall, avoiding the soldiers when I see them patrolling a block, dragging my fingertips along the brick, wishing I could see inside.

My heart leaps into my throat as the warm, low tones of a song rise through the air, taking me hostage as I press my ear to the stone, pleading for more.

> *The sky is dark and gray*
> *but behind the clouds, it's blue.*
> *Lovely days will come*
> *soon for me and you.*

Luka? I claw my fingertips into the grooves of the brick wall, trying to find a way up. "Luka?" I call out in a whisper.

> *Keep me in your dreams,*
> *and I'll come to you each night.*
> *Hold me in your arms*
> *until the morning light.*

I try to climb up to the top until my fingers become raw,

until the singing stops, until it's clear no one hears me calling Luka's name. Maybe he's on the very other side, trying to reach me, too.

It shouldn't be this way.

A scuffle along the curb startles me into jumping away from the wall, searching for whoever else is on this darkening street. The steps don't sound like they come from a soldier's boots, but I won't chance the risk. I hurry across the street to hide along a protruding arch entrance to a building, waiting for the person to walk by.

I breathe a sigh of relief when I confirm they aren't a soldier, but they are walking swiftly with an assault rifle tucked under their arm, a satchel hanging from the other, and dressed in dark civilian clothing. The members of the resistance try to blend in, but I've become more cognizant of their presence lately. I want to know where he's going, especially this close to the enclosure.

I follow, but with space between us, trying to be quiet with each step. The man moves along around corners and blocks, checking the surrounding area once every few steps. After reaching a protruding corner, he bolts to the left, crossing the street to head in a different direction. I hesitate to follow, now unsure if he's here for a similar reason to me. I wait until he's two blocks ahead, watching him move along at the same pace he's been going, and make the quick decision to continue pursuing him. Where there's one man of resistance, there must be more.

He finally comes to a stop where three other men are waiting for him, and descends into a hole in the ground. The sewer tunnel. No matter how many times I've followed Tata and Miko, it's only been to a decrepit hole in the wall where they go in through a cellar door.

I watch for a while, wondering if anyone else will go down the sewer tunnel. No one does, and one of the others who must be guarding the sewer hole says his goodbyes to the other two and heads in my direction. I back myself into a nook of a building, but when he passes, I can't help myself.

"Excuse me," I call out. The man stops short and turns toward me, his hands gripping tightly around his rifle. "I didn't mean to startle you, but I'm wondering if you can help me."

He steps toward me, his face still dark until he's within reach. "Arte Bandoa?" I recognize him from secondary school.

"Ella?" he searches around for prying eyes and ears before continuing. "What are you doing over here, alone in the dark?"

"It might be too much to explain."

"You shouldn't be over here. It's dangerous." He shuffles his satchel higher on his shoulder and conceals his weapon, tighter beneath his arm.

"I understand, but I'm looking for someone in the ghetto."

"You can't. Tomorrow, an announcement will be made public that no one else will be coming or going from inside. The Jewish people will be locked up in there for good."

"The tunnels...they go beneath the walls, don't they?"

Arte exhales sharply. "Yes, but it's not a corridor. It's a sewer with water knee high."

"I'll join the resistance. I'll help," I offer.

"Have you hit your head or something? You're talking nonsense. I'm going to walk you home."

"No, no, Arte, I haven't hit my head. Can people from within the walls go through a sewer tunnel on their end?"

"Yes, that's why we're—"

"Show me, please."

"You're out of your mind. I'm taking you home. Your father wouldn't want you here."

ELEVEN

LUKA

January 1941
Warsaw, Poland

The wagon putters over every stone, its wooden wheels grumbling in protest. Each stone that catches beneath a wheel sends a tremble through my arms as I grip the worn handles tighter to steady the load of bodies piled up on the bed.

Mother and Grandmother were spared from work duties, but as Apollo, my tenement-mate stated on the day of our arrival just over two months ago, I would likely be assigned to work the next day, and I was. I was assigned to maintenance duties, with little to no instruction other than to keep the streets clean.

I want to be a singer and composer. It's all I've ever wanted. Mother and Father told me I would have to fight hard as an artist, and it would come with challenges, but I didn't expect this sort of challenge. After the other Jewish children of Warsaw were kicked out of public schools, I had little else to do but sit in my apartment, writing lyrics and composing music on Grandmother's piano. I didn't consider a trade because I knew what I wanted to do. So now, I'm here without a physical skill set aside from singing a tune. I suppose that's why I've been assigned to cleaning up deceased bodies from the sidewalks.

With winter upon us, there are new challenges to face, ones I hadn't considered in the autumn weather. A young boy stumbles past me, barefoot and coatless, teeth chattering. His tiny legs, bare beneath his kneecaps, are covered in sores. His lips are cracked and layered with dry blood, and his cheeks are covered with streaks of dirt. He reaches out his frail hand toward a man selling scraps of bread to a line curling around a corner, but the man shoos him away while shielding the pile of goods he plans to barter off. Everyone here is forced to beg the street tradesmen for food, fabric, leather, anything and everything because they have nothing. Some steal, but who can blame them?

Overhead, the cloudy sky hangs low, the color of ash. Snowflakes flutter, melting into the grooves between the cobblestones. The air bites at my face and hands, and freezes my heavy breaths, forming short puffs of fog.

"Luka!" I hear between the clattering of the wagon's wheels. I turn, in search of whoever called me, finding Apollo trudging toward me through the mass of people. His factory-issued overalls are too thin for winter, and his breath clouds in front of him as he rushes over. His hair is a pile of dark, greasy curls. He's tall and lanky like me, and walks with long, gaping strides, giving him a goofy look. But then he also has a sly, crooked smile and mischief in his eyes, making it hard for me to predict what he's going to approach me with next. He keeps me entertained at least, and it's been nice to have a friend here.

"Why aren't you at the factory?" I ask him. He spends his days crafting tools for Germans, while I cart dead bodies away from the sidewalks.

"I have to talk to you," he says, breathless. His somber-looking eyes dart around, searching for whoever might be listening.

"What is it?" I follow, scanning the area for any Jewish Ghetto Police or members of the Judenrat. They linger everywhere with their sharp stares, and dark souls sold to the Germans for crumbs.

He nods his head toward a quiet corner, and I follow him, dragging the wagon behind. "The black market," he says.

"The one no one can find?" I add.

"One of the other men at the factory was talking about it this morning. There's a black-market underground in the sewer tunnels. People are exchanging goods with folks outside the ghetto."

"I'm sure the Germans are down there, too," I tell him. It's not that I haven't considered every possible way to get to the other side of these walls, but I've watched many try, then, the moment they'd make it to the other side, I'd hear one sharp blast of rifle. Their attempts have been a warning but not a deterrent to all.

"It's like a maze. They can't be everywhere, and we wouldn't be escaping, just trading. I wouldn't want to be the one sticking my head out of a hole to reach the outside, I understand your worry there."

"You overheard all of this?" I press.

"Yes, many people know about the tunnels, but I didn't realize there are trades between us and the non-Jewish Poles."

I know about the tunnels, too. Ella mentioned that her father and brother go down there for their work with the resistance. However, there isn't much talk about access points.

"I'm going down there tonight. I'm going to see what I can get my hands on," Apollo says. "Come with me."

"I can't go with you tonight. I promised to help my mother with something. Maybe another night?"

"You never take risks, huh?" he questions me.

I'm not surprised to be accused of this when he's right. The number of thoughts I've had since walking in through those black iron gates in October. I've considered sending Ella letters, asking Poles who used to come through here for business to bring a message to her. I stood in front of the gates, watching the other side for hours, wondering if I might spot her among the crowd. Then I realized if I sent her a letter and it was intercepted by a German soldier, they could go after her. If I gave the wrong person a message to deliver, the same thing could happen. There have been so many people passing by the gates daily that it's likely impossible to spot her among them. I want to protect her, which means living with a heavy heart and wondering what pain I might have caused her. I tell myself they can't hold us in here forever, surely...?

"I can't do that to my mother or grandmother. They aren't well. I need to care for them," I explain.

Apollo twists his mouth from side to side as if he's pondering the same thoughts. He has a mother and two younger sisters to care for, too.

"I want to do what I can to care for my family, and this might be the answer." He curls his hands behind his neck and stretches, staring up to the cloud-covered sky. "You're right. I should think on this."

Apollo taps my shoulder and heads back toward the factory. I wish I didn't know about this tunnel, it'll be weighing on my mind now.

With a tug of the heavy wagon, I weave between the tradesmen on the street, searching for the next lifeless body lumped alongside a building. A pile of black fabric catches my eye, and I stop, my breath hanging in the icy air. Beneath the fabric, pale feet poke out, frozen and bare. Snowflakes cling to the folds of the cloth.

I tug on the fabric, revealing the face of a young girl. Her porcelain skin is untouched by the dirt of the street, her long lashes resting peacefully against her cheeks. Her lips are blue, and her eyelids carry the faintest tint of frost. My fingers press against her neck in search of a pulse I won't find. It doesn't matter how many bodies I scoop up daily, the same tight pain in my chest drains more life out of me for each lost life.

Frail like paper, with bones dangling over my arms, I curl her into my arms then rest her down in the wagon as if I was putting a little girl to bed. She's no older than seven or eight. She's someone's little girl and there's no saying whether this someone is still alive or looking for her. "I'm so sorry, little princess," I whisper. Why am I so numb inside? It's as if I've run out of tears to shed. Or this pain has simply become a fiber of my being.

* * *

Apollo hasn't come back to the apartment before midnight once in the last week. He's still asleep when I leave in the morning, but I assume he decided to take the risk and venture down into the sewer tunnels. I'm curious as to what he found or didn't find.

Though there are more than a dozen of us living in this one apartment, what belongs to each family isn't shared. It would be impossible to share evenly. We all must fend for ourselves.

"You're back," Mother says, wrapping her frail arms around me. "My wonderful mensch of a son."

"I'm back, yes. Are you well? Where's Grandmother?" I peer around the crowded floor, not spotting her anywhere.

"She's not right," Mother says, shaking her head and staring up at me with wide eyes. "I'm scared something's wrong."

"Where is she?" I ask again, more urgently.

"Between the kitchen and the single bedroom. I didn't want anyone to disturb her."

I step over others who are already asleep at this early hour and turn the corner, finding Grandmother curled into a ball, asleep. She's pale and her breathing is labored, a whistling sound passing through her lips.

Mother wraps her arms around mine as I ask, "What is she sick with?"

"It could be anything," Mother says. "I would do anything for some of my herbs. I can nurse her back to health much quicker. We've gone through everything I had. I should have set some aside. I don't know what I was thinking." Mother's voice breaks as a quiet cry escapes her lips.

"What is it we need to help her?" I've watched Mother chop, dice, steam, extract oils from seeds, and then concoct it all over boiling water—turn a bunch of leaves into a serum or tea. I never paid much attention to the process though. Herbal remedies became her focus after our doctors were forced to leave their practices and consider their licenses to be void. She would tell me we're on our own and must take care of ourselves somehow, and nature can help with that.

There's no nature within the walls of the ghetto. Even in the late summer and fall, there were hardly any birds, never mind patches of grass, trees, or wildflowers.

"Anything would be more than what we have," she says. "Garlic cloves and ginger would be helpful, or thyme and honey. Have you seen anyone selling them on the streets?"

People are trading goods more than food. Food is scarce for everyone, inside and outside the walls. Though there are more sources outside than there are here.

"I'll search tomorrow when the tradesmen are out. I'm not sure I've seen anyone selling herbs."

"I figured as much," Mother says. "She's a fighter, your grandmother. She'll pull through this, I'm sure."

But my mother's words lack the confidence of the promises she would make to me when I was younger, assuring me everything would be all right, when really, nothing would be. *To fear*

fear, is the worst form of fear, is what she would always say. It makes too much sense now.

Mother resettles herself on the pile of blankets we have, and I sit down beside her. I sit, holding my knees against my chest, staring toward the last lit candle in the center of the room.

The quiet enhances the number of us coughing and sniffling. It isn't just Grandmother who's sick. There's no heat in this building. We all quiver through the night, sleeping in our coats and boots.

The front door opens and closes, pulling me out of a daze between being awake and asleep. A hand drops to my shoulder. "Luka, come out here with me, quick."

Apollo's back early tonight and with something important to share. I push myself to my feet and carefully avoid stepping on anyone as I follow him back to the door. We're out in the dark hallway with no light other than a slice of the moon glowing into the cracked window above the stairwell.

"I was down in the sewer tunnel. There's life down there. There are a lot of people, selling, trading, entertaining. There hasn't been a German in sight. Not yet at least. I was talking with a few men tonight, taking in information from outside the wall on the advances Germany is making through Poland and then I heard someone calling your name."

"Me?" I question.

"It was unmistakable, brother. I went through three different tunnels to find where the sound was coming from. I thought I was losing my marbles but then I found the person calling for you."

"Who was it?" I ask, struggling to catch a breath.

"She didn't give me a name. I told her I knew you and she shoved a paper into my hand and pleaded that I make sure you get it. I asked what the name was, but she wouldn't give it to me. She said she's been looking for you for months, but no one has known your name until tonight."

Apollo grabs my wrist and shoves the paper into my hand. I unfold it and try to read it within the darkness, unable to see a thing. I move closer to the stairwell and the window, waiting for the cloud to move across the moon to offer more light.

Then I see.

Luka,

I'm searching for you. I've been down here...every night, praying someone will help me reach you. My heart is broken into so many pieces I'm not sure I'll be able to put it back together, not knowing where you are or if you're well. I love you so very much and I can't think of anything else but you. I will do whatever I can to find you. If you find this letter, please know I'll keep looking. I'll keep waiting. I'm here. I have been and will be.

Yours Truly,

E

* * *

I fall backward, landing on the top step of the stairs, and press my hand through my hair, unable to believe what my eyes are reading. She's down there in the tunnels—the place I've been fearful to go because of the risk involved.

"Did she leave, or did she stay?"

"She walked away after handing me the letter," Apollo says. "Who is she?"

I press the note to my chest and stare out at the moon. "My love, on the other side."

TWELVE

ELLA

January 1941
Warsaw, Poland

No one can see inside the walls, and they can't see out here. Our city is divided like black and white colors without an ounce of gray between. The brick layers don't stop the sounds from escaping—children crying, women and men pleading with others, and ghostly screams that mimic the whistling of wind.

I've overheard people in the store saying things like the walls are an enclosure for the burial ground of Jews, which isn't shocking with what I see in the underground tunnels at night. For months, I've done nothing more than work then map my way around the sewers, calling out for Luka with hope of finding him or someone who might know him. I was losing hope until last night someone finally responded to my calls. Whoever that man was, he agreed to take Luka my letter. The odds of this happening seem too slim. Many of the Jewish people I've seen underground are in a mentally ill state of mind, talking to themselves, pleading with the air in front of them for help, keeling over, and worse.

I climb down the cold, wet metal ladder to the bottom of the tunnel where three passageways meet. I've explored all three but found only one that connects to the passages where the Jewish people wander from within the walls.

From this tunnel and its wading water that rises to my knees, several other tunnels branch away. I keep a note in my pocket with the directions I've followed because my fear is that I'll run out of matches, or my torch will become too damp to light. Without fire, I'll be blinder than a cloud covered night in an endless field.

The narrow confines are the tunneled walls that breathe a life of their own, exhaling cold air filled with a foul odor of rotting waste from the city streets above, then inhaling the air from my lungs, leaving me unbalanced and dizzy. As the water splashes against me with each step, flickers of light and shadows pass by slight openings to other tunnels, a mystery of who else might be traveling through the dark underground. I try to glide to avoid extra movement within the water, but it's a strain moving against the current. That and the cold temperatures against my wet stockings and boots leave me numb after a few short minutes of walking.

I keep promising myself my persistence will pay off and I'll find Luka before he becomes a part of this enclosed cemetery people speak about. It's hard to notice others down here until we're right beside each other. Many choose narrow divots in the wall to set up shop and sell whatever they hope the Jewish people will buy with whatever they have to offer. It won't be long before the Germans are tipped off to the great amount of activity occurring down here each night but until then, we all forge ahead.

I drag my hand along the damp stone wall, searching for the next extruding tunnel where the black market is the busiest as there's extra space between the connecting tunnels in this one area. It's also where someone responded to my call for Luka last night.

It's lit up with more torches and the water level reduces to puddles. Crates are used as tables and people form lines to conduct trades.

"Luka," I call out above the hum of chatter, holding my torch out in every direction to scan my surroundings. There isn't a familiar face among the crowd, and I must sound like I've lost my mind after doing this night after night here. Each call for his name tears away another small piece of my heart as silence returns with the answer I keep dreading. Between the flares of light from the torches, the people are lost in the shadows walking around as silhouettes. I imagine his face, the thought of finding him, the pain that would ease knowing he's at least still alive. With a tug, I tighten my coat around my chest, turning in each direction to call out his name as my voice breaks from the cold.

With my arm out to the side, I search for the nearest wall, making sure not to walk into anyone on the way. "Luka?" I call out again, holding up my torch.

I will myself not to cry from holding on to too much hope after last night.

A lick of fire flashes in front of my face, briefly blinding me. When the darkness returns, a hand presses to my cheek, fingers curling around my ear. My heart pounds, fearful of who's touching me, and what they might want. I gasp for breath when a mouth closes around mine.

Familiar lips, plump and consuming, his body pressed against mine, pinning me against the wall, offering me a warmth that spreads through the numbness. My eyes close as I lose myself in his touch, his embrace, his gentle but affirmative movements that define the meaning of longing. For a moment, the tunnels vanish from around us and we're beneath the golden sun setting above us as we dangle our legs from the tree branch, laughing and listening to the songs he wrote just for me —a place where the world didn't exist.

His heart fights mine, pounding against each other as he envelops every part of me, refusing to let go or take a breath. He inhales without moving his lips from mine, then claws his hand through my loose braid, cradling my head. Words aren't needed when this moment could last me a lifetime and beyond.

When our lips break apart, I open my eyes, finding a gentle glow from above us, his hand resting on the wall above my head with a lit torch. "My girl, my love," he utters. "You're here in the center of unimaginable danger."

"I've been trying so hard to find you. I was beginning to think I never would," I say, my voice cracking into a squeak of despair. "I've been so scared something happened. The rumors are so ugly, Luka."

"They're all true," he says.

I reach for his cheek, finding his face even thinner and more defined. His hair is longer on the nape of his neck. "When someone told me they knew you here last night, I thought I was dreaming. I thought I had driven myself so mad trying to find you that I was imagining it all. But in the chance that I wasn't, I brought food, as much as I could pack into my satchel."

Luka sweeps his nose to the side of mine, kissing the corner of my lips, and I wonder how easy it might be to take him home with me and hide him. "I can't believe you've been searching for me all this time. I was afraid to come down here, not knowing the risks involved. And yet, here you were, risking it all for me."

"I will keep doing it, for however long it takes to make sure you're well."

"It's so dangerous, Ella. People are shot coming in and out of the sewer holes."

"The one I've been using is guarded by the resistance," I whisper. "If I could, I'd take you, your mother and grandmother home with me. I would hide you, keep you all safe."

He swallows hard and exhales heavily. "My grandmother isn't well, and my mother is falling apart. I wouldn't be able to get them down here and—"

"I understand," I tell him. The risk would be enormous, but I would do it if it meant helping them. I wish there was a solution that could help the three of them. "What is your grandmother sick with?"

"I'm not sure. Whatever it is has made its way into her lungs, though."

"What can I bring you? Your mother can fix her some herbal remedies, right?"

Luka tilts his head back, staring up toward the burning torch. "How much of a risk will it be to you?"

"Don't worry about me. Tell me what you need. Let me help. Let me see you again."

"Thyme leaves, honey, or garlic and ginger. But I don't want you going anywhere you shouldn't to find these items, Ella. I don't want you to go outside the city. You must listen to me. I wouldn't be able to live with myself if something happened to you when I'm stuck here and can't help you."

"I'm stronger than I might appear," I tell him. I won't let fear take me down.

"I never questioned your strength," he says. "I just love you too much to be the reason you are ever in danger."

A clatter against metal rails above our head means the resistance guards are calling everyone back up, but it's hard to decipher if the demands are coming from inside or outside the ghetto walls.

Luka inhales sharply through his nose and closes his eyes then kisses me again. He feathers his knuckles down my cheek, my neck, and across my shoulder. "If I ever get the chance to keep you, I hope you'll be mine forever."

"And ever," I utter in return. "But until then, I'll be back tomorrow night. Same time, same place, with more."

"I love you so much it aches through every bone in my body," he says.

"I'm familiar with that pain." I rest my cheek against his chest, memorizing the rhythm of his beating heart. I slide my fingers between his and squeeze gently as a heaviness presses against my shoulders. He lifts my hand and kisses my knuckles.

"Tomorrow, my love."

He steps away but doesn't take the satchel. "Wait," I call out.

He turns back and I hold out the bag. "Take it."

His chin trembles as he takes it from my hand. "Thank you," he says with a faint breath. We part ways through opposite tunnels, not knowing if tomorrow will come.

THIRTEEN

ELLA

August 1941

Since Luka was banished to Warsaw's ghetto last October, I searched for nearly four months until fate finally reunited us. Now, ten months into his imprisonment between the walls, night after night—through February's frozen waters to August's stale heat—nothing has stopped me, and nothing will, from making my way to him in the dark world beneath our city.

His grandmother is better and they have more food. His cheekbones were less defined, making me think I've done something to help them at least. It will never be enough. I want to take them all away from the ghetto and keep them somewhere safe, but with each day that passes, more German soldiers are flooding the street. There's no end in sight and there's no saying how long anyone can continue surviving within those walls.

The German soldiers are preparing for something, another something we're all in the dark about. All we can do is speculate and fear the worst. I want to block it all out and pretend these horrors don't exist and our forbidden exchanges aren't anything more than a little secret, but even if I could, it would be impossible for Luka to imagine this is all a nightmare.

Then I'm left wondering how long this luck will last—how long will Luka and I get away with our rendezvous? Each night the walls of the tunnel squeeze tighter, as if they're closing in on me, threatening to close completely and never set me free.

"Papers!" another German shouts at me from down the block. It's rare to go a day without having to prove my identity now. It makes me wonder how many Jewish people have managed to escape relocation to the ghetto, and if they have, whether they dare step foot on the street.

I retrieve my identification out of my pocket, staring at my hand as if I could summon it to hold still. The soldier glares at me, his eyes narrow and beady as if I'm vermin he's forced to share the same air with. To think I've spent my life looking for friendship, ensuring I show kindness to all, and still question myself if someone doesn't take a liking to me, makes me realize my attempt to please everyone is impossible. I will never be able to get everyone to like me and it's something I must live with. Still, I wonder who could hate a person they've never met. I tell myself it shows their true character, not mine.

Regardless, the nerve and fear hasn't diminished in the face of these German soldiers parading through our city as if they're royalty. Despite how many times I've shown my papers and been sent along on my way, my conscience gets the best of me just knowing I appear innocent when really I'm elbow-to-elbow with many of the resistance members of our city every night. Do they see the guilt in my eyes?

"Papers!" the soldier shouts to someone behind me as he hands mine back. I hurry around the next corner where trees line the center of the street so I can move more freely, until reaching the street connected to the sewer entrance.

"Good evening, Miss Ella," Arte greets me from his usual guard spot behind the open sewer cover.

"Arte," I reply, before handing him a loaf of bread and a paper bag filled with flour for his mother. It's an agreement we've made. He won't tell my father what I'm doing or where I am, and I'll give him extra rations in return.

My family's routine is rigid, Mama tends to her embroidery while Tata and Miko venture out into the night with an unusual amount of understanding from Mama who rarely questions what they're doing, especially with the threatening ten o'clock curfew hanging over all non-Jewish citizens' heads. I suppose she lives by her infamous motto of "A secret is a burden of the truth." If someone is gossiping, she'll remind us of how she feels. It's understandable, being forced to live with information we'd rather go without.

As for me, I climb out my bedroom window each night, thankful we live just above the awning of the grocery store with a trellis on the side. Unlike Tata and Miko, I make sure to be home before the instituted curfew.

"Thank you," Arte says.

"Thank you," I reply.

I wade through sewer water, holding my dress up above my knees, moving quicker and quicker each night so as not to waste a single moment of our time together. With every encounter, a renewed sense of relief fills my heart, knowing he's still holding on to hope as much as I am.

His hands always find me before I spot him, stealing my breath once again when he claims my lips. Tonight, his muscles are tense, neck stiff, palms are hot and clammy, at least much more than usual.

"Is something wrong?" I ask, grasping at the loose fabric on his sleeves.

"I'm just delighted to see you," he says.

"Something's wrong. I can hear it in your voice."

Our torches both flicker and crackle as we stare at each other and I'm trying to understand why he isn't responding, why his eyes look more lethargic than they did yesterday and the day before, why his lips won't hint at even a small smile.

"I want these moments to be the light in my day," he says.

"Tell me," I plead, my heart racing as questions flash through my mind like wind-blown pages of a book.

He takes my free hand within his and smoothes the pad of his thumb over my fingers. "Everyone is sick. People are dropping dead right before my eyes every day, and that's not including the bodies I collect from the streets. Grandmother is sick again. It's worse this time. Every time she regains her health, something else hits her. She's so weak and fragile. It's as if she's aged ten years since last October. My mother is terrified. She hardly speaks. She spends her day chopping up whatever herb you've sent to her and stares at walls without blinking. *Everyone* just stares lately—it's as if our bodies have become shells of the people we once were."

"Luka, you are a fighter—a survivor. You can't think otherwise. Not now. Not ever."

"I've checked in with the Jewish council a dozen times now and there's no record of my father or grandfather anywhere. I haven't told my mother this, fearful of where her mind might go if I do."

There is so much pain in his eyes. I doubt any amount of food or supplies I give him will be enough to help. I loop my arms around his waist and rest my cheek on his chest, listening to the fast beat of his heart, his heavy breaths, the tremor when he takes a deep inhale.

"I'll go on a hunt for more herbs tomorrow. The crops are drying up in the heat, but I'm sure the farmers have something."

"The farms? Ella, those are outside the city. How will you get there?"

"I'll find a way."

"No. I can't imagine what the rest of the city is like right now, but I'm sure it isn't much better than what I'm living with."

"I'm not going to let your grandmother stay sick."

"Please. I—I can't—promise me you're not leaving the city tomorrow. This is why I was hesitant to say anything. I shouldn't have told you."

"Stop it, Luka. You're talking nonsense now. I asked you what was wrong. I knew something wasn't right."

"Promise me you won't leave Warsaw. If you can't find the herbs in the city, we'll find another way to help her feel more comfortable."

Luka slides his hand beneath my chin, forcing me to peer up at him—forcing me to witness the plea within his tired eyes.

"I'll search the city, high and low," I utter. "I won't leave."

"Thank you," he murmurs, pulling me back into his chest, folding me into his arms and resting his chin on top of my head. "I could convince myself this moment is a dream. What more could I ask for than you in my arms?"

* * *

I'm at odds with my brain and heart, one telling me to go one way and the other saying something else. His poor grandmother. I can't stomach the thought of how much they're all suffering. I must find whatever herbs I can tomorrow. They've helped her regain her health each of the three times she's fallen ill since arriving within the encampment ten months ago.

I climb up the wet, metal rungs of the ladder until I make it to street level. "Hurry, Ella, they're close by. Too close tonight," Arte says. "Was there anyone else behind you?"

"No, not that I saw." He pulls me away from the sewer hole and drags the cover into place. "Come on now, let's get you home." He tugs my arm, pulling me down the block and to the main street I'll take home.

"Arte, I can get home just fine, but I appreciate the offer," I say, curious why he's determined to walk me home tonight. He hasn't since the first night I found the tunnels and bargained the exchange deal with him.

"Ella, please...I received a warning that officials were heading in our direction," Arte whispers. "I just want to make sure—"

"Ella Bosko, is that you?" someone calls out from behind us with an unfamiliar sound of glee.

My heart leaps into my throat as I clutch the collar of my dress, feeling choked. I recognize the voice, and I'm thankful I'm not too close to the sewer entrance.

A former acquaintance I haven't seen in years steps out of the shadows of a dark road. *Daniel Kuziakow.* We went to school together. His father was a police officer, often patrolling the streets bordering the school yard. All the children knew him. He was a nice man who knew everyone by name, greeted us on the streets daily. It was never a question of how much he loved his job. Therefore, it isn't a surprise to see Daniel follow in his father's footsteps. Except, Daniel isn't an ordinary police officer—he's one of the Blue Police, working for the Germans—a traitor.

"I didn't realize you had become a Blue—"

"I'm with the Polish Police," he states as if I don't realize there's a difference. Their affiliations are marked by uniform.

A laugh threatens to come out in the form of anger and resentment, but for the purpose of getting home safely tonight, I hold my tongue.

"How wonderful of you to follow in your father's path. I'm sure he's proud," I say.

"Indeed, he is. And you, how are your family?" he asks. "I haven't seen Miko in a while. What is he doing with his life?"

"Everyone is well," I say, keeping my response short.

"Ella, I promised your father you'd be home on time," Arte speaks up.

"Yes, he's right. I should be going," I say, wanting to end this rendezvous.

"Are you two...?" Daniel asks bluntly.

"No, just friends," I say. Immediately, I regret my answer. If I had said yes, Daniel would walk away. Luka had popped into my mind before I could think it through.

"How nice," Daniel says. "Arte, if you don't mind, I'd love to have a moment to catch up with Ella. I'm happy to make sure she makes it home on time."

Arte's eyes light with terror, but it might be due to the two of them not getting along well in school. I shared common friends with Daniel and there was a time when he was persistent about the two of us dating, though things never turned out that way.

"I'll be all right," I assure Arte. I'm sure he can hear the lie in the strain of my voice. I don't want to cause any bad blood with someone on the Blue Police. He'll take me home and that will be the end of it. Arte is hesitant to walk away, but my forced smile tells him he must.

"Have a good night," Daniel tells Arte. "Nice to see you!"

His friendly salutation to Arte isn't fooling me.

"How have you been?" I ask Daniel, hoping this walk and conversation go by quickly.

"Well, and you?" he asks, walking alongside me in the direction of home.

"As well as possible, I suppose." I could only wish for an awkward silence to follow my response.

"You sure look beautiful," he says, jumping right to his plan of attack. I should consider myself lucky that the night's sky hides the sewer grime covering my bare legs beneath the hem of my skirt, and my black boots hide the rest. Since the city reeks of sewage from overcrowding in the ghetto, lack of running water, and broken sewer lines, the clinging odors seamlessly blend into the air, shielding the truth of my earlier whereabouts.

"That's kind of you. You look sharp in your uniform." My words come out dry and lifeless, hard to make them sound any other way.

"It's been so long since I've seen you. We should really spend some time together."

"I work a lot of hours in my family's store. I don't get out much except for a quick walk before curfew most nights."

"I understand," he says. Without waiting on another breath, he continues. "Say, my family is having some people over this weekend. An end of summer hurrah of sorts. Would you be interested in accompanying me?" He clears his throat and coughs against his clenched fist. "I assure you the party will make you forget about the grimness of the city for a bit."

I clamp my teeth together and catch the side of my tongue, anger seething out of me. The copper taste of blood fills the back of my mouth, and I regret telling Arte to leave. I should have let him walk me home. But I'm confident this conversation would have been much harder to steer if Arte was walking with us too. This city is grim because of the Wehrmacht. Who could throw a party to forget about life when innocent people are being starved and caged between walls just blocks away? I wouldn't have expected his father could be capable of such disgrace.

"I'm not much into hurrahs," I say, repeating his disgraceful word.

"Come on, Ella, you belong with the elite crowd. Come join us. There will be entertainment and life will seem somewhat normal compared to what we've all been living through." This must be a nice way of calling my family poor since we live above our grocery store. Or maybe he's inferring that I'm just another hungry Polish citizen with no rights.

"Your offer is truly hard to pass up, but I am in a relationship, just not with Arte. In fact, we're likely getting married soon. My love is visiting some relatives for the next week, and so it wouldn't be appropriate to join you as your guest this weekend."

He clears his throat again. "My apologies for assuming you're free. I should have known someone would sweep you up. You're quite a catch."

The fight to stop myself from making a sound or rolling my eyes is becoming painful. "Thank you."

"Ah, how about the two of you join us when he returns then? Maybe in a few weeks? I would love to meet the man lucky enough to capture your attention."

"I don't think that will work out." I speak too quickly. It's a telltale sign I'm hiding something. He'll read right into it.

"Well, why not?"

"I just don't think it's a good idea."

Daniel stops walking and grabs a hold of my wrist. "We used to be friends, Ella."

I yank my hand away. "People change. War changes people. I should get home before my father comes looking for me."

"I'm quite sure he'll understand if you're with me. We used to get along great."

I'm losing my ability to take a full a breath. He's crowding me and I can feel his hand all over me despite shaking it off. "No, I don't think he will. It was nice catching up, Daniel. Have a good night."

I take my chance and run, praying he doesn't chase me.

FOURTEEN

LUKA

The daytime hours in the ghetto carry on as if they might never end, especially in the dead heat of summer. By noon, I'm exhausted to the point of wondering whether I'll make it back to our tenement. Yet somehow, here I am. The lights are out as some try to sleep. Others lie awake all night. Some never wake up at all.

The heat inside is worse than it is outside, even with the windows open. The walls sweat along with the constant fog of heavy breaths that clings to every one of us. It's no wonder Grandmother can't seem to get well. Today might be like the longest day I've faced since arriving in the ghetto ten months ago. All day beneath the grueling sun dragging loads of bodies through the streets, my mind spun around the conversation that Ella and I had last night in the tunnel. I might have put too much pressure on her to find herbs for Grandmother. I shouldn't have said anything. She promised not to leave Warsaw, but every crumb of bread is a challenge to find, and there's no question in my mind that she would go to the ends of the earth to help.

It's hard enough living with the fact that I can't keep her

safe from inside these walls. I also know her life would be much easier without me, and it's a hard concept to sit with. Am I selfish for holding on to her? The thought of her is the only thing that keeps me going here. None of the four-hundred-thousand Jewish people imprisoned within these walls should have to fight for their lives. The Germans have ensured this by making certain everything has been taken away from us.

But I do have a reason to fight.

With little space between any one of us, I sit here in silence between Mother and Grandmother, who are trying to sleep through the deafening symphony of sickness while I wait out the minutes until I can move again. Mother is aware I leave every night, but by waiting until she's asleep, it saves her from having to question where I'm going and when I'll be back. What matters is that I return with extra food for us. I fear causing her extra worry, especially in her weak state. She isn't sick like Grandmother but she's beyond pale, almost gray some days. The skin on her face sags and her eyelids are heavier than I've ever seen them. It's as if her soul has left her body. She's living in agony, worrying about Grandmother's health and wondering if Father and Grandfather are well. I'm sure she's imagining the worst, just as I am.

Grandmother doesn't talk in her sleep, but she falls into a state of unconsciousness each night that often scares me. Before leaving, I lean in closer to make sure I can hear her still breathing, for peace of mind. We aren't sure what she's sick with, but I fear it's something more than what can be cured. She coughs so hard, there's a rattle in her resting breaths, and she hardly moves when she is awake.

Watching her has caused me so much desperation—to the point of asking Ella for help, possibly endangering her. God, I hope she's safe and okay.

I stare over at Apollo to see if he's ready to leave the building and head down to the tunnels, but one of his sisters is whimpering and he's brushing his fingers through her hair, smiling and talking. His mother is lying down with his other sister, doing the same, trying to assure them both that everything is okay. The poor girls never leave this room. Apollo tries to bring them home "treasures" every day, scraps from the factory that he bends into shapes. He gives them parts of his portioned food and reads them stories, teaches them math and English. He does all of this after working all day. It's as if he's taken on the responsibility of being their father and he's only twenty years old. I don't envy the additional amount of worry he carries on his shoulders. He's a better man than I.

FIFTEEN

ELLA

Tata and Miko's silverware clash against their plates nearly at the same moment after they both shovel in the small portions of potato stew with legumes. "That was wonderful. Thank you, dear," Tata says to Mama as he dabs his face with a napkin. We're eating much later than usual. Missing inventory at the store caused a hold up with reconciliation. People steal from us daily and there are so many in the store at once, it's hard to spot.

"Yes, wonderful, Mama," Miko echoes.

"It isn't a race to see who can swallow their supper first," she reminds them. "It takes me hours to prepare the food you devour in mere minutes."

Despite my urgency to get up from the table, too, it's the same complaint every night—one I can't quite blame her for. Mama is tired of Tata and Miko running out of the apartment after dinner to their resistance meetings—or "citizen-aide-meetings" as they call them. It breaks my heart to see the despondence and worry in Mama's eyes as she watches them walk out the door.

"I love you, my darling," Tata tells Mama, giving her a kiss on the head. "And you my, sweetheart." He kisses me next.

Miko grabs his satchel and pulls it over his head, crossing it over his body to hang by his side. "Be home soon, Mama," he says. "Ella...stay out of trouble," Miko utters to me as he passes by.

"Did you hear about the increase of SS troops?" Miko asks Tata as they walk out the door.

"What am I going to do with the two of them? They leave every night, thinking they're helping the city in some way, and nothing has gotten any better. If anything, it's just getting worse. This is just another reason I don't ask questions. It's better not knowing. Of course, unless someone forces information upon me. Then I must sit and stir over it," she says with a grumble. "Although I did hear something quite interesting from a neighbor today."

"Mama, it could be gossip—" I say.

"It's not," she says, her stare widening as she continues. "The Germans killed a woman for smuggling food in through the ghetto wall. They killed her right on the spot without warning. And apparently, it isn't the first time this has happened. It's unfathomable, really."

Sweat from my chest soaks through my work dress, hearing the looming threat I face every night. I understand the risks involved in helping Luka and his family, but I can't sit here day after day knowing what they're suffering through, and do nothing for the sake of fearing the soldiers.

"Here, I'll do the dishes so you can go sit down and rest," I tell her, standing from my seat at the table.

"No, that's all right. I'd rather stay busy, but thank you, dear."

Guilt slithers through me like slime every time I walk away from Mama at night. "If you insist. I'm going to go read for a bit before bed," I lie.

"I'm so glad to see you reading so much again," she says with a faint smile.

"Me too," I say, swallowing hard against the continued lie.

Mama knows me better than anyone else, which leaves me wondering if she's aware of what I do at night, but chooses not to say anything. She doesn't ask about Luka, and I don't mention his name, not since he was taken to the ghetto. I don't want her to ask me questions about whether I've tried to visit.

"Goodnight, dear."

I close myself into my bedroom and turn my radio on to a silent hum of classical music—one of the few stations we still receive. Of course, this classical music is by German composers only, and other than at night, the station is filled with German cultural programs and news. The sound, however, masks the creak of my window opening.

I stare down at my watch again for the fourth time in fifteen minutes, bouncing my knees as I wait on the edge of my bed, making sure it's been long enough since Tata and Miko left that I won't run into them. I'm running out of time.

I retrieve the bundle of goods for Luka that I've been storing beneath my bed. I made an exchange with an apothecary tradesman I spotted in Castle Square, just outside the ghetto walls. I was there before sunrise this morning, waiting in the man's line, hoping he would have what Luka needed for his grandmother. I'm still surprised I was able to acquire everything.

I gently shove my window open, then climb over the sill, swing my legs through the opening, and hop down to the flat overhang above the store. I shut my window then tiptoe to the side edge and scale down the trellis.

The street is quiet at this hour, leaving me with only the sound of horse and carriage passing on a nearby main street, and the crackling rubble beneath my boots as I scurry down the sidewalk.

"Ella, stop," Miko shouts, his voice jarring, making me gasp and clutch my chest.

"What are you doing?" I shout in a whisper. "You nearly scared me half to death."

"What are *you* doing?" he turns the question back to me.

"Nothing."

Miko exhales heavily and takes a hold of my arm. "What's in the bag?"

"Nothing," I say again.

"Ella, I know you go into the sewers every night. A change of clothes, soap and water can only conceal so much."

My heart pounds, wondering why he's not with Tata and what he's going to do to prevent me from bringing these herbs to Luka. "Have you been following me?" I ask as if he's to blame rather than me.

"You're my little sister, and despite what you might think, I love you and worry about you. It's hard for me to tell you not to do the same thing I'm doing every night, but I have resources of information that I can use before making decisions. Do you?"

I shrug because there's no sense in lying about that. I'm not an actual part of the resistance like he and Tata are. Therefore, I wouldn't have access to the same information. "No."

"I wouldn't take the risk tonight. There's a lot of German soldier activity, beatings, shootings—it's bad."

"I'm careful. I have people, too."

"Arte? He's your people?" I should have figured Miko knew more than he was letting on. "Ella, please listen to me. Give it a few days. Hopefully the increase of the SS troops' activity will quiet down."

That's not true. Nothing ever becomes quieter than it was.

"I need to bring Luka something. His grandmother is going to die if I don't."

"Do you think he'd rather you die trying to get him something that he may never receive? I've been in love before. I know what it's like to put everything on the line and throw the thought of your own safety to the side for someone."

"You're still in love, Miko. That's why you're in the resistance, too. Katja is in the resistance, too, isn't she?"

Miko releases a heavy sigh. "All right, fine. Yes. But I'm not going down into the sewers. You must listen to me."

"You're lucky you don't have to go into the sewers for a moment with Katja. Try to understand," I argue.

"Tata has no clue what you're doing right now. I didn't rat you out. I won't say a word to him, but please go back home."

My throat is dry and my muscles ache as I battle against the fear that keeps so many from doing anything to help those who can't help themselves. I don't respond, because I'll only be agreeing to letting Luka down, and not helping his grandmother.

"Be safe, Miko," I tell him, hoping he will turn around and go back to wherever he's supposed to be with Tata. "Thank you for looking out for me."

Miko checks his watch. "I have to get to Tata."

"Go. I'll be fine," I say.

"Please, Ella. Think about what I'm saying."

SIXTEEN

LUKA

Apollo finally gets his sister to sleep and tucks a thin sheet around her just before bobbing his head around to get my attention. It's his cue that he's ready to go.

We slip out of the apartment, avoiding the wooden planks that moan and whine, only opening the front door enough to squeeze through the space so the hinges don't squeal, then weave down the stairwell, skipping the stairs that sound like they might collapse with each footstep.

"Is your Ella bringing you herbs to help your poor grand-mother tonight?" Apollo asks as we head down a quiet alleyway between two buildings.

I shrug despite knowing he can't see my gesture in the dark. "Everything is becoming harder to come by, and I didn't think this was possible just a year ago. She promised to do what she can, but I told her to stay within the city. God only knows if things are worse outside Warsaw."

The summer heat funnels between the walls regardless of the time of day, making it so the air is constantly as oppressive and thick as it is inside the building. There is no fresh air anywhere, only the smell of sweat, rot, and waste suffocating us night and day. The cobblestones of varying subdued colors are now covered with dust and dirt, littered with scraps of newspaper, broken belongings, and weak people who can't make it back to their living quarter for the night.

There are bodies everywhere, not just the ones of the dead, but ones like mine that are hollow, frail, pale, and barely functioning. I'm grateful to avoid my reflection, but I do wonder what I look like in comparison to others walking around with limbs too thin to hold up their frail frames with unrecognizable skeletal faces.

Just a year ago, my heart ached watching neighbors sit on their front stoops in torn clothes, living off essentials and losing weight by the day. Never did I expect how much worse it would become.

We're all trying to survive without reason. It's just what we're supposed to do. This is what we tell ourselves even when looking up to the top of the brick walls the height of two people, one on top of another, fixed with barbed wire.

Each corner I walk around unfolds into another length of space holding a line of people waiting and begging for a crumb of bread, or a possibility to barter for bare materials.

On the side streets I pass through, I overhear whispers of resistance, and rumors of life outside the walls. The other side of the walls is like a foreign place now.

"I don't blame you, telling her not to leave. It's scary enough to wonder what's happening outside these walls," he says. "What I do know is...that girl loves you. You're lucky to have someone, even if you can only be with them in secret." Apollo has mentioned before that he wishes he had someone to love, to give him hope and a reason to smile. I tell him there will be plenty of opportunities once the Germans are gone. We both realize it's nothing more than wishful thinking.

Apollo doesn't go down into the tunnels for the same reasons I do, but he's found a group of men who play cards for money and despite playing with one cent coins most of the time, it's a small escape each day—a hint of an ordinary life.

We search around for stubs of scrap wood to use as a torch once I'm inside the tunnel. It's very difficult with the number of broken wagons and deteriorating building structures are on every corner. Together, we lift the sewer top and shove it to the side so we can make our way down the ladder.

My heart thunders with each rung I descend, knowing I'm a step closer to pulling Ella into my arms. I'm not sure she realizes how many ways she's saved me from falling into a hopeless pit of despair while we've been stuck here between the encumbering walls. She's my last breath, the thread that keeps me dangling over a ledge—the thread I hope never breaks. I want to say all these things to her but I'm afraid of the burden I'd cause. We're both putting ourselves in danger by climbing through the sewers every night but sometimes the wrong decision is the only choice left.

Apollo closes the sewer cover from within, the thud echoing between the walls. I grab a match from my pocket and strike it against a dry crag of flint above the water level and use the glow to guide me through the maze of connecting passages.

It amazes me how many people meander down here regularly—everyone with their own unique reason, whether business, trading, meetings with members of the Polish and Jewish resistance. Except for some Jewish and Polish police, most Polish citizens are desperate for the return of our freedom. No one questions each other down here. We might all be naive in thinking the Germans aren't aware we're down here, but no one can afford to make assumptions either way and the underground passages are our only way to contact anyone outside the ghetto walls.

"All right, brother, I'll meet you back here in a bit," Apollo says. "Tell Miss Ella I send my hello and thank her for the cheese she brought for us yesterday."

After months of meeting one another down here, Ella and I found a split between three tunnels, one that leads to an enclosure, a place for a bit of privacy unless someone is lost and trying to find their way to a sewer hole. She's usually already here waiting for me, as she's said she doesn't want to waste even a short second of time before the resistance guards on the Aryan side close the entrance for the night. The Germans make their rounds around the city blocks outside the walls a half hour before curfew every night and no one wants to be caught in their sights then.

I wedge the torch between a few rocks, finding that I've arrived here first tonight. My mind doesn't wait for logic or reason, but my blood runs cold, my limbs stiffening with worry. Maybe she got held up with her family. Or the guards might have delayed the entrance time due to a change in the Germans' schedule. I just need to be patient. She'll be here.

SEVENTEEN

ELLA

The streets are quiet as usual, no increase in soldier activity from what I've seen thus far, and I'm just a block from the sewer entrance. Luka must be worried that I'm not already there. I hate making him wait and I'm rarely late. Arte is in his usual place, offering me a bit of relief to see everything is how it always is at this hour.

I rush to his side beneath the trees, out of sight from the main area of the street. "I'm here," I say, handing him the parcel of legumes he requested last night.

He pushes my hand away. "Not tonight. You should get home."

"What? Why? I'm late—I'm sorry. I was held up, but the sewer is already open. No one is around," I say, panic laced around my words. "I only need a few minutes and I'll be out at the usual time still."

"Ella, I need you to go home," he says, his statement unwavering as he stares at me with a firm look of concern.

"It's Miko, isn't it? He was here," I ask.

"No."

I shove the parcel of legumes against his chest and push by him towards the entrance to the sewer tunnel.

"Halt! You're under arrest for resisting German law," a man barks. My heart stops. Everything inside of me is frozen as a flashlight blinds me.

"Please, I—I'll go home. I didn't break any laws. I'm not resisting your laws. I wasn't—"

"Shut your mouth. Curfew began two hours ago, and here you are at the not so infamous entrance to the sewer tunnels. Looks like your old friend Daniel was right about you being a sewer resistance rat. You shouldn't have been so rude to him when he was kind enough to invite you to a nice outing," the man clucks his tongue several times. "Shame, shame." His thick German accent sends a painful chill up my spine. *Daniel.* I should have assumed he's still incapable of handling rejection, but this—this is beyond something I could imagine him taking part in.

The light grows brighter against my face and then someone grabs my wrists before patting my body down, stripping me of my bundled goods and discarding them to the side. As if the fear of what's happening isn't enough, the sight of the bag lying on the ground, knowing Luka won't receive it, is tearing my heart into shreds.

Arte is detained at the same moment, and side by side we're pushed forward down the road and around the corner, finding a line of other Polish citizens standing in a row, all with their hands tied behind their backs. *Are they part of the resistance?* Without warning, my hands are roped behind my back just before I'm tossed to the end of the row. Arte soon joins me at my side, restrained as well.

* * *

It's been well over an hour of waiting here between a line of others as the German soldiers decide what to do with us. My pulse continues racing, making me dizzy and weaker by the moment. They want to terrorize us. It's clearly their only objective. I don't know where the others even came from, but I assume they fell into the same trap as I did. Luka must be thinking I abandoned him and his grandmother after not showing up tonight like I promised I would. I've let him down in every possible way.

A truck rolls up to our side and a slew of German shouts and demands are whizzing overhead as we're shoved forward to the truck. Everyone is thrown inside, me included, as if I'm nothing more than a bag of rubbish. My body smashes into others, knocking them around as I search for an empty spot on the metal bottom.

There were ten of us scattered around the exterior walls of Warsaw, waiting to descend through the sewer entrance. The gestapo, on the prowl for anyone involved with the resistance, must have been tipped off about our nightly activity.

I peer through the opening between the tarp and metal bed of the truck as the gestapo police scream in the faces of the others, including Arte. Each of them are searched, hands clawing at their bodies and stripping them of weapons before shoving them into the vehicle, too.

No one told us where we're going or what they plan to do with us, but anyone affiliated with the resistance in any way knows how few options exist. Interrogation then execution or transport to a labor camp.

My body is numb, soaked in sweat, pinned between others on every side of me. I didn't fight the Germans, not like some of the others. Yet, we're all here just the same. I knew the danger and risk involved in helping Luka every night but, if anything, I've gained more confidence as time crept along without getting caught. I thought maybe they didn't care to waste their time on the people trudging through sewers.

"We attack when given the chance. I'll signal to everyone when it's time. It's our only hope," a man whispers between us. "Do we all agree?"

We have no weapons, only our hands. The gestapo police are armed. We won't stand a chance against them. I don't want to die. I don't want to raise my hand and volunteer to be executed. Everything I've done until this point has been to help Luka and his family. What information could they want from me? Would they even believe me?

Maybe this man is right. Our only chance at survival could be to fight them off. I'm not sure I know how to punch anyone properly. I've never laid a hand on another being. Arte is in the truck somewhere, but I can't see him. I wonder what he's thinking. I'm not sure he heard the comments about me rejecting Daniel. If so, is he blaming him like I am? Or, is he blaming me for telling him I could handle Daniel? Would any of this have even mattered either way?

Luka is most certainly wondering where I am and thinking the worst. Mama and Tata won't realize I'm gone until tomorrow at some point. Everything I've been fighting for has brought me to this—a dead end, with no hope. I've failed.

EIGHTEEN

LUKA

I check my watch one last time, already knowing it's well beyond the hour either of us have been together down here. She hasn't missed a day. I haven't missed a day. It's the only thing that gets me through.

I blew out the flame on my torch an hour ago and have been standing here in the dark for the past hour, waiting for a sign of life, another flame, the sound of a footstep, but there's been nothing but utter silence except for Apollo, silently waiting beside me.

I spark another match and light the torch, forging light ahead of me to the vacant tunnels. "Maybe I should go in the direction she'd have come from just to make sure—"

"We shouldn't go to the Aryan side, brother. Nothing good will come of that," Apollo says.

"I need to—just take a look. Wait here. I'll be quick about it."

Apollo clears his throat, making it clear he disagrees, but I'm desperate to find her. I do debate turning back toward Apollo, several times, knowing I'm going against my good common sense. Maybe one of the sewer covers is up, and I could escape. I wonder how far could I get without being spotted, questioned, asked for papers?

If anything happened to her, I'm not sure anyone would know where to look. Not even her family knows she's been coming every night. At least, I don't think they do. She mentioned bartering with the guard who had threatened to bring her to her father. She's been giving him bread and other small commodities.

I keep walking until I spot a sewer cover, but it's closed. I'm not sure how close or far away the next one might be, leaving me with no other choice but to return to Apollo.

She would have been here. Something's not right.

Apollo's torch is lit and waiting as I turn the last corner. "Nothing?" he asks.

"No one was in those tunnels and the cover was closed."

"Maybe there were gestapo police out there tonight. She's a smart girl. She'd avoid trouble."

"I hope you're right."

My thoughts are overwhelming as I wade through the water toward the ladder we used to make our way down here. I start climbing up first, holding on tightly to the torch with one hand and ascending the rungs with my other. I use the top of my head and hand to push up the sewer cover and push it across the gravel, the severe scrape echoing around me. I put out the torch and push myself up to the ground level, but before I have a foot up, someone grabs hold of my collar and yanks me out of the hole. "You think no one would know the two of you have been scrounging around with the rats down there," the man says, shoving me to the gravel, before reaching in for Apollo next.

A Jewish Ghetto policeman. "I don't care," I tell him. I'm aware of what my words could cost me, and now my anger is consuming me.

"Why don't you do the same? You aren't hungry like the other Jews?" Apollo spews out at him.

A sadistic chuckle rumbles in the man's throat as if he's only a bit humored by us, but more annoyed to be in our presence. "I'm not hungry," he says.

"The only Jew in this country, huh?" I argue.

The man grabs me by the throat and slams my back into the wall. "Watch your mouth."

"Or what?" Apollo shouts. "Are you going to proudly beat a fellow Jew to a pulp for some extra recognition? Maybe an extra ration? You turn on your own people and we're supposed to bow down to you. There may not be a hell where we Jews go after we die, but you—you are an exception."

The policeman growls and slams me into the wall again, my head thudding against the brick as a cold sting strikes down my back, making the world spin around me. A sequence of movements blurs before me but it's clear the policeman is reaching for his pistol.

"I didn't turn on my people," he barks at Apollo. "I am surviving like everyone else. It's each man for himself here. You're a fool if you haven't come to realize this."

"I still have my dignity," Apollo grunts. "You are nothing but a Jewish gestapo."

A pop blasts between the buildings, ringing through my eyes, quaking through my body. The sight of Apollo's body falling to the ground is clearer than everything else around me.

"No, no, Apollo," I utter, gritting my teeth.

My head throbs, and a buzz zings through my ears as I crawl toward the only friend I have here in this hell.

The police officer tosses me to the side. I land on the ground next to the cracked-open sewer. I've lost all my physical strength. I can't even fight this man off me. Blood is dripping down the sides of my face and this man is gawking at me with a stark expression. "You're the singer from the Leszno Street square, aren't you?"

"Apollo," I mumble his name, ignoring the policeman.

"Get the hell out of here before you end up like your mouthy friend, or worse, deported on the next train."

I push myself up, staring at Apollo's lifeless body. I can't leave him here.

"Go, now!" the police officer shouts.

The gravel kicks up against the backs of my legs as I run through a blur back to my building, gasping for air with each step. Sweat drips down my face and my heart thuds like a hammer against my chest while coming to terms with what just happened. Until tonight, Apollo and I have managed to make it back from the sewer tunnels, into the apartment, quietly, without making a peep or disturbing anyone.

I can hardly breathe by the time I near the top of the stairs inside our assigned building and lunge for the door, catching it before falling to my knees. I claw my way into the dark apartment and close the door behind me. Everyone is rolling around or sitting up. I can only see as much as the moon's glow will let into the cracks between the curtains, but the reflection bounces off the sets of eyes watching me, wondering what I'm doing at this hour—why I'm crawling into our apartment.

"Luka," Mother hisses. "What in God's name are you doing?"

"I'm sorry," I cry out in a whisper.

"Where have you been? Do you do this every night? Is that how you procured—" The extra food we've been sharing with this extended family we've inherited.

"Yes," I answer softly.

"You go by yourself? Why would you do such a thing?" Mother continues to scold me when the last thing I need at this moment is a lecture.

"I—" I peer across the room, wondering if one of the curious stares belongs to Apollo's mother.

"Apollo goes with you every night." Her voice comes from

beneath the window where she sleeps beside her two daughters, Apollo's little sisters.

"Yes."

"Where is he?" she asks, her voice shaking as if she's already assuming the worst.

As my eyes adjust to the little light available, I slide my boots along the floor, careful not to step on anyone, making my way over to Apollo's mother. I kneel in front of her and take her hand in mine. My throat tightens around a sob.

"No. No," she growls. "Where is he?"

"The police—" I gasp for air.

"No," she cries out again, more guttural and from deep within her gut.

"He shot him. He's—"

A cry like I've never heard another human make fills the room, echoing off the walls, slicing into my ears.

Tears barrel down my face as I squeeze her hand tighter, my chest bucking with sobs. "It's my fault." To take the blame, it's all I can do for her.

"Wh—what did you do?" she croaks.

I didn't have an answer prepared. "We climbed out of the—uh—the sewer tunnel. We were caught right away. I couldn't save him. I was thrown against the wall; my head was spinning. It all happened so fast."

"Apollo?" one of his sisters calls out. "Mama, what happened to my brother?"

I embrace the three of them, unsure what else I can do but hold them as tightly as I can, wishing there was a way to undo what has happened. If we had come out a few minutes sooner, we might not have been caught. But I was scared to leave and miss Ella. He died because of my selfishness.

NINETEEN

ELLA

The gestapo truck lurches to a stop, throwing all of us into each other and the unforgiving metal walls. I gasp for breath as if my lungs have given out upon impact. Around me, the sound of shuffling and sliding as everyone tries to straighten their position is punctuated by the glow of hollow eyes and pale faces from a dim light filtering in between the tears of the tarp over our heads.

Doors at the front of the truck open and slam closed in the seconds before the back is opened, and a hot burst of air filled with gaseous fumes swooshes around the inside of the truck, choking me.

"Raus!" a soldier barks at us, sending a jolt of terror through my veins.

Everyone shoves one another as if we're in a race to jump out of the truck first. I want to hide in the dark corner where they might not see me, but it's my attempts to defy these terrorizers that have led me here.

We spill out of the truck into an unruly line. My legs are shaking, and my arms feel like they're weighed down even though it's just my wrists bound with rope. I make it past one of the soldiers just as a thud against metal quakes around us. On instinct, I turn to see what happened, finding one of the men traveling with us flat in the bed of the truck.

"Stand! Get up!" a soldier yells at him before using the butt of his rifle to jab him in the head. I recoil as the man lets out a strangled cry.

I gaze around, seeking a familiar face—Arte—knowing he was captured, too. I spot him in the back of the group, his face baring despair but his jaw clenched tight. I want to call out to him, but that will only cause more trouble. The soldiers already saw enough of an interaction between us tonight. It can only be used against us, I'm sure.

All of us with our wrists bound by rope are shoved forward, across a dark yard toward a brick building with a small glowing window flush with the ground. Around me, all I hear is gravel crunching beneath boots or people like me tripping over their own feet. Sweat covers me from head to toe, making my arms itch and scratch against the sharp rope. My heart thuds with a sharpness and the fear building within me is taking over. I should have listened to Miko. He wanted to protect me, but I thought I knew better. Arte too—he tried to save me before it was too late, and I wouldn't listen.

We reach the building just as a soldier begins to shout more orders, splitting us up into smaller groups, the moment Arte and I are separated and sent in different directions. There are only a few of us going in the same direction as me, down a narrow hallway lined with stone walls. We descend a set of uneven stairs into another dark space with a glow in the distance. With people on either side of me, I continue forward through damp air reeking of mildew.

The glow comes from a bare room with two light bulbs hanging from the ceiling, subtly swaying back and forth. A soldier takes my arm and yanks me down to one side of the room, shoving me onto a wooden chair. The other few people are taken to opposite ends of the room, out of hearing range.

My throat is so dry, I can't swallow and I'm shivering though I'm sweltering. Another soldier in a more decorated uniform, one with pressed pleats and shined boots, clicks his heels with each heavy step before stopping in front of me, where he hovers.

I can't see his eyes beneath the shadow of his cap but there are scars above his lip and across his nose.

"Name?" he presses.

I consider lying, but my papers are in my pocket. "Ella Bosko."

"And who do you work for?" the soldier asks, his voice calm, unnerving, and yet, I'm confident that would change within a blink.

"No one, I swear. I'm not part of anything or working with anyone." My voice is hoarse from breathing so heavily throughout the ride here and the walk into this building.

A backhanded slap comes out of nowhere, so fast that I choke on air. My cheek burns, hot and sharp, but I hold back my tears. I won't give him that.

"You think we're fools, idiots, yes?" he snaps at me. His German accent tears through me like a knife.

"No, no, I don't think that at all!" I clench my eyes, but nothing follows except a weightless flutter as specks of light freckle my vision. The soldier's voice is more distant now, but shouting.

"Liar! You were caught at the entrance of the sewer where the resistance gathers."

"I was visiting with a friend who lived nearby," I mutter, telling myself that isn't the right answer as it will still be considered resistance since I was out after curfew.

My vision takes a moment to clear, but the blurriness lingers, making me question whether I'm seeing one soldier or two now. "It appears she might need more convincing," the second soldier with a different voice says.

I don't see it coming, but a heavy strike to my ribs tosses me off the side of the chair and onto the ground. Still unable to move my bound hands, I draw my knees into my chest to press against the throbbing pain, but it's relentless, searing through every nerve in my body.

"Who is Miko?" the second soldier asks, his voice softer than it was a moment ago as if this question is more sensitive and I should be more forthcoming. How does he know Miko? "You mentioned his name at the sewer entrance."

"No one," I choke out. "I don't know a Miko." I'll die before I give up information on my brother.

"Such allegiance, wasted on something that lives and will die in a sewer," he says.

But Miko isn't the one in the sewer. It's Luka. *Please don't hurt him.*

The room spins around me as another thrust strikes my head. The flicker of light above me burns out into a stark blackness. The image of Luka swishes through my mind, his touch, his hold, his voice and words..."*If I ever get the chance to keep you, I hope you'll be mine forever.*"

It's hard to imagine we'll make it there now.

I'm so sorry, Luka.

TWENTY

ELLA

October 1941
Oświęcim, Poland

The cold floor stings against my back, stealing the little warmth left in my body. The cell is dark, the only form of light comes from a window with bars at the top of the wall where the ceiling joins. I've lost track of time, the hours and days spilling into the next since I arrived here.

The interrogations are less frequent now, but the silence is never ending. I think they're waiting for me to break. They must think I have more information than I do. I'm not worth their time otherwise. Though it doesn't explain why they haven't killed me like they did with half of the others. I witnessed each instance, was covered in their blood, then sent into this cage of metal bars—where I've slept night after night.

There's more movement down here today, but it's hard to tell where the sound is coming from until my cell door opens. An unfamiliar soldier grabs me by the arm and drags me out the door and out to the courtyard, dropping me like a sack of pota- toes onto my knees in front of a running truck. A dozen others are on either side of me, all of us bruised, lined with purple and red welts, swollen, and deformed.

The bumpy drive jolts us in every direction, forcing us to endure more pain against the contusions we're already suffering with. However, at the next stop, we're tossed from the truck at the foot of a steaming train. Without long to wonder where we're going, we're herded into one of the overcrowded cattle cars and sealed into darkness. Fingers poking into every wound —the grinding, squeezing, and pulsating, relentless. People are falling on top of me and at first, I think they're trying to torture me, but then I realize their eyes are closed, unconscious.

For mindless and endless hours, the people within this car sway in only four directions, front, back, side, or side, and as one unit together. It's as if the air has been sucked out of the train, holding us in a stale space.

I squeeze my eyes closed as the thought of what I've caused everyone I love flashes before me like a horror film reel. I wanted to help. Luka's grandmother—she's probably gone now, and he might think the worst of me. Mama and Tata, they tried so hard to keep me sheltered and I wouldn't allow it. I couldn't sit back and let the world fall apart. Now, they're the ones enduring the consequence for my actions. And Miko, we've bickered and poked at each other for as long as I remember, but he was trying to keep me safe. Always trying to protect me despite me never wanting that protection.

A screech rips through the car as the pile of us lean sharply to the left, then quickly to the right, before using one another to try and push ourselves upright. Screams and shouts bellow from outside the train, coming from every direction. The people closest to the door try to lift the latch, but it's locked. My body is as weak as a rag doll and I doubt I'll make it off the train to wherever we are now.

The sound of people walking back and forth past our closed car door as if they don't realize anyone is alive in here goes on and on. Then the door slides open with a crash of metal against metal, a gust of cold wind blasts us before the shouts and screams grow louder, echoing between the walls we're still stuck between.

It takes minutes before people find a way out. My knees won't lock, and I can't hold myself up no matter what I grab onto. Hands wrench around my body and toss me off the train, dropping me against stone rubble. A woman around my age pulls me up to my feet. "You poor thing." She weaves her arm around mine and holds up more of my weight than I'm holding myself. "I think we're at Auschwitz. You must look healthy and alive. A distant uncle of mine heard from a reliable source all about the makings of this place. You either work or die. There is no in-between. He scared us all terribly, but I suppose I'd rather know how to act competent than not." I'm taking in everything this woman is saying but struggling to comprehend it all.

"Work or die?" I repeat.

"Yes. That's right. So, pull yourself together before the SS spot you look like you're about to collapse right here."

Why does she care enough to help me? If I've learned anything since my arrest, no one has much compassion left to help anyone when they can barely help themselves. We're all fighting for our own survival now.

"Are you here alone?" I ask, my throat constricting.

"My sister and mother were put on another train. So, for now, yes. What about you?" She tries to press a smile onto her lips, but her chin trembles instead.

My shoulders slump forward from the reminder of defeat. "Yes, very much alone."

We're walking across a concrete platform past the train, still expelling billows of hot steam that silence the world as we move closer to SS officers with snarling dogs by their sides.

"You're a typist or an administrative clerk if they ask," she says.

"Why is that?"

"My uncle said the healthy women will likely end up working in administration if they have the skill set."

"Your uncle sure knows a lot about this place," I utter, wondering how.

Out from a crowd of people, an SS officer steps in front of the two of us, demanding our names, birthdate, country of origin, and occupation. The questions aren't challenging, but the way he's staring at us could make me forget my name.

"El-Ella Bo-Bosko." I answer the next questions a little quicker, but stall when thinking about my occupation. If I'm trying to survive, I can't give up now. The thought of telling Luka I'm stronger than people give me credit for is nearly laughable now. But maybe I should believe my words. "I'm a typing clerk and a bookkeeper for a business."

The woman still holding on to my arm with a display of causality goes on to answer her questions. "Tatiana Malinka, 4-10-1918, Poland, and my occupation is a record-keeping managerial clerk." Her pale blue eyes hardly blink as she speaks, staring directly at the officer as if she doesn't fear him. She squares her narrow shoulders and lifts her chin, forcing a strong and rigid appearance along her slender frame.

"To the right," the officer shouts, spit flying out of his mouth. "Report to registration."

A set of wrought-iron gates in the distance come into view, confirming Tatiana's suspicions of our whereabouts. Among the chatter I used to hear in the lines in the grocery store, I had often heard mention of a concentration camp named Auschwitz. The words "concentration camp" eventually morphed into "death camp" over time. I had told myself it must have been a figure of speech, but the closer we walk toward the gates, the more I feel as though I'm about to step into the mouth of a hungry beast. Work or die. Or just die...?

The air is heavy with smoke, burning wood, cigarettes, and

something sour. The combination pokes at my empty stomach, causing nausea to rise within me. I search around, attempting to take in all my surroundings, including what lies beyond the gates. Barbed-wire fences, watchtowers, identical long brick buildings neatly stationed in rows and columns stare back at me as if they're about to swallow me up.

People in blue and white striped uniforms slug around. Some are carrying buckets, others tools. But they all look the same, lifeless.

The gates, now above my head, encase the words Arbeit Macht Frei. "Work will set you free," I utter beneath my breath.

"See," Tatiana says. "Just like my uncle mentioned—you either work or die here."

We're led into one of the buildings sprawled among the many others within the overwhelming expansive space. The low ceilings and dim lighting give off a sense of suffocation or strangulation. The walls are bare, and the floors are cracked and dusty. A stench of urine and vomit, so potent, hangs in the air.

Guards or officers, whoever they are, holler orders from every direction, dizzying me. I turned to see if Tatiana might know more than me, but we've been separated, and I'm alone again.

The line I'm in moves in slow increments, stirring my nerves and worries for what I'm waiting for next. When there are only a few people left ahead of me in line, I watch the exchange of personal information for a scrap of fabric with a stamped, inked number.

Once I receive my number, proof of condemnation, I keep moving in the direction I'm shoved until another guard steps ahead of me and shouts, "Strip! Can you not hear me?" His breath cloaks my face, rancid coffee and nicotine adding to the nausea already sloshing through me.

He can't possibly expect me to remove—

After another look around, I find everyone in the nearby vicinity stark naked.

My hands shake furiously as I peel off my layers of clothing —avoiding the gawking eyes of nearby guards. Never have I been more exposed and defenseless, even after all the beatings I've endured.

My belongings are torn from my hands and thrown to the side, even my shoes are taken—the ones Mama had dotingly mended for me at least a dozen times over the last few years. I can hear myself from the past, telling others, "*They* have already taken everything from us. What more can they take?" I never should have spoken that way. I shouldn't have assumed we had seen the worst. It can always be worse.

Shouts and commands sound muffled as the line I'm in is continuously shoved to the next location, leaving me to fear what lies ahead. A running swish of water with droplets hitting a drain is what I hear before I'm pushed beneath a stream of freezing water, like icicles scraping down my back. I squeeze my hand around the scrap of fabric with my assigned number, protecting it from the water—out of fear for what it will be used for. There are many other women around me, everyone moving in closer to each other, shaking, holding their arms around their bodies, and huddling into the person beside them. The touch of arms against mine is a gift now.

There is nothing to dry our bodies with except a heap of worn uniforms tossed at as us as we're shoved away from the streaming spouts of water. I dress as quickly as I can, my uniform three sizes too large, hanging off my shoulders like a shawl. Wooden clogs replace my shoes, pinching my feet as I scoot my damp feet into the tight fit. I try not to think. I don't look at the others around me. I focus on wavy stripes on the person's uniform in front.

Cries and moans filter through the air, warning me of the

fears I'm trying to avoid the thought of. "Hurry. Move. Move. Move!" a guard shouts.

The line moves much faster than anticipated and then when I'm just a few spots away, I get a clear view of a woman slicing numbers into the arm of a woman sitting across from her.

When it's my turn, I move along to avoid being yelled at. I sit down and roll up my sleeve, lay my arm out flat and drop my focus to the dirt-covered cement ground. I picture Luka's hazel eyes, the way they glow beneath the sun, his smile unfurling into deep dimples, the sound of his voice, calling me his girl. It's not fair. We never got the chance to love each other as much as we wanted. There should have been a future for us—something more.

A cold liquid spills over me and my eyes flash open, finding ink filling the deep scratches engraved into my arm. The burn searing through my nerves is nothing compared to the understanding that I've just been branded.

"Next!"

The sorrow bearing on my soul is inescapable. Now stripped of everything that makes me human, fear embraces every step, knowing I'm moving forward in complete darkness.

How can I push forward alone without knowing what I'm fighting for? I want to ask Mama and Tata. They would have a wise answer, and yet, I can hardly hear their voices in my head now. I might as well be a world away. They haven't a clue where I am or what's happening to me.

TWENTY-ONE

LUKA

October 1941
Warsaw, Poland

This isn't survival. It's something different. With little hope and an overwhelming amount of guilt over what happened to Apollo just eight weeks ago, I still travel into the tunnels each night. I've found another entrance within the cellar of an uninhabited building that was destroyed in a bombing last year. My desperation to find Ella is wreaking havoc on my sanity. Every night, at the same time, I go to the spot we had met every night before she stopped coming—each night since I waited too long down here and paid the consequence with Apollo's life. It was his rage toward the ghetto police that ultimately got him killed, but it was my fault he was there.

I've had to cut down on the time I wait for Ella each night, which pains me, losing more hope in her returning, but I have business to conduct with a black-market tradesman.

"Where are you?" I whisper in our corner. "I need to know you're safe somewhere." It hurts too much to consider the alternative. My mind goes to dark places every night while I try to sleep, and the thoughts torment me. If something happened to Ella, I would be to blame, and that's not something I can live with.

"What do you have for me?" It's the same man I visit most nights. His shoulders are pinned up by his ears, hiding his neck. His face is long with a hanging jaw. Bags of skin droop beneath his eyes and he can hardly keep a steady hand as he reaches out for what I'm retrieving from my pocket.

"A gold watch..." he says. "There must be piles of them somewhere I bet." He's aware of the labor work I tend to all day. Jewelry and watches constantly fall to the ground while pushing a wagon full of deceased bodies. I tell myself to leave it behind but also realize someone else will take it and do exactly what I'm doing right now. I'm bartering for food, enough to help Mother, Grandmother, Apollo's family, and whatever I can spare for the people I live with. It's wrong, but it's the only means of preventing starvation. The ghetto has been restricted to less than two-hundred calories worth of food a day, and all I can imagine is the soldiers watching us from windows of nearby tall buildings, betting on how long people can survive severe starvation.

"Not piles," I say.

In return, the man takes my satchel, fills it with goods from beneath a black blanket and hands it back. I check inside, ensuring I'm getting a fair exchange, then return to the opening of the sewer to get back to Mother and Grandmother.

The autumn chill sends aches through my body as I trudge back to the tenement. Painful chills weaken my muscles even more and I grapple the railing to yank myself up the stairs and into the unit.

The lamps are still flickering at this late hour, and several people are circled around the corner where I sleep. "What's happening?" I ask, keeping my voice down for the few who are asleep.

Heads turn, pairs of eyes catch mine before falling, as if their stares are too heavy to hold. The small crowd is hard to push through before finding Mother hovering over Grandmother, holding her hand and crying. I fall to my knees beside them, Grandmother's eyes open as she finds my gaze. She slips her hand out of Mother's and struggles to hold it up toward me, grasping the air until I give her my hand in return.

"I—I'm scared," she utters through a breath. "I'm not ready, Luka. I don't want to go anywhere without your grandfather. I need someone to tell me he's all right. I can't die without him. I'm afraid to go alone."

"Shh, shh," I hush her. "You're not going anywhere."

"Promise me I'm going live, my Luka," she says, pleading in a way I've never heard her speak. She has always been tougher than any woman I've known—ready to take the world by storm, even if just with a snippy comment under her breath.

Her plea chokes me, and I tell her what she needs to hear, or rather, wants to hear. "I promise, Grandmother. You're going to live. We'll find Grandfather."

Her smile trembles as she slips her hand from mine to pat my cheek. "That's my good boy." She hasn't said that to me since I was young. Whenever I would get her a cup of tea or a blanket, I was her good boy.

"You're the strongest person I've ever met," I tell her.

She gives a gentle nod and folds her hand over her chest just before gasping through a sputtering breath.

"Mama," Mother cries out, placing her hands on her cheeks. "Mama, open your eyes. You can't leave. I need you still. We need you. Please, Mama."

Tears roll down my cheeks, watching Mother regress into a young girl, pleading with her own mother not to leave her behind. Everything within me shatters into a million pieces I'll never be able to piece back together.

Mother rests her head on Grandmother's chest as another sob bucks from her chest.

"She's gone. My mama's gone. I couldn't save her."

I pull my mother into my arms, holding her tightly as she cries with everything she has left inside her. I can hardly breathe through the grief, watching Mother writhe in agony next to my grandmother's soulless body. I clasp my hands, still holding on to her, and dig my fingernails into the soft flesh of my wrists, seeking an external pain to mask my internal agony.

TWENTY-TWO

ELLA

March 1942
Oświęcim, Poland

For five months, I've been holding on to my memories of the life I had before Auschwitz—perfect in comparison to what's around me—as if they will save me. I can't find any semblance of warmth here, even with the hundreds of people sharing tight quarters in this barrack. I'm back-to-back with one woman and holding a thin blanket in front of my face for separation from another woman's face that's within a fingertip's reach. She breathes so heavily all night; the sound and smell often keeping me awake with my heart racing. It's hard to breathe through the blanket, but it blocks out some of the bodily fluid stenches that I've yet to grow used to.

Mama used to make my bed for me even after I was far too old for it. She said she enjoyed adding a touch of love to every room in our apartment. She would line up the doll, stuffed elephant, and a pink teddy bear, all of which Tata gave me for birthdays as a little girl, in front of my pillow. The sheets taut and the quilt perfectly folded. Everything in my small bedroom would be neat and tidy. She would spray a touch of vanilla in the air and close the door. Meals were on the table every night, no matter what our days would bring. She always greeted us with a smile, but she must have been tired from taking care of us. I never appreciated how much work it was to keep a clean home, food on the table, clothes pressed, bills paid, and errands completed. A thankless job that I took for granted. How can I apologize?

I squeeze my eyes closed, pleading for a dream to take me away from where I am. I picture Luka, the same image every night. It's almost as if he's with me but frozen in my memory, stuck in the same place we were that last night I was with him in the tunnels, promising to help him find herbs for his grandmother. I was as worried about him as I was about her, with how thin he was becoming. I don't want to think of him that way but even when I sleep, my fears sneak in and take over. That's why I stick with the one image—a favorite moment in our tree. The touch of his lips on my fingertips still lingers in my mind. His melodic murmurs, just out of reach, leave me pleading for the sound of his voice.

The darkness of exhaustion pulls me under...

* * *

"Sing for me," I whisper, searching for him in the dark. "Tell me you still love me, and everything is all right."

His fingertips sweep across my cheek and a glow along his face teases me with his beautiful smile as it grows along his lips.

"My heart sings for her..." he murmurs. "For you, my beautiful."

"No," I say through a grave exhale. "Luka..."

"Even if my voice can't be heard..." he continues.

"Not that song..."

"Our moments are no more," he sings. *"We'll be trapped like a caged bird."*

"I never told you I heard you singing that night from the other side of the wall in Warsaw."

"I'm so sorry," he says. *"I wish things could be different."*

"No, don't say that. Shh," I hush, holding my finger up to his lips. They're ice-cold.

* * *

A deep echoing hum thuds through my ears. I gasp for air and bolt upright, crashing my head off a beam of wood. "Luka, no!" I shout, then immediately slap my hand over my mouth.

"Quiet, you're going to get us in trouble," the heavy breathing girl next to me snaps.

I blink, finding darkness with a faint light, and a pain swelling through my forehead. My moments with Luka were alive in my head, but even there, he's taken from me. Is it because he's truly gone? The thought of the vivid dream quakes through my chest. *It was just in my head. It wasn't real.*

A chill zips down my spine, followed by another, and another—the next one always looming. Yet, sweat glosses my skin, beads trickling down my torso and back adding to the raw coldness. I roll onto my side, scraping my brittle hands and jagged fingernails beneath my chapped cheeks as I will myself back to sleep. But it's too late...

The first morning gong bellows between the walls, screaming at us to move faster.

I drag my hands out from beneath my cheek as the lights flicker from the ceiling. I squint against the tired ache and wait for my vision to clear.

The sharp pointy bones along my wrist are what I notice first every morning. If they become any thinner, they might snap. I try to push myself up to slide off the bottom edge of the bunk, panting from exhaustion with such little movement. My breath lingers in a ghostly fog, drifting away until disappearing.

I skim down the side of the wooden frames, flinching from each splinter I scrape against. Other women are moving in every direction as if blind and disoriented, each bumping into one other, into me, their warmth almost inviting in an unnatural way. We're surviving off a few hours of sleep each night and worked to the bone before starting the horrific cycle all over again.

A quick visit to the latrines to use the toilets and wash whatever body parts time allows.

Then, it's disbursement of watered-down, cold coffee, and a slice of stale bread. I eat so fast, my jaw aches and my stomach muscles tense.

Before the last bite of bread falls to the pit of my stomach, the second gong rings, causing another atrocious headache.

Now, it's roll call...again.

As the general direction of movement leans to one side, I slink along in the middle, taking in various stenches as I walk. A combination of unbathed skin, sweat, and fermented sickness assaults my nose and wrings around my stomach. I swallow against an acidic burn and continue making my way toward the arctic blast outside.

With my arm over my eyes as a shield from the flood lights striking us from both directions, I imagine the glow being from the sun instead, and rather than the frost bitten air, the breeze could be warm, a scent of wildflowers in a meadow, Mama calling my name to return home after picking ripe herbs. My dress would twist and bloom around me and I would run with the wind's hands pushing me forward like a swing in motion.

"Aufstehen!" A shout tears me from my hallucination. All of us move in a line, shoved forward with impatience. We fall into rows, for roll call. Eyes graze over us, up and down, staring with a telescoping glare to find something out of place—

someone where they don't belong, doing what they shouldn't be doing, breathing the wrong way.

I try to block out the action of standing still for so long by holding my breath in increments of fifteen seconds each, hoping my legs won't shake. There's no escape. Every one of us is out in the open, but restrained, waiting for an inspection.

Francine, the block-elder, a Polish member of the resistance, stands before us, her shoulders as square as her jaw, her eyes narrow with ire. She holds a clipboard and a pencil as she moves back and forth in front of the rows wearing a man's overcoat with an armband that denotes her as a block-elder—the person in charge of us. The person who will rat any one of us out to an SS officer for any small infraction. She spews hate through every word and all I can do is stare at her day to day, wondering how anyone who referred to themselves as a Polish resistance member could treat others as if we were the Germans she spent her days fighting. She must have forgotten what she was fighting for or realized she's the only one worth fighting for.

The resistance was trying to help. That's what Tata and Miko spent their days doing. I wasn't an official member, but I wanted to help Luka's family. Help is all any of us wanted to give. Even until the last moment as the gestapo police were coming for us.

The air nips at my face with every step I take following the end of our roll call, walking to my designated checkpoint. I keep my eyes pinned to the ground, focusing on nothing more than the old frozen snow crunching beneath my feet.

Though I can't see the stares, they weigh on me. Every day, I sense people watching me just as I watch them when they walk by, wondering what they did to end up here, whether it was because they were just simply Jewish, or standing up for their country. What innocent purpose could so many people have to be here, living like this with the never-ending fear of being sent away, never to return. It's become apparent those people are sent to their death. The train stops at Auschwitz—or so I've heard through murmurs of others.

A gust of wind showers me with freckles of snow, blowing my scarf back along my shaved head. I yank it back into place, holding it until I come to the guard post.

"Here for clerical duty in administration," I say, pushing the sleeve of my dress up to show the dried ink of numbers beneath the top layers of skin.

The guard grunts and nods, then releases the gate for me to pass through where other guards line the short walkway between that gate and the administration door. They all stare at me as if I'm some creature from outer space.

The moment I step inside the building, the intense cold ceases, turning into a more manageable chill. The air is filled with the scent of cigarette smoke and old coffee, with the sharp zing of paper and ink. The walls are covered with maps and propaganda posters and my clogs create a hollow thud with each step I take down the corridor.

An SS guard follows behind me, making sure I go to where I'm supposed to. His eyes burn against my back and he's walking too closely. I reach the end of the corridor and enter the open area lined with desks. I approach the one I report to each day, finding a stack of papers spilling out of a folder. The guard walks past me, presses his finger to the pile and taps twice.

Each paper is a single prisoner record, all needing to be entered into a catalog along with their numbers and block assignment. I see so many names every day and have no idea who anyone is, what they look like, or what their fate is. I can't afford a mistake. Consequences await mistakes. I sit down on the oak wooden chair and pull myself in closer to the desk and take a pen from the lonely tin can. My hand is still cold and shaking from the walk over, but I need perfect penmanship. They said that's why I was chosen in the first place. No one has ever told me I have perfect anything, especially not my handwriting, but it appears it might be the one thing saving my life now.

"Psst," a hiss grows from the desk behind me. I look around, making sure the guards aren't within sight, and twist around, finding Tatiana cupping her hand around her mouth. Maybe it was coincidence, luck, or the two of us listing off similar occupations, but it was a relief to find a friendly face here the first time I reported for duty. "Open your hands."

She unrolls her sleeve and plucks out a small object from the cuff then tosses it into my hands. A warm, foil wrapped strawberry candy rests in the center of my palm, calling for an angry stomach growl—a reminder of how little I consume each day. "Where did you get this?" I ask, keeping my voice to a whisper.

"Many people here know someone who knows someone who can get things most of us can only dream of, and well—I received information. The guards in this building keep a stash of sweets in a narrow, inconspicuous closet behind the door guard's post. Apparently, they never lock it, and the door guard leaves for twenty minutes at noon every day. It'll be the most delicious treat you've had in months."

I don't waste a second before peeling off the wrapper and shoving the tart candy into my mouth. My cheeks clench and lips pucker. For a moment, I'm in heaven. It is the most delicious taste and I had almost forgotten something so sweet existed.

As I crunch through the candy, I realize I don't have anything to offer Tatiana in return. I cover my mouth to stop the drool from pooling at the corners of my lips and stare back at her. "I don't have anything for you. I'll find something. I'll do anything. What can I do?" I ask.

"Stop it. We're friends. I want to share."

"Friends. Always," I tell her. It hasn't been long, but anyone who shows empathy to another person here is someone to hold on to for as long as possible—a thought I cling to all day.

For endless hours, I listen to my pen scratching against paper with background drone of boots clomping down the hallways or hushed conversations between guards. The hanging light above my head flickers all day, causing spots to float in front of my eyes, landing on the papers I'm trying to focus on. Then the click of the flicker becomes a repetitive silence that makes my heart pound with every inked letter I form.

The sweetness from the candy has worn off my tongue and my stomach has grown a new level of anger and hunger from the delectable tease. In the final hour of the work day, the dark thoughts always return, reminding me my life has an expiration date—friend or no friend, and this is how I'm spending whatever final days I have—a slave to the Wehrmacht who believe they have a right to whatever they want.

TWENTY-THREE

LUKA

April 1943
Warsaw, Poland

Sitting in this apartment with thirty or so others, each holding a loved one, or a reminder of a loved one on this first night of Passover—a day in which we are to be thankful for our freedom and the ability to hold on to faith even when the odds are against us. To celebrate when we're suffering and being treated as slaves here, seems nonsensical, but I keep that thought to myself. Mother has her arm locked around my waist and I have Grandmother's favorite scarf pressed against my chest. I trace my eyes over the spot on the floor where she slept beside me, trying to understand how she's already been gone for six months. I lied to her and told her she wouldn't die.

With time to think about the promise I made to her, I have tried to come to terms with being thankful for her freedom—the end of suffering, days without starvation or sickness. Therefore, though we continue to suffer, Grandmother can be a symbol of Passover this year.

"Chag Pesach sameach," Mother says out loud to the others

around us. "May this Passover bring us a reminder of the freedom we were once strong enough to acquire and may our faith carry us forward."

"Amen." The echoes of tired, weak people, young and old, sound like an old untuned organ.

"Luka, sweetheart," Mother says. "Would you sing?"

The tear-filled eyes of cohabitants in our tight quarters are lit by only a shallow candle in the center of us. They're staring at me, waiting.

A memory of Ella staring up at me while I sang stings my heart. I haven't sung a word since I last saw her nineteen months ago. It seems like only a day has passed, but also, yesterday feels like a lifetime ago. She gave the words to my song a meaning.

"Please, dear," Mother urges me again.

My eyes clench tightly, searching for the strength to sing.

And thus, it—

My voice trembles as I begin to sing, soft notes filling the quiet—but the melody is shattered by an explosive succession of booms.

Everyone cowers, throwing themselves flat to the ground. "What's happening?" someone cries, panic rippling through the room.

The booms grow louder, endless. My chest aches as I weave through everyone, making my way to the window. I pull back the black fabric curtain covering just enough to peek outside. My shaky breath escapes me when I spot armed Jews of the ghetto ambushing the SS with their smuggled firearms and homemade bombs. The SS are running in various directions, shouting with clear panic and shock. They weren't expecting this. "The Jewish resistance are attacking the SS," I tell the others, unable to believe the words coming out of my mouth. This is the uprising I heard whispers about while traveling through the tunnels—a plan to attack the Germans and push them out of the ghetto, and Warsaw. The threats sounded like an unrealistic ploy. The Germans have had us all under their thumb for so long.

"What do we do?" Mother shouts from the other side of the room.

"Lie low, beneath the window, and stay quiet. We don't have anything to fight with or protect ourselves."

All of us are curled up on the ground, eyes wide open, staring at each other, listening to the ongoing attack. The gunfire eased for a short time but returned with a vengeance not long ago. With the sunlight breaking over the horizon, the truth is waiting outside the window. I claw myself up against the wall to steal a glimpse, and I can only wish my eyes are deceiving me as war sprawls through the street.

SS, gestapo, and German soldiers flood the streets in large quantities. They've brought in tanks, and artillery to continue the fight.

Another earth-shattering explosion shakes us as a German truck explodes down the street, not too far away. "Our people are still fighting," I utter to the others. "I'm not sure for how much longer though."

Soon after I drop back to the ground alongside Mother, a loudspeaker bellows through the chaos, commanding: "All Jews must surrender!"

"No, no, we must stay quiet," one of the older men says. "We aren't the ones fighting. We have nothing to surrender but ourselves, right?"

I don't want to be the one to answer, but I'm sure the SS are expecting all Jews to surrender themselves regardless.

"We can't give in to them," a woman says. "We've done nothing but follow their laws."

My heart pounds and I fold onto my knees, wrapping my hands around my head, trying to think through the panic raging through me. "I agree, we should hide for as long as possible. The resistance is likely still fighting against the Germans. Our only hope is to stay here for as long as we can," I announce, praying it's the right decision. Ignoring German orders is never the right decision, but if we walk out there, they might kill each of us on the spot.

A few others try to catch a peek of what's happening outside, reporting similarly with shock and disbelief.

"I don't see any other Jewish people surrendering," a woman cries out with a hint of hope in her fear-filled voice.

There are as many Jews out there as there are Germans, except our resistance utilizes men and women, young and old, all of them armed with acquired weapons. I'm not sure how the resistance has managed to make it through the night, but there are dead German soldiers and gestapo on the street. Their efforts have not been in vain, but I doubt this battle is anywhere close to being over.

"We'll continue to wait it out as the others must be doing," I reply.

In the last couple of hours, the ghetto has filled with smoke. I can hear buildings crumbling around us. I'm sure the Germans are trying to decimate every bit of the ghetto and smoke us all out.

Without an end in sight, I'm questioning what we should be doing. What if we're all sitting here, waiting to be caught in the fire?

My question only lingers for so long before smoke weaves in through the cracks of the window, choking us. Mother begins to cough violently along with some of the others. It's becoming impossible to breathe through the heavy smoke filled with burning wood and gun powder.

"We can't stay," I tell Mother. "We need to get out of here before the building burns to the ground."

Her chin quivers as she takes my hand and I head for the door, opening it onto what looks like a solid wall of smoke.

The stairwell isn't visible. We can hardly see two feet in front of us.

"The building is going to burn down. We must all leave now," I shout into the apartment.

I block out the cries and hysteria, knowing I must focus on getting us down the stairs, hoping there isn't a fire blocking the entrance. I thought I would make it out of here, even after all this time. I told myself I'd find Ella, and we'd both be fine. It's become too easy to lie to myself and build myself up with implausible hope. I just wanted to see her once more. I would take only and forever once more over never again. Everyone we love is gone, or so we have told ourselves. It's been over two years since Father and Grandfather were sent away. I haven't been able to find their names on any list the Judenrat has control over, which just leads me to believe the worst.

I must take care of Mother. It's what they would all hope I'd do.

Apollo's mother is having trouble with her two girls, both hysterical and terrified. I lift one of them into my arms. "Come on, darling. I've got you. We'll be all right." I hold her thin blanket over her nose and mouth, blocking out as much smoke as I can.

"I'm scared," she cries, the words muffled against the blanket.

"But you are so brave. So brave," I tell her.

I hold Mother tightly to my other side and get us all down the stairs as quickly as possible. We burst out of the building, gasping for air, coughing between each breath. I pull Mother to the side of the building, keeping us among the smoke until we reach the corner. Apollo's mother takes her daughter from my arms and squeezes her tightly.

"Come with us," I tell her. "I'll help you with the girls." Just as Apollo would have.

Apollo's mother shakes her head, her mouth quivering. "No,

Luka. We must all fend for ourselves now," she says. "But thank you. Be safe. God bless." She presses her fingers to her lips and gives us a teary-eyed wave.

There isn't time to beg, though I'm running as blindly as she is now. We could very well be running into a trap, but most of the fighting was coming from the other side of the building. Mother's hand squeezes mine so tightly, like I'm her lifeline, the thin frayed rope hanging between jagged rocks. "Come on, Mother. I have you," I utter between chokes.

I have you, I keep repeating in my head. I keep pulling her along down narrow passages between buildings. So many of them are burning down.

We end up at a sewer opening with a displaced cover. People are down there, and they could be Jews or Germans. But there's only one way in and one way out from this direction and if we run into the wrong people, it will be the end.

A broken-down brick building without a roof comes into sight and I consider the thought that no one would try to destroy this building again seeing as it's already mostly flattened. But there's a black cave through one side. It could collapse. It could be bombed. It might be our only chance to survive.

"In there. It's already been demolished. Let's try for now," I tell Mother.

She doesn't argue. She doesn't have a better idea. She's relying on me as if I'm Father, as if I'm in charge, and trusting that I'll keep her alive. I can't let her down.

I help her into the crawl space of a hole, finding a small open pyramid of space between the stacks of bricks. 'This is the end, isn't it, my dear?" she says.

"It's not the end. We'll fight beyond the end. They want us to give up. That's why we can't."

Mother grabs my hand, hers shaking and covered in sweat from the steam and heat of the surrounding fires. She wraps her arm around my back and pulls my head down to her shoulder. "My sweet boy, the one who made me a mother. You have always been the love of my life, you and your father's."

"Stop talking that way. We're going to make it out of this," I tell her.

She squeezes my hand a little tighter. "Perhaps, but I fear there will be a next 'this,' my son."

I swallow hard, trying not to give in to this fear, to this desolate end. "Remember the song—the one you always sang to me before bed when I was little?" I ask.

"Which one is that?" she asks.

I suppose she sang many but only one was my favorite. One always led to sweet dreams. I begin to sing softly, reminding her of the past:

> *There's a place for you*
> *Warm, inviting, bright, and true.*
> *A dreamland waiting to be found,*
> *Where peace and beauty both astound*
>
> *So, rest your eyes my dear*
> *Let colors burst and skies grow clear*
> *Flowers bloom in endless hue,*
> *A world of wonder just for you*
>
> *Those vines are yours to climb*
> *To touch the rainbow's endless time*
> *This magic place, so safe and near*
> *Exists for you—right here, my dear*

A tear from Mother's eyes falls onto my wrist. The ground rumbles heavier than before, like an earthquake that won't end.

"Luka, I must confess something to you," Mother says, grabbing hold of my chin to look at her.

"What? What is it?" I wish she would stop saying goodbye. I need the strength to get us out of here somehow.

"I had a friend who worked at city hall, one responsible for supplying lists of citizens to the Germans. I paid her a large sum of our savings to remove your name from the list of eligible male laborers. Your father and I agreed it would be the best use of our money. I wish more than anything we had enough to keep all three of you off the list, but the three of you being in one household would have raised questions. Your grandfather made it clear he has lived his life and would give whatever he had left to you. Your father, though far too young for such morbid thoughts, said the same. We all wanted the same: for you to have a chance to make it through this so you can experience the life you deserve."

"Mother, how could you—why wouldn't you tell me—" I lived all that time in fear of a letter. I can only imagine what people must have thought about me walking around after all other men my age had been taken. I must have looked like a coward.

"Because of the thoughts going through your mind at this very moment. You would have chosen to protect your father or grandfather over yourself. You would have turned yourself in. That's the man you are, the man I'm proud of, but the man—my son—who I will protect until the day I die whether you like it or not."

As if shock hasn't already taken its toll on every part of me, my gaze lingers on Mother, a mix of emotions tearing through me. Have I done right by her? Have I done enough to deserve what she and Father have done for me?

The bricks begin to fall, one by one, giving us little warning to move before it's too late. I pull Mother out just in the nick of time before the rest of the building caves in.

"Jews! Jews over there!" a German police officer shouts.

"Put your hands up," I tell Mother. "They'll know we aren't here to fight."

"What will they do with us?" she asks.

"I only know we shouldn't run now."

It isn't long before a truck rumbles through the piles of burning rubbish and we're harshly shoved inside with a load of others. An SS soldier punches his fist against the metal body of the truck. "Take these ones to the train station. They're going to Auschwitz."

Auschwitz.

Mother cups her hands over her face as tears fill her eyes. "I've heard of Auschwitz. That's where they're killing our people."

TWENTY-FOUR

LUKA

April 1943
Oświęcim, Poland

Were we spared or being sent someplace worse? No one on this train is any more aware than we are. There's only darkness, except for a few cracks along the outer walls of this speeding train. We can't sit or move without pressing into another person. We're pinned together like rolled up socks in an overflowing drawer.

Mother sways slightly forward and backward, only moving along the side of my arm tirelessly with every bump and turn. Our skin is raw, covered with dirt, smoke, and rubble, scratching and scraping with each touch we can't avoid. Her eyes are closed, and I believe she's being held up by me and whoever is on her other side. I wonder how much longer this never-ending ride will last. Will it go nowhere until the end of time? "Mama, you can rest your head on my shoulder."

She doesn't respond and I can't lift my arms to help her.

I've been staring into the dark scarfed head in front of me for so long I'm not sure if my eyes have been open or closed, but my body is stale and numb. My toes and my fingertips are cold as ice, numb to the touch. The temperature keeps falling even though there's no air to breathe.

When the train comes to a sharp halt, we all bend and straighten together, a frozen tidal wave. The door opens and people fall out. We all lose our balance and tumble forward like dominoes. I manage to catch Mother with my back then pull her to my side as we prepare to step down from the train onto the platform.

It's daytime, but the sky is covered with a thick blanket of dark gray clouds, rain expanding within and threatening to pour out on us all at once. I would drink it. I would take the wet cold in exchange for drinking the rain.

"Line up," SS officers shout at us as they pull others who didn't move fast enough off the train.

The crowd of people move in one direction carrying us along with them. Suitcases crash into my side, and I try to keep my arm around Mother, so she isn't knocked down. "I'm all right, son. I'm all right. Thank you for taking care of me," she says.

"I've been worrying about you."

"No need. We're here. We're together."

Her eyes gloss, as if she doesn't realize what's happening here. She has so many moments of confusion and then she speaks clearer than ever before. She's been through so much. We both have, but she's fragile now.

"Move! Keep moving!" I'm jabbed again with something else sharp, sent forward into the person in front of me.

We walk past dogs growling and barking, white foam spilling out of the sides of their mouths as if we're their next meal. An officer ahead is asking people questions I can't hear, then sending them away in different directions.

"Can you hear what they're asking?" I ask Mother.

She shakes her head. "I'm not sure."

When we make our way closer to the shouting officer, the question becomes clearer. "Occupation?"

When it's our turn for questioning, the SS officer looks pointedly at Mother, stares for a long second and says, "No, off to the left you go." He points to our left. "And you, your occupation?"

"Where are you sending her?" I ask, terror racing through me.

"I asked you a question. What is your occupation?" He then shoves mother to the side with all his strength, throwing her right down to the ground. I lunge for her.

"Are you all right, Mother? All you—"

"Let her go!" the guard shouts before thrusting his boot into my back, forcing me face first to the ground. I ignore the thrash of throbbing pain and push myself back up. "My mother is a seamstress. She has useful skills."

The officer laughs at me with cynicism. "Oh, does she now? Fine, then. You go to the left. She can work."

"I need to stay with her," I argue.

"Don't take my son away," Mother follows, her voice deep and loud.

"Enough," the officer hollers. He grabs Mother by the arm and flings her off to the right and holds his arm up, blocking me from moving toward her. "You want to work, in your condition? You want to do that instead of having your son work? You think that will save his life?"

"We can both work," Mother cries out.

"Nein," the officer says, shooing his hand at me. "You, old lady... You think you can work in place of your son?"

"No, no," I argue. "We can both work. Please, let us stay together. We'll work hard." Mother can barely stand, but we must stay together and work...it seems to be the only option.

"You..." the officer shouts in my face, the tip of his finger nearly touching my nose. "Go to the left!" He points toward a line of mothers and young children. "And you..." The soldier points his finger at Mother now. "Go to the right." He nudges his head toward a line of men. "You will work in place of your son. Then you will learn not to question authorities." He's punishing us, sending us into two directions—neither of us going in a direction it seems we belong.

"I'll find you. Don't worry. I promise. I'll find you," I shout to Mother as I follow the line to the left, praying she will be able to care for herself with her skills. She holds her arms around her body as she keeps her eye on me until she's forced around a corner. "I'll find you." My last promise comes out in just a whisper.

When I arrive at the end of another line, I find myself behind mostly women and young children, wondering why I was sent this way and Mother, the other. With no direction or instruction other than to remain in line, and for hours on end, none of us can predict what lies ahead. The mothers are cradling their children within their arms, old and young. Many are sitting on their suitcases or in the dirt. I've searched in every angle, trying to understand what it is we're waiting for here, but the SS walk by us as if we're nothing more than tree stumps. Yet an orchestra perched on a short hill off to the right, has been performing since we arrived. Some melodies I recognize, others I don't. The music has distracted me, making me believe there's something better at the end of this line we're waiting in, but that wouldn't make much sense after what we've already endured.

The mother ahead of me has two young children, both crying their hearts out. The mother has tried everything to calm them, but without luck. One of her little girls with chin-length hair and eyes bigger than coins stares at me as tears trickle down her cheeks. She couldn't be older than four or five, but she's looking as if she's waiting for something.

I kneel, bringing myself down to her height, and begin to sing. I try to keep my voice quiet, not to disturb anyone.

The sky is dark and gray
but behind the clouds, it's blue.
Lovely days will come
soon for me and you.

A darkness within my mind takes over, stealing the dream of belonging to this world, the hope that this will all end and bring all people closer together.

Keep me in your dreams,
and I'll come to you each night.
Hold me in your arms
until the morning light.

"What is it you think you're doing?" someone interrupts me.

My eyes flash open, finding an SS officer standing before me, the shadow from his cap darkening his complexion.

"Trying to cheer up the folks standing in the path before me," I say.

"You're a singer?"

"Yes," I utter. My gaze drifts past the SS, finding a crowd of others watching me with handkerchiefs pressed up to their mouths, tears falling from their eyes, stares of concern—a form of worry I should hide behind. "I didn't mean to disturb anyone."

"We could hear you down at the other end of the platform," the officer says.

"Again, I apologize for disturbing anyone."

The officer lets out a groan and grabs me by the elbow, pulling me up to my feet and dragging me away from the line. All I can do is stare at the little girl with short brown hair, watching as I'm pulled away. She's no longer crying. In fact, there's a small smile poking at her lips as she waves her small hand in goodbye.

The officer doesn't release me to any other line. He just continues dragging me along at a speed I can't keep up with, forcing me to trip over my own feet as we go. It isn't until we reach a row of buildings that he throws me to the ground and whispers something to another officer standing guard at a gate. The other officer stares down at me, his brows furrowed in confusion.

"It's your head to risk," the other officer tells the one who dragged me here.

Another exchange of whispers continues before the new officer points his baton at me. "Stand up." I push myself up to my feet, trying to hold myself upright, as straight as I can. "Follow me."

I follow his orders, walking in his shadow, looking around at thousands of others in every direction, dressed in blue and white striped uniforms, dirty, and sickly. They are all surveying me as if they've never seen a person who looks like me before, but that isn't the real reason for their stares.

They all have Star of David badges. They're all Jews. Is this where they've been taking our people? This muddy encampment that reeks of rotting flesh and manure? I can't move my eyes fast enough, searching the entire area for a sign of Mother, unsure whether she's been taken to the same area or somewhere different.

The air is almost unbreathable, solid and thick with ash and musk. To my left, I spot a set of gallows with ropes tied into nooses, hanging from each block. To my other side, I witness someone eating crumbs from a pile of dirt, shoving them into their mouth as if someone might steal them away. A dry ache burns through my chest. My voice will not save me here. On the contrary, my voice may become the end of me...

TWENTY-FIVE

LUKA

The officer stops short as we arrive in front of a set of narrow, red-brick buildings joining at a point in the shape of a V where a line of people are walking into the building. A large, open central hall blurs before my tired eyes, filled with rows of desks and groups of people waiting in a line at each. The farther I walk inside, the danker the air becomes, the smell of sweat and pungent chemical cleaner swirl together, forming a nauseating stench. Everyone watches each other, trying to understand what's happening, as I am. Again, I search every face, desperate to spot Mother among them. But I don't see her.

"Here, stand in this line," the officer says to me, shoving me into the woman I'm standing behind.

"I'm very so—"

I trip backward, a hand grappling the back collar of my shirt. "I didn't tell you to speak," the officer says, shoving me forward again.

With a breath scraping my throat, I scan the area without moving my head, searching for Mother, but there are so many people in here, dressed in drab, dark clothing with their heads covered, it's impossible to pick anyone out of the crowd.

The line moves at a slow place, and I can't hear what information the clerk is seeking up ahead.

"She said next, did you not hear her, fool!" another SS shouts from ahead, striking a man across the back with his baton.

As time passes, the light within the open area dims, the sun faintly glowing through the barred windows. Eventually, lights hanging from the ceiling flicker on, adding a subtle orange glow.

I'm next, waiting to step up to the tattered wooden desk where a woman sits with an open logbook spread out in front of her. A black scarf conceals her head, and she's dressed in blue and white striped garb, a Star of David pinned to her chest.

"Next," she calls out, her voice hardly audible.

I've seen what happens to others if they don't jump fast enough in response, so I move quickly, stopping within reach of the desk's edge.

The woman keeps her head down, staring at the open book as the guard who pulled me inside steps around the desk to watch over what she's doing.

"Name?" she asks, pressing the tip of her pen into a jar of black ink.

For a moment, I consider lying but the papers in my pocket will speak the truth. I'm not sure a name makes any difference anyhow. "Luka Dulski," I reply, a tremor obvious in my annunciation.

She writes out my name then slides her wrist to the left, placing the tip of her pen in the next column.

"Date and birthplace?"

The scratching of pen on paper, murmurs of others in line and distant shouts make it difficult to recall simple information about myself.

My vision blurs for a moment as I speak, "The second of February 1918 in Warsaw, Poland."

"Nationality?" she continues.

"Polish."

"Occupation?"

The SS officer reaches over the clerk's shoulder and points to a different column. I can't read the headings from this angle. "Entertainer, singer," he tells her.

The girl looks up at me as if questioning the truth. The only truth between us is the red vein webbing across the whites of her eyes, the dark circles beneath her lashes, and her sunken, raw, chapped cheeks.

I nod, assuming she's seeking confirmation.

"Religion?" she asks, her question softer this time.

By the matching withering armbands on both our sleeves, she can see I'm the same as her. "Jew," I reply, the word cloaking me like a contagious disease.

She jots down a series of numbers in the last column then reaches beneath her desk, retrieving a thin, rectangular scrap of white canvas. Then she lifts a stamp and arranges the pieces of rubber with metal dials and presses the rubber onto a pad of ink then directly onto the white scrap of canvas.

"You are no longer who you were before," the SS officer spews, needling me with cold, dark eyes—the stare of a raven carrying warning. "Now, you have no name. Your number is your name. This is how you will be addressed and identified. Your family and home no longer exist. If you forget this fact, you will face severe consequences. Here, you are to work and follow orders, nothing more. There will be no rights or privileges. Your survival depends on you and your ability to follow instructions." The officer speaks so fast, I'm trying to process everything he just said but it's clear this new number represents me as an object, and no longer a person.

I take the scrap of canvas from the girl's raw hand and clutch it within my grip.

The officer moves along without direction, and I scramble to stay behind him and his casual pace between lines toward a connecting corridor.

He stops walking just after passing an open door. "Inside," he says, pointing into the almost bare room where another line of people wait. The tripod mounted camera centered in the room offers a blink of relief, but also, time to consider why an officer is escorting me around alone. Everyone else is in a line of some sort.

A middle-aged man in a prisoner uniform shoves each person onto a bench, then snaps photographs from three different angles. Without a word of exchange, he then grabs each person by the elbow and shoves them to the side to leave until it's my turn. I go through the same form of humiliation, and for what purpose?

It isn't long before I'm following the officer again through another corridor to an exit where we briefly step outside to cross the grass-matted dirt into another building labeled: Sauna.

The new cement room holds dozens of naked men waiting to be sprayed down by metal shower heads protruding from the ceiling.

"Strip. Leave your clothes in the metal bins. Nothing shall remain on your body. All belongings should be left behind," someone shouts.

The spray isn't water. It's cold, burns, and carries an acidic stench. Now naked, my scrap of canvas which was taken from me before being sprayed down, is handed back as I'm shoved into the next room where hair is flying around the room like falling snow.

Again, I wait, already coming to terms with what's next. A rough shave and all hair buzzed from my body. Blood drips from several nicks down my neck and my face.

Another line forms toward the next door in sight and I follow it into another open space filled with rows of tables. It takes a moment to understand what I'm looking at. When it's my turn, I sit on a wooden stool and reach my bare left arm out onto the table as the man across from me avoids eye contact while dipping a needle into a jar of ink before the first sharp sting and the grasp of rough hands squeezes at my wrist. The process of being poked over and over by hundreds of small dots of ink brings beads of sweat to the nape of my neck, the anger hurting me more than the sharp needle. The coppery and acidic scent from ink and blood floats through the air and I refuse to look down at my arm. Others around me grunt or utter a quiet groan through the pain. I bite my tongue to bear the pain, until a metallic taste sloshes through my mouth. Nothing masks the burn writhing up my arm.

Still naked, bare to the bone except for my identifying number etched into my raw skin, I'm escorted outside and through a set of iron gates with the words *Arbeit macht frei* arched over the top.

Barefoot, I walk in a line with others down a long row parting brick barrack blocks. The roads are all rock and gravel, slicing my feet as we continue to parade through this compound, bearing our pale, limp bodies as we cover our privates for a sense of modesty in front of whoever is watching us.

By the time we stop in front of one of the identical buildings within the endless row, the sun is scraping along the horizon, a warning of impending darkness. A man in a striped uniform pulls up to our side with a wagon full of roped bundles and proceeds to hand one to each of us. I stare down at the load dropped within my arms, finding a striped uniform, a pair of clogs, a blanket, and eating utensils.

I then enter the open door into the building, finding a large, crowded space with rows of bunk beds, four rows high. The first open space I spot is just a few columns down on the right and up on the third tier. I place my bundled belongings down and retrieve the uniform and clogs, wasting no time in slipping them on and covering up.

The shirt loosely fits over my shoulders, and I futz with the waistband of the pants to try and roll it over, so they'll stay above my hips. This uniform is meant for someone twice my size—odd, seeing as all the Jews have been starved over the last two years.

I turn my attention back to the space I've claimed within the bunks, finding a middle-aged man lying on his belly to the side of my spot. His arms are folded beneath his chin, and he stares at me with a scowl, but shifts a smidge to the side to make more room.

I climb up, careful not to jostle the first two tiers of beds. I start on my back, realizing there are only two ways to find comfort here—on my back or on my belly like the man next to me. My hips certainly wouldn't thank me for putting my weight on them here. My shoulder scrapes against the bunk above as I shift to my front.

I grab the blanket I received, and a matching striped cap falls out of the pile. I slide it, along with the utensils and bowl, to the small amount of space next to my waist. I keep the blanket folded and pull it over my arms to rest my head, finding the first moment of rest since Mother and I were taken from Warsaw.

The voices around me grow louder through my stillness. Whispers in Polish, Yiddish, and German slur into one indecipherable conversation. Though, I hear snippets of statements of survival tips, work assignments, and warnings to stay away from the buildings where thick smoke rises into the air.

"First night is the worst," the middle-aged man mumbles. His eyes are half open, but my head is facing in his direction. I was trying to look elsewhere to be respectful of his space, but I suppose that's impossible here. "Don't ask questions. Do what they tell you. And pray none of them have a reason to talk to you."

I let his words sink in and I nod against my rolled-up blanket. "Thank you."

My stare lingers on the wooden beams holding up the bunks across the row, the spots of dry blood painting a picture I can imagine far too easily.

TWENTY-SIX

LUKA

The metal clang of a bell sends a spark through my chest as my eyes flash open. Dim lights glow along the center of the building and men are scrambling to their feet, pulling on their caps and sliding into their clogs.

Another man standing by the front door makes his presence known by shoving and yelling at anyone in his way before shouting, "Outside! Line up for roll call!"

"He's a kapo. He works for the SS. Do as he says, too. Roll call is twice a day and you must be present," my middle-aged bunk mate says.

I disjointedly make my way out of the barrack, the cool, damp spring air licking my skin as I step outside. Prisoners in striped uniforms stand rigidly in rows as SS guards pace back and forth with a grip on their growling dogs.

Roll call drags on and on as SS guards shout prisoner numbers and a series of commands. I listen intently for my number, unfamiliar despite it being inked on my arm. The number finally rings through the air, following a direction to join a group off to the left where a shovel is smashed against my chest. "Go," a prisoner says, one with an armband that depicts him as a kapo, like the man who'd shouted orders at us in the barrack earlier.

We follow him past several rows of buildings until we stop at a trench-like pit. "Dig."

I follow the speed and pace of everyone around me, noticing some are slower than others. I assume being faster must be safer. Though in less than an hour, the pain from shoveling hard dirt without a break sets in. Then blisters begin to form on my hands. The sting and soreness are a stagnant feeling that grows worse by the hour, but I keep my head down, avoiding eye contact with any passing guard.

"She's a seamstress." Did I save Mother from this type of work by telling the SS of her skill? The thought of her digging like this all day makes me sick to my stomach. At least she isn't in this group, digging alongside me. I couldn't watch her go through this.

By the time I return to the barrack, hours after wreaking havoc on every muscle in my body, I'm nearly numb as I lift a measly bowl of soup to my mouth. The middle-aged man already warned me to only eat half my serving of bread to ensure I have food for the morning. They plan to starve us here, too. It's no surprise.

I drag myself up the wooden rung toward my bunk, ready to black out from exhaustion. "Wait. You." Something sharp pokes me in the back and I stop, frozen, wondering who is behind me and what they want with me. I peer over my shoulder, looking into the eyes of an SS officer. He grabs my arm just as I step back down to the floor and shoves my sleeve up to inspect my number. "Yes, come with me," he demands.

The blood drains from my face as I notice no one else is stepping back out of the building currently. Just me. We walk the length of the camp once again, exiting the metal gate and taking a different path around the exterior of the camp past three long and narrow buildings on my left and a barbed-wire fence on my right where more brick barrack rows extend into the darkness of the night.

The officer hasn't said a word about where we're going or what's happening and, like everything in the last several hours, I'm supposed to keep walking without asking a question. I've noticed every weapon draped across his body, the baton in his hand, the whip sticking out of his back pocket. He's likely eager to use any one of them, or so I can only assume by the behavior of most gestapo police.

We enter a grand foyer, two stories high, outlining the interior opening. Polished wooden floors beneath my feet and dark wooden beams line the tall ceiling. Symbolic German Reich statues and gold fixtures decorate the walls along with ornate torches near every floor-to-ceiling pillar.

People are dressed in formal attire, like that from a time I can hardly remember. There is no war inside this building, just common life for high-class citizens. No one looks at me or finds my appearance appalling or out of place. It's as if I'm a flea that slipped in through a door crack—impossible to notice.

"What songs do you sing?" the officer asks, his voice quiet in comparison to the rumble of cheer surrounding me.

"I—I, uh, write my own, but I'm familiar with many classics."

"Fine then. The people here need cheerful, uplifting tunes. Nothing melancholy."

The officer stares me in the eyes, something most avoid. In the momentary exchange, I watch his Adam's apple struggle to slide up and down his throat. I hear him swallow, as if sand is caught in his throat. By the look of him, he can't be much older than me. We're the same height. He has dark hair and pale skin like me, at least before my head was shaved bald. The only visible difference between us are the clothes we're wearing, the authority given, and most distinctly, the race and ideology flowing through our veins that no one can see.

"I understand," I reply.

But I understand nothing. How can anyone expect me to sing for these monsters and with uplifting cheer, too? Ella always told me I was giving so much to others just with my voice—happiness they desperately needed. The people in this room don't deserve happiness in the slightest. They are the thieves and murderers.

"In the back corner, you'll find a pianist who will accompany you," the officer says, pointing through a crowd of people.

No one acknowledges me as I move forward, seeking openings between people to avoid brushing up against anyone or asking for their pardon. My feet squelch and squeak in these clogs from sweat and puddles.

Once I make it to the back of the room, where a row of open windows greet me, I find a dark portrait-like scene unfold: the first row of prisoner barracks is no more than a stone's throw from here. Perhaps this location is purposeful, allowing the prisoners to overhear the merriment that's just out of reach. *Despicable.*

I find the pianist sitting behind a grand piano. He's a middle-aged gentleman, maybe Father's age. He has sprigs of white hair poking out of his scalp, matching the lower half of his face. The skin beneath his eyes sags like skin-colored prunes and his eyelids are swollen. I wonder how long he's been here, how long he's been playing the piano for these people.

"Hello," I greet him, keeping my voice down.

He nods his head and widens his eyes, frightened.

No speaking, I gather.

He lifts a hand from the ivory keys and points to the sheet music in front of him, his finger trembling. I've heard the artist's name and his music; however, I haven't sung in German before. The pianist pulls another sheet out from behind the one I'm looking at, one with German lyrics that he sets beside his sheet music. The man's fingers feather across the piano's keys, as his hands float, and I wait through the introduction, before singing out the first words.

The words crooning from my tired throat are a lie in every possible way. To sing a song about every person needing a home that can bring them happiness when all the Jewish people have had their homes taken from them is cruelty at its finest. If I could block out the people swaying back and forth around me, I would, but I have to read the lyrics.

The guests of the party begin to sing along with me as if they have no idea what they're staring at, who they're watching —no one, a man without a home. They don't care. Not one of them.

The next song is a contemporary piece used in a film years ago about a woman yearning for love and happiness. I know the lyrics and can imagine a world where I could be happy, full of love. My voice fills the space around me, trembling through me in a way I can hardly remember. If I could forget I'm here, singing in German, it would be quite magical, but my heart knows nothing but the cold chill I've become accustomed to.

As the song comes to a slow end, I open my eyes to see the crowd of high-ranking men and their wives watching me with hands clutched to their chests as if they believe every word I sing to them. A few applaud but the gesture quickly ends as hushes move through the crowd. They must have forgotten where they are, too.

Hours of singing and dehydration break my voice into a slur of scratched notes. I don't envy the pianist either. His hands must be sore and aching. I haven't slept in so long; the room begins to wobble around me as if I'm dancing along with the others. I try to take in a sharp breath to shake the dizzying sensation away.

"Almost over," the pianist utters. "They'll kill you if your voice cracks. You know that, don't you?"

"I'm well," I say as a cough rattles my chest. I shove my hand against my ribs, holding it back.

"They will leave soon."

Hunger rakes through my stomach, pinching and burning, reminding me of how little I've consumed in the last few days. Yet, I watch the latest round of food passed around to the guests, still eating, still nibbling, for hours on end, while I would do anything for a mere crumb. Do they know how hungry we are? Would they care? And Mother...has she gotten water? Has she been fed anything at all? All I can do is wonder what's happening to her, and it's breaking me down.

My breath becomes weak, and the swaying of my body is happening on its own. I spot the edge of the piano to my right and consider pressing my hand down to hold myself up.

The main doors open and close repeatedly. They must be leaving.

I continue to stare over at the side of the piano, responding to the cold zing working through my veins. I'm not well. I watch a woman shrug on a fur-lined coat, her blonde curls bouncing along her shoulders. Ella's hair looked that way the times she wore it down, which wasn't often since she found her hair to be more of a nuisance than anything. She preferred to have it woven into a long braid. I loved it any way she wore it. The woman links her arm with a man in a suit, a cigar nipped between his lips and laughter rumbling between them. We never had the chance to attend a formal event or a fine dinner. I dreamed about taking her to a nice place, staring into her eyes all night by candlelight and holding her hand for as long as she would allow me to.

Despite never having the opportunity, I would take back our days in the sewers over all else. We were together and she brought me warmth and contentment like these people seem to have, as well as their ignorance of the reality of our world existing outside this building.

Bells from a grand clock ring out, calling my attention to the golden minute and hour hands hovering over the twelve. The last song ends, and the pianist pulls the cover down over the keys. I peer over at him, wishing I could ask him what we're supposed to do now. He nods to a door behind us. I follow him into a corridor with another door ahead of us.

"This is the door we should come in and out each night, not the way you were escorted in. Now, we return to our block for the evening."

"What about tomorrow?" I ask.

"You'll receive a daytime assignment, I'm sure. You might not assume so, but there are several opportunities for Nazi chosen musicians here. However, you won't find any to be gratifying, I'm afraid."

"I see."

"Do as you're told and you'll have a chance..."

"A chance?"

He looks back at me as he's about to open the exiting door. "To live another day, young man."

I may not make it another day if I don't have water and food. I follow the pianist outside, where an SS guard waits. He doesn't speak to us, just follows in our muddy shadows. I wouldn't know where to walk if it weren't for the pianist leading the way, but we weave in between two other long buildings before arriving back at the main gate I entered through earlier today.

The SS guard continues to follow us. The sound of his footsteps now accompanies a crunch—the man chewing on food. The thought of food makes my stomach cramp again, forcing me to clutch my arm around my waist.

We arrive at the block I was assigned earlier, realizing the pianist has also been assigned to live in this block. Before dismissal, the guard tosses something into a nearby muddy puddle. I spot a piece of biscuit and a slice of sausage floating. I lunge for the food, scooping it up and shoving it into my mouth, ignoring the foul taste of flinty dirt.

The guard laughs, a high-pitched squeal. "Damn rat," he says, trying to catch his breath through the scornful laughter.

He grabs me by the collar and shoves me into the block, face first, sending me skidding across the splintered floor. I hit the bottom of my chin, and my chest burns as I push myself back up in the pitch darkness of the block where many are either asleep or pretending to be asleep, leaving me to find the slim, empty spot where I left my assigned belongings earlier, before I was taken away to perform.

TWENTY-SEVEN

ELLA

May 1943

I know it's May. It's been a year and a half since I arrived here
in Auschwitz. A year that has dragged on as if ten. It's the repetitive cycle of doing the same thing every single day that causes
the days to blur into one. I wouldn't know it was May unless I
was forced to write the date down over a thousand times a day.

The memory of a May when we set up part of the grocery
store out on the front stoop flashes through my mind. Tata
would be waving at everyone on the street, inviting them over
with his friendly smile. "This is how you find happiness, Ella,"
he would say. "When you offer a smile, you give someone else a
reason to smile." He was right. Only in front of our store did it
sound like the bees were singing rather than buzzing, and
daffodils would blossom for months. Birds would weave
between customers' feet as if we were all one of a kind, and
everyone knew our names. Life felt magical then, almost unreal
compared to this. It might as well still be winter here with how
cold the air is and the relentless dense fog that hovers over us
like another imprisoning wall or gate. Would Tata tell me to

smile now? Would he tell me it would work, fix everything around me? I'm not sure.

Day after day, I question whether I'm alive or in some form of hell, but there's no answer.

Rain falls in fat plonks as I amble away from the roll-call square to the administration building. The mud is thick and sticky, sucking the clogs off my feet just to splash back at me after I place my foot back down.

I once loved the rain. I thought it was magical and romantic —a perfect setting for a first kiss with a symphonic background made of drips, drops, and plonks that would silence the world's chatter. If I could have that moment back, that one kiss, the only first kiss I might ever experience—I would love the rain again. That was a dream, it had to have been. How can one person go from living a life like that to one like this?

I push my sleeve up to show the guard at the gate my number and wait for him to let me through. The world around me becomes a blur as I walk down the corridors into the room where I will catalog names until the muscles in my hand seize.

The stack of papers on my desk grows taller each day, despite making it through the full pile daily. More and more innocent people are being brought into these confines. By the over-population of Polish resistance members now imprisoned within these walls, it's hard to imagine there's anyone left to rescue us. And worse, I'm terrified to think what might have become of Tata and Miko—if they've been caught.

"Ella..." the whisper of my name tells me the coast is clear of officers, guards, and kapos in the near vicinity. I peer behind me, finding Tatiana with her hand cupped around her cheek, calling for me. I've come to learn she'll only call for me here if there's a reason worth taking the risk.

She waves me over and I scan the room to make sure there are no watchful eyes before scurrying to her side with my back arched to conceal myself behind the front row of typists.

"What is it?"

"I've made a friend," she says, her eyes growing wide as if I should understand what she means by her statement. We all have "friends", but there are varying forms of friends here: those we can trust and rely on, share emotions and secrets with, some who offer help in exchange for help, and then, of course, there are the foes who act as friends but will rat out us out to receive an extra crumb of bread. Without knowing who each of these people truly are deep down inside, it's easy to walk into a deadly trap.

"Go on," I tell her.

"Iza, she works in a room down the corridor, processing incoming and outgoing post. She's looking for a name—her sister to be exact—and she's desperate to know what barrack she's been assigned. I told her I would look and ask you and the other girls the same. If we manage to find this name, she's offered to help clear a letter for each of us."

My mouth falls open, shock swelling through me as I consider the thought of sending a letter out of this place. Then I remember how feeble our luck has been upon trying to locate names in our logs. We tried to find Tatiana's mother's and sister's names before, but we couldn't. She's convinced herself they were sent somewhere better than here and that's why she can't find them. I think that thought helps her sleep at night.

"What about the restrictions and SS reviews?" We had once been told we could send an occasional note out of Auschwitz, but that "generous" offer came without any ounce of privacy. Every letter would be reviewed before being sent to the addressee and anything found to be stated negatively against Auschwitz would be a violation and result in severe punishment, torture, or death. That's why I haven't sent anything home.

My notes would be full of lies, forcefully positive and upbeat, as well as offering false hope to Mama and Tata. They might find relief in knowing I'm alive, but no one in Auschwitz is promised a tomorrow.

The guilt I live with, knowing they must assume I'm dead or held prisoner somewhere showers my mind with images of them grieving for me daily, especially after Miko warned me not to go help Luka that night. He's likely aware of what happened to me and there isn't a doubt in my mind that Tata and Miko will travel to the ends of the earth to find me. That thought alone leaves me with more dread than anything else.

"She's a Funktionshäftlinge, a functionary prisoner who screens letters under SS supervision, but her supervisor wanders about more frequently than most," Tatiana says. "It's something, a bit of hope for us."

I stare through my friend, knowing tears should be filling my eyes, but I'm not sure I remember how to cry through the staleness of my mind. "Thank you—what—what is her sister's name? What should I be searching for?"

"Zofia Jonowicz. She's seventeen from Krakow."

Tatiana scribbles down the name on a small note card, folds it up and presses it into my hand, folding my fingers over the note. I offer a small smile, the only form of a smile I'm capable of here.

I rush back to my desk and pull out a piece of note paper to hide beneath the catalog of names—a blank sheet I can use if I find the name we're searching for. I could search previous pages, one or two at a time between entering a column's worth of new names.

I take the top paper from the pile and set it down next to the open catalog. I dip my pen into a bottle of ink and script out the prisoner number, surname and first name, date of birth, place of birth, nationality/ethnicity, religion, date of arrival to Auschwitz, reason for imprisonment, occupation, and assigned block.

I flip the paper over and set it to my left, then take the next paper from the pile to scan before jotting down the information.

I blink, holding my eyes closed for a moment to clear my focus as I recenter my stare on the name:

Family name: <u>Bukowski</u>

Forename: <u>Lukasz</u>

Born on: <u>4.5.1918 in: Krakow</u>

Status: <u>Unmarried</u>

Religion: <u>Jew</u> Country of Origin: <u>Poland</u>

My blood turns cold, despite the words "it's not him" rushing through my head. Luka. 1918. Polish Jew. I wouldn't want him to be here. I know what they do to most of the Jewish people here. But my Luka is Luka Dulski, not Lukasz Bukowski. Same age, but Luka was born in February on the 2nd of the month in Warsaw, not Krakow. My heart splits down the center, the fibers of tissue tearing like a thin fabric, filling me with a pain that will never subside. In a humane world, I could write to him, but in this world, it could endanger him under the policing laws of the ghetto.

I see people who look like him every day, making me feel like I've gone mad. Every man here is bald, left only with their eyes, nose, and mouth as their only discernible features, making many of them look nearly identical to one another. That's the point. We've all been stripped of our identities, left with a number, striped uniforms, and hollow eyes. We're objects used to work and make the daily lives of the SS easier.

I force my hand to scribe the information across the page,

spelling out the man's name as my heart continues to bleed onto the desk beneath me.

* * *

The nights are the hardest, even worse than working twelve to fourteen hours a day. I've found that when there is less time to think, the better off I am. At night, after we've eaten the second half of our daily allotment of bread, our stomachs still angry for something more, we are sent to our straw-filled mattresses to sleep elbow to elbow with others in the same block.

There's no reason I shouldn't fall asleep within seconds of lying down. My body is always in an extreme state of exhaustion, yet my mind refuses to concede as it searches for sustenance to fill the gaps of the thoughts that I actively avoid from the moment I wake up, until right this very moment when I'm staring at the back of a shaven head, counting the beauty marks along her scalp. I suspect none of us had ever questioned how many beauty marks or freckles we had on our scalp before arriving here. To be so unfamiliar with our bodies makes me realize we, as humans, think we know far more than we do.

With a deep breath, I let my eyes drift closed in search of sleep, but instead find Luka's presence in the darkness of my mind—his beautiful hazel eyes filled with hope and determination. That was the Luka from over a year ago. I'm not sure if he's even still breathing. I tell myself he is, knowing the likelihood is slim. Too many people were dying in the encampment within Warsaw. I was bringing him and his family extra food. Without that, they would likely be just as worse off as the rest of the people living there. To know I could have kept him alive, but didn't listen to Arte in that one passing second, will haunt me for the rest of my life.

The lights flash back on as if a strike of lightning breaks through the barrack. "Roll call, now!" Francine, the block-elder shouts at us. We've already been through roll call, just after we ate our crumbs of supper. "It's been brought to my attention that several of you didn't return from the latrines before lights went out."

Who would tell her such a thing? No one converses with Francine unless necessary. I, for one, can't understand the reason for the pure cruelty behind her actions. She treats every woman in this barrack as if we're the German soldiers who dragged her away and imprisoned her here, when we are the same as she, if not worse off. The Jewish women here were taken from their homes or plucked from the streets. Many, separated from their families.

We all pull ourselves from our beds, our bodies landing heavily to the ground against the day's imposed weakness. No one speaks. We all slip our clogs onto our feet and shuffle toward the door into the cool, dense fog, walking through mud toward the roll-call square within the orange glowing lights. I stare up at the closest light, watching flying insects swarm the glow in masses, fighting for something better than the darkness can offer. We're living a similar life down here.

Francine disappears, leaving us in rows, cold to the bone and tired. One woman falls into the next and that woman begins to fall in the same direction. The women behind her grab hold of their smocks, fighting to help them remain upright. Whoever was behind them would decide their fate tonight. Some of the other women no longer converse or attempt to help another. They move when they're told and carry on like walking corpses, unaffected, or maybe unknowing of whether they're even alive or dead.

My eyelids become heavy the longer we stand in silence, listening only to the buzzing of the bugs and heavy breaths of the women on either side of me. And then, warm melodic notes weave through the air with a rich silky tone that breaks into a smooth vibrato between a bow and a violin's strings. Am I dreaming? The music softens, blending into the silent buzz around us, welcoming a tune carried by a male voice.

> *Through battles of a time long ago*
> *Triumph and victory will carry on*
> *Through smoke and whispers of foe*
> *It is all we must see, the light, so very strong*
> *Very strong...*
>
> *It is for us to achieve, bravery for free*
> *For one and all, this, is our solemn vow*
> *Set forth and though shall not see*
> *What is left behind, then and right now*

The weight of my eyelids lifts, the wind burns as I forget to blink. That sound, the hum, muffled but clear, traveling through the few trees and gates between the barrack behind us and the Commandant's villa on the other side. My heart goes still, then gallops up into my throat. I clutch my chest.

Is it another delusion? I've seen him in so many faces, felt the warmth of his endearing stare from people I've never met.

> *Through battles of time long ago*
> *Triumph and victory will carry on*
> *Carry on...*
> *So strong...*

My breath hitches, the weight of exhaustion lifting like a fog. That voice—unmistakably his. It awakens a part of me that has been asleep for so long. Where is the sound coming from? It's close by, but faint. My chest tightens as the song continues, each note pulling me in closer.

> *We are one and the same*

Alive with courage and heart
Time will come when they chant your name
The heroic tales of war's subdue art...

The way he carries the last note, lifting it to travel like a silk scarf twirling through the air. I've only known one person to sing like that. Only one.

But it can't be. It can't. He wouldn't be here. Please, don't let him be here.

The thought twists in my stomach with a mix of hope and terror.

I can't allow myself to believe it's Luka.

TWENTY-EIGHT

ELLA

My hands are unsteady today, or more unsteady than usual. The papers slip in my fingers, but I keep moving, hoping it doesn't show. My mind isn't at its sharpest, going over and over the question of whether I might have unknowingly written out Luka's name as if it was just any other name, monotonously grinding my pen against lines over and over all day. Or one of the other clerks could have logged his name and wouldn't have given it a second thought because they don't know anything about him. There are too many variables to consider, which leaves me desperate to come up with a way to confirm whether it's Luka's voice I've been hearing.

I could ask the others to look for Luka's name the way we've been helping Iza search for her sister, Zofia. Though part of me thinks it's foolish to look for Luka's name because if I was to find it, it would mean he's here. It would mean he's no longer promised a tomorrow either. I wouldn't dream of that for him. It's the last thing I want for him.

Furthermore, I can't avoid the reality of odds that he would end up in the same place I am—they must be slim. I already know my mind has been playing tricks on me, making me think

I see him in others. This is the last place he should be. He was already a prisoner of the walls in Warsaw. This place—this is intended for torture and death.

Something sharp strikes me in the shoulder and I whip around, terrified I've been caught flipping through the pages of the log rather than continuing to enter the names. I find a small, triangular folded card on the ground behind my chair and scoop it up. Upon returning upright, I glance at Tatiana's desk, then at Tatiana, who's shooting me a questioning look. "Everything all right?" she mouths to me. She must have noticed I've been moving quite slow.

The sharp angled card pokes the inside of my hand. I turn around to face the front, look around to make sure there aren't any watching guards and unfold the paper to scribble out a quick note:

I heard a man singing last night.
    I recognized his voice.
    If it is him...It's my Luka.
    Or I might just be going mad.

I fold the note card back up into the triangle and flick it back over to her.

She catches it and unfolds the paper swiftly and reads what I wrote. Tatiana places her hand on her chest then turns the note card over to jot something down. Within seconds, she folds it in half then tosses it back to me.

I catch it, mid-air, open it and read what she's responded with:

Oh gosh, we'll search the logbooks!
    What does he look like?
    I'll keep a lookout for him, too.

I respond beneath her short paragraph:

Thank you. I must know, either way.
He's tall, slender, sharp facial features,
and striking hazel eyes.

It's hard to describe him when we're devoid of our identi-fying features—our hair, starved, and tortured into a quiet submission.

Again, I toss back the note, but it swoops beneath her desk this time. She doesn't waste any time retrieving it, but then hits her head beneath the desk, causing a loud thud. Tatiana jumps up, her mouth hanging open as we both scan the room. Just then, an officer saunters by the open door, his hands clasped behind his back as he stops and glares inside, scoping out all the women working.

A woman two desks down from me fumbles with whatever she's doing and spills the jar of ink on her desk. The officer pivots and steps into the room, making his way into the room with long, slow strides toward the woman who's trying to move all the papers away from the ink spill.

The sound of whimpering and heavy breaths forces me to squeeze my eyes shut, predicting what's to come. The clatter is loud, echoing and too easy to imagine. Her bones hit the desk, and she cries out in pain. "You...foolish imbecile," the officer spits out. He's thrashing her around on the desk. "This is what happens when you spill our ink."

When the racket stops and the clicking of boots against the floor grows quieter, I peek out of the corner of my eyes, finding the woman pulling her dress together, holding it where it's torn and covered in ink. Her face is red, and blood is dripping from the side of her mouth, falling against the smudged ink stained across her body. We aren't allowed to console her. Acts of kind-ness are forbidden, punishable by beatings, or worse.

The officer lingers in the doorway, the long moment stalling, before finally walking away. I release a breath, and my shoulders fall. I'm afraid to turn around to face Tatiana so I continue entering names from the pile of papers beside me.

To think of how I used to complain about helping Tata and Miko with inventory for our store needles at me. I was young and didn't know what life could look like.

* * *

"I don't want to be here. It's not fair. I was in school all day," I complain to Tata as I stack jars of pickled vegetables on a shelf, one by one, ensuring the column is straight with each jar's label facing me. Tata's rules, not mine.

"Ella, this store is part of our family. If it was me or your mother who needed help, would you say that isn't fair, too?"

"The store isn't a person," I argue.

"No, but it brings life to others. We keep people fed. It's an important job, and this store has been in our family for generations. You should take pride in that."

I will take pride, but when I'm older with nothing else better to do. The other kids in my class don't even invite me to do anything with them because they know I'm never available. This store has become my only friend, and it's still not a person.

I sigh in response, trying to hold my tongue rather than be disrespectful. Tata is the one who always tells me I'll only be a child once and I should enjoy life without so many responsibilities. He must not understand that sitting in this store all day is stealing my youth. "All right."

"Ella," Tata says, taking me by the hand. "Place that jar down and come with me."

I stand up from my knees, as he pulls me toward the back room of the store and taps on a milk crate.

"Sit." He sits down across from me on another crate. "You're sixteen. I understand your frustration. I do."

"Then why not let me be a young adult like the others at school?" I argue.

Tata folds his hands together and rests them on the knees of his worn brown pants. "There are many people in this city who were born into families of wealth. There are people who barely get by on the money they have. Then, there are the people like us, who weren't born into a family of wealth, but were fortunate enough to have a business passed down to us, which acts like a money tree of sorts. We have what we need so long as we continue to put in the effort to keep the tree growing. Many years ago, your mother and I decided that we were not going to raise you like many of the other young girls in this city."

"Why not?" I ask, frustration bubbling through me. "Why do I need to be treated differently?"

A small smile curls into Tata's lips as he reaches over to squeeze my knee. "Sweetheart, your mother and I don't think you are a simple young lady who will someday be content serving as a housewife to any man you choose to spend your life with. We see the desire for adventure within your eyes and we want to make sure that whatever it is you want to do as a grown woman, you can do. Whether that is working in this store, exploring the world, or being an amazing mother and wife—we want the choice to be yours, but if we don't teach you how to survive, how to earn a living, and take care of yourself, your options will be limited."

"There's more that you aren't saying," I whine. If he wants me to have freedom when I'm older, he will allow me some room to grow now.

"You're correct, my darling. We have lived through the world's worst economic crisis over the last eight years, and we are just now starting to rebuild, but there is no guarantee that our country and the world won't fall again. Therefore, we need to put

*everything we have into this store to make sure we continue to
live a stable life, and we need your help to do so."*

"Are we poor?" I ask, wondering if that's what he means.

*"We have spare change in our pockets, food on the table, and
a roof over our heads. We are fortunate. Let's always remember
that and never take it for granted," he says, pinching my cheek.*

Now, I work and don't get paid. I'm fed just enough to keep me
alive, and the roof I sleep beneath is just another form of prison
within a larger prison. Everything Tata tried to explain then
finally makes sense now, and it's too late. I may never get to
experience anything more than entering names into a book.

The ten-hour workday mark strikes with shouting demands
from the corridor outside the clerical room. We fold up our
catalog books and funnel out the door and into a line where
we'll be escorted back through the main gates. The girl who
spilled her ink earlier in the day is hunched forward in front of
me. With blood stained across her uniform, and tears in the
fabric gaping below her neck, a dark bruise of fingerprints tells
the story of how she was grabbed earlier.

She's limping and dragging her feet, trying to hold her
uniform together over her chest. Throughout the walk toward
the main gate, I listen to her heavy breaths, struggling more than
the others. She slows down, causing a gap to form in the line.
She stumbles to the left and I lunge to grab hold of her, but
catch the eyes of an SS officer standing at the gate, watching the
scene unfold. The girl thankfully rights herself back to two feet,
but again, stops walking. Her knees buckle and she falls face
first into the dirt. For a brief second, I question if she will stand
back up, but then a blitzing crack of a pistol fires past me, a
bullet lodges straight into the back of her head.

She won't be getting back up.

* * *

The lights in our barrack go out, marking the end of another dreary day I've managed to survive. My pulse races within my ears, my nerves fraught with impatience as I listen for another ghostly hint of Luka's voice, knowing I shouldn't want to hear it. I want him to live and find a way to survive, and he's already been depleted of so much. The idea of hearing him in the first place makes no sense. I'm not sure who he or anyone would be singing for or where the singing would be coming from.

The longer I lie here in the darkness amid the thick air of bodily stenches and sounds of whimpering and moans, the more my mind races. My eyes fall shut, trying to block out the surroundings and the hunger pains growling from within my body.

Then it happens again...

A hum of music drifts by, but so quick and faint, I can't convince myself it was a voice or a song. It's easy to imagine, though. Too easy.

Another brief wave of notes tickles my ear, and I prop my head up on my folded arms, listening for more.

"Are you all right?" the woman next to me asks. I must have woken her up with my sudden movement.

"Yes, sorry for bothering you. I thought I heard some music."

"Oh, yes, like last night? It was lovely, wasn't it?" she asks, her voice croaking through her words. She heard it, too. More of the melody flickers through the air, the sound almost out of reach. "It's harder to catch tonight."

I slide forward and turn onto my back to pull myself out of the hole between the bunks. "It's much harder to hear tonight," I reply as I scale down the wooden ladder.

"Where are you going? You know we aren't allowed to leave the barrack after the lights are out."

"I know," I whisper back. I don't want to say much else, fearing her saying anything more.

"What are you doing?" someone else utters as I pad bare-foot toward the door. "Using the latrines downstairs is forbidden at night."

The warnings are clear. I know the rules. I'm aware of all the consequences for just breathing the wrong way in Auschwitz.

"A kapo could be guarding the corridors," someone else shouts in a whisper. "You shouldn't leave." At this hour, the kapos are as exhausted as anyone else, and sleep while they can.

I drown the women's voices out through my desperation to know where the singing is coming from. I open the door to the corridor and make my way down the one flight of stairs, grip-ping the handrail with all my might so I don't stumble through my blindness of the night. As I make it to the bottom, more notes fill the air, and I follow them, finding the sound growing just slightly louder the farther left I walk.

An open door catches my attention. I don't usually come down this way as the main entrance and exit is to the right of the stairwell. Sweat forms on my forehead as I glance behind me, finding nothing but more darkness.

I pass the open door, finding an administration-like office setup with boxes of paper stacked in dozens of columns. There's a small window along the back wall and I creep into the room, cautiously peering around each column of boxes until I step up to the window, which sits just between two moving spotlights that don't cross over one another.

There isn't much to see of course, nothing but a barbed-wire fence. But the music is continuous now, just soft. I pull up the window, slow movements to avoid any squealing or crackling. The music grows louder, reeling my focus to the right, beyond the fence, where I've been told the Commandant's villa stands.

Why would the music be coming from there of all places?

From now until tomorrow
The moonlight will—

A crash echoes through the corridor, startling me into closing the window and scrambling for a place to hide. The front door, that's what it was. Two sets of footsteps follow, and I realize there's nowhere to run. Someone is coming down this way. The other is heading up the stairs.

Terrorizing heat boils through me, sweat dripping from every crevice of my body. My breaths are heavy and short, and my knees are shaking as I crouch behind one single column of boxes. A breath catches in my lungs as the footsteps grow louder. Whoever is here enters the room I'm in and walks toward the window, coming into my view. An SS guard.

I lift a foot to shift around the column, away from the swishing glows of nearby spotlights. My other foot sticks with sweat, making a soft squelch. I clamp my hands over my mouth.

The guard takes long, slow strides, the movement sounding as if they're weaving around the columns, but I can't tell where the sound of their footsteps is coming from now.

"Second floor is cleared." The voice travels down the corridor.

The nearby footsteps continue, then stop, followed by heavy breaths, expelling air filled with coffee and cigarettes.

Someone might have me right in their sights, but I'm too afraid to open my eyes. The person snuffles and clears their throat.

Please, no. Please God.

"Ernst?" the other person calls out.

He lifts a foot, scratching against the grimy floor.

"One moment," the man in the room—Ernst—replies.

TWENTY-NINE

LUKA

I can speak fluent German. It's something we all learned years ago, but I don't know what I'm singing about. I'm following the tune of the piano. My mind is somewhere far from here, in the corner of the open foyer where a small party of SS officers and their wives mingle.

I could be anywhere else, far away from German soldiers and their wives. Ella could be with me, standing as my wife, perhaps, both of us mingling with others as I lovingly wrap my arm around her lower back. I would be watching her laugh at a joke, reveling in the sound and beauty she emits through happiness. She would flash me a glance, loose curls framing her face, a complexion of porcelain, flawless. I'd squeeze my hand around her a bit tighter, a silent gesture between us. Then I'd ask myself how on earth I was lucky enough to have my arm around this perfect woman, to call her mine.

The sharp clang of glass jolts me back. Ella isn't by my side; my arm isn't around her. I'm not among the crowd mingling with other couples. I'm a slave to the SS.

She's all I want and everything I'll never have.

"What are you singing?" the pianist, Franc, utters, glancing at me with quick blinks as he sprawls his long fingers across the tops of the ivory keys. He seems as if he's been in Auschwitz a while, or at least much longer than I have. He must be around my father's age, too, and the thought of what he's doing at this moment sends a queasy wave through my stomach. "The words are on the music sheet," he says, pointing at the papers resting atop his piano. "You must sing the right lyrics."

I stare straight out ahead of me at the small crowd, wondering if they've noticed I lost track of what I was supposed to be singing. Just as I make eye contact with the officer who brought us here tonight, a champagne flute comes flying toward me, spinning in the air. I duck, trying to move out of the way, but I'm not as fast as I once was and not fast enough now. The edge clips the top of my scalp before breaking against the post I'm standing in front of. The glass shatters, shards spraying along my back.

"What about *German uplifting music* do you not under-stand? You will not sing in—" an officer snarls as if his next word is bitter on his tongue, "Polish." He's shouting at me from across the room, making a spectacle that creates a silence between all four walls.

"I thought it was quite beautiful," the woman beside him, I assume to be his wife, says. "It's nicer than the folk songs that are supposed to bring a smile to our faces. This man is singing about love. Clearly." The outspoken woman takes a sip from her glass and turns around, placing a hand on the officer's back.

"Less folk...and sing in German. We don't speak your language," the officer says, giving his presumed wife a ques-tioning side-eye stare. "Go on. Continue." He flaps his hand at me as if I'm a fly he's shooing away.

"I'll follow you," Franc says as sweat glistens across his fore-head, reeling in a slight reflection from the ceiling light.

When you think you know

The meaning of love,
But it's only a tale for show

The heart bleeds with tears
Broken, shattered dreams,
Wrapped in a cloak of fears.

Reasons we refused to see
Can you hear me? Please, let it be.
Tell me it was love, or take my heart,
Hold it close—or set it free.

A light round of applause startles me and ends as abruptly, a warning that I've crossed a line I didn't intend to cross.

"Did you write that yourself?" Franc asks, talking without moving his lips. He repositions himself on the piano bench, his stocky pale frame causing a creak and moan beneath him.

"Yes," I reply in the same way.

"You're gifted, and I'm sorry you're in so much pain."

I won't rest until I find her.

"Aren't we all in pain?" I ask him.

"Only if you can still feel it," Franc says, pointing to his ear with a sweeping gesture.

Blood drips down the side of my head, falling onto my earlobe. No pain. It's the agony in my chest I'm afraid will never go away. I run my hand over my head, pulling it away and finding it covered in blood.

"Let's go—the two of you. You're nauseating the crowd. Get yourself cleaned up and in one piece before tomorrow night," the SS officer snaps before grabbing the two of us by our arms and yanking us toward the back door. He's the one who threw the glass at my head. What did he think would happen? Everyone witnessed the behavior and not a person flinched at the scene. It was as common as throwing a rolled-up napkin at someone. The anger rages inside of me bringing words to my tongue, but then I remember the look on Apollo's face after he spoke his final thoughts out loud, the shocked look in his eyes before he was released from this torture.

Maybe that's all it takes. A few justified words to this mongrel and I'll be set free like all those whose insides were painted along the execution wall today. But I can't do that to Mother. I can't lose her. I must know she's okay.

THIRTY

ELLA

By some measure of luck, I went unnoticed last night while hiding in the administration office on the first floor of the barrack. At least, I don't think I was spotted. Though it's possible that with my eyes closed in the face of fear, the man lurking around could have taken mercy on me and left to clear the rest of the floor. The thought just seems extremely unlikely, given I've yet to meet one guard to consider letting anyone get away with anything here.

Once my heart settled into a steady rhythm a long hour after I made it back to the tiers of bunks, I began to wonder why I could have heard Luka's voice coming from the Commandant's villa of all places. After those brief seconds of clear sound, I couldn't be more sure that it's him. By why, how— could he be there?

This block isn't very far away, but with the barrier between those buildings and these, I can only depend on what I hear. I'm afraid to ask anyone else in the block if they hear him, too. They might tell me I'm hearing voices. That's a sign of mental incompetence here and if our block-elder, Francine, or any kapo hear about any of us losing the bearings of our minds, we'll immediately be sent elsewhere—likely to Block 10 where people are tortured through medical experiments, some even dissected while still alive. The rumors have circulated and though unfathomable, nothing should be questioned here in Auschwitz.

So many women are coughing, sniffling, and groaning tonight, suffering from an array of illnesses sweeping through the barracks like the plague. It's a warning for those of us who haven't gotten sick. It's only a matter of time until we catch something. As hot and humid as it is within these walls, I often cover my face with the wool blanket while I sleep, convincing myself it will keep the germs out.

Tonight, I stare through the dark blanket, the prickly fibers scratching along my cheek as I imagine Luka's voice, praying to capture just a hint to give me a sense of peace before I fall asleep. Though my eyelids are heavy, my heart pounds too hard and fast to rest. Most of the others have found a position they're comfortable enough to fall asleep in, eliminating some of the surrounding static noise.

"Does anyone hear that?" someone whispers from several rows down. I clutch the blanket tighter, pressing it against my chest.

"What? What do you hear?" another person whispers.

A creak from the window startles me as someone attempts to crack it open—something we haven't done since last summer.

"Oh, that," another voice adds. "That's the new singer the SS have enslaved as their nightly entertainment."

"Who's speaking?" Even though there is a dividing wall between the rows of bunks and her closet-size space to sleep, Keely has the hearing of one of those German shepherds. She's the privileged kapo in our block who answers to Francine with behavioral logs each morning before roll call.

No one responds, as usual. Keely isn't as brutal as Francine, or she simply doesn't have the strength to investigate every single sound throughout the night.

"If I hear another word, I will find you, and you will be reported," she says. I can't see her, but I can almost hear her nose pointing into the air. When I can see her, her arms are folded over her chest, she sucks her cheeks in to highlight her cheekbones that don't need highlighting as prominent as they are in all of us from the hunger we endure. It's become apparent that people don't change, despite our equalizing circumstances. If they saw themselves as being above others before being imprisoned here, they still do now. The SS seek out those people like Keely and give her privileges above everyone else, knowing she cares more about herself than anyone else around her. Maybe all kapos aren't like her. Some are worse, as I've seen, but most wouldn't remain in their position without giving the SS what they want.

The silence after she returns to her small private space invites a melodic breeze in through the cracked window. My ears tingle though I can't make out the words of this song, but the familiar sound of his voice, the highs and lows—the smooth notes that carry for longer than a common breath—embrace me. My eyes slide shut as I think back to stolen moments in the nook of the tunnel. The glow from the flame blocked out the surroundings, allowing me to imagine we were anywhere but there, but really—I was with him, and that's all that mattered. The way the fine hairs of his cheek tickled mine whenever he would nuzzle his face into the crook of my neck, and the way his arms would wrap all the way around me and hold me so tightly, convinced nothing could ever tear us apart. And our conversations, our talks about our future when the war ends and we're free to be who we are, and together. One of the last nights we were together, we planned out what forever would look like for us.

* * *

"Where will we live?" I ask as Luka strokes his knuckles gently down my arm.

"Anywhere but here, in a tunnel or a sewer," he says with a silent chuckle, as he tugs me tighter into his chest, nuzzling himself into the corner of this dark nook we hide in every night.

"I want to live on a farm, have a wooden swing outside the front door where we can rock back and forth all night and stare up at the stars. You can sing your heart out and have nature be your orchestra."

"And you, Miss Ella, what will you do with all your freedom and happiness?"

"I'll tend to the farm, make sure no one ever goes hungry again." Food brings people happiness and after watching so many suffer from going without it, I wouldn't want to do anything else. I didn't understand why Tata held on to the family store with everything he has left within him until I realized how much he's given to others, how much those others rely on him. He fights and struggles daily to bring food into the store, gathering it from places he never talks about. All that matters is that he gives to those who need it most after they've been sent away empty-handed. I want to do the same.

"Sounds like a beautiful life to me," Luka says, placing a kiss on my neck.

"Dream of it tonight, and I will, too," I tell him.

He sighs gently against my ear. "At least I can dream about you when we aren't together. Once you're mine forever, our farm will follow."

* * *

After the gong rattles through the block and everyone scatters to prepare themselves for a day's worth of work, I slide down the side of the bunk and make my way over toward the window someone cracked last night. "Who mentioned the singer working for the SS?" I ask, keeping my voice low between the scuffles.

"Me," a woman says, sliding off her bunk with hesitation, pain pinching at her eyes. "I'm Magda."

"Ella," I reply, waiting for her to say more.

I've seen this woman every day, but haven't spoken to her. Our paths haven't crossed until now. In fact, I'm not sure I've heard her speak until last night. She must be around Mama's age, and it pains me to think how much harder this life is affecting her than me. Mama's back was always hurting, her shoulders would have pinched nerves that would cause her headaches, her knees ached if she was standing too long in the kitchen, and the joints in her fingers swelled just from knitting. She would tell me there's nothing fun about aging and to stay young for as long as possible.

"Do you mind if I ask you how you know about him?"

"Personally, I don't know the man. A kapo, Evie, who works in the communication office with me transports messages between the SS buildings. She mentioned something about a new male singer the SS are torturing at their evening meetings and dinners." We never found his name registered. But it's his voice. I need to know.

Torturing. The word slices down my spine. "She said that?" I was under the impression that kapos don't speak poorly of the SS. They're typically loyal.

"Evie is one of the few good ones."

"What do you mean?" I'm speaking quickly, knowing we're running out of seconds before we need to hustle for roll call.

"A few of the kapos will help us if the price is right."

"Price? Money? You pay her?" It's like we're living in two different places right now. I'm very sure no one here has any money.

"Not with money, with food rations," the woman says, buttoning up her smock.

Without thinking of what else I would need to forfeit, I ask the burning question: "Do you think Evie would help me with something?"

The woman laughs through a breath. "With what?"

The other women are rushing past us in a hurry to make their way to roll call as we should be doing but I'm stuttering on the words stuck in my mouth. "I—I, well I think—I know the singer. We were torn away from each other in Warsaw. I love him and he loves me. I would do anything—truly anything in the world—to get a message to him."

"Careful about who you express your desperation to here, Ella..." she tells me, her motherly tone grasping a hold of my attention. "What room do you work in?"

I swallow hard before responding, thinking before I speak after the last comment. "The log-room, cataloging incoming prisoners."

She nods and glances past me toward the door we need to be walking out through. "I'll tell you what... You find me the name of someone I know is here, find out what block they're living in, and I'll do what I can to convince the kapo to deliver a message for you so you can confirm whether the singer is who you think. Save up your rations, though."

The woman pulls a scrap of paper and a pencil the size of my little finger with jagged lead out of her baggy sock. She scribbles out the name and hands me the paper. "Deal?"

"Yes, yes, of course, thank you."

"Don't thank me yet," she says, her voice flat and unwavering, as if she has little faith that I'll come through. I don't have much faith that I will either, seeing as none of us have had much luck finding the names we've tried searching for so far.

I hurry to roll call, catching every single puddle on the way. The lines are already formed, and Francine is already making her way between us as I squeeze in between two women in the back row.

"Watch it," the woman to my right says. "Just because you can't get here on time, you think you can shove all of us?"

"Shh," I plead, staring at her with dread. She grits her teeth and grinds her jaw from side to side.

"You'll get us all in trouble if you show up late again," she hisses.

"I won't. I promise. I won't."

She curls forward with a deep, wheezing cough that won't relent. Without Francine in sight yet, I place my hand on the woman's back and try to calm her so she can catch her breath between coughs.

"Try to inhale through your nose," I whisper.

She presses her lips together and shakes as she pulls air in through her nose, holding it for a moment before standing back upright. From the corner of her eye, she peers over at me and her chin trembles. She swallows hard and clenches her eyes. Blood and mucous dribble from her nose just as Francine turns down the next row. I nudge her and gesture to wipe her nose. She'd be sent right to the infirmary if Francine sees her like this. People don't usually come back from there.

"Thank—" she tries to speak but her knees give out and she keels over, face first into the ground, heavy as a log.

Francine shoves everyone to the side to make her way over, finding the poor woman unconscious in the mud. She blows her whistle and shoots her hand up in the air, signaling for someone to come take her away. For good.

THIRTY-ONE
ELLA

More women have begun clerical duties in the small office ten of us were sharing. Previously, five of us were assigned to cataloging incoming prisoners, and the other five responsible for typing up punishment logs—records of disciplinary actions taken on prisoners who committed violations. Today the additional five women settle into desks with typewriters. I would choose a typewriter over handwriting logs if given the option.

A kapo who meanders around the room off and on throughout the day is spewing out a list of rules and objectives to the new women. The clang of typewriters overtakes the swooshing of papers and scratching of pen tips against paper.

Guards pace by the open door of the office once every few minutes, stopping to dart their sharp stares in every direction, ensuring each of us is on task. As the current guard steps away from the door, I reach down to my sock and retrieve the scrap of paper Magda gave me, studying the name for a moment before replacing the paper. *Elizabeth Gacek.*

With my pen still full of ink, hovering over a nearly completed page of entries, I gape at the list above, knowing it won't matter how many pages I personally search through for a name when there are at least five of us alone in this office entering information.

I twist and glance over my shoulder toward Tatiana. "Psst."

She lifts her head, her eyes wide but red, a sign of a sleepless night. "What's wrong?" she asks, her gaze flickering toward the door. I know we have at least another moment before the guards return.

"I need help from you and others to search for another name," I say, leaning closer toward her desk. There's less space between us today than yesterday, thanks to the newly added desks in the room. "There's a woman in my barrack. She's looking for someone. If I find them, she might be able to help me find out where Luka is working." Despite our efforts, no one has found his name in our logs yet either.

Tatiana's shoulders fall at just the sound of Luka's name. "Did you hear him singing again?"

I nod. "It's his voice. I think he's truly here."

Tatiana's fingers lift to her mouth, her eyes widening in response to finding out that someone I love is a prisoner here, too. I wouldn't know whether to smile or show my sympathy either. "Sure," she says. "I'll pass the request along." We've set up a communication line of whispers between desks, for when the five of us need to share information. "But, Ella, you know how hopeless our searches have been." Zofia's name is still unfound, too. Defeat weighs on us for letting Iza down, but also, it means our letters will likely never be sent home. Every attempt seems hopeless.

"I know," I say, a heavy doubt settling into my chest. "Please, if I can help her and she can help me—I need to know if Luka is here somewhere."

The hours crawl by in measures of metal plunks and paper swooshes, the second hand of a nearby clock adding an offbeat annoyance as well. My writing hand is red and cramping, the side of my fist is covered in black ink, and my fingertips are as brutal as they are at this hour each day.

A sharp breath interrupts the flow of monotonous sounds. "I found it," one of the other women whispers. My heart tumbles in my chest and my breath falters, waiting for her to say which name she means.

"Who?" Tatiana asks in a hush.

"Elizabeth Gacek."

The woman who sits to the other side of Tatiana scribbles out the information on a scrap of logbook paper torn from the back of the book and hands it to Tatiana, who passes it to me.

The name and information blurs within my stare as I'm struck with disbelief. It *is* possible to find someone in these lists. I can hold out hope to find Luka's name, too, but with Elizabeth's information, maybe Magda can help me, too.

Twisting around in my seat, I turn to offer the woman a silent thank you when the swift clunk of boots returns to the open doorway. I crumple the paper in my hand, scorning myself for not putting it directly in my sock, or watching the time between the guards checking on us. I know better.

"What is this?" the guard shouts.

My stomach turns sour and twists in pain as the guard stares at me with a beady look in his eyes. What is there to say? As if I'll find the answer in front of me, I search my desk while the guard steps in closer. The memory of what he did to the woman who spilled ink forces an acidic burn to rise through my chest. "I was—I was checking to see if there was extra ink in anyone's bottles since mine is nearly empty. I didn't want to open a new bottle at this hour."

The guard leans over my desk, peering into the ink bottle as if he can see where the ink line ends. With the little amount of light we have here, there is no reflection on the liquid. If he lifts the jar, he'll end up with ink on his hands. But he picks up the bottle and swishes the liquid around. My throat squeezes in on itself and my chest aches because I'm not sure how much ink I have left.

"Give her some ink," the guard demands from the woman who found Elizabeth's name.

She stands from her table and hands her jar to me. She doesn't have much left either, but I pour a bit from hers into my bottle, my hand shaking viciously as I try my best not to spill a drop.

I place the bottle back on her desk and return to my seat. "All taken care of now," I tell the guard.

He stares around the room at each of us, glaring as if we've all done something to disturb him, but then thankfully leaves, the moment allowing me a breath of sharp relief. It's best if I don't talk to anyone else for the remainder of the day now.

* * *

Moments before the lights are set to go out, I locate Magda in front of her tier of bunks and retrieve the piece of paper. I take her hand in mine and smile. "It's the first one we've successfully found."

She pulls her hand away as her eyes fill with tears. She turns away, facing the bunks, leaving me with the view of her arms moving about by her waist. She turns to face me again as a tear tracks down her cheek. "Elsie is in room four in the administration building. She wears a navy-blue scarf with small black polka dots around her head and she has a tear in her uniform across her right shoulder. She also has a kapo's armband. You'll need to tell her: 'The smell of rain is in the air,' code for the exchange of rations for information. I will make sure she knows to expect your request."

"In four days, I'll have two rations saved up to give her. I'll seek her out then."

"Thank you for this," Magda says. "It's everything to me."

"Of course," I say with a tight-lipped smile, trying to be emotionally supportive. Though, really, I think she'll soon realize it's not so wonderful knowing someone you love is a prisoner here, too.

* * *

Four days of cutting my food intake from little to scarce is taking a heavy toll on my body. It's weaker than gelatin and every limb shakes uncontrollably, but it's worth it if I can find Luka. It will all be worth the hunger and risks to my safety. In a haze of lightheadedness, ambling through the administration hallway, I pass my assigned office. Upon approaching office number four, I peek inside, finding it free of SS guards. Though, my nerves don't ease, knowing one could walk in at any moment.

The office is filled with waist-high green filing cabinets and just a few desks, compared to the ten in the office I work in. There are only a few people in here, too, which makes my presence more obvious. I take a quick glance at each woman, finding one with a navy-blue scarf and black polka dots, and a tear on her right shoulder. This must be Elsie. While reviewing a sheet of paper in her hand, I step up beside her and clasp my hands behind my back.

I don't want to address her by name as it's forbidden here, and only those of us who consider ourselves friends take those liberties. We are nothing but numbers here.

"The smell of rain is in the air," I recite the sentence Magda quickly fed me when explaining what I would need to do when approaching Elsie.

She steps to the side and weaves between two filing cabinets, stopping by one near the corner of the room where the two lower halves of our bodies are concealed from the open door. She holds out her hand by her waist, never moving her stare from a paper she's still studying in her other hand. I hand her slices of bread equaling two loaves first and she drops them into her large overcoat with pockets—a perk of being a kapo. She holds her hand out again and a flood of emotions rushes through my chest as I hand her the note I have carefully crafted for Luka over the last couple of days.

"Luka, he's the singer performing for the—"

"Yes, I'm aware of who I'm delivering to," she says, interrupting me. Elsie tucks the note away then turns to face me for a brief second. "I'll see what I can do. It might take some time as I don't know when I'll be given the next SS message to deliver." She points her nose to the ceiling and takes in a tired breath before uttering her next words. "And don't expect a miracle."

I wasn't *expecting* to hear self-doubt in her abilities. Maybe she tells everyone the same to protect herself if something doesn't work out in the requestor's favor. I would do the same, I suppose.

"I understand," I say in a hush.

She leaves my side, tending to a filing cabinet on the left side of the room so I take the opportunity to head to where I should currently be.

An SS guard turns the corner just as I'm stepping in toward my office. His stare is direct, cold, and sharp. His direction changes just slightly, aiming for me. "Where are you coming from, when you are to report to this office?"

Lie. Lie, it's the only option. "I—I'm not sure. I walked past the office and didn't realize it until I reached the next one down and didn't recognize the room. I turned around and returned here, of course."

The guard stares at me, his eyes burning a hole through my head, then he peers down to my chest at my number marked on a patch and the red triangle badge signifying I'm a political prisoner. "Consider yourself lucky that you're not a filthy Jew," he says, spitting in my face. "Get to work!"

Without another round, I scurry into the office and take my

seat, keeping my head down as I sort through the stack of papers sitting on my desk. I can hardly pull in a full breath as another wave of dizziness overwhelms me. I squeeze my eyes shut and swallow hard. *I'm breathing and the sun is in the sky.*

I'm alive.

THIRTY-TWO

LUKA

June 1943

Become hollow. It's the only advice I could give anyone who just arrived here. It's been six weeks of somehow surviving on less than a handful of food a day, a mere few hours of sleep each night, and the constant pushing and shoving from the SS on where to be and when just so I can entertain the SS—and now, also the dying prisoners.

Every note I sing is a lie, offering fellow prisoners the falsest sense of hope—a tease seconds before a bullet strikes straight between their clenched eyes.

Everyone still here, walking around beside me, are just skeletons with flesh, moving in the direction they've been told to go. I wonder every second if my mother is among them.

* * *

"Don't go out in the cold without a coat, Luka, you'll get sick,"
Mother shouts as I storm out the front door to run to school.

"I'm twelve, Mama, I'm all right. I'll keep warm by walking fast," I reply.

Less than a moment passes before Mama grabs my ear, stopping me from rushing down the stairs of our apartment. The yank makes me groan, wondering if an ear can be torn off someone's face. I don't want to know if it's possible. "And don't think I didn't notice that you didn't eat your breakfast either. What is with you, my son? Without food, you'll starve. Oy, and what would your father say when he got home from work? It would be my fault, Luka. I was placed on this earth to keep you alive, and I will do just that. Do you understand me?"

"Yes, Mama, I understand."

"Good. Now, do you want to get sick from the cold and starve?"

"No, I don't," I say with a huff.

Mama shoves a pastry into my mouth. Then she yanks my knapsack off and drops my coat over my shoulders, holding out the sleeves, waiting for me to comply. I slip my arms in quickly to spare myself the argument she will always win. Once she places my knapsack back on my shoulders, she grabs my face from behind and gives me a wet kiss on the cheek. "I love you, my darling."

"Love you too," I say, taking back off down the stairs.

It's a myth. People don't get sick from the cold. And no one dies if they miss a meal. It's just something all mothers say because their mothers told them the same. Someone needs to break the news to them at some point.

* * *

Mother never said how cold it would have to be for someone to get sick, or how many meals they would need to miss before starving to death. Maybe she didn't know, but I've followed a regular pattern and seen which degradation hits first. It's starvation, then the cold, and now that it's summertime, people die from the heat, too. I was wrong. Mother was right. To think I once fought her over wearing a coat and eating a warm pastry for breakfast...this may very well be my punishment.

The orchestra and I continue playing through the final execution of the day, playing a romantic tune that contrasts everything happening in front of us. A male prisoner is dragged toward the execution wall. He's the type who doesn't fight back. Some do, some don't. I'm not sure anyone realizes that the ones who fight back get shot quicker. They're put out of their misery faster than the ones who comply.

The officer with his grip on the man's wrists shoves his nose up against the wall and mutters something in his ear. They always say something—some last words that I never hear, nor want to.

The blast from the rifle drowns out the music, replacing our notes with a deep, throbbing crack. My eyes fixate on the back of the man's head as words pipe out of my lungs—words that come out on their own, it seems. I've memorized the lyrics and no longer think about what I'm singing. Instead, my eyes are locked on a bullet hole oozing with blood, wondering why I no longer feel a sense of sickness in my stomach when witnessing murder.

Some prisoners fall before the blood oozes. For others, the blood oozes first before they fall. I wonder what causes the different bodily reactions. Would I fall then bleed or bleed then fall?

The violinists speed up their tempo, racing alongside the cellist uphill then downhill into a hush of silent tones that fade into the warm stale air. They drop their instruments by their sides and my shoulders fall lower. We all take a quick look at one another and nod our heads, knowing it's time to turn back for roll-call square where we'll be directed to our evening assignments.

We walk past the guards, keeping our heads down, moving in sync with one another through the soggy grass. The shuffle of footsteps bleeds into the distant shouts from various soldiers and their constantly barking dogs. Every step forward takes more effort than the one before. There's nothing left inside of me, yet I prevail—despite the pain—to breathe, talk, swallow crusty stale bread, and even drink water...never mind the singing. My voice is broken. I'm broken. My head is heavy but empty, and my body threatens to fall forward with each step. My legs are too heavy to lift. These thoughts terrify me, realizing I'm much stronger than Mother. It's becoming harder to convince myself she's surviving through this torture. I don't know how I'm still alive. Can it really be simply because I'm still breathing, and somewhere above the gray clouds, the sun still exists?

A short line of others moves toward us and I force my head upright, lifting my gaze, ready to give a hello with just my eyes— the only form of greeting we're allowed to share with one another. It's something human.

This is the first line of women I've passed here as they keep us separated between fences, but I suppose they must be moving to wherever their job takes them, leading to the rare crossover. I can tell they're women from a short distance, but only because they're forced to wear smock dresses instead of pants and a buttoned shirt. They look as miserable as we do. Shaven heads, hollow cheeks, frailty, we're all moving closer to the end, whenever that might be.

A figure among the women catches my eye. Though she looks like the women before and after her in the line, there's something about her that makes my steps falter. A rumble within my ears blocks out all sound from around me as my eyes meet hers.

A moment—surreal, impossible, maybe delusional, continues endlessly, the world closing in on us from each side until it's just the two of us. My breath catches, and again, I question my sanity. Is this real? Our eyes meet and I find a mirrored disbelief there as time struggles to keep up while moving past one another. Her lips part, mouthing one word that steals the wind from my body.

"Luka?"

No. No, no. Please, no. Not here. It's her. It is. Her voice, so soft, broken, and painfully familiar. I clutch the fabric over my chest, trying to grab my heart. The lines push us past each other, my body moving on its own as if mechanical. I try to respond, call out her name, but my throat tightens, and I can't make a sound. All I can do is twist my neck to keep staring at her—to keep her in sight before she disappears.

She lifts her hand in front of her chest, just slightly, trembling before dropping it back by her side. Her bottom lip hangs open with despair as tears spill down her cheeks, leaving streaks among the dirt.

"Ella!" My voice breaks, hoarse and weak. I stumble on the heel of the person I'm behind, righting my direction before I fall or knock someone over, but as soon as I can, I turn back around, searching for her. Where did she go? My breaths quicken. I would stop walking if the person behind me wasn't about to step on my heels, too. Where is she? I need to know where she went.

A hand shoves me from behind, "Keep moving, songbird," a guard growls.

No. I need to go back. It's Ella. It's her. I know it is. My body continues to move forward, but my heart has left my body. It's twenty steps back, being trampled all over, covered in dirt, shattered into a million pieces. How can she be here?

THIRTY-THREE

LUKA

Two weeks later, another gathering in the Commandant's Headquarters means another reason to walk the length of the camp, with an opportunity to spot Ella again. There is no single way for me to locate her otherwise. I've looked at every person who has passed by me since I saw her. I know it was her. I'm sure of it. Yet, without a list of those trapped here, and the replacement of peoples' names for numbers, finding anyone seems impossible.

A violinist and cellist have been assigned to join Franc and me tonight for our evening performance. In any other place, time, and world, it would be an honor to play alongside these gentlemen. But here, it's an act of disgrace, one I will never forgive myself for. I should have chosen death before entertaining murderers. I could still choose death, but I'm afraid to die. I'm just a coward.

Franc lines up the music for the evening. "Did you get any further with your search since I saw you earlier in the week?" he asks, words forming without him moving his lips.

"No, I don't know anyone with access to prisoner logs and I haven't seen her." Hearing my words out loud makes me question whether I ever saw her at all. I dream of her every night, and exhaustion overwhelms me so greatly that I should be able to slip into a dream even with my eyes open.

"Sorry, my friend," Franc utters before sharing the lineup of music with us before placing the stack on the stand attached to the piano.

The guests are just arriving, which is our cue to begin. However, a female kapo rushes through the breezeway past us, and into the growing crowd. The way her eyes dart in every direction hints at a time sensitive delivery. I've seen this woman here before, never without a paper or envelope in her hand. She seems to be a courier of some sort, delivering messages from officers in one administration building to officers in another. Just another privileged prisoner surviving by proving a form of loyalty to the SS.

There are so many kapos here, I can't fathom what could make them betray their own people. They're still hungry and exposed to every terrifying disease that sweeps through the barracks. Maybe there's something I don't know—something I could never trade my soul for. They've learned to hate their own kind. It's the same as the Jewish Ghetto Police in Warsaw, like the one who killed Apollo. They're somehow much worse here—I don't trust any one of them.

The kapo finds her target, hands the officer a memo, pivots, and heads back this way. She glares at me as if we know each other, but we don't. The three or four times I've seen her, we've never made eye contact. Why now?

The kapo shifts her gaze almost immediately as she passes us. Still trying to decipher the reason for the cold stare, I notice a square folded note fall from her clenched fist. It wasn't an accident. She would have retrieved it, but instead, continues toward the back exit.

I scan the surroundings ensuring no one is looking in this direction. I lunge for the note and curl it into my fist.

"What is that?" Peter, the violinist asks.

I shrug. "The kapo dropped it on her way out."

"She'll come after you once she realizes it's gone. You should leave it on the floor." Peter worries more than anyone I've met here. We all worry, but his personality matches the vibrato he plays so beautifully. He's constantly unsteady and fearful of every breath he takes. It makes me wonder how he's able to keep the bow moving so smoothly across his strings.

"I should look at it first," I say.

"Are you out of your mind? It could be confidential," Peter hisses, his eyes bulging from their sunken sockets.

Franc shakes his head and locks his stare on the notes in front of him.

I run my free hand down the side of my pants to dry the sweat and quickly unfold the note. My gaze settles on the top line, and I forget to breathe. I clutch my hand to my neck as I read:

15th of May 1943

Luka, is that you?

I've told myself it's impossible, but I know it's not. If I had a wish, it would be to find out that I only heard someone who sounds like you. Then I'd know you aren't here in this horrible place, but hopefully somewhere safer.

I blink for a long a moment, trying to reconcile what month it is. A flash of a bulletin runs through mind, a warning I saw hanging on a post earlier. It's the middle of June and just a week ago, I spotted Ella. She must have known I was here before we passed each other. How is that...

I hear you almost nightly, or whenever the weather will comply with carrying the sound of your voice.

If it's you, I must know. I must know you're all right.

I'm doing as well as I can manage, caught a lucky break with being assigned to clerical work.

I've seen what unlucky means, and I wouldn't wish it upon anyone.

Luka, if you're here, I need to find you—I will do anything, even if it's the last thing I do.

I think about you day and night, feeling like a trapped mouse, searching for a way out of an enclosed maze of walls, knowing there is no way out—and I've yet to find a way to you.

I love you so much it hurts every single bone in my body as I pray to the heavens above to set us free from this torture and misery.

I still dream about a future with you, a house on a farm, stargazing to the sound of your beautiful songs. The image is so vivid in my mind when I fall asleep at night. If only it were possible to escape through our dreams, be together, and never return to this reality.

If it's safe and you can hand a note back to the messenger who dropped this note for you, she will bring one back to me.

I'm sure you're worn and living in a state of starvation, struggling to move each day, but your voice breathes life into me, something to hold on to.

Forever my love,

E

Hot tears burn the backs of my eyes and my chest quakes. The thoughts in my head are telling me to race out that back door and run, shouting her name until I have her attention. The room spins around me, the chandeliers rattling, crystals clashing.

"Ready?" Franc says, reaching for my arm that has fallen by my side. "On three."

"No, I'm not—"

"What do you mean? We must begin now. We'll all be in trouble if we don't."

I turn and glance at the back door, my heart caught in my throat...

THIRTY-FOUR

ELLA

July 1943

It's been nearly two years since I arrived at Auschwitz and was assigned to work in the administration office, and yet we've only managed to successfully locate one name through our searches in our logs. We all are desperate to find loved ones who might be here. The five of us who are responsible for the prisoner intake logs have attempted another round of searches for any name we previously tried to find, only to come to an end, empty-handed again. We still try to tell ourselves there's a chance the people we're looking for truly aren't here, but of course, we've proven that theory wrong in the past.

Because...Luka is here. I saw him. It was a few weeks ago now, but I saw him—clear as anything I've ever seen. It was Luka, without a doubt. Yet his name is not in our registers. We've all checked multiple times—it doesn't make any sense.

I can't sleep, despite my exhaustion. It's impossible to rest my mind, knowing he's here somewhere just out of reach. All I can do is continue searching for him in any possible way. Even to just know what barrack he lives in, would be something.

"Ella," Tatiana whispers my name. Her voice pulls me out of a trance I didn't realize I was drifting within. I give a small shake of my head to refocus, glance toward the door to check for guards then back at Tatiana. "You haven't logged a name in over five minutes."

I squeeze my eyes shut for a brief second. "I know. I keep losing focus, trying to think up a way to find Luka."

Tatiana shifts her gaze to the door, checking for a guard as I did. "What more can you do without asking for trouble?" she asks, despondence lacing each word. "You know...I've been thinking..." Tatiana's eyes dart back and forth between me and the door. "There are so many people being admitted every day, some might just slip through the cracks and never be registered. That might be why we aren't finding names." I think she's trying to tell me there's no way to find him unless by happenstance again.

The thud of boots warns us to put our heads down and be doing what we're assigned. A guard steps into the doorway, scans the room for a long thirty seconds then continues down the corridor.

"I'm sure you must already realize that those who are sent directly to the showers never go through the process of registration," one of the new typist girls says quietly. She doesn't know anything about my situation, but she's speaking the facts.

"I'm aware," I tell her. Every name we enter is accompanied with a number and an assigned barrack. Those who never receive a number wouldn't end up on a list. But I've seen Luka walking through the camp in a uniform. He wasn't one of those people.

"I've heard they send over five thousand people a day to the shower rooms," she adds. "Imagine how many more people you would be logging if that weren't true."

Over five thousand people a day? That can't be right. We all know the truth of what happens in the showers. But I didn't know how many people were being sent each day.

With an entire world still living outside these gates, how can no one know what is happening here? How many people need to disappear before someone takes notice?

* * *

The monotony of the day is abruptly interrupted when a succession of whistles, shouts, and gunshots whip through the air outside the administration building. All of us women jump in our seats. I clutch my chest, searching among us as if someone here might know what's happening outside. Two guards race past the opening to our office toward the exit of the building.

Tatiana stands from her seat and rushes for the door and eases her head out just enough to look at what's happening. The main door opens and closes several times before she turns around. "All the guards just ran outside," she whispers. "We should know what's happening out there." Tatiana rushes out the door without a second thought.

There won't be much time before they return, I'm sure.

I stand from my desk, too, and rush out into the corridor, but I don't see Tatiana anywhere. I'm not sure where she went.

And I need this moment for a different reason.

I scurry down to office four and step inside, finding Elsie standing to the side of the window they're lucky enough to have in this office.

I weave through the maze of filing cabinets until I make it to her side. "I need your help. I'll give you whatever it is you want in return, four rations, six, eight... I'll do anything."

"Someone else just tried to escape," she says, her words drifting from her mouth like a fog as she continues to stare without blinking. "The SS just killed a dozen people for one person's decision."

I swallow hard, hearing the risks and threats. I can see them flashing in my head. "That's awful," I reply.

"What are you doing here?" she hisses, eyes refocusing. "I told you if I had a note from him to give you, I would, and we could make bartering arrangements then."

"Have you seen him, the singer?"

"Yes. He's with the officers many nights where I'm delivering messages. I gave him your note."

He hasn't been sent to the showers. I haven't heard him in the last few nights, but it's been raining heavily, likely drowning out any hope of sound.

"You're sure he received it?"

"I'm almost certain," she says, focusing her eyes out the window.

"What do you mean by *almost*?"

"I couldn't make a formal showing of handing him the note. I did what I had to do to put it within his reach. I'm sure he received it."

"Have you seen him again since?"

She continues staring outside, her jaw grinding back and forth. "I'm not sure. The nights blur together here. It's possible. The delivery of messages between high-end officers is incredibly nerve-wracking."

"Was there someone singing when you delivered a message last?" I want to shake this girl by the shoulders. My question isn't difficult.

"I can't remember if it was before or after I delivered the note to him. I'm sorry. There are some high-level officials coming into town next week and I'm quite sure I'll be relaying messages between buildings then."

I can't be at the mercy of this woman's tired mind. "I will

give you a week's worth of rations if you agree to help me once more."

"You plan to starve yourself for one more favor?" she asks.

"I would give up everything..."

"What is this favor?" she asks, her tone uneasy.

Blood pumps viciously through my veins after Elsie agreed to my barter, but as I return to my desk, listening to the shouting and disorder continue outside, I notice Tatiana hasn't come back.

"Do you think she left the building?" one of the other women asks.

I shrug. I don't think Tatiana would go as far as leaving the building to find out what was happening outside. Would she?

I bounce my knee for hours, staring back and forth between the door, clock, and the log I'm writing in, wondering why Tatiana still hasn't returned.

The guards came back hours ago, but haven't said a word about her vacant desk.

By six o'clock, the reality sinks in... Tatiana must have gotten caught somewhere she shouldn't have been. My heart cracks. She can't just not come back. I don't know if I can do this without her.

THIRTY-FIVE

LUKA

August 1943

The Commandant has been hosting dignitaries throughout the last week, and rather than host formal banquets at the headquarters, he's shifted to the more intimate setting of the gardens outside his personal villa next door to the headquarters. For me, only the scenery has changed. The fumes from the crematoriums still fill the air the same as they do inside the prison camp.

Outside amid the Commandant entertaining his guests, I observe them, wondering why they don't react to the putrid stench. If you were to take a photograph of just this square of grass and botanicals, no one would know about the thousands dying less than fifty steps away. Except, these people know, and it seemingly has no effect on them. I want to shout out to all of them that my mother is somewhere within those gates, possibly dying, and they're here reveling in laughter. Then I'd tell them they also stole the woman I love, and they're torturing her, too. They should know they took away my father and grandfather and were the reason my grandmother died earlier than she should have. Not only that, but they've stolen most of my voice.

There's hardly anything left of it now. They have taken every-thing away from me and yet, here I am, offering them entertain-ment while they continue to torture helpless victims just footsteps away.

I wanted to be a musician, entertain people, do the same thing night after night, and that wish came true in the most horrifying way possible. What's worse is that every time dark-ness folds over me during a song, I pray Ella will be standing before me when my eyes reopen. My mind knows better, but my heart is in denial.

Ella wouldn't be here in the Commandant's villa though, nor the Commandant's Headquarters. I don't know where she is and despite searching through every line of people who pass me, I haven't seen her. If I didn't receive a letter from her after, I might still be questioning whether I'd imagined seeing her in the first place. But I know she's here and I don't know if she's safe or well, and that thought keeps me up at night, my stomach aching, and my chest throbbing. Those pains are often worse than the relentless burn clawing at my throat and chest.

It's harder to know she's here than thinking she gave up on me back in Warsaw. I would rather live through that heartache over and over again in exchange for knowing she's being put through the same brutality as me. I'm trying to live. I'm trying to stay on my feet and upright. For her and for Mother, if she's still alive, somehow. But I'm not sure how long I'll last. My body is failing me. I have fevers come and go, and a cough that won't relent. I've choked up blood and I don't know if it's from an illness, or injury. Regardless, I know a body can only handle so much before it succumbs to the inevitable.

Franc and I are the only two here from our usual quartet tonight. I don't know why, and I likely won't find out the reason. We act as though nothing is different and no one is missing, and I follow Franc's lead with the music he's been given.

While tuning out the grotesque patriotic German folk song,

I observe the different servers and functionaries reporting from the prison like us, most of whom I've never seen, including a kapo with a stack of papers in her hands. She's shorter than the usual kapo who delivers messages.

I keep my focus on the kapo handing one of the Commandant's men the stack of papers. She stumbles, almost nervously while taking a few steps back, giving the men their privacy and space. This new woman could be connected to the other kapo who typically delivers messages, or she may know nothing of her. I may never find out if Ella ever received my letter.

It's just a letter.

I need to see her—hold her in my arms.

After two full songs, the papers are handed back to her and she's gestured at to wait a moment longer as the man who handed her the papers stands from his table, pulls his wife's chair out for her and takes her by the hand to walk alongside one of the taller gardens.

The messenger glances in our direction, her eyes squarely focusing on me.

My heart stutters.

Her lips part...

My breath shutters.

How—how can it be?

She's...so beautiful, with her doll-like gaze.

Ella.

It's her. She's here.

In shock, my voice hits an off note, and I clutch my chest, trying to clear the congestion there. My throat aches relentlessly. My voice has been changing, weakening, becoming more brittle. I push through the air in my lungs, straining to sound unaffected. I wonder what they will do with me if my voice gives out.

I know the answer.

I maintain the tune, but alter some of the lyrics, my eyes transfixed on Ella...

> *It's you, in the battle of the night*
> *With stars that sparkle high above*
> *Your eyes, your beauty, such a sight*
> *The moon aglow for my love*
>
> *How could nothing else feel true*
> *When I dream of soaring through the sky*
> *While sitting here, so close to you*
> *A melody so pure, it's no lie*

Why is she here? How is she here? What did she do?

> *Say the words, my dear*
> *You're all right tonight*
> *Oh, tell me not to fear,*
> *For tomorrow will bring sunlight*

Tears fill her eyes, and they sparkle beneath the glow of the moon. A gesture so subtle, I might be imagining it, but she shakes her head. I hope she's telling me she's all right.

Another one of the Commandant's men approaches her with a sealed folder and I switch back to the proper lyrics.

"What the hell do you think you're doing?"

An officer approaches me from the right, tears the microphone out of my hand and grapples the back of my neck. "What —I don't understand what you—" I stutter.

"You're given lyrics for a reason." The officer narrows his stare at me before saying anything more, and the wait pales me as my breaths become cold. "Your voice..." The officer steps in closer, now just a nose-length distance from my face. "It sounds weak...weaker tonight than last night and the night before that."

I stare back at him, trying to keep my fear masked. My gaze flickers to Ella. She's watching this confrontation; her eyes wide, filled with worry. I swallow hard and return my focus to the officer breathing down my neck, wondering if he's waiting for me to respond to his statement or expecting me to simply listen.

"It's just a chest cold," I say before clearing the phlegm from my throat, making a show of proving my point.

The officer leans to the side of my face, the hot air from his breath fogging over my ear. "You know what will happen if you're no longer useful to us?" he hisses spitefully.

I nod, still unable to swallow against the back of my tongue. I need water. I might as well be swallowing sand with how dehydrated I am. "Yes, bu-but—"

"The stupidity with you people runs strong, doesn't it? Surely you weren't going to question me?" The officer winds up his arm and thrashes his fist into my left eye, knocking me backward right off my feet. My stomach sinks in between my rib cage and sharp pains ache through my head. I try to open my eyes, but find only black spots floating above me, and a ringing in my ear. "You better find a way to strengthen your voice before tomorrow night, or you'll soon run out of nights altogether."

It isn't the first time I've been beaten for singing the wrong words, whether forgotten, misread, or simply exhaustion getting the best of me. There isn't an allowance for mistakes. A consequence always follows. I'm not sure how many consequences I can survive, or how many they'll deliver before I'm sent away for good. At least tonight, I know my altered lyrics were no mistake.

THIRTY-SIX

ELLA

September 1943

My vision blurs as I walk back to the barrack from roll call, imagining Luka's face contorting in pain after an officer blasted him with his fist. I had to bite back a cry as I watched Luka fall to the ground. The images are burnt into my mind, haunting me at night as I condemn myself for not doing something more than just watch it happen, even though I know I would have gotten us both killed if I had reacted. Luka didn't do anything to deserve the beating. His voice was strained, hoarse, and it's clear he's sick or his vocal cords are injured. Before the officer stood up from his seat to charge toward him, Luka was holding his hand around his throat. He hardly sounded the way I remember, but regardless, it was still him.

The threat the officer made to him to fix his voice or *"you'll soon run out of nights,"* sits inside of me like a pinched grenade —one I'm losing a grip on.

I drag myself up the flight of stairs to the second level and then hoist myself into my bunk, leaning my body to the right side of the straw mattress while unrolling my sleeve cuff to retrieve a handful of strawberry candy suckers I managed to steal from the door-guard's unlocked and unattended closet at noon today. If I could thank Tatiana for sharing her secret with me, I would, but I might never get that chance now. The kapos don't even call her number out at roll call. She's simply not here anymore and it's killing me to be reminded of this fact every single day.

I hide the candies under the corner of my mattress, along with a third of my dinner ration to add to the others I've been saving for the past week and a half. The bartering with Elsie is costing me—I'm growing weaker by the day. However, if it means helping Luka in any small way, I don't care. I'll do it for him. The candies will soothe his throat. He needs much more than this, but it's something at the very least. I just need to make sure I can offer Elsie enough rations to ensure she gets Luka the candies before it's too late.

I'm thankful to still hear his voice at night, despite the weak broken notes. At least I know he's still alive for now.

Unlike Tatiana.

Everything that has happened to everyone I care about feels as though it's my fault. I haven't done enough.

* * *

I drag my limp body into a narrow spot on the second-level tier and squeeze in between two others who are already lying limply on top of the thin straw-filled mattress we share.

In my thin canvas blanket, I wrap myself up tightly, hoping that it will protect me from bedbugs and lice. Yet, I know the blanket has been exposed to whatever crawls around this room all day. I can only try to convince myself it's clean and will keep me safe.

Now settled for the night, I wait for the second gong to rattle the walls and the sound of the light switch clinking, darkness taking over. The other prisoners do the same—we're all mindless bodies moving in the same pattern flow, doing as we're told. We're all just waiting for the day to end.

Outside, the wind whistles, and then the rain ends, a hum of silent static filling the air.

My heart hammers in my chest as I lie motionless, confined to this one spot for the long hours of the night. But then—a sound breaks the silence.

I pull in a breath to silence my body, straining to catch every note until the song grows clearer, the gentle melody a caress against my fractured heart.

He's still alive. That's what matters. We've made it another night here.

Despite the torture we all face, Luka's voice still somehow defies the despair surrounding us, carrying a sense of comfort and hope, even with the growing damage in his tone. It's as if his life depends on each word...

> *The sky is dark and gray*
> *but behind the clouds, it's blue.*
> *Lovely days will come*
> *soon for me and you.*
>
> *Keep me in your dreams,*
> *and I'll co—*

A blunt crack slices through the air. The song halts mid-word, choked by Luka's sudden gut-wrenching howl of pain. Then there is only silence...

I can't blink, breathe, or move. My body stiffens like ice as I wait for what comes next. Or is this...the end?

THIRTY-SEVEN

ELLA

The morning gong strikes as if a mallet smashes against the top of my head, bringing me back to a form of consciousness I'd rather not find. Luka's unfinished word and cry of pain plays in my head like an echo. Everything in my body tells me the worst has happened.

By late morning, the sound of the repetitive scratches from pens against paper and the clinks and clanks from the typewriters are like nails being driven into my head. The guard's boots thudding in their methodical pace adds to the relentless pain slicing through me.

I can't keep my hands steady as I make entries into the report logs. Out of habit, I glance over my shoulder, finding a new woman sitting in Tatiana's seat, doing her work. Anxiety gnaws at me, but Luka—wondering if he's all right is all I can think about.

I can't continue like this.

I shove my chair back, the wooden legs scraping against the terse floor, garnering several sharp stares from the other women. "What are you doing?" one of the typists asks.

"I—I can't sit here. I can't be here. I need to do something," I say, my words running into each other.

"They'll notice you're gone," she continues.

I look down at my desk, lift it up and shimmy a few footsteps to the right, adjusting my seat so it's directly behind the woman who sits in the row before me and blocks the view of the doorway. I move the chair next, and gather the paperwork on my desk, before hurrying toward the corridor as my heart throbs against my rib cage. The guards aren't in sight, but I know it won't be long before they return. I just need to make it past the intersecting corridor to the front door before they return.

My pulse thrums in my ears as I poke my head out into the other corridor, checking for guards. Two of them are walking away from this direction, one on each side. I slip my clogs off and tiptoe to the door as quickly as I can. I open it just enough to squeeze through and hold the handle until it swishes closed. I drop my clogs, slip them back on and head toward the main gate.

The guard at the gate, his rifle locked in position, watches me as I approach with the stack of papers. Before he asks me what I'm doing and where I'm going, I say, "I've been assigned to deliver these papers to Block 10, it's urgent, and I'll be returning just as soon as I hand them off." Block 10 is often requesting records from us for medical purposes, which doesn't make much sense to me, but it's not information I would be privy to.

For whatever reason, everyone shivers when they hear about Block 10, even the guards.

The guard clears his throat and nods. "Go on." He drops one hand from his rifle, checking the time on his watch as he turns away from me.

I let out a slow breath of air, trying to regain my strength through the crippling fear rushing through me. I keep my head down as I continue down between the barracks, moving with purpose to avoid questioning, though knowing I have no true destination.

If I can just lay eyes on Luka and see he's all right, it will be enough for me, for now.

I pass around the first building, out of sight from the gate, when a clash of music from two violinists and a cellist catches me off guard, shocking me into nearly tripping backward. Thankfully, I catch myself on the edge of the building. I wasn't aware this is where the musicians sometimes played. I hear them, but didn't realize it was just beyond the main gates. They aren't playing when I go to the administration building or when I'm released at the end of the day.

The musicians might live in one area or block. The cellist is giving me a look from the corner of his eye, likely wondering why I'm standing here staring at him and holding a stack of papers.

I walk up behind him so I can ask him a question he'll hear over the music. "Sorry to bother you, but could you tell me if all musicians live in a certain barrack or area?"

The man's eyes shift from side to side. I don't know if he had trouble hearing me, or if he's wondering why I could be asking this question. Possibly both.

"I believe most of us are in block twenty-four," he says before recentering his focus in front of him rather than peering over at me.

"Thank you."

It doesn't take me very long to make my way over to Block 24, since it's close to where the orchestra was playing. Two kapos are standing outside the barrack having what appears to be a firm conversation. A shudder runs through me as I straighten my limbs to avoid looking nervous. "Pardon me, but I've been asked to deliver these papers," I say, my voice strong and steady despite the panic driving through me.

Both male kapos narrow their eyes and knife me with their stares. "Who sent you?" the kapo on the right asks.

I can't swallow against the strangling tightness encasing my neck. I can hardly breathe. "The—the SS Administration office," I say, lying through my teeth. With sharp inhales through my nose, I try my best to steady my racing heart.

The kapo questioning me peers down at the stack of papers then shoots his glare back up at me. "No. You're not allowed in there. Shoo."

"Please," I utter, my words sounding more like a cry for help. "I must get these—"

"Leave, I said," the kapo shouts, taking a menacing step toward me.

I jump backward to distance myself from him. The man is seething, his eyes blaring at me as if he's a tortured animal.

But I can't give up. There must be a way I can find him.

I've already been away from the administration building too long, but I continue around the row of barracks, weaving between them, the latrines and workshops while scanning every face I pass. My efforts are useless, in vain and dangerous, and I'm forced to return to my desk. I'm not sure if anyone noticed I wasn't there today, but if it was noticed, I'll find out, I'm sure.

I retreat to my barrack for the night, tears threatening to spill out of my dry eyes. Despite living with three times the number of women who should fit within this space, I've never endured more alone than I do now. I've risked everything to find him, and even though I managed to that once in the Commandant's villa, the only thing I gained from that was the memory of watching him be beaten by an officer. And now I don't know what's happened to him...

I lie awake long after I should have fallen asleep, waiting for a hint of Luka's voice, but it never comes. Not tonight. Not after the last broken word. *Where are you, Luka?*

While straightening the blanket out over my slim section of

space along the bunk to roll onto my side, a hand brushes against my arm. It isn't uncommon, given the little space we have in which to move, but this passing touch consists of a sharp scratch against my skin. I untangle myself to reach for whatever it is that's scratched me. With little light available, I brush my fingertips across its edges, determining it's a folded piece of thick notepaper.

I whip my head to the other side in search of whoever just left it here and recognize the back of Magda as she walks toward her bunk. She's a short, stocky woman. Her body shape is different from those of us completely wasting away. She's lucky.

My heart races as I fidget with the note, trying to unfold it and straighten it out, twisting myself in every direction to steal a stream of light from the spotlight shining into the window down the row. When I manage to catch a hint of light, my eyes settle on the handwritten note, heart pounding faster.

17th of July 1943

My Dearest Ella,

My chest tightens, stealing my breath as hope ignites... Then, I notice the letter was written two months ago. This letter doesn't mean he's safe—not after what I heard last night. But it's something...

It is me. It's Luka, and yes, I'm here in Auschwitz, too.

My heart aches, knowing you, of all people, not Jewish, a person fighting against the Germans, ended up here in this hell. I imagine you were caught trying to help me and that's something I've been trying to process without success. I'm ashamed of myself, Ella. I shouldn't have let you continue to visit me in a place where neither of us should have been. I could have stopped everything that has happened before it was too late. To you, that is. I take full responsibility for your imprisonment here. It's not something I will ever forgive myself for.

Like you, I'm sure, I'm given little opportunity to do much else besides revisit old memories, rethink past decisions, and try desperately to find a meaning in all this.

When I saw you that one day in passing between the barracks I questioned if I had imagined you. Then I received your note. It's given me a ledge to hold on to here. I read it every chance I have.

I spend my days, as mentioned, watching so-called criminals, who I believe to be innocent, murdered with one bullet at the execution wall. Then, I spend my nights entertaining comrades of the Commandant, singing until my throat tightens and sound no longer forms. I see people enjoying themselves, dressed in formal attire, drinking champagne, laughing, and smiling. Then I return to my barrack, finding grown men crying in soiled clothes, sitting in their own sickness, barely breathing, and I ask myself why? Did we do something so wrong to deserve this torture? Are the Germans so right to deserve this victory?

Ella, my heart is torn into shreds. I don't know how to find you, but I have tried. Every step out of line is considered a crime. But I love you and will love you until I become the man with my nose pressed against the execution wall. I know my words are morbid and you would tell me to stop thinking the way I am, and you would remind me of the words I used to say —if I'm breathing and there is a sun in the sky, I'm still alive. But, Ella, I'm not sure I even know who I am at this point. I'm not sure if I have a family. I'm not sure if I trust the woman I handed this note to to deliver it to you. Worst of all, I'm not sure I'll wake up tomorrow.

I'm so sorry I've let you down. I'm weak and falling to pieces. I'm not sure we can save each other. Or even ourselves.

I know this isn't the response you were hoping for, and if I could see you—touch you—maybe...

I don't know what I'm saying. That's my truth.

I'm dying. Every bone in my body says so.

Remember, what happens here doesn't define us.

I'm sorry for us. I'm sorry for what could have been and will likely...never...be.

With love,

Luka

Next to his name is a stained streak of darkened paper. A remnant of a tear. Now, my own tears flood down my cheeks, one falling to splash on his note before I shove it beneath my blanket. I convulse with silent sobs, wondering what the SS have done to him. This note was from two months ago and Luka's words were already hollow and hopeless then. What's happened to him now...?

THIRTY-EIGHT

ELLA

October 1943

It's been weeks since I've heard Luka's voice, and I refuse to believe I never will again. The hole in my heart grows wider every day and the silence is unbearable, but I can't let it break me. I must believe he's still here somewhere, fighting for his survival. I'm not foolish enough to ignore that the SS use people until they become useless, then kill them. But Luka isn't useless, and neither am I.

Each night I'm forced to fall asleep in the oppressive silence, I remind myself why I can't give in. I've made a promise to myself that I will see this through and continue holding on to whatever sliver of hope I can grab onto. If I stop fighting, stop searching, the SS will win.

Through the rain, I walk behind the others toward roll-call square, my back aching, my legs heavy with exhaustion. The rain soaks through my skin, turning my muscles into stone, but I grit my teeth and press forward. I can't concede to weakness. Not now, not after how far I've come.

Francine shields the roster under her coat, reading off

numbers as thick raindrops putter over us. An SS officer steps up to her side, whispering something that makes her stiffen. "What about me?" she asks, no concern for discretion. She's always acted as if she's untouchable but it's clear she doesn't truly think that way.

The officer places a piece of paper over her list then strides off, an umbrella gripped in his hand, unaffected as if whatever he just handed her was no big deal.

"Block 2," Francine shouts, her voice hoarse. "Some of you are being transferred to Birkenau with new assignments, some—elsewhere. A small selection will remain here, but the majority of Block 2 will now be utilized for other needs."

Elsewhere.

The selection of women step forward away from the sedentary rows, trying to analyze if they have anything in common with one another. It's becoming harder to spot who is sick and who is just weak to the core from hunger and endless hours of work. However, the numbers she's calling—the women all have more meat on their bones, a sturdier step, and a sixth digit in their number. They are all newer arrivals.

I inhale sharply and hold it in as Francine moves to the next group. Then she calls numbers I recognize.

My pulse whomps between my ears. The administrative workers—like me. This must be the group staying here. It must be.

The rain turns to hard pellets, sleet, weighing on my shoulders. Francine continues calling out number after number, and I wait.

I wait and wait.

My number never comes. *I'm not meant to stay.*

I look around at the other women grouped with me, remaining in the original line. We're all emaciated, pale, hunched forward and shaking at the knees, but so are the group of administrative workers she pulled away. I will not be marched to my death without a fight.

This isn't about fate—a higher power determining what comes next for me. I will decide when my time is up.

"Excuse me," I call out to Francine, the rain drowning out the sound of my voice.

She turns toward me, her expression sharp with a sense of evil darkening her eyes. She doesn't respond. Just walks toward me as if she might walk right through me.

Keep still, stare back at her, and stay upright, I tell myself.

"What are you doing?" she hisses, stepping in closer. Her hot breath assaults me, but I don't flinch.

"I've followed your every order since I arrived at this—place. Now, you're—what? Transferring me?" I lift my chin and take in a sharp inhale. "You've taken an oath to support the SS, but you're still Polish, like me. You know what's happening here. You've sold yourself for extra bread, for a larger space to sleep. And for what? Power?" I take another breath, my heart pounding like a fist against my ribs. "You don't have to tell me where I'm going. I already know. But why don't you look me in the eyes and tell me...tell me you're sending me to my death."

She watches me, her lips sneering into a hateful smile. But she doesn't know I see something beneath it—a hint of who she used to be, and the realization of the choice she still has. "You've worked so hard and no one has done anything to repay you for your efforts," she scoffs. "You poor thing. Let me see if I can fix that for you."

THIRTY-NINE

ELLA

For two hours, I've stood in this short row, scolding myself for speaking out against Francine. I know better. I've seen what she's capable of and how she turns people over to the SS. My outburst punished not just me, but the others still standing here, waiting.

My legs tremble and my body has never felt so heavy. I don't know how much longer I can keep standing.

Francine might have made us stand here anyway, but kapos pass by us as if we're invisible. Everyone else has been sent elsewhere.

"I'm sorry," I whisper again to the women beside me. They know they're still standing here because of me.

"I wish I had the courage to say what you did," one murmurs.

"Me too," another follows.

It wasn't courage. It was desperation, anger, and grief.

For years, my purpose has been clear—find Luka, help him, hold on to him. Now, I fear I'm too late. And without that purpose, I'm left with a single choice—grasp for false hope or let go.

A young kapo steps in front of us, her eyes narrowing in on me. Where is Francine? I'm not sure I should be grateful she's gone.

"Straighten up," the kapo snaps. "Move."

We follow her toward the main gates where the train station waits beyond. Are we being transported? To another camp? Or to the other side of Auschwitz—Birkenau—the place no one returns from?

What if Luka was sent there? What if he's still here, sick in an infirmary, and I'm leaving him behind? Could he still be alive?

We walk between the barracks, toward the metal gates. A guard adjusts his rifle, angling it at us while speaking in private with the kapo. If they won't say where we're going, it means we already know.

The guard presses his fingers to his bottom lip, zipping out a whistle. With a rigid wave, he calls more guards. They arrive at once, saluting *Heil Hitler*.

The wind pushes against my weak body. The autumn chill nips at my face. I can't leave the last place. This is the last place I saw Luka. If I have any chance of finding him, it won't be outside these gates.

The guards and kapo corral us through, forcing me to leave my heart behind me.

We reach a wide empty road, fields stretching endlessly on either side. There's nothing to block the wind, as if nature itself is shoving us back toward Auschwitz.

Dirt and rubble whip through the air, blinding me. My clothes billow like a worn flag, fabric pulling away from my skeletal body—leaving me naked.

My legs falter again and again. I've nearly tripped twice, but I keep moving.

A woman behind me stumbles and falls. If I turn back to check on her, I'll be punished.

"Get up, you cow!" a guard shouts, charging toward her.

She cries out, pleading for help.

Pop. Pop.

Two shots.

I flinch, clutching the few belongings pressed against my chest. I don't shut my eyes. I keep them wide open, letting the wind sting, forcing myself to look—to witness another end.

The first bullet was enough. The second was out of hatred.

Does guilt drown them in their sleep? Do they think about who they have killed? How could they not?

The road stretches on, watchtowers appearing like ghosts in a patch of fog. A train rumbles past, the pressure deafening as it shakes the ground. We stumble out of line as the guards grip their caps and forge ahead.

The train is endless, red and black cattle cars rattling along the tracks. When it finally passes, a wail lingers in the air, haunting and hollow.

Through the fog, a wide shallow building looms ahead. The arched opening over the railroad tracks and a wooden sign confirms we've arrived.

Birkenau.

My metal bowl slips from my grip and clunks against the ground. My fingers are frozen. I didn't realize I'd lost my hold. It rolls to the side, and I scurry to pick it up. We don't stop walking, no one does.

"What is this?" a guard shouts, charging toward me like a bull with sharp eyes and plumes coming from his nostrils.

I stand frozen within his stare, clutching the bowl back into my belongings.

"Your hands aren't broken, are they?"

I tilt my head to the side, unsure whether I should speak.

He snatches the bowl and hurls it toward the barbed-wire fence.

"Go get it."

I force my legs to move, my steps careful as I near the fence. The buzz of electricity hums through the wires and spikes up my spine.

I grab my bowl and race back. The guard waits with his arms crossed.

"Next time, I'll throw it over the fence," he says, his voice playful. "Let's see how you get it then."

I say nothing, and I clutch my things and keep moving.

Through the gates of Birkenau, beyond the tracks, is a platform where people are falling out of cattle cars as if mistreated farm-animals.

Finally, a vast landscape of barracks appear—rows upon rows of dark wooden structures. More prisoners. More guards.

We walk the perimeter, past a few brick barracks then along a line made up of mostly women and children, weaving around a nearby building.

Their eyes lock onto mine and mine to them, wondering what the difference between our lines are.

A child wails.

A gunshot fires.

I jump. I always jump.

A mother collapses over her child, wailing, pleading. A second gunshot.

They're together now.

"This is your barrack, check in with your block-elder for assignments," a guard shouts.

A kapo waves us forward.

I follow the others toward the wooden barrack, unable to stop myself from looking over at the dead mother and daughter once more, this time finding another daughter, a young girl, staring at the other two with wide eyes full of shock and terror.

I cup my hand around my mouth as bile rises in my stomach. I step inside, between the walls of what looks like an animal pen with bunk beds.

Another gunshot shatters the air. Silence follows as the door slams behind us.

The odor of human waste mixed with filth and rotting wood are reminiscent of the barrack I came from. But it's worse here. It's harder to breathe. Women walk between the tiers of bunks, hunched forward, unsteady on their feet, their jaws hanging low. Is this what I look like, too?

The barrack stretches on endlessly, wooden bunks stacked high. Not one is empty.

I gasp for air as my head becomes heavy, then I reach for a wooden post to keep myself upright.

A faint cry pulls my gaze. A girl—maybe thirteen or fourteen, clutching her blanket as dirt riddled tears streak down her cheeks. Her fingers tremble as she strokes her fingers over the fabric's folds.

Then, softly, she sings. The words are foreign, but I know the melody. Hebrew, I believe. I don't understand, but I listen.

With another step toward her, she stops singing, her lips straighten across her mouth, and she stares back at me, unblinking.

"Are you all right?" I ask her.

She shakes her head in slow movements, side to side. I don't know how to help her. I'm afraid to ask her if her mom is here because she might not be. She might have been sent to the showers. I don't know who they keep and who they kill.

"Excuse me," a woman says, brushing by me with a metal bowl and water sloshing around. She kneels in front of the young girl and tips the bowl against her lips.

My heart pounds and my breath stutters as I reach toward the woman.

"Tatiana?" I ask hesitantly, knowing how unlikely it is that I would find her again, and here.

My chest tightens as she turns toward me. Her jaw falls open. It's her. She's here, in this barrack.

"Ella?" she cries. She gently hands the little girl the bowl of water as she continues to feed herself, then pulls herself up along a wooden beam before wrapping her arms around my neck. "You're here."

I nod my head, having a hard time forcing sound through my tightening throat. "I don't know what's happening. I thought they were sending me to die." My words fumble together.

She leans away briefly and stares at me for a long second. "If you can work, they'll keep you alive, usually," she says.

My throat clenches. "And if someone is sick or unable to work as they had been?" I already know the answer. I don't need her to tell me.

Her gaze falls between us, and she takes my hands within hers. "They send those people to the showers, Ella."

"Right," I say, the word floating on a short breath. "Like Luka. His voice broke one night. Then—there was a distressing cry of pain, a sound I can't forget. That was it—I never heard him again. I think the SS got rid of him. I didn't want to leave the other section because I was holding on to a bit of hope that maybe he was in an infirmary, but I couldn't find him anywhere. I tried. I don't know where he is, and I'm dying inside. I'm not sure I can do this any longer," I say, my voice croaking into a quiet cry.

"Oh, dear," she says, pulling me in for another embrace. "I'm so sorry. I know how hard you worked to find him. Everything you've done has been because of him."

"None of it mattered," I whimper.

"You didn't want him to be suffering. I know this," Tatiana says.

"I want to help him, save him, whatever I can to—"

"Ella..." Tatiana interrupts me and shakes her head as her lips unfurl into a grimace. "I—I don't know how to tell you this..."

The veins in my head pulsate as I stretch my gape wider,

staring at her, urging the seconds between her breaths to go faster. "What, what is it?"

Tatiana pulls in a trembling breath. "The other women here —I overheard them talking about the male singer, the young one with the beautiful eyes. They said the SS sent him to one of the shower rooms. I tried to ask them if they might know anything more, but they stopped talking and shook their heads. I don't know if—"

The room tilts to the side as nausea rushes up my throat. I reach back for the bunk but miss and my body falls heavily to the ground, my cheek hitting the wooden plank floor. I feel nothing...

FORTY

ELLA

As my senses start to come back to me, an ache spreads through my head and I blink, finding splintered wood to my side, my cheek pressed against it.

Luka.

I push my face away from whatever I'm leaning on, every muscle in my body repelling each slight movement. My lips are parched, cracking as I open my mouth to inhale the dry, dusty air. Tatiana? Where did she go? The memory of her urges me upright. She was right here. It's impossible to sit up straight in a bunk with how narrow the openings between each tier are.

A thud beside me makes me jump and gasp, finding Tatiana pushing a bowl up to my mouth just like she did to the little girl. "Drink, quickly. As much as you can."

I do as she says, the quick few gulps inducing nausea. "They're about to assign you to labor. I'll be here tonight. Don't give up. Please. You matter, too. I've missed you and now that you're here, I don't want to lose you again."

"...six-three-nine-four," I hear someone shouting my number and I glance around. A kapo stands at the open door, wearing a men's blue overcoat over her striped smock, but with the armband labeled with the word "kapo" next to a Jewish star. That says all I need to know.

I pull myself up and give Tatiana one last glance and a nod. "I'll be back," I whisper.

Luka.

He was sent to be gassed.

That's why I collapsed.

Luka was sent here. They discarded him just as I assumed.

Though...there could be another singer, maybe? Could I make myself believe that instead?

"The young one with beautiful eyes."

My chest is hollow and my heart only aches like it's been battered with a bat. I need a moment. I need to cry. I need to scream.

But my body just moves forward as it was told to do.

I approach the kapo with the clipboard in her hand, sneering at me as if she's already lost her patience, waiting the long seconds for me to make my way across the block to her. "That's my number," I utter weakly.

"Outside," she says, pointing to another line, then shouts the next number on her list.

My knees shake as I walk over to the other woman standing in a single line, facing another kapo. Snow is falling now. A snowflake lands on my hand and I stare down at it, wondering why there isn't an accompanying chill. More fall over my shoulders and arms, and on my cheeks as well.

As I go to sweep the flake from my sleeve, I realize why the snow isn't cold—it's not snow. It's dust. A small pebble falls into my hand, and I take it between my fingertips and examine it—a particle of bone. I pinch the bridge of my nose to stop tears from forming, but in the darkness of my mind, I find Luka singing in the Leszno Street square, reaching his arm out toward me and the crowd, releasing his beautiful words and sound to fall upon us. Then he falls to the ground like a steel beam, his arm still outstretched, his eyes still open—but he's gone.

"No," I whisper to myself. "No, I won't believe it." An acrid burn swells in my chest as I dust myself off.

Two lines emerge from the one I was standing in and we're moving forward, heel to toe as if a caterpillar squirming along as one unit. We take a turn away from the barracks, out between two barbed-wire fences and return to the central path, bordered by more fences.

We drag our feet, unintentionally kicking hard dust up at each other until we approach a closed gate, guarded by an SS officer. "These women are reporting to Kanada," the kapo tells him. He walks down the short line, grabs my arm, pinches his fingernails into my flesh and checks my inked number against whatever is written on the list in his other hand. Kanada is where I was assigned.

Once all of the women's arms have been matched to the list, the gates open to a series of long, wooden and brick buildings. Set out in front of the wide barn-like entrances to the buildings are carts of luggage and piles of various personal belongings. The sounds of gates opening and closing ring constantly as other prisoners walk in and out of the barrack's doors, carrying bundles of items. Kanada must be a warehouse of some sort.

We're directed inside, swallowed by dust, burnt wood, and the stench of bitterness. Guards stand in every direction, rifles slung over their shoulders, eyes scrutinizing us. The hanging dim light flickers, blending with the streaks of sun slipping through the thin cracks in the walls.

Shelves line the room, piled high with stacks of a variety of items confiscated from incoming prisoners—clothing, shoes, suitcases, and kitchenware. Prisoners work methodically, sorting through them with vacant stares and mechanical movements. None of them stop to look at us.

A kapo steps forward in front of us and begins to read our

numbers off again, followed by assignments appointing us to a landmark of goods.

"Teeth—remove all gold teeth and set them in the crate," the kapo says, her voice lacking inflection.

She calls my number and points over my head. "Handbags —empty them, sort valuables and non-valuables."

I move toward the pile, passing whispering workers and the scrape of crates on concrete—the factory-like hum, suffocating.

I find the area where women are sorting through handbags, each of them moving quickly. I grab a bag, mimicking the others.

A sharp gasp breaks the steady rhythm of repeating tasks. The girl next to me stares at her bleeding palm. I spot a broken mirror shard on the ground, grab the handle and toss it into the worthless pile.

"Can you not handle such a simple task?" a kapo's voice snaps from down the row. The kapo thrusts herself down the row, grabs the girl's handbag, and dumps the remaining items over her head. "Hurry!" she growls before storming off.

The girl scurries to pick up the fallen items, her hand still bleeding, blood dripping down to her elbow. I search my bag until my fingers graze over a handkerchief.

Luka's voice drifts through my memory. *I've heard women can keep an entire pharmacy stored in one small bag.*

"Here," I whisper, handing her the cloth beneath the bags we both have open.

She doesn't dare look up, but her lips press into a faint smile.

"Thank you," she utters. "I'm Galina."

"Ella," I reply.

I take the next bag, a black leather purse, pulling out a pill box, a wallet, a small Bible, and lipstick. I place everything down to sort through after checking through the bag once more, touching every silky surface of the interior until something crumples like newspaper beneath my fingertips. I find a small hole, reach inside, and retrieve a worn letter.

"My darling, how do I share the amount of love my heart holds for you?"

I find scripted ink with sharp edges to each letter, like Luka's handwriting.

The clunk of heavy boots spooks me into dropping the note and tossing the empty bag into a wagon set out before us for the empty handbags. This woman, wherever she might be, had a last note for her love, something to hold on to.

Hours of monotonous rummaging pins me in a mindless rhythm, disconnecting me from every object I touch. To survive, I can't let myself care.

A harmonious cry of a violin zips overhead as a guard enters a nearby door, the sound trailing behind. There's music? Here?

"Are you all right?" Galina asks, the movement of her lips subtle.

"Did you hear that?"

Her brows furrow. "Hear what?"

"Music."

Galina releases a quiet sigh. "Sometimes musicians play outside the shower rooms."

My stomach snarls at the thought. What a cruel way—to...

"Is there ever a singer?" The question flies out of my mouth.

Her brows furrow as she peers up in thought. "There was, once. A Jewish man. The guards mocked him, then called him a waste of talent."

Luka? I clutch a scarf to my chest as if it's the one last thread that can keep me connected to something real. Luka's real. He's still alive in my heart. It must mean something.

Tatiana's words ring through my head again. *"The male singer, the young one with beautiful eyes... He was sent to be gassed."*

My thoughts come to an abrupt stop and the room closes in

on me when the door opens again. For a split second, a voice soft and faint hums in the distance.

I freeze, gripping the bag in my hands.

The sound wanes.

"Did you hear that?" I ask Galina, my question frantic but quiet.

Galina watches me and gently tilts her head to the side. "Ella...there's no singer."

It disappeared as quickly as it came. I lower my chin, shaking my head in disbelief, wondering if my mind is playing tricks on me.

My mind wouldn't betray me like that. It wouldn't. I know I heard something—a familiar melody—a sliver of hope, or maybe pure madness. But it's like a flicker of light from a match that doesn't want to burn out.

FORTY-ONE

LUKA

February 1944

From the moment I arrived at this death camp, I no longer questioned whether there would be a final night in Auschwitz. A final night on earth. The thought loomed liked a brewing storm. When the beatings dealt by an SS officer became a nightly occurrence, growing harsher and longer, I wondered why they didn't kill me. I can only assume they wanted me to keep singing, even though they weren't satisfied with my performance.

I should have been more grateful for those days rather than questioning why I was there.

During my final performance at the Commandant's Headquarters in September, five months ago now, I was so ill and weak, I couldn't make it through one song without gasping for air. The brutal officer, the one who often took pleasure in beating me, came toward me once again. This time, somehow, with a darker look than I had seen before. I was halfway through a song when he took his first swing. He didn't stop. Not that time. He kept thrusting his fist into my stomach again and again, then kicked me in the chest until the wind left my body.

Everything went dark, and the next morning I woke up in an infirmary with signs marking the location of Birkenau. Immediately, it was clear I had been brought to the other section of Auschwitz—the side Jews went to die, as rumors went. With a swollen face, blood everywhere, and bruises marring my entire body, the pain ignited just seconds after I woke up. But I couldn't scream. All I could do was stare at the wooden beams crisscrossed above my head, asking God why I was still alive.

Again, I wondered why they didn't just finish me off. The SS kill for far lesser reasons here.

It's because this place isn't done with me yet. That's why.

I've been in Birkenau for five months. As soon as I became well enough to be assigned a block and labor, I ended up in front of a shower room—a gas chamber—the place where Jews go to die. When will it be my turn?

FORTY-TWO

LUKA

I'm not stationed by the chambers because they've decided I shouldn't die...yet. I'm here to entertain those who are waiting their turn to step inside. I've spent time at two of the four gas chambers until this point. The longest line appears to wait here —in front of chamber number four. We were moved here earlier in the week.

"Jetzt kommen die lustigen Tage," Etan says, giving me a quick glance. He's the talented violinist I've been grouped with here, a young fellow, around my age, a skeletal body like myself, eyes protruding from his face. He's been separated from his entire family, too. He said they were all sent to the left when he was pushed to the right, and like me, he didn't realize that was the last time he would see them. We all have a story, but it's odd to have such similar ones. "On three."

A favorite song of the SS—German folk music about the cheerful times ahead. A musician's job here, among the endless line snaking around us, is to put on an act, lie as the SS convince these innocent people that they are truly here for the promised shower—the death-trap behind the brown painted door I examine all day.

"Ready," I reply in a whisper, saving what's left of the sound in my voice.

The SS don't appear to care how broken my voice still is or that my vocal cords never healed from whatever virus I was ill with. Rather than waiting to be beaten to death, I will wait until I sing myself to death, and with a forced sense of cheer behind each word.

"One, two—" Etan continues.

In the dead of winter with frigid temperatures and blades of wind slicing through me, I shiver relentlessly through each word. The line of people in front of me come into a sharp focus as I begin to sing, wishing I could change the lyrics to: "Run, there is no shower inside, just vents that will release a deadly gas and kill you."

But I would only cause them panic and fear, and that would be worse than not knowing. The guilt is like black tar, filling my soul, and I'm ashamed to think that the faces are all beginning to look the same to me while passing through this line. Regardless of which of the four gas chambers I'm assigned to perform outside, I can't stop wondering if Ella could end up in one of these lines. What if she's passed me and I've glossed over her? I could have let her walk right into one of those shower rooms and... *Breathe*, I remind myself. *Breathe*.

She must think I'm already dead, now she can no longer hear my voice where she is, which leaves me wondering what she might be doing to find out what happened to me—how much she would risk for an answer. Ella doesn't give up. She's made that clear again and again. But now I'm here, in Birkenau, any chance she might have had of finding me is gone. Almost all Jews are sent here—whether to the shower rooms, or to labor. I didn't realize it was unusual for me, as a Jew, to be in the main camp of Auschwitz for as long as I was. That area of the camp holds mostly Polish political prisoners, so it's where Ella will stay.

Mother might have been sent to Birkenau, too. She could be here somewhere. But it's been ten months of this brutality and starvation since the train spit us out into this hell. The thought of her living through what I've been—it turns my stomach inside out.

No one should have to live like this. Dying would be easier. I consider this thought each time before falling asleep.

"I can't stand upright any longer, Mama," a little girl hollers from the line during the instrumental verse of this folk song.

"Hush, hush. We're almost there. See, darling. You can see the door. We'll be receiving a nice warm shower in just a few minutes from now. Won't that be nice?"

My chest swells with grief and my throat tightens into a sore knot—a pain that won't cease. She's just a little girl.

FORTY-THREE

LUKA

Moments after the first gong strikes, warning us of how little time we have before roll call, Etan slaps his hand over my shoulder as I'm pulling the blanket over my narrow space on the bunk. I don't know how he moves so fast in the mornings. We're the same age and he's been here a while, too. I try my best to keep up with him, so I don't look like I'm becoming one of the weak. Many men are not moving at all. Some of them will die in their beds today and they'll be gone when we return. Others will hold up roll call, requiring all others to stand in the row longer, only to be physically assaulted with punishment after. It's hard to think past the moment we're living in, I guess.

I step outside and a gust of powdery snow stings my face before I step foot into an unmarked path toward the latrine. The march through the partially frozen snow soaks my socks. My ankles will be wet and cold for hours just so I can relieve myself in the latrines and possibly steal enough time to wash my body before it's time to claim breakfast.

There's never a change in the food we receive, except for the occasional slab of margarine or jam they spare for us to scrape a thin layer over our leftover evening bread. I wash it all down with a cup of warm water mixed with floating coffee grinds. I've forgotten what something savory is like. Even my imagination fails me. No amount of food ever satisfies my hollow stomach. If anything, a deeper hunger follows my final bite.

A second gong informs us it's time to line up at roll call, which is as brutal here as it was in the other section of the camp —long, drawn out, and cold. The wind traps between the buildings, swirling around us as if we're caught in an icy vortex. All I can do is shiver and try not to crack a tooth while my teeth chatter.

Once dismissed, I report to my designated location where I will sing until I damage my voice even more while straining through the painful cold for the next ten hours. I find Etan standing by the gas chamber, adding rosin to his bow then fine tuning the small knobs at the base of the strings. I notice a slash along the side of his face that I didn't see when I was half awake this morning.

"What happened?" I ask, keeping my voice low.

He shakes his head. "It was nothing."

"It doesn't look like nothing. It's bleeding."

"I was rewinding a string, and it fell," he says, before nudging his head toward a nearby guard. "He got to it first."

Etan continues to tune his violin, and I wrap my hands around my neck, trying to keep my vocal cords warm for as long as possible. I no longer attempt to vocally warm up my voice as I don't know how long it will last throughout the day as it is. I can't afford to waste the sound.

I could easily mistake the line weaving around for the same line that was here yesterday when I left. It's as if I've seen the same group of people walk in over and over when I know that's impossible. The only difference between them all aside from their gender and age is the slight differences between their personalities. There are those who appear to have some form of hope. Others seem to sense the doom as they stare, unblink-ingly, at the foreboding door.

Then there are the mothers. One places her hand on her child's shoulder as she exchanges whispers with another, even sharing a smile or two. The quiet bond between them is a glimmer of light, yet casts a deep, vacant shadow within me. Another mother gingerly straightens her young son's collar, the gesture so natural and ordinary it makes my chest ache for them. Still, I force myself to pick up the next verse of lyrics awaiting me in one measure.

Despite being amid music and singing, albeit the damage in my lungs, nothing distracts me from the rusty hinges squealing as the door to the building opens.

It must be near noon.

The door only opens two to three times a day, since more than one thousand people enter at once. I've noticed a pattern of timing and can now predict when the door will open next, depending on the last time it opened.

Etan told me it takes less than ten minutes to fill the cham-ber, then another ten to twenty minutes for the Zyklon B gas that's dropped in between the slats of the roof. All of this takes place at the back side of the building where no one in line can see what their future holds. SS guards will stand watch at a peephole along the wall of the interior chamber and wait for the complete stillness of each body before sending in the Sonderkommandos, the forced Jewish laborers assigned to the task of removing the corpses, extracting gold teeth, shaving all hair, then transporting the bodies to the crematorium. This process takes up to three hours before the next group is sent inside.

The most gutting part is the excitement the line of people share with each other when the door finally opens. They think they're about to be properly taken care of once inside. What else could they think when we're forced to play uplifting music full of cheer and promise?

As the noon time group enters, two walk through the door at a time. As if on instinct, I glance toward the families edging closer to the door, but then I freeze.

My gaze catches on a woman who moves just within my range of sight. Her figure is bent like a question mark, but her movements are stern and deliberate, as if each step carries more than just the weight of her body. She isn't wearing traditional clothes like those who step off the train. She's a prisoner, dressed in a familiar blue and white striped smock, her head covered by a black scarf with a red floral pattern that ties in the back and falls to her shoulders into frayed edges.

I blink, telling myself I must be imagining things again, but when my eyes reopen and I focus back on the scarf, my chest fills with an icy numbness. I know that scarf. I remember the way I would tug at it when Grandmother tied it around my head, telling me I needed it more than she did. I would be embarrassed because it was covered in red flowers, and argue that I didn't need to be warm. But it was warm, and the fabric was soft as it swept against my cheek. It smelled like Grandmother's favorite vanilla fragrance. I held on to her scarf after she passed away. I slept with it at night as if it would bring me the same comfort she did.

When we were taken from Warsaw and shoved onto the train, I took the scarf out of my pocket and placed it into Mother's, knowing she might need it more than me. My lungs are like stone walls in my chest as I fight to breathe and exhale the lyrics I'm meant to be singing. My voice bleeds into the air as I search around, wondering if anyone has noticed. But the guards are too busy escorting the line in through the door of the chamber.

My eyes lock onto her face, the features becoming clearer the closer she gets to me. She's watching the children in front of her, smiling weakly as she offers them a gentle wave. Closer and closer she comes, and her profile sharpens, the line of her jaw, and the faint tremble of her chin and bottom lip.

She's here. In this line. My mother.

My legs weaken at my knees. They shake from the cold, from the fear, from the incredible pain slashing through me. My body wants to give up and fall to the ground again as it's done too many times before here, but I hold myself steady, willing myself to stay upright and think of a way to pull her out of this death line.

During the brief, momentary pause between songs, I open my mouth to shout her name, but stop myself when a guard snaps at someone for being too slow. There are too many guards around. They'll hear me shouting. Frozen with terror, I gawk at her without blinking, praying I can somehow get her attention, but she's unaware of me standing here. She must not even recognize my voice with how damaged it's become here.

The music restarts, giving me just a few more seconds before I will be forced to start singing again. I'm counting the measures, making sure I stay in time, but then Mother glances over at me, her eyes meeting mine, and I clench my fists. My eyes bulge and I shake my head, trying to warn her without being able to say anything other than:

> *There's a place for you*
> *Warm, inviting, bright, and true.*
> *A dreamland waiting to be found,*
> *Where peace and beauty both astound*

She mouths my name, but I can't hear her voice over my own until the music softens. "Luka," she shouts, her words frantic, pleading, and full of relief to see me.

I wave my hands at her by my waist, telling her to stop. I try to mouth the word "run" instead of singing the lyrics to keep with the music. My eyes are about to fall out of their sockets, trying to warn her to do something, not to come any closer, but she doesn't see the words I'm trying to speak. She sees me, her son who she's probably assumed dead.

She lunges out of the line in my direction, crying out for me. I move toward her, leaving the music behind. Leaving everything in this world behind for this one single moment.

FORTY-FOUR

ELLA

February 1944

When I think it can't possibly get any colder outside, I'm proven wrong. Despite how many of us work within this warehouse, Kanada, there's no additional warmth inside than there is outside, but I'm thankful to avoid the wind and frostbite.

Each time the door to the warehouse opens, I brace myself for the sting of cold to follow. A kapo has been holding the door open for minutes now. It will never warm up in here.

A hazy melody floats in with a gust of wind, carrying notes into my ear.

> *There's a place for you*
> *Warm, inviting, bright, and true.*
> *A dreamland waiting to be found,*
> *Where peace and beauty both astound*

My jaw falls and I choke on air. Galina peers over at me with a look of confusion in her eyes. "I did hear that—the singing," she says. "I've never heard anyone singing outside this building."

I stand up without thinking of the repercussions. I keep my hands gripped around a handbag.

"Luka!" a woman calls out at the top of her lungs.

Luka.

My stomach folds in on itself as I run for the door, holding my hand over my mouth as if I'm about to throw up. I might.

The cold wind pushes against me as I step outside.

"Aufhören!" an officer shouts, but not at me. The music that was playing just a second ago comes to an abrupt stop.

A woman in the long winding line around the warehouse steps out and trudges forward with her arms outstretched. I take another few steps forward toward the barbed-wired fence. I recognize her...

"Hör auf, sagte ich," the officer shouts again, warning the woman to stop moving.

No.

No, no, no. It's Luka's mother, Chana. The closer I step in toward the gate, the wider my view grows, finding a violinist, cellist, and—is it...

A metallic, sharp and scratchy "clink-clink" bellows from a rifle's chamber round.

"No!" a man shouts. "Don't shoot!"

It's him. I can see him. It's Luka. He's alive.

Luka. I come close to grappling the barbed-wire fence before the buzz of electricity reminds me I'll be killed if I touch the metal. *Don't shoot. Don't hurt her,* I plead silently, my heart exploding within my chest.

The rifle swings in Luka's direction, pointing directly at his head. "You fool. Sing

or—"

"My mother. Please—don't—" Luka begs.

FORTY-FIVE

LUKA

My plea for the officer not to shoot Mother has brought the world to a stark halt. The world is caving in on me. I can't breathe. I can't move. All I can do is stare at the horror consuming Mother's pale face.

"Aw, you mean you'd rather be the strong heroic son and take the bullet for your dear old mama?" the officer coos, toying with me as he continues to aim his rifle at my head.

My body shakes uncontrollably even though I want to be strong—to show Mother I'm strong so she doesn't feel the need to be brave and save me. I need to save her. I must. "Please," I whimper.

"Luka," she cries out again. The sound brings back a memory of the time I tripped along the edge of a fountain and fell headfirst to the ground. The terror of me getting hurt. That's what her voice cries out now, but she's the one meant to be walking toward the gas chamber.

Another guard steps forward and lifts his rifle up in front of my chest, preventing me from moving any closer to Mother. "Please don't hurt her," I cry out. Why must they make me beg?

"Schießen," the guard standing beside me shouts. Shoot.

"No, no!"

A metallic "click" shatters the air before a defining crack and the ground beneath me shudders. My world collapses on top of me and I scream.

I try to run, but the guard keeps the rifle aimed at me. "Unless you want to be shot, too, don't move. Keep singing," he says, gritting his teeth.

"No one told you to stop the music!" another guard shouts at the other musicians.

My eyes fill with tears as I absorb every detail of my mother, blood pooling around her head in the fresh snow. My heart won't beat. My body won't move.

"Sing!" the guard beside me snaps, shoving the butt of his rifle into my side, forcing me to choke out in pain.

I crumple inward, gasping for the air that was stolen from my lungs. My lips part, but phlegm gums up my mouth. The strings from the violin scrape against their bows, the sound of hesitation. The cellist follows, a beat too slow. Their bows all tremble into a sound of disarray and I force sound out to cover the sound of the others, trying to protect them before I do something to hurt them, too.

My voice cracks, despite the force I'm pressing against, and Father's words echo in my head, "You've become a fine young man, Luka. I'm proud of you. Always, and I know you can handle whatever comes our way."

I've let my entire family down. I was supposed to protect her and Grandmother, and I didn't.

My vision focuses on everything around me, the people watching me with intent. I'm not as invisible as I thought. The guards continue to glare at me. All of them now, three rifles pointed at me with the threat to end my life right this second. Maybe that's what I want...

More shouting commences around the music, and the guards move back to their original places to continue shoving people along into the chamber. My focus stops on Mother again, her body melting into the snow as if she's becoming one with the earth. Her scarf floats over the snow, the red flowers blending with the blood. I can't look away. How can I stop looking at what's left of her now?

The guards' voices grow louder, fiercer as they begin to forcibly shove people inside as fear rivets through every set of eyes as they all begin to question if it's truly a shower they're walking toward. Why shoot a woman walking toward a shower unless someone was about to expose the truth? Their panic is my fault.

People step over her body in fear of not complying with the orders. It's as if she's a rock lodged in the center of their path, an object they can't avoid any other way.

I choke on the last word of the verse, coughing up the air in my lungs.

"Sing, you worthless rat!" a guard shouts from near the open door.

I open my mouth again, but no sound comes out. I can't sing with my mother lying dead to the side of me. My voice will not work, not like this.

The guard at the door lifts his rifle, pointing it at my head once again. His fingers twitch on the trigger.

"Wait!" another guard shouts from behind me, his boots crunching along the snow. Prisoners in line step aside, making space for him to pass, and as he does, he stops in front of Mother to inspect her dead body as if it should be of interest to him, then his icy eyes stare at me. I recognize him, one of the higher ranked SS often at the Commandant's Headquarters.

"This one," the familiar SS says, "the voice of an angel, yes? But clearly not anymore. Now, you're just as weak as a tiny little mouse." He flaps the back of his leather gloved hand at me. "Take him with the others. He must need a...shower...too."

"No!" I shout, and my voice comes out strong and sharp.

The desperation pulling something out of me. "Please, I'll sing. I'll do better."

The officer smirks and shakes his head. "It's too late," he says, clicking his tongue. "Such a shame."

"No one else knows the music," one of the violinists says. "We don't have another singer. How can we entertain these people who are patiently waiting for their showers?"

The officer shoves me in the shoulder, pushing me into the violinist. "No talent in the world can save you here," he utters. "You're not worth the space."

FORTY-SIX

ELLA

My body is frozen. I can't move. I can't cry. I'm about to fall to my knees, as the horror continues to unfold before me. Luka's mother is dead, just a few steps away from me, but with a fence between us. She's dead. There's blood everywhere. I gasp for air that won't fill my lungs.

"Are you sending the singer into the showers?" a guard shouts from the chamber door to the officer pointing his rifle at Luka's head. He's alive. Let him stay alive. A cough spills out of my lungs, and I slap my hands over my mouth as the officer drops his rifle and grabs Luka by his collar.

"What do you think I should do, you filthy Jew?" he growls.

"What are you doing out here?" someone shouts from directly behind me and grabs me by the collar, dragging me backward. "There are no breaks. This isn't a theater for your entertainment purposes. Get back to work!"

I fall to the ground inside the warehouse after being tossed in through the door. A boot clobbers me in the back, forcing all the air out of my lungs. A wave of black dots floats in front of my eyes as I take a breath. I gasp against nothing.

Again, I try to take a breath, and this time air flows but pain radiates through my back. Someone shoves their arms beneath mine and drags me through the warehouse, dropping me in front of the pile of handbags. "You all right, Ella?" Galina's face is in front of mine, her hands pressing on my cheeks. "Breathe."

I stare her in the eyes, but all I can see is Luka's mother, dead in the snow. The rifle pointing at Luka's head. The shower door, open and waiting for him.

"It was him," I say, my voice raspy and barely producing sound.

"Who?" Galina asks, keeping to a whisper.

"The voice—the one I keep telling you I hear. It's him. My Luka. They're about to kill him. They just killed his mother. I watched it happen," I blurt out.

"Are—are you sure?" Galina asks.

Tears form in the corners of my eyes, and a tickle fizzles through my nose as I clench the muscles in my face to stop myself from reacting. "Yes," I utter. "He isn't dead, but he's about to be."

FORTY-SEVEN

ELLA

"Here's another bag. Keep going," Galina says, pushing my hands inside the bag as if I'm a useless rag doll.

"I have to make sure he's still here," I say while mindlessly plundering through a bag.

"You can't go back out there," Galina says. "You'll be punished much worse next time if they find you out there again."

She's right, but I don't care about being punished. I need to see if Luka's still alive. It's been a few hours, and I haven't heard his voice, only the other musicians still playing their instruments. I don't know how many bags I've handled, what I've found, what I'm doing right this second. Nothing else matters.

"I have to go," I tell Galina again.

"Ella, listen to me," she says, grabbing my wrist, poking her fingernails into my skin. "If they sent him—if the worst has—he would not want you risking your life, would he?"

I stand up, shoving her words to the side as I keep my focus on the door, finding it clear of kapos and guards once again today. Fear doesn't flicker through my veins as it normally would. Apprehension of what I might or might not see does. I claw at my chest as if I need to physically hold my heart still as I slip out the door into the metal pen we're corralled within. I walk around the side of the building, closer to the gas chamber, searching for the musicians.

They're playing but there are no lyrics. I can see the backs of the performers. They're standing close to the adjoining gate between us. A retching sound captures my attention and I spot a man on all fours, less than a footstep away from the gate, vomiting, blood spraying out onto the snow.

I walk closer, forgetting about any guard or officer who might be within view. "Luka?" I whisper, wondering if sound will carry far enough to reach him.

He struggles to lift his head, his eyes bloodshot, his bottom lip hanging. He lifts a hand, reaching it toward the fence.

"No, no!" I shout through a breath. "You'll be electrocuted. Don't touch the gate!"

A thunderous cough bucks through with a whistle and a wheeze so strong, I don't know how he's breathing. More blood sprays from his mouth, but he swipes the sleeve of his arm across his face. "Ella," he groans. "Ella..."

"I'm here. I'm here," I cry out.

"I'm dying. I can't live," he says through a shuddered breath. "I'm sick. And my heart—it hurts so much. But—" he swallows hard and gasps for more air. "You're alive. I thought—I don't know." Tears spill from his eyes.

"Shh-shh-shh, it's all right. I know what happened. I'm going to help you. I'm going to help you. You must be strong, for your mother. She'd want you to be strong for her. I love you, Luka. I love you so much. I'm going to help you. However I can. I'm going to help you. You can't die. Don't let them—"

Shouts from kapos echo within the warehouse and I look back toward the door.

"Go back," he says, between tremors. "I don't want you to get hurt. Please. It's too late for me."

I give a firm shake of my head. "No," I say, gritting my teeth. "Don't say that. You hold on. Do you hear me?" I cry out, clenching my arms around my stomach from the pain. Again, I turn to look at the door, knowing I need to stay alive now to help him. "I'll be back." I run to the door and slip back inside, crouching behind taller people and scurrying over to the pile of handbags.

Galina gives me a quick glance, her eyes full of concern. "They just caught someone stealing. I'm glad you're back," she whispers.

"Yeah, me too," I say, grabbing the next bag from the pile.

I continue sorting through the handbags, cleaning each one out, forced to catch glimpses of photos packed away in these belongings—photos of families, loved ones, and times of happiness. The things in these photos are particles of history now. I'm not sure there's any form of happiness left in this part of the world.

After tearing through hundreds of bags this afternoon, I open one of the last few in the pile, emptying it of its contents: a compact, a few photos, a handkerchief, a pill box, a prayer card, and the smallest jar of honey I've seen in all the items I've separated.

A memory flashes before my eyes of the first night I finally found Luka in the sewers beneath Warsaw when he told me his grandmother was sick. I remember telling him not to worry about me and to just tell me what he needed so I could help him. He didn't want me doing anything dangerous, but I made him believe I would be fine no matter what. He finally confessed what could help.

"Thyme leaves, honey, or garlic and ginger. My mother would use those to help my grandmother, but I don't want you going anywhere you shouldn't to find these items, Ella. You must listen to me. I wouldn't be able to live with myself if something happened to you when I'm confined here and can't help you."

Honey. I squeeze my hand around the small jar and reach back into the bag for the last item, a change purse. I let the jar slip down my sleeve as I retract my hands from the bag and empty the change purse onto the table before lifting my arm up and over to a bin of discarded items to release the puckered leather accessory. The jar slips further into my sleeve where I'm able to pinch the upper part of my arm against my rib cage to keep the jar pinned. All of us women could use pockets in our smocks like some of the men have on their uniforms, but the SS don't want us to have pockets for this precise reason so we're forced to come up with other ways of hiding items—an act that could be punishable by execution.

Following evening roll call, I return to the barrack in search of Tatiana, not finding her by her bunk. I pace around, shoving my hands over my spiky, shaven hair.

"Ella," Tatiana says, grabbing my wrist. "What's the matter? You look mad."

I pull her in by the bunks and step in closely. "I saw Luka today."

"I was coming to find you, to ask if you heard him singing. I don't know where he came from, but there were performers outside crematorium four today. The man I saw was young and he does have beautiful eyes, so I was praying for you that it's him. It is him?"

I nod, trying to hold back the sob squeezing through me. I shove my fingers to my temples, and swallow back a lump. "They shot his mother, right in front of him. She came from the line of people waiting for the showers. They threatened to kill him, too, but then spared him. They must not have noticed how sick he is, how sick he's been... I'm not sure he ever got better from when his voice was breaking back when we were all in the main section of Auschwitz. He told me he's dying. We spoke between the fences. I need to do something. I need to give him something."

"How?" Tatiana asks, her shoulders tense and rising to her ears.

"Are you still working with the Sonderkommandos in the crematorium?"

"Yes," she says, talking as if she doesn't want to be reminded of her job at this hour.

"Will you switch jobs with me tomorrow? No one checks numbers after roll call anymore. Please. I'll do anything for you."

"Uh, well—I—of-of course. I'd do anything for *you*," she says as fear glows within her eyes.

"Lights out," the kapo shouts.

I make it into my bunk, still pressing the jar of honey between my arm and ribs. This plan might cost me everything, but it's a chance I'm willing to take to help Luka.

FORTY-EIGHT

LUKA

The morning is cold, damp, the air thick with the sound of misery and the smell of death. Mother's screams still shrill in my head like a scar that won't heal. The blood on the ground from when she was shot is still there, with no fresh snowfall today to cover over it.

I take a glance at Kanada, the warehouse beyond the barbed-wire fence, looking for a hint of Ella. I can't believe she's close by. I don't know how long she's been here because, before now, I was performing at another gas chamber in another area of this compound. Men and women rarely pass each other here. But there she was, finding me at my weakest moment—a moment where I was debating whether to throw my body up against the electrified fence like many others have done at the end of their road. I wasn't in my right mind. I'm still not. I'm not sure I ever will be again.

I want to walk right into that warehouse and find her and tell her everything I need her to hear before it's too late. She deserves to know how much hope she has given me when I needed it most. She needs to know how much I love her and how sorry I am if I succumb to the sickness within me that I can't fight—both of body and of mind.

But no one will let me in through those gates.

I shake the hands of the three men I continue to play with in front of Gas Chamber number four as we prepare for another day in hell. There are orchestras or other forms of musical talent peppered along significant areas of the camp, too. They have a group performing at train selection lines, and the other gas chambers. Sometimes a group will be placed in a certain spot to entertain a visiting officer being taken on a tour through this hellhole. I suppose their need for multiple performers is the reason I wasn't sent to the gas chamber yesterday. The officer threatening my life was also pulled away for an incident more pressing than the demand for a grief-ridden song. Still, I know a threat is a threat and never assume someone won't make good on their promises.

Through the lingering notes of my damaged voice, I try to focus on something other than the relentless pain in my chest, and continue watching the movement between the disrobing barrack and disinfection zone to my left. Between each song, I cough up more blood and scoop up whatever clean snow I can find to drip down the back of my throat. The cold numbs some of the pain at least.

The piece we play each morning drawls on and on, the notes repetitive, the song forcefully uplifting. I can't remember if we're on the fourth or fifth verse when a metallic shriek of the gates opening punctuates our music. Another wagon creaks through, ready to collect items from the gas chamber to take back to Kanada discreetly. The SS wouldn't want those who are waiting in line for their turn to take a shower to see a pile of gold teeth, heaps of human hair, or prosthetic limbs passing through. However, the vision of Jews working, laboring, pulling wagons, gives the people in line hope that once they step out of this building, they'll be put to work, too.

Three women enter the gates with an empty wagon. Their heads are down and movements stiff. I can hardly see their faces. The heavy clouds manage to part for a moment, a glow from the sun shredding through the smog, highlighting the women passing by.

A perfect nose with the tip upturned just a smidge, covered in freckles I can't see from here. The sunlight blinds her, marking her eyes with a rich cerulean-blue hue. My heart blasts against my chest as I lock eyes with her, refusing to blink and chance losing sight. I would have seen her come through before. But then she turns her head in my direction, just slightly, just enough to be completely sure it is her I'm looking at. To be unequivocally positive that the light in my life is standing ten footsteps away from me. She's thinner than I remember, her face sharper, her eyes surrounded by a heavy darkness of exhaustion. I forget the words in the song and continue to hum them before filling the missing words with her name.

"Ella," I sing.

No one notices. No one except Ella. She's trying to say something to me, but I can't read the words, and the music drowns out any hope of sound from outside our small circle.

I take a few steps forward as I often do, unable to stand perfectly still while singing, but I haven't tested how far I could move before the guards in the watchtower take notice. I glance up. The guard's back is to the window. I take another step in Ella's direction.

She raises her hand in front of her chest as if she's about to wave, but a square of fabric wavers from her grip as something falls to the ground, rolling in my direction through the dead grass and remnants of melting snow. Once more, I look up at the guard tower then to the gates, finding a moment clear to move a few more steps to retrieve whatever it is Ella just dropped. My pulse races as I slide to my knees, grasp the small jar and return to the circle of musicians, trying to hold a note that clashes painfully with theirs.

My gaze returns to her as she meanders forward, dragging a wagon. She looks at me once more, her lashes flutter heavily over her cheeks, and subtly touches her finger to her pursed lips and releases the kiss in my direction. She continues to move, her position no longer parallel to mine. I can only see the knot of the back of her scarf.

I unclench my hand from the jar, sneaking a quick peek, finding a shimmery amber glow. Honey. It's honey. I would recognize the texture and color anywhere. My throat tightens, not from the strain or relentless pain, but from the ache in my heart, the want, desire and plea to just be next to her when she's so close. Yet, she couldn't be farther away with every obstacle between us.

I'm still watching her walk away as the moment shatters with the growl of a guard's voice. Ella stiffens in response and moves quicker to catch up with the other two wagons in front of her. The square of fabric she had in her hand falls behind her, drifting to the ground like a feather. She must know she dropped it. The guard moves past the entrance to the gas chamber where we're performing and utters something under his breath as he readjusts the rifle on his shoulder.

I slip the jar into the pocket of my shirt; thankful the fabric is baggy on me with all the weight I've lost. It doesn't look like anything is in my pocket since my chest now caves inward.

My hand lingers on the jar, realizing it's still warm from her touch. It's the only warmth we've been able to share here. Mother would have told me I needed honey to heal my injured vocal cords. Ella knew. She remembered. She somehow found honey and now it's in my pocket. More importantly, Ella is alive. She's still walking. She's still working. She's still trying to take care of me.

The guard now following them spots the fabric and grabs it

from the ground, inspecting it closely. My chest tightens as I strain to see if Ella is still making her way around the bed of the building, but I've lost sight of her.

Another guard follows from the gate, passing in front of us. "Louder. Play louder!" His demand is sharp and impatient.

I nod and press against my throat to force out more sound at a higher volume. A shard of glass sliding down my windpipe would hurt less.

"Did you see where this came from?" the guard who retrieved the square of fabric asks the one who just shouted at us. He takes the fabric from the other's hand, inspecting it.

"It must be from one of them with the wagons," I hear from the guard who's still moving ahead, following the wagons.

The guard who shouted at us, now holding the piece of fabric, turns in our direction. His eyes scrutinize me as if he knows I'm the culprit, which I will gladly be if it's between Ella or myself. With the increase of volume in the song, the jar of honey vibrates against the bones in my chest as I arch my shoulders forward to make my shirt hang without a bulge. He's still looking at me. I force myself to sing even louder than I am, praying my voice doesn't give out in return. I'm just hoping the volume is to his liking, enough to make him turn back to whatever he was doing a moment ago.

A cough threatens to break the song, and I clamp my hand around my neck, trying to prevent my body from its habitual workings. The guard's narrowed eyes pierce through me, as if he can smell fear and guilt. A wheeze scrapes the inside of my chest, waiting for him to walk away as thick phlegm and congestion form.

Time remains still until the guard turns his back to me, finally satisfied, or perhaps, bored with mentally torturing me. The piece of fabric still dangles from his gloved fingertips as he strides toward the wagons, his boots crunching on the frozen dirt. He pauses where Ella had stood moments ago, his stare cast to the ground in search of something that isn't there.

Air lodges in my throat. *He knows.* He probably read the guilt branded across my face.

He calls out to the other guards, his voice sharp and demanding but muddled with the music. I didn't hear what he said.

My knees threaten to give out, but I force myself to keep singing, the music scraping against my throat. My gaze is frozen on the indentations from the wagon's wheels in the hard snow. The guard walks through the wheel tracks and points ahead of him. "That one," he shouts.

I want to scream, run, pull their attention back to me and away from her. The honey in my pocket weighs my chest down, a reminder of Ella's sacrifice. The guard's focus on the square of fabric hasn't wavered. I know he's going to find out where it came from, one way or another. That's what they do. Anything they find that shouldn't be here—it tells a story, it rats someone out, it's the demise of someone's life regardless of how insignificant the meaning of the item is—even a scrap of fabric that could have simply belonged to someone whose ashes are rising into the sky at this very moment... Except, it didn't.

FORTY-NINE

ELLA

My heart thumps inside my chest. Luka has the honey he needs. He's alive. I'm alive. That's all that matters. Except, the guard behind us is now shouting at me. I haven't turned around, afraid to catch his eye. What if he saw me drop the jar, or Luka pick it up? It all happened so fast.

Tatiana switched scarves with me since hers has a distinct pattern and mine is plain black. She also let me borrow her Sonderkommando armband, denoting certain prisoners' access to the gas chambers to remove gold teeth, hair, and prosthetic limbs from the bodies before they're taken to the crematorium. The thought of this job would normally be enough for me to stay away from switching roles, but my desperation to see Luka and make sure he received the honey is all I care about. I don't know if the honey will help, but it's something more than what he has. He was so pale and thin, his body hunched forward as if he's carrying something heavy on his back. I may look just as bad... But even if it doesn't help him physically, it could be the boost to his spirits that he needs, and that means everything.

The fabric of my smock scrapes against my back as I'm

jerked backward. "You," a guard seethes in my ear. "Is this yours?"

His spit splatters along my face, but I tell myself it's mist from the sky, so I don't budge or blink. He holds a piece of fabric up in front of my face. "Is it?"

It is mine. I must have dropped it when walking away from Luka. My muscles tense and my grip tightens around the wagon's wooden pull-handle. "What is it?" I ask, nausea rising in my stomach.

"What does it look like?" He holds it closer to my face, nearly pressing it to my nose.

"It's not mine," I say, forcing each word out without a change of inflection.

He drops his hand, slapping it against his side. "I see," he says, clawing his hand around my arm to inspect the Sonderkommando armband that doesn't belong to me. "Go." He points to the back door of the gas chamber. "Do your work first."

He steps away and his words ring through my head over and over, the threat of punishment to follow the cruel labor I'm about to endure—the labor Tatiana endures daily. He didn't look for my number. He didn't write it down. Will he remember me by my pale face that looks like every other female I work alongside?

I catch up to the other two wagons, stepping inside the gas chamber for the first time. I wasn't sure what to expect or what it might look like inside. I've been wondering if the other prisoners still think they're getting a shower once in here, or if they know something else is about to happen once the doors close on them. Or is it not until they fall from the fumes poisoning them that they realize they've been sent into a trap?

The two other women with me line their wagons up just outside the door and pull their scarves down over their noses. I do the same.

I turn away from the overwhelming stench that smacks me

in the face. Even with a scarf covering most of my face, it's worse than the filth I live in. Much worse. A sharp, bittersweet, nutty smell mixed with body fluids, sweat, and rot. You might easily believe they were leaving the deceased bodies in here for weeks with the level of smell, but that isn't the case. I taste the odor, and it seeps down my throat and shrouds my stomach, forcing my throat to constrict. *I can't allow myself to become sick in here.* Someone who does this day in and day out would be numb to their surroundings.

I must get this done with. I force my eyes back open, finding the rectangular chamber sprawled out before me and much larger than it appears from the outside. The walls are white-washed brick, covered with fingernail scratches—the markings outlined with dry blood. There are no windows, only iron caged lights along the ceiling which offer little visibility.

I'm wasting time as I fight against looking down to the ground where the massacre lies. I take in a lungful of potent air and hold it until I become dizzy. The concrete floor is covered with dead bodies, most people having fallen into piles beneath the ceiling vents. They must have thought the water would be coming in that way. There are children's limbs poking out beneath their naked mothers' bodies. My breaths are erratic and short. I'm lightheaded and my stomach pinches painfully.

"What are you waiting for?" one of the other girls whispers to me, knowing we're being watched, though we can't see from where. I bow my head, taking in another trembling breath. "You get the children. We'll lift the adults."

"I thought we were supposed to retrieve hair, teeth, and—" the hushed words stick to my tongue as I struggle to comprehend what we're doing.

"We bring the bodies to the workroom next to the crematorium first." The girl's words come out quickly and while she's moving around, reaching for arms to pull—a reminder not to be caught standing still in here.

There are only three of us and an adult body needs more than one person to lift. I follow the other two around, waiting on them to lift the mothers off their children so I can retrieve the small bodies. I will never forget this image for as long as I live, however short that time might be now.

One by one, I drop each into a wagon as if they're a sack of potatoes rather than lifeless little angels. Tears swell in my eyes and sweat beads on my forehead, seeping into my eyes with a burn. After an hour, it seems we've hardly made any progress and yet we've taken the wagons to and from the crematorium several times already.

Eventually, we carry the last few people to the wagons and leave the chamber empty and prepared for the next victims to meet their demise. I will never be able to close my eyes again and see anything else. How can the German military and police live with themselves knowing what they are doing to all these innocent people? They walk around with smiles on their faces. I don't understand.

Our last pass to the workroom outside the crematorium brings us to organized piles of sorted bodies other Sonderkommandos must have taken care of while we were retrieving. An SS officer steps inside, holding a rag over his nose, and reaches his hand out with a pair of clippers. Neither of the other two girls take it from his hand, so I do. I assume I'm responsible for removing the hair.

I spare myself from watching the other two with their tasks of removing gold teeth and prosthetic limbs. I cut the hair of each person as close to their scalp as I can, taking handfuls and dropping them into a large set of sacks to my side. I don't ever want to know what they do with this hair. I hope my imagination is too weak to ever come up with a possible thought of where it goes next.

A thick film of grease or residue shrouds the hair, making it difficult to cut through. But the other two are moving along much faster, which means I need to keep up. My mind is in a haze as we make it through the bodies. It's been hours and my arms are weak, my head is heavy and my back aches from being hunched over for so long.

We're escorted out of the crematorium building with our wagons full of hair, teeth, and limbs, then led back to the warehouse buildings by a guard. We don't leave the same way we entered. There's a backside passageway into Kanada, away from the line of prisoners waiting to enter the gas chamber. I assume the SS know better than to let the line of people spot us walking by carrying body parts. It would give away their intentions and cause mass chaos.

We stop outside the building where teeth, hair, and limbs are collected within Kanada and lift the sacks two at a time to bring inside. I follow the other two, but before I can step into the building, someone grabs hold of my arm. "Your number?" a man demands from behind me. The man takes the sacks of hair out of my hands and hands them to another prisoner passing by.

"It's—" I hesitate.

"What it is?" he shouts, flinging me around to face him where I find a second guard holding onto Tatiana's arm. Her eyes are wide, full of fear, and it's all my fault. I did this. I asked her to help me, again. I'm still wearing her armband. They must know.

The guard with his grip on me pushes my sleeve up to check my number, since I never answered his question. The other guard holds a clipboard out for him to check. "Foolish women. You don't know when you're lucky, do you?" he snaps. "Now you're about to realize how lucky you were."

Tatiana is shaking, while I'm frozen in place. Say something. I have to say something. "This isn't her fault. It's mine. I forced her to switch places with me."

"Why? No one would choose to carry dead bodies over

working in one of these buildings. You must have had a reason. What was the reason?"

A reason. Anything I say won't be the right answer.

"My back was aching," Tatiana says. "I thought a day's break would make it so I could continue working as normal tomorrow. I didn't want to hinder the work that needs to be done."

The guard standing next to her glares at her as if he's expunging a confession to her lie.

"Is this true?" the guard next to me asks. "You risked both of your lives to help her—a Jew, of all people?"

"Her back hurt. I forced her to switch jobs with me so her back could get better." The lie continues to grow but fits with my previous lie.

The two guards release us and step to the side to speak indiscreetly, leaving Tatiana and me to stare at each other with hollowed eyes. "I'm sorry," I mouth the words to her.

She shakes her head, telling me no.

Movement behind her grabs my attention and I glance at the barbed-wire fence between us. Luka is facing the gate, but from the other side where Gas Chamber number four is located. I've never had to enter these buildings in Kanada as my work has been done on the other side within a different set of buildings.

Our eyes lock for an instant, and I want to tell him to turn back around and continue singing or doing whatever he's supposed to be doing. Watching whatever might happen here isn't going to do him any good.

"Twenty-five whip strokes for each of you," the one closest to me says, grabbing a wooden barrel from near the door of the warehouse, then flipping it upside down.

The other guard steps aside and pokes his head into the warehouse. "All prisoners report outside at once," he shouts.

A wave of dizziness washes over me as I inhale ice cold air that somehow burns my lungs.

All the women within the warehouse congregate outside as directed. "This is what happens if you make the foolish decision to switch jobs with another person. Let this be a lesson to you all."

The guard who checked my number grabs the backside of my smock and tosses me into the barrel, and lifts the smock to expose my entire backside. I'm forced to stare through the barbed-wire fence between Kanada and the gas chamber—from where Luka keeps turning around to see what's happening.

The first whip whistles through the air before striking me like a set of knives searing into my back with a burning pain that radiates across my body. I gasp for air, but choke as the next lash strikes.

Again.

Through the darkness that falls over me, I see Mama's face, her eyes full of worry as she reaches out her arms to lift me up as if I'm just a child who's fallen off my bicycle. And then there's Tata, his calloused hands cupping my cheeks as he presses a kiss to my forehead, his way of telling me everything will eventually be all right. I'm sorry, I want to tell them. I'm so sorry I didn't listen to you... I'm scared. I'm so scared. I need you.

Another slash.

And the dark haze becomes a heavy burden I can longer hold up.

The pain is too much.

With one last deep breath, I let go...

FIFTY

LUKA

January 1945

It's the middle of winter, early morning, but sunlight is seeping in through the few clouded windows. Using every ounce of strength I push my head off my folded arms to glance around the barrack, finding everyone still in their bunks or scattered along the ground. There wasn't a gong ring to wake us or the common shouts of roll call. Those of us who had become used to waking up on our own before five in the morning lost the ability to fight our bodies demanding more sleep and rest. The sound of the gong is all we had to go by. Surely, we didn't all sleep through it.

I place my hand on Etan's shoulder and shake him gently, hoping not to startle him. He was sent to live in this barrack a few weeks ago when people were being separated due to a viral illness sweeping through the buildings. I made room for him on the bunk I share with several others. Aside from Franc, the pianist, on the other side of Auschwitz, Etan is the only other good friend I've come to trust here. In a situation like the one we're in, you might assume that we could all rely on each other in some way or another, but we're forced to protect ourselves, and only ourselves. Any visible sight of camaraderie is a crime fit for punishment.

Etan and I spend our entire days together, which have made it easier to communicate without drawing attention. I can read the look on his face and he reads mine. I know he lost his father and brother upon arriving here, and the woman he was supposed to marry was taken away the night before his deportation to Auschwitz. He has no way of finding her. I've shared my similar woes, except for Ella being here in the same prison camp —that was my burden to carry alone. Now, I don't know how I can carry on any longer...

It's been almost an entire year since Ella took the risk in delivering me the honey. The images from that day have been branded into my mind as I was forced to watch and listen to her brutal punishment from the other side of the barbed wire separating us. Her lifeless body was dragged away, taking what remained of my heart and my hope with it...

"What's happening?" Etan asks, lifting his head so quickly he bumps it on the bunk above ours.

"There was no gong or roll call this morning. Everyone is still asleep or in their bunk. I'm not sure why..."

He pulls himself closer to the edge of the wooden bunk and peers out down the row of others. "Something isn't right."

Nothing has been right for longer than I can recall.

The sound of boots crunching in the snow is followed by a stale whistle working against the cold sounds in the nearby distance outside the barrack. "Hear that?" I ask him.

He twists his head to face the door at the end of our row and the whistle sounds again.

My pulse speeds up as I shake the remaining haze out of my eyes and heaviness from my head.

The door flies open, an officer standing in the opening, a silhouette with the glare of the sun swallowing him whole.

"Everyone out. Now! Gehen! You won't be returning," he shouts, stomping his boot onto the wooden floor then crashing his baton against the door. Snow squalls into a narrow tornado behind him just as the cold air bites at our exposed skin. The officer hits the door three more times, each time with more vehemence than the last. "Gehen!"

All at once, everyone throws their bodies out from between the tiers of bunks and shoves their feet into clogs or boots. Etan and I are among the few fortunate people with boots. I received them with my uniform upon being assigned to perform for the SS. He was in a similar situation before ending up as a performer at one of the gas chambers. Some of the physical laborers have acquired boots, too, but for the most part, the wooden clogs are the standard, and impractical, especially with the frequent snowstorms in the winters.

I grab my blanket, bowl and spoon, not knowing what it means to know we won't be returning. Is this finally the end for me?

Everyone from the barrack is shoved into an unmoving line within seconds following the order, heel to toe as we shuffle forward toward the door. The SS have never failed at their attempts to bring us elements of surprise to disorient us. Once outside, within the freezing temperatures, we're diverted into a few different directions, but led through gates most of us have never passed through before in a direction no one is familiar with. There are plenty of guards manning the line of prisoners along the way as we move closer to the tree line ahead.

Before making it to the trees, two men fall, one bringing the man in front of him down, too. All three of them are subsequently shot without warning then kicked and rolled away from the moving line. I jerk my eyes away. I will never become used to seeing a man lying dead on the ground.

The sight of blood-splattered snow turns my heart into stone. My last memory of Mother was the same, blood blooming away from her head into branches that grew other branches, endlessness until her blood ran dry.

We could all be walking to a mass grave just to get us all out... Etan and I overheard guards speaking about the Soviets' location growing closer. This must be their solution to evade what's coming for them, using us as their shields, most likely.

Our line merges with others, creating an endless thread of weary men dragging their feet through the slushy snow without an end in sight. I've wrapped my blanket around the upper half of my body, using the top as a hood to shield the windblown snow plowing against us.

"Keep moving!" the guards shout, as if we need the constant reminder.

The longer we walk, the less I believe we're walking towards anything more than a grave. But without Ella, without the knowledge that she's alive—I don't know how to continue like this. I don't think I can...

Snow is stuck to my eyebrows and eyelashes despite my attempt to block out the elements. The freezing wind burns my throat with every breath, an addition to the pain I live with daily from damaging an injury over and over, ensuring my vocal cords will never heal. I should be dead from infection. I don't know what has kept me alive. I may never know.

Our trek takes an uphill turn alongside a rocky cliff where another line of prisoners in blue and white striped uniforms are walking in the same direction. The other group all have scarves and must be groups from the women's barracks.

I can wonder all I want, hope or not hope Ella is among them, but the intelligence I used to believe I had would tell me otherwise after what I watched her endure. Everything she did from the moment she stepped into my life was a risk to help me —always just to help me in whatever way she could. Her life's purpose had to be something more than offering me longevity...

but maybe that's all she was ever destined to achieve. And now she's gone...so will I be.

A gunshot echoes between the trees, and I spot a fallen body from the line of women. How many of them have been killed throughout this day-long march? Too many from the line of men have been left behind in the snow after giving up or falling.

What am I fighting for? I need to know.

Etan stumbles a step ahead of me, his boot catching on a patch of icy terrain. I catch him just before he loses his balance, shaking as I strain to hold him upright until he catches a solid footing. "Thank you," he utters through a shaky breath.

The line slows as another incline becomes an obstacle, even for the guards who slip with each step. A German argument ensues from ahead at a gathering of tall pines where the ground is partially thawed beneath the long thick branches covered with a dusting of snow.

"Do you know what they're saying?" Etan utters over his shoulder.

I listen for another moment. "They're arguing over what direction to take."

"No, please, no," I hear from around the bend of trees. It's one of us crying out, followed by a grunt and the thud of a rifle thrashing into something.

Etan glances back at me with terror flashing through his heavy eyes. We watch the guards as they shove others at the top of the hill with the butts of their rifles, forcing them to move faster. Is this it? The end?

Etan moves another few steps forward then stops as my toes reach his heels. "What is it?" I ask him.

I look around him and down, finding the edge of the cliff to our right crumbling into fragments and falling into silence as the distance swallows any noise. There's nowhere else to move with the tree trunks rooting from mounds of snow on our left.

"Move along," I hiss to the men in front of us. "The ground is giving out."

Where the guards aren't actively pushing us off the cliff, the cliff is taking us down itself. Instinct forces the man in front of Etan to turn toward us rather than do as I said. A louder crack rumbles beneath us and the man finally jolts forward into the line of others.

Etan takes a step forward, too, just as the weight of the world becomes too much for the one spot we're standing on. His hand shoots out, grasping for a low hanging branch above us, but it's too late. His face contorts with horror, his jaw drops as if he's about to scream, but there's no sound.

The ground beneath us growls as it crumbles into dust, and we're pulled down the side of the cliff among jagged pieces of falling earth. Shrapnel of snow and rocks rain down around me as I fight against the force of gravity. Desperately, I reach for something to grab hold of, my fingers grasping at nothing but air. But there's nothing—just the ice-cold air I've been a victim to since I arrived here.

The world blurs into streaks and sounds fade into a hollow silence. Images flash through my mind—my family and wonderful childhood full of warmth and love, the fruition of my dream to entertain a crowd with my voice, and Ella. Ella is where my life came together and when I was whole, complete— perhaps that's why this is the end. She was what I was always looking for and I found her. She found me. And now if she's gone, I will be gone, too.

The world tilts and spins, leaving me weightless. The blur of colors fade to black, the cold, pain, and torment of what has been devours me into a void.

FIFTY-ONE

ELLA

January 1945

The cold air bites through my skin, whittling my brittle bones. I've forgotten the sensation of warmth. Yet, somehow, I'm still alive. Then again, *being alive* means *living*, and I'm not sure I can call this *life*. For Luka, my spirit struggles on, but my body... it's starting to fail me. I don't know how long I can keep going for him.

The whipping I took as punishment, almost a year ago, for trying to keep Luka alive, nearly took my life. The deep slashes carved into my back and legs remained raw and open for weeks, the wounds weeping blood and pus through my uniform daily. I fought to keep them clean, but battling infection was nearly impossible. A fever plagued me with bouts of delirium as I trembled on the barrack floor, too weak to move. I should have died then. Perhaps, it would have been better if I had.

Instead, the SS reassigned me to brutal, physical labor. I hadn't appreciated the shelter I had while working in the Kanada warehouses. That work had been its own kind of torment, but this...*this* will kill me.

Another change is upon us, and I've given up trying to predict what will come next. All I know is that for the past week, the gongs have fallen silent—no demands for roll call in the morning or at night.

The first day the gongs didn't ring, the kapos stormed into the barrack, shouting as they forced us outside. We were separated into different groups, though I had no idea where anyone was being taken. Many of the other women I lived with were sent elsewhere, while I was pulled from a line and ordered back to my worksite—the ash pit outside Crematorium number five, where I've spent my days digging trenches to bury human ash.

"Dig!" the kapos keep shouting at us.

I don't understand what they expect from any of us assigned to this job. The shovels aren't making much of a dent in the frozen ash-ridden soil.

My wrists bend and strain against every attempt to break through however many layers of frozen earth they want us to get through. The scabbed cuts along my knuckles stretch, threatening to reopen. The open cuts along my fingers, between my thumb and forefinger begin to bleed again, as they do daily.

It's no surprise Tatiana was sent to continue shoveling, too, after we were caught. Neither of us ever make much progress, but they don't spare us either by death or another ruthless task. Burying ash is our only option even as we watch most of the other prisoners walk through the gates, holding what looks to be their belongings as they leave the premises. No one has ever been allowed outside, and yet, we are watching it happen before our very eyes. Are they going on to live? To have freedom?

If they're being released, why aren't we? Our punishment for switching roles the one time has been ongoing since March, trapping us in a barrack farthest away from where we work each day. Rather than imagine what I must look like to anyone else, I've watched the decline of Tatiana's health, her body becoming a dying, frail tree within the icy grips of winter. One strong gust of wind will take her down.

She is me.

She is Luka.

If he's still here...still alive... Does he look like us, too? Has his body shriveled into nothing but thin bones like ours?

We continue making very little progress throughout the day, but any guard left behind is breaking down buildings and throwing furniture into burn pits.

"The Soviets. They must be almost here," Tatiana says. She's hardly spoken a word all day. All week, really. I'm not sure when she's said more than a few words. Neither of us talks much at all. It takes too much energy we don't have.

"Do you think they'll save us?" I whisper to her. I don't see any guards in near sight, but they're always everywhere.

Tatiana shrugs, her shoulder bones protruding against the fabric of her smock.

"We're getting rid of the evidence—that's what we're doing..." I say, coming to realize what is happening around us.

"I know," she says.

"Tatiana..." My voice cracks as I stare down at my brittle body, skin white as the snow with blue veins swelling across my limbs. "We...are also...evidence."

Tatiana stares at me, her shovel shaking within her hold. She scans the area around us just as I've already done, noticing how few of us there are left. "They still need us. Until they don't, there's nothing more we can do."

We won't know when they will be through with us. They won't give us a warning.

"Yes, there is," I say, my breath escaping me.

Her forlorn eyes stare back at me, and I can see she doesn't have any fight left in her. I never wondered how much the human body could endure, how much damage it could take, the amount of deprivation we can withstand. It seems impossible to still be alive after over three years of fighting to survive in this inhumane prison.

Tatiana doesn't ask any further questions about what I plan to do to prevent us from being tossed into a fire—our existence leaving no trace behind. The longer I stir over potential plans to keep us safe, the more challenges seep into my head, making me rethink my statement of telling her there is something we can do. I'm not sure there actually is.

But if there's a chance Luka is still alive, I must persevere. I promised myself I would never give up—not if there's still a chance. Not if there's hope... *I'm still breathing* and the sun is in the sky.

As the sun slips behind the clouds, a stronger cold front falls over us, bringing along a deeper level of freezing pain that breaks through the dull numbness we burden through every day. My bones ache from weakness while my muscles tighten beyond my control, making it impossible to shovel even a particle of dirt.

The lights on the watchtowers don't power on as usual and the quiet around us is eerie. The others digging along the ash pit have given up and are lying next to their shovels or have gotten up and left. We didn't hear anyone stop them.

"Come on, we should go back to the barrack," I tell Tatiana.

She isn't moving, just staring ahead, her hands still clenched around the handle of the shovel. "Follow me," she whispers.

"Where?" I ask.

She doesn't answer. She drops her shovel and stumbles toward the back electrified fence, but then takes a left turn toward a cluster of trees, leading us behind Crematorium number two, one of the three that's still intact. Crematorium number four, the one Luka had been performing in front of, was burnt down by a group of resistance members within Auschwitz three months ago. I considered us lucky to be away from the uprising outside the Kanada warehouses, but then we heard some people were able to escape. Although, whoever didn't escape and took part in the act, was killed—or so we heard through other whispers.

Could Luka have been among them? Did he make it somewhere safe before it was too late?

I try not to think about what might have happened to Luka if he was still performing over there. I don't know what happened to him after I was caught last March. I want to believe he's still okay somewhere, still alive, maybe even one of the lucky ones who managed to escape. But once I was moved away from the Kanada warehouses, there was no possibility of hearing him sing. Sometimes, I hear other orchestras play, their sound traveling only on the wind, but that all stopped a week ago, too, when most everyone here was taken away. Any hint of music disappeared with the others, leaving us behind in silence.

The quiet is unbearable. *If all the music is gone, Luka must be, too... Is there even a chance for him now?*

I glance up at the dark watchtower, having never been within mere footsteps of one. I can only assume there isn't a guard up there because there isn't a spotlight or any lighting for that matter. They would have already seen us by now, I suppose, and being directly beneath them is likely safer than being within their view. There's another watchtower next to the trees, and it's hard to see if there's anyone in there. Tatiana takes another left, bringing us to the other side of the gas chamber and crematorium.

The trees become less dense the farther we walk, offering visibility to the two-cylinder sewer plants on the other side of another fence. Tatiana stops to the side of a small wooden warehouse, peers around the darkness as if she could see much of anything more than what's in front of us, and rattles the door handle.

It's hard to believe the door might be unlocked, but nothing is as it was ten days ago. "It's unlocked because they removed all the cans of Zyklon B," she says, as if she already knew what I was thinking.

I wasn't aware this was where they kept the gas, but as a Sonderkommando she had access to more areas than I did when working in Kanada.

She closes us inside the dark building and paces around blindly until I hear her hand bump against something hollow and metal.

A squeal from a hinge echoes around us, sparking my heart into heavier thuds, bringing along a wave of dizziness. The sound of metal scraping against more metal disturbs our attempt of silence, and I have no idea what she might be doing.

"It isn't much," she says.

"What isn't?"

"The guards kept a stash of food taken from the one of the buildings in Kanada. I'm not sure if any of this is edible since it was taken from personal belongings, but it's something."

Tatiana has gone from staring out into a void all day to possibly finding us food in an SS warehouse. I'm not sure how we'll manage to bring whatever she's carrying back to the barracks without being spotted, but she seems confident despite the number of guards still here.

A thud startles me, but it's followed by a light scratching noise. "Are you all right?"

"Come down to your hands and knees," she says. "Follow my voice." A panel of wood flooring creaks and shakes the ground. What is she doing? "Hurry."

My knees swell upon dropping to the ground—agony throbs through each stretch, scratch and pull while searching by touch for Tatiana in the dark. Another wooden panel creaks. "What is this?" I ask.

"A place to hide. Help me lift these floor planks up and to the side." I scoot around until my hands catch on the wobbling plank she's tugging away from the floor. I help her move it and then four more panels to the side. "That should be good. We can fit now. I'm climbing in."

I keep my hand on her back as she lowers herself into the opening. Then, I slip down next, finding the depth to be just the right amount of space for us to sit upright. There's concrete below us. It's cold, frozen maybe, but it's not dirt or water. *Water.* How long does she think we can hide in here? *Why* are we hiding? What are we hoping for?

I want to believe she's thought this all through, but neither of us are in our right minds. She reaches up to slide the floor panels back in place over our heads. I follow her lead until we're completely concealed beneath the floor of this small warehouse.

There's no telling when they'll burn this structure down. We've been watching them decimate everything around us. We won't be able to escape once it's up in flames.

"I'm not sure this is a good idea," I tell her. "There may not be a warning before this building goes up in flames, too."

"Let's just pick through the food first and maybe have a meal before we decide where to go next," she says, already plundering through loose items into what sounds like a canvas bag. "Sausage. It's sausage, Ella," she cries out. "And biscuits." The thought of sausage draws a groan from my stomach. I hear her tearing at a paper wrapper, struggling through quiet grunts. "I've got it."

She's quiet for a minute then slaps her hand against my chest. "He-re," she says, her mouth full. I find a thin sausage in her hand and bite down on it gently, wondering how stale it might be. I haven't chewed on anything harder than a potato in years. It's firm, and a bit tough, and my teeth ache, but I manage to tear off a bite and hold it in my mouth, savoring the mild spices mixed with fat. Drool pools at the corners of my lips and I chew the bite as many times as I can before swallowing. It hits the bottom of my hollow stomach and a frenzy of violent hunger ravages through me.

"Here," I say, handing the sausage back to her, knowing she's just as hungry.

"We'll split it, don't worry. You can open the packet of biscuits. We can share those, too." The moment I tear open the paper around the biscuits, I question if we should be saving what we can. There's no telling how long we'll be stranded here with whatever is left of the piles of rotting potatoes. We've barely received a full slice of bread in the past week.

But the justification of preserving food is forgotten with each bite I take, reveling in the sweet and smoky spices swelling against my tongue and dancing down my throat.

We finish the sausage and eat most of the biscuits before leaning back against the short cement wall and resting our heads against each other's. If we burn inside of this building, at least we got one last taste of flavored food.

I didn't think we would fall asleep, but the sunlight filtering in between the floorboards yanks me awake. My neck is stiff from not moving all night and my behind is numb from the cold floor. Why is light leaking through the wooden floorboards above our heads? There aren't any windows in this warehouse.

I shake Tatiana and place my hand over her mouth before whispering in her ear, "Don't say a word."

The wooden planks above our head groan, following heavy footsteps. I'm breathing so hard I might faint. There's no telling who is in here or what they're looking for, but if it's a guard, they won't hesitate to bury us with this building.

The metal closet whines and groans as someone swings the doors around. "It's empty," a man says.

"I doubt that," a second man says, following another set of footsteps above our heads. "This one is loose."

The floorboard right above us creaks and more light spills into the crawlspace as the wood begins to lift. I hold my breath as if it will save me, and wrap my arms around Tatiana.

"Are you Poles?" a man asks, his Russian accent thick and surprising.

"Yes. Yes, we are. What's happening?" I cry out, shoving my feet against the dirt, pushing away from the men.

The man standing closest to the hole we're in holds his palms up. "Let us help you."

Tatiana grabs my arm and shakes her head. "No, no. The Germans—they'll kill us. Don't tell them we're under here, please. We beg of you."

The Russian man crouches and reaches his hand in again. "They can't hurt you now." I look over at Tatiana. She's shaking, as am I. How do we trust anyone in a war? But what other option do we have now?

With hesitation, I glance up at the man, noticing his Soviet military uniform. Vehicles are rumbling in the near distance, but I don't hear gunshots. I don't hear combat.

"We should go with them," I tell Tatiana.

She stares at me with wide eyes, unblinking, unsure. Still, I reach for the soldier's hand, and he carefully pulls me out of the hole first and places me down against a light post. The other soldier with him helps Tatiana out and sits her by my side. "The Germans ran when we arrived. We're going to do all we can to help you and the others still here. You can trust us."

I look into the man's eyes, telling myself I need to see a hint of trust before I can believe the word.

He stares back at me, and I notice the struggle in his throat as he swallows. He's human, like me and Tatiana. I can see the pain in his eyes. He's likely already seen too much today from what he's walked in on here.

"Will you help me find someone?" My voice squeaks above

a whisper. I don't even know if Luka is still alive, never mind here in Birkenau still, but I must ask. I need to know.

"Of course. We want to help all of you. We have aid to offer and food."

"Is it over?" Tatiana asks, her voice soft and hesitant.

"Almost. Almost."

FIFTY-TWO

LUKA

February 1945
Unknown Location

My eyes are heavy and burn against the bright light above me. I try to blink, but the ache makes it hard to fight through. I rest for another minute before trying again. This time, my eyes open enough to make out a blurry image of a wall. With hesitation, I peer down at my legs, finding a sheet over them. The hazy view of my hands resting on my stomach is clearer than the wall and my legs, but unfamiliar all the same. Blurs of motion move between my feet and the walls, and I can't turn my head to see who or what is passing by.

"Good morning," a woman says, lifting my arm as if it belongs to her instead of me. "Can you tell me your name?" Her accent is thick and hard to understand. I've never seen her before. She has short black hair and a round face. "Your name?" she repeats. I open my mouth to speak, but a film of phlegm prevents sound from forming. Even if I could speak, I wouldn't know what to say. "It'll come back to you in a few minutes. It always does."

The confusion of where I am and who this woman is sucks the wind out of me. "Where am I?" I force out, my words only floating on air. "Who are you?"

"Let's help you remember who *you* are first," the woman says. "You'll remember, don't worry."

My stiff neck makes it hard to twist my head in either direction, but I spot a row of beds, which doesn't help me piece together anything more now. "I don't—"

The woman's unwavering expression relaxes as she pulls a wooden chair away from the wall and up to my side. She touches her hand to my arm, and I don't like the sensation, which makes me flinch. She moves her hand and nods her head. "You are safe now. That is what's most important."

Safe? What does that mean? I continue to look at her as my eyes focus more clearly. I notice lines on the sides of her eyes, curving downward like a frown, but she maintains a tight-lipped smile. My chest muscles tense despite the friendly nature of this woman, but she isn't making any sense. "Who am I safe from?"

Again, my throat produces very little sound other than a rasp, despite my effort to speak up. A burn radiates down my neck, forcing me to clutch the fabric covering my body. The woman reaches to her side and brings back a metal cup, edging it closer to my face. I don't move away from the cup, but peer inside as she pushes it close enough to touch with my lips. The cool sensation against my mouth is followed by a gentle swig of water rushing over my tongue, instantly soothing the raw dryness in my mouth and throat. I swallow, but not without effort, which doesn't feel right—as if I've forgotten how.

"Take your time," the woman says. "Disorientation is common. You've been through a lot."

My mind spins in circles but won't stop to grasp onto any solid thought or memory. "What have I been through?" These questions come out on their own even though I don't want to ask her anything.

Her brows knit together as if she's the one who doesn't understand what's happening right now. "We'll talk about that soon. Let's focus on getting stronger first."

Her refusal to give me answers sends frustration shooting through me. I blink a few times, trying to see through the foggy darkness inside of my head, searching for the answers on my own. Flashes of images come and go, but so fast and unsteady that it's hard to put anything together aside from the shape of faces, or a field of snow, cold air, a tannic smell that gnaws at my stomach.

"Why can't I remember anything?" I ask, my voice breaking, sound piercing through my panic.

The woman takes in a deep breath then drops her shoulders. "When a person goes through an immense amount of trauma, the mind will find ways to protect itself to allow time for healing."

Trauma. She keeps saying different words that only scare me more, rather than clarifying anything. The way she says the word "trauma" makes my head heavy, like it's full of water swishing back and forth. I clench my fists and slide them up higher on my chest, finding red lines across my knuckles and white scars over the top of my hands. These aren't my hands. They can't be. I haven't done anything to injure myself. Or is that why I'm here?

I focus on her face harder now, trying to hold my eyes steady to look at hers. "Tell me the truth. Tell me exactly where I am right now."

A sigh expels from her throat, and she glances to her side for a moment. "This doesn't get any easier," she mutters.

"I don't understand," I follow.

She looks back at me once more, still with a sympathetic expression. "You were brought here from Przczyna, about a day's walk from Auschwitz."

The name hits me like a hammer against my head, filling

the space around me with a shrill noise I can't block out. Auschwitz...thick fog floating over barbed-wire fences, snow everywhere, boots crunching around me before the shouting begins and then a smell so potent it forces a wave of nausea through me.

"No, that's not right," I utter through a whisper. "I—I wasn't —what is Auschwitz? You must be mistaken."

Her chin trembles and I don't understand why. She doesn't know me. I don't know her. Why would she feel anything at all? Maybe I'm missing a face. Is that what this is? She's letting me down easily. How would I have lost a face? I can't recall anyone's face, even my own.

"You were in Auschwitz. You've been through—you're alive, and that's all that matters."

"Alive? How? I'm here and I haven't the foggiest idea where here is. Is this it? Is this how I'll always be now? Lost in this body that may or may not belong to me?"

"I understand this is hard, but I'm trying to help you. Do you recall your name now?" She's asking again as if something has changed during our uncomfortable conversation.

I drop my hands to my side, fabric brushing against the inside of my palms. I refocus my stare at the wall ahead, noticing it's no longer blurry. It's yellow, a pale yellow. Again, I glance down at my legs, still covered with a sheet, and then realize I'm on a bed, but nothing around me is familiar. Nothing belongs to me.

"No," I finally say, my eyes burning from a hard stare at this stranger.

"It's all right. Some days are better than others. You remembered your name and many other details yesterday. It's still early in the day," she says, another forced smile returning to her lips.

As she continues coming up with reasons for me not to worry, my attention draws to the ticking of a clock and the swoosh of a broom, and a murmur of static from a radio. Other voices grow louder, some with accents I don't recognize, some with a slur in their words, some speaking clearly with a sense of logic, and some like this woman, just calm and gentle. I turn to face the rest of the room once more, looking beyond my immediate sides this time, finding more than just beds in a row. People are on the beds—injured people with bandages, some who look like skeletons lying in a cloud of fluff, others stiff and staring at the ceiling as if they're dead. Other women dressed like the one who has been speaking to me weave in between the beds helping the other people, each of them with a forced smile and careful movements.

I take another look at the injured people to my side and stop at a person a few beds away from me. He's one of the people who looks like a skeleton and is also staring up through the ceiling. An unexpected pull to him makes me wonder if I've met him before.

"Who is that?" I ask, nodding in his direction.

The woman sitting beside me follows my gaze. "That's Etan," she says. "He arrived here around the same time as you, but he hasn't spoken much yet."

His name is familiar. It is. I want it to be. *Etan.* I say it to myself again and again, waiting to retrieve more information about him. "I know him. I think I know him." Maybe I don't. But if I do, it might mean my memories will return like they did yesterday.

"I'm not sure. You were both found in the same clearing of the woods, unconscious, but breathing. The Soviet soldiers who rescued you said it appeared you both took a significant fall off a cliff, which explains your head injuries and the memory loss as well as the other physical trauma you've sustained. But we're here to help and we're taking good care of you now."

FIFTY-THREE

ELLA

February 1945
Unknown Location

The voices of the Soviet soldiers still repeat in my ears as I sit on a hard bench in the back of a transport truck. "We haven't found any record of Luka Dulski," an aide said upon answering my plea to help me find someone.

The relentless battle to survive, pushing myself beyond limits, and forcing myself to hold on just another minute, hour, and day has rendered me helpless—unable to find words, stay upright, or fully understand what's happening. The fight inside of me has left my body.

And if Luka is gone after this relentless fight—what was it worth?

The word liberation waves in the air like a flag in the wind, but the meaning seems open to interpretation. Who won? Did anyone win something? It seems we all lost. Our friends, our family, our humanity, our lives... Is the war even over?

Tatiana's head falls heavily on my shoulder, her breaths short and quick but steady. The soldiers promised us food and medical care, but the look in their eyes spoke a different truth. Maybe I've lost the ability to trust another person, but something tells me they were offering a sense of hope to keep us alive a bit longer. They gave us bread and soup, the warmth of the liquid was like new blood being pumped through my veins, and though the bread was as stale as what we've grown used to, it was bread to help us, not to keep us alive for the sake of being a slave.

The journey from Auschwitz to a displacement camp is foggy. I'm not sure how long we've been in this truck, how far we've traveled, or where this location might be. The other faces of people around us are unfamiliar, gray, and I keep wondering if some of them are still breathing. *Would Luka be unfamiliar? He could be looking for me, too, but would he recognize me?*

Tatiana mumbles something against my shoulder but as I peer down at her, I see she's asleep, dreaming perhaps. Her words don't make sense. Perhaps that means she's somewhere better within her mind now.

If I could sleep soundly, maybe I'd dream of Luka—him waiting somewhere for me. But I don't dream anymore. Maybe I'll wake up and find out that everything I experienced over the three and a half years was a horrific nightmare. What if I never wake up again?

The truck stops and we're assisted out and into a collection of connected tents. The air inside is warm but only from the amount of people surrounding us. The smell of smoke is strong, mildew, sweat, and the decomposition of every living thing.

Doctors and nurses run in every direction. There are many, but I can't imagine there are enough for the number of decaying people standing about. They won't be able to help everyone, no matter how hard they try. It's impossible.

I'm holding Tatiana up, but losing my grip. Her ankles drag behind her as I pull her along from under her arms. The fight has left her body, too.

A nurse comes by and takes her by the arm, hoisting her upright to remove her weight from me. "I need to take her with me," the woman says.

"No," Tatiana groans but doesn't fight against the nurse holding her. She can't.

"They need to help you," I tell her, placing my dirt-covered hand on her cheek. "Let them help you. You're safe now."

My words linger in the air after they take her away. I just hope I'm right...

FIFTY-FOUR

ELLA

May 1945

Many weeks have passed, and I remain in the same haze as the one I was in when I arrived, dormant on a cot, staring up at the crease of a pitched tent. Conversations drift around me, some I hear, others float by unnoticed, but someone said Warsaw was no longer unreachable. I don't know if someone can find my family, if I even still have one. The odds seem impossible, but if I've heard proper information, transport is being organized to take citizens of Warsaw back home. Within hours, I'm escorted onto a bus. "You're going home," someone said. "We'll do whatever we can to help you find your loved ones once you arrive there." The words are hollow.

The bus travels harshly over broken roads and rubble, leaving me to do little else but wonder if I'll recognize Warsaw. It will never look the way I remember. The other people on the bus aren't talking either. No one has any idea what we're traveling toward, aside from a place we used to call home. What will be left of it? And can I even call it home if Luka won't be there to greet me...?

I fall asleep for brief spurts of time, but only fully open my eyes when the squeal of the bus brakes slashes through my ears. I'm not sure where we are. I don't recognize anything outside the window. Yet, Red Cross volunteers are helping us off the bus, one by one, and walking us toward a brick building. I should recognize this building if it's in Warsaw.

When it's my turn, I hold my focus on the steps leading off the bus then the curb, and the broken blocks of pavement and rubble, walking down a narrow path toward the building we're being taken into. I can walk, but the volunteer holds on to me as if I can't.

Another bench awaits me inside the building, next to others who have departed the same bus. There's a lot of people talking, but not those of us who came from the bus. People passing by stare at us as if we're unearthed dinosaurs. They aren't sure what to think of us. I suppose I might act the same way if I was seeing us all for the first time.

A figure walks toward me but I don't look up properly until they're within reach. Then suddenly he's on his knees, grabbing my hands. "Ella," he cries out.

For a long moment, I fixate on him—recognizing him, but having trouble finding my words. All I can do is ask myself if this is real. I don't know anymore.

"Ella, it's me..."

My heart—it's torn in half.

My gaze settles on his eyes, awakening my nerves.

"Tata," I utter.

It is him. He's here. He gathers me in his arms and pulls me to his chest. "My baby. My Ella."

"Tata," I say again, my voice croaky. "I'm home."

He kisses my face, my forehead, cheeks, and nose before scooping me up into his arms and walking away from the bench with me. I rest my head on his chest and let my eyes fall closed while listening to his heart race. "This is my daughter. My papers are in my left pocket. Her name is Ella Bosko. She's twenty-three years old, birth date is the tenth of July 1921—born in Warsaw."

"Yes, sir, the information matches. You can take her with you, but she will need further medical follow ups."

"All right," Tata says, moving ahead with me toward the front doors. He nuzzles his cheek on top of my head then pulls the collar of the donated coat I received at some point in the last few weeks. "Keep warm, sweetheart."

"Ella!"

"Dear me—"

The voices are a dream. I recall them so well. They sound so real.

"I'll take her, Tata."

I blink my eyes open, but I'm blinded by the sun glaring down. I'm shuffled from Tata's arms into Miko's.

"Miko?" I utter.

His chest bucks in and out, rattling me around. "She's alive," he cries out.

Mama's hand presses to my cheek. I would recognize the touch of her hand out of all the hands in the world. "My sweet girl," she squeaks through a held breath. "I didn't think—" Her words trail into a grim sob, one I feel in my chest, but doesn't do anything to me. I've forgotten how to cry. I've forgotten how to live.

"Come on, let's get her home and out of the cold."

Miko cradles me like Tata, but squeezes me tighter against his chest and walks harder with heavier steps.

"This is real," I whisper. I clench my eyes shut again, trying to convince myself. If I say it enough, it must be true. But also, no one is looking for Luka—or waiting for him here at home. *That, too, is real.*

* * *

Mama lets me sit in her rocking chair with the knitted blanket I used to sleep with when I was little. Our apartment is the same, unchanged, but also, foreign. I can't differentiate the life in Auschwitz from the comfort of a home.

Mama, Tata, and Miko haven't left my side in the two weeks I've been home. The grocery store is closed temporarily, even though I asked them not to do that to the people who might be depending on them. "There are plenty of other markets around. They can go elsewhere for now," he said.

Mama keeps replacing the cup of hot tea I hold in my hands most of the day. It never becomes cool. They all stare at me most of the time, as if they're waiting for me to start talking and tell them what I've gone through. But I've decided I won't do that to them after putting them through the torture of thinking I was dead. They've dealt with enough and don't deserve the added burden of the truth.

"I'm well enough to start looking for Luka," I finally get the courage to tell them. I'm not sure how they will react. It's hard to assume what they might know about my arrest or what is still a mystery to them.

"Luka," Tata repeats. "You were trying to save him when you were arrested, isn't that right?" I suppose he gathered that much. He was part of the resistance; I shouldn't be too surprised at his insight.

"Yes," I say, staring down into the honey brown liquid in my cup.

"God made you good, my sweetheart. No one can fault you for that. I blame myself for not realizing what obstacles you were moving through to care for him and his family. Arte's father found me shortly after the two of you were arrested and told me what had been going on. He blamed himself as much as I did. Arte was helping you so he could help his family with the food you were bartering with, and you were helping Luka by risking your life. Your acts of bravery far surpassed anything your brother and I were ever doing, and I would have stopped you had I been aware of the danger you were putting yourself in. But none can fault you for having a heart of gold."

"It might have been for nothing. That might change your mind," I say.

"For nothing? How can that be?"

"He was taken to Auschwitz, too. Luka. I'm not sure if he survived. If he didn't, all I did was keep his family alive long enough to endure the most unthinkable—"

"Endure what?" Tata asks, pressing me to finish my statement.

I stare past him, my eyes blurring. "Auschwitz."

Tata reaches for the coffee table behind him and tears off a piece of the newspaper.

"Miko, grab a pencil." He stands from the corner he's been sitting beside me every day and does as Tata asks, hurrying back within a few seconds. "Jot out his name and birthday."

"Luka?" I ask.

"Yes. Whatever information you have about him, write it down."

Mama takes a book from the mantel and places it on my lap, trading it for the teacup I'm holding. "There you go," she says.

Tata places the torn newspaper down on the book and Miko hands me the pencil. All of them watch as I carefully jot out Luka's information. I place the pencil down and Tata takes the scrap of newspaper and folds it up as Mama takes the book and pencil.

Tata steps away, his movements filled with tension. He trembles as she slips his coat over his shoulders and slips the folded scrap into his pocket.

"Where are you going?" I ask, pushing myself up from the rocking chair, the blanket slipping from my shoulders. My voice cracks, punctuating how frail my strength still is.

Tata glances at me, his eyes tired with a web of red veins.

"I'll find the right people to speak to, dear. I won't let it all be in vain if I can help it. Stay with your mother and rest."

"I need to—I need to know," I whisper through my tight throat. "I can't bear—"

"We will find answers," Miko says. "We will. I promise."

The two of them leave the apartment, and the door closes with a hollow thud leaving us in stark silence. Mama bends down to lift the fallen blanket and wraps it back around my shoulders, leading me to the sofa rather than the rocking chair. She helps me sit and takes the seat beside me, holding me within her arms. "It wasn't for nothing," she says. "It was for love."

"Love. I might have to live forever without it now," I say.

Mama tightens her arm around my shoulder. "Ella, at the end of life, we die. Every one of us. A lesson almost every person must learn is that with love comes inevitable consequence. You could be with the person you love for fifty years and live a beautiful life together, but one of you will have to endure losing the other at the end. Grief is a consequence of love, young and old."

Mama's words bring an ache to my chest. I realize what she's saying is true, but it isn't just grief I will live with. It will be the horrors we both faced leading up to an untimely death.

* * *

I've been watching the clock since Tata and Miko left. Nearly three hours have passed and each creak of the stairs in the building causes my heart to race and my stomach to twist in pain.

If Tata finds an answer—the one I'm most fearful of—I might regret giving up any chance of hope in finding him. There won't even be a gravestone with his name. None of the people who were sent to the gas chambers will have one. Even those who were executed were sent to crematoriums. There are no remains.

Just as the sun dips beneath the horizon, I recognize the two pairs of heavy footsteps hopping up the stairs. It's them. They're walking fast, which tells me they know something.

I stand up from the sofa and clutch my hands over my chest, waiting for the door to open.

They burst in, both with their shoulders slouched forward and a curious lack of expression on their faces. I notice an envelope dangling from Tata's fingers, covered in inky fingerprint marks.

"Tata," I whisper, trying to speak against the agony riveting through me. "What did you find?"

Mama stands and holds her arm around my shoulders, waiting for him to answer.

Tata releases a slow exhale and shifts his gaze to my eyes. "We found information," he says.

I'm still holding my breath because information could mean anything. "Is he—" I can't get the words out. I can't breathe.

Miko nods, but his expression doesn't change—still flat, nothing. "Yes, he's alive," he says, swallowing hard after his last word.

I gasp, as the air is sucked out of my lungs. "He's alive?"

"Yes," Tata confirms. "But..."

"But what?" Mama follows sharply. "Say it."

Tata hesitates despite Mama's demand. His fingers tighten around the envelope. "We don't know everything yet," he says. "But, sweetheart, he's in a displacement camp. He's not well."

"Wh-what do you mean? Wha-what does that mean?" I ask, my eyes searching between Tata and Miko as I step in closer to them. "What's wrong with him?"

"He's in a trauma unit for people suffering from severe memory loss whether from injury, psychological conditions, or both."

Tata hands me the envelope and I push myself to lift my arm to take it from him. "He won't recognize me?"

"Sweetheart, I don't know anything more than what I've told you. His location is inside the envelope."

Mama takes the envelope from my hand and pulls me into her chest, embracing me tightly. "We'll figure it out," she whispers. "We will."

FIFTY-FIVE

LUKA

May 1945

Time: *Nine weeks and three days,* I write at the top of my journal entry after peeking at the previous page that says: *Nine weeks and two days.*

Name: Luka Dulski

I graze the tip of my pencil to the blank space following the prompt.

What do I remember today:

While staring at the red marked scars lining my knuckles for a moment, I collect my thoughts before jotting them down.

My family is dead, but I'm alive.

Etan. I know him. We're friends. He's doing much better than I am. He's here with me.

I like to eat and listen to the record player.

That's good enough for today. I close the journal and place my pencil down. A man in uniform passes by my bed with a little girl by his side, holding his hand. His shoes are loud on the floor, making my ears hurt. I blink and the black uniform becomes green, and the little girl begins to scream as he drags her down the row of beds. I blink again, and his uniform returns to black and the little girl is calm and walking on her own. Every time I drift into a dark haze, I see something different— something other than what's in front of me. I try to grasp hold of the image just to understand the meaning, but no matter how hard I try, it fades away.

"Luka…"

I open my eyes, giving up the fight. Etan is standing by my bedside, his hands tucked into his pockets. After nine weeks, I can finally see his face is becoming fuller, less hollow around his cheeks. He looks healthier. I'm not ready to see what I look like. I won't recognize the reflection.

Etan said we were prisoners together in Auschwitz, performers together, he a violinist, and me a singer. It's hard to imagine anyone performing in a prison. It's hard to imagine me as a singer when my voice sounds like I've swallowed a bunch of rocks. Most of the time I still whisper, feeling less pain that way.

"Are you doing all right? You look a bit lost today," he says, pulling up a stool from behind my bed.

"Sure. I wrote in my journal," I say, gesturing to the closed notebook on my lap. "The nurse says it helps."

Etan's lips curl into a half smile. "She's right. You're getting better every day. You remember much more now each day than you did weeks ago. It's progress."

"I suppose." I glance at my hands again, flexing my fingers while watching the scars stretch and shrink as if they'll speak to me in some way, or fill in the missing pieces I can't find. "There are still so many gaps. There are still so many things that don't make sense."

"They will," Etan says, his head tilting to the side. His empathy is pure, full of optimism. "Give yourself time."

Time. The word on everyone's lips here. Time will do this, and time will do that. In time, we'll all be better. Is it true though?

The man in uniform returns from whoever he was visiting, the little girl still holding his hand. "Come along, Ella, we have one more person to visit before we go," he says.

Ella... Ella.

I open my journal and flip through the pages until I find the one where I've been keeping track of names that come to mind. I find the letter E with a dash following. It could be for Etan.

E could be for—the vision of a long flowing braid with wisps of golden hair flying against a face covered in light freckles. A sweet, gentle laugh. She turns her head and—Etan is waving his hand in front of my face.

"Where did you go?"

"Do I know someone named Ella?" Etan stares at me without answering and I don't understand why. It's a yes or no answer. "Well?"

"You tell me," he says.

"Blonde hair, a braid, a beautiful laugh..." I describe the vision.

Etan shifts his weight from one foot to the other. "No one really had much hair where we were—"

I repeat her name in my head several more times, trying to call for another vision to appear in my mind. I shut my eyes and say her name once more. A reel of darkness steals my memory again. I reopen my eyes, finding a nurse passing by.

"Did I mention the name to you before?"

"Yeah, yeah you did," he says but with unease like he doesn't want to say anything more about this person.

By dinner time each day, I've exhausted my mind past the brink of being able to form new thoughts and I easily fall asleep, ready to chase memories through dreams, hoping to capture them and keep them with me when I wake up. I imagine a long braid, blonde wisps of hair against a face full of freckles. I reach out and sweep the hair off her face, finding a glittering smile with dimples at each end. A nose that turns up just slightly at the end like a doll's face. And eyes the color of the Mediterranean Sea. She's beautiful. Her cheeks blush after holding her stare to mine for too many seconds and she looks down, but her smile remains. My heart thunders in my chest and my stomach fills with nerves that make me happy.

The smell of coffee and eggs pushes the image away and I open my eyes to the sun shining in through the window, marking another day here in this bed, in this place where I don't want to be anymore.

"Good morning," a nurse says, placing a tray of food down on my lap. "How are you feeling this morning?"

"Fine, thank you," I say.

"Can you remember what your name is?" she continues.

"Yes. My name is Luka Dulski."

"That's music to my ears, my good man," she says.

The nurse continues delivering trays down the row of other patients like me, but then returns to the foot of my bed. "I haven't had a chance to finish my food yet," I tell her.

"Take your time, dear. When you're through with breakfast though, there's someone here to see you. I can bring you into a more private space so we can make sure you have quiet, and a bit of time to process your thoughts to see if you remember this person. Does that sound all right with you?"

My family is dead—my mother, father, grandmother, and grandfather. She's the nurse who told me so. "Of course," I say.

I scrape up the food on my plate and eat faster than I should. Though it's been a while since I've gotten sick from eating too quickly.

"You're supposed to take your time with that, Luka," the nurse says, returning to my side.

"I did. I would like to see whoever came to visit."

The nurse helps me into a wheelchair, not because I can't walk, but because of the risk of falling. The injury I sustained to my head will need time to heal, though it doesn't hurt anymore. But the nurses and doctors insist I be cautious for a while.

The nurse wheels me out of the ward and into a closed off space with a small window. "I'll be right back with your guest," she says.

I wheel myself over to the window to look outside from this angle of the building. There isn't much to see other than another building almost within reach.

"Luka..."

I suck in a breath before turning around, searching for a memory of the voice, but nothing flashes through my mind. I twist my chair around, finding a young woman with short blonde hair, rosy cheeks. She's frail, with a lot of uncertainty in her bright blue eyes.

"Yes, that's me," I say with a hoarse rasp.

My response makes her chin tremble, but she walks closer to me. "Do you remember who I am?" she asks, her voice unsteady.

The longer I take to answer, the more sorrow fills her pretty eyes. "What's your name?"

She shudders an inhale. "Ella. Ella Bosko."

"Ella," I repeat. "I know—I know your name." But how are we connected?

"You do?" she asks, her voice full of hope.

"There's a girl with a long blonde braid, freckles, and the sweetest laugh—I see her in my dreams," I tell her.

Her eyebrows furrow as she stares at me. "I did have a long braid," she says, weaving her fingers through short strands that end at her chin. Again, she takes a few more steps closer to me and kneels so she's not hovering over me. The light that filters in through the window behind me highlights freckles across her cheeks.

"You're Ella—the one in my dreams."

She smiles and sniffles. "Yes, it's me. I don't know what you went through after I last saw you..."

"Were you in Auschwitz, too?"

Her eyes gloss over and widen. "Yes, I was, but there were many months between the time I saw you last and—"

"When I suffered a head injury and lost my memory," I say, finishing her sentence.

She nods and places her hand gently on my knee. The warmth of her fingers sends a chill up my spine. "We loved each other very much, but we were separated in Auschwitz, so it was hard to see each other."

"We loved each other?" I ask, a smile lifting my cheeks.

"Yes," she says, her voice breaking. I'm hurting her and it's the last thing I'd ever want to do.

"Are you—my wife?"

Ella laughs through a gentle sigh—and the sound paints a picture in my mind... *I see her sitting in a tree beside me. Both of us are swinging our legs. I wrap my arm around her and hold her tightly.*

"No," she says.

"Was there a tree—did we sit in a tree, and did I wrap my arm around you? Or am I imagining something that didn't happen? It's hard to tell the difference lately."

With another trembling breath, she nods, hope flashing in her eyes. "We had a tree. It was our tree. Our favorite of all the trees."

"You mean to tell me I sat in a tree with a beautiful girl who I loved and didn't ask her to marry me?" Suddenly, a form of desperation pleads for the answer.

"Someone else you love once told me, 'Marriage is nothing more than a binding piece of paper, and nowhere on it do the words describe the meaning of love.' That was enough for us."

The words drawl in my head as a voice different from Ella's. "My grandmother said that, didn't she?" I whisper.

Ella smiles again. "She did."

"She must have loved you, too."

"The world was once filled with love, and we'll have that again soon, I believe," Ella says.

"I hope so," I say.

Ella sighs and drops her gaze. "I don't want to take up too much of your time today. I'm sure you—"

"Time. Too much time? There's not enough time," I tell her. "I almost ran out of time. Don't go. Please. Don't go."

She presses her hand to her chest. "No, no of course not. I won't leave if you don't want me to. I just—"

"Don't be so courteous. If I've learned anything about myself in the last couple of months, it's that I don't like when people are careful when they speak to me. I already know I'm broken."

"You're not broken, Luka."

"May I hold your hand?" I ask, holding mine out. She doesn't hesitate to lift hers and weave her fingers between mine. "Just for a moment."

With a struggle, she rises, wincing a bit as she does. I recognize that pain. I drop my feet to the ground and pull the brake on my wheelchair.

"What are you doing?" she asks, looking behind her to make sure I'm not doing something I shouldn't, which I am.

I use the handle of my chair just enough to get my knees to straighten out so I can stand upright. Once I'm up, I'm steady. "Could I—"

She's staring up at me with curiosity and hope and what I imagine to be love because my heart is telling me to hold her closer, in my arms, right where she's supposed to be. I wrap my free arm around her back and ease her against me. I rest my cheek against the top of her head and close my eyes.

I see her lips—I stared at them for a long moment once upon a time, before I realized I couldn't stop myself. Her cheek was damp from the sudden rainstorm, but she was warm and sent sparks shooting through my body. I told her—I told her...

"I remember our first kiss. I compared you to a song—one I would sing over and over to recall that perfect moment," I whisper in her ear.

She pulls away but doesn't let go of me, staring up into my eyes, her breaths hard and heavy. She rests her hand on my cheek and presses up on her toes then, her lips brushing against mine.

She's part of me—inside of my heart. If I lose her, I don't know if I'll still be myself. It's hard to breathe as I pull her closer, and kiss her harder, desperate to remember this moment and never forget.

We both tug away for a breath, our chests heaving against each other's.

I cup her cheek and murmur, "I do love you. I need you. You're the missing piece to the broken parts of me."

Tears fill Ella's eyes. "I didn't think I could cry ever again, but my heart—it's been aching for you for so long. I sing myself to sleep every night with a song you wrote for me—I've kept you with me that way. I can always hear you if I need a reminder that you're with me."

Tears fill my eyes, too. "Will you sing it to me?"

A quiet, sweet hum utters against my ear as she sings to me:

> *The sky is dark and gray*
> *but behind the clouds, it's blue.*
> *Lovely days will come*
> *soon for me and you.*

The melody wraps around me like a blanket of comfort and safety. And then it happens—a memory, so clear and vivid. The two of us talking about forever, a swing beneath a tree, stars covering the sky over our farm, our quiet, peaceful place to call our own. The song she's singing comes back to me all at once, filling my soul. I interrupt her with a whisper, my voice joining hers:

> *Keep me in your dreams,*
> *and I'll come to you each night.*
> *Hold me in your arms*
> *until the morning light.*

Ella's voice falters, her breath catching on the last word as she presses her cheek to my chest. "You remember the words," she says, as a tear falls to my arm.

"I do remember," I tell her, my voice cracking. "I remember you, my darling Ella, and now I know you're a beautiful singer, too."

"No, no I'm not," she says, her breath catching in her throat.

"Don't be so humble," I tell her, words that fire through me as a memory of one of our first conversations.

"Humble," she whispers, closing her eyes and smiling.

The melody lingers in the air as I hold her, swaying back and forth. The music between us, it's a bridge of the past and future, leading us to a fresh beginning—the life we fought for, a love worth living for, and hope that will never die. From the moment I laid eyes on her, I knew she would be the reason I would keep breathing and searching for the sun in the sky. She saved me the first day she saw me, and she kept on saving me—against all odds. No matter the risk.

For her, I would fight any battle, like she's done for me. In my heart, I always knew that one day, our love would be strong enough to pull us back together. To survive for.

The Beginning.

A LETTER FROM SHARI

Dear reader,

I'm thrilled you chose to read *The Singer Behind the Wire*. There's nothing I love more than sharing my books with readers from all over the world. If you would like to keep up to date with all my latest releases, just sign up at the following link. Your email address will never be shared, and you can unsubscribe at any time.

www.bookouture.com/shari-j-ryan

I have a profound interest in the way of life and humanity during World War II, a topic with endless lessons and understanding. I'm passionate about bringing these unique stories, based on true accounts, to preserve a history we must never forget. My focus on the Holocaust stems from my Jewish heritage and upbringing. As a descendant of two Holocaust survivors, I'm deeply committed to providing accurate details through extensive research, including firsthand accounts I've been fortunate to receive. While the subject matter is heavy, I believe that the opportunity to educate through my books strengthens me as a writer and allows me to honor my family's legacy.

I truly hope you enjoyed the book, and if so, I would be very appreciative if you could write a review. Since the feedback from readers helps me grow as a writer, I would love to hear what you think, and it makes such a difference helping new readers to discover one of my books for the first time.

There's no greater pleasure than hearing from my readers—you can get in touch on my Facebook page, Instagram, Goodreads or my website.

Thank you for reading!

Shari

www.sharijryan.com

 facebook.com/authorsharijryan

x.com/sharijryan

 instagram.com/authorsharijryan

ACKNOWLEDGMENTS

The Singer Behind the Wire was another remarkable journey within my writing career—one that will stay with me forever.

I'd like to thank Bookouture for being an exceptional publisher—the professionalism, generosity, and hard work is something I appreciate with every exchange of communication. I'm thankful to be a part of such an incredible team.

Lucy, working with you is such a delight and I couldn't be more fortunate to continue learning from you with each book we work on together. You are incredibly brilliant, which is a tremendous help to me while crafting each book. I'm beyond grateful for the opportunity to work with you.

Linda, thank you for everything—for always encouraging me to be true to myself. Our friendship means the world the world to me!

Tracey, Gabby, and Elaine—thank you for sticking by my side and being my sounding board. I'm grateful for the time and support you offer me, but mostly, your friendship.

To the wonderful bloggers, influencers, and readers: There isn't a better industry to be a part of than this one with you. Thank you for your endless support and encouragement.

Lori, the best little sister in the universe. Thank you for always being my number one reader and my very best friend in the whole universe. Love you!

My parents—Mom, Dad, Mark, and Ev—to know how deeply you love and support me daily continues to give me the motivation to keep going and reaching higher. I'm a lucky girl! I love you all.

Bryce and Brayden—my amazing sons—I love watching you follow in my footsteps with the way you've learned to write. To know you've chosen to express your thoughts through beautiful words will forever make me proud. You both continue to inspire me every day, and I love you so much.

Josh, a manuscript doesn't leave my hands before I've taken a minute to appreciate the support you continuously offer me. I'll continue to remind you that you are the one who motivated me to begin this journey, and I'm surer than ever that I couldn't have done any of this without you by my side. I love you so much!

PUBLISHING TEAM

Turning a manuscript into a book requires the efforts of many people. The publishing team at Bookouture would like to acknowledge everyone who contributed to this publication.

Audio
Alba Proko
Sinead O'Connor
Melissa Tran

Commercial
Lauren Morrissette
Hannah Richmond
Imogen Allport

Cover design
Eileen Carey

Data and analysis
Mark Alder
Mohamed Bussuri

Editorial
Lucy Frederick
Sinead O'Connor

Copyeditor
Shirley Khan

Proofreader
Tom Feltham

Marketing
Alex Crow
Melanie Price
Occy Carr
Cíara Rosney
Martyna Młynarska

Operations and distribution
Marina Valles
Stephanie Straub
Joe Morris

Production
Hannah Snetsinger
Mandy Kullar
Ria Clare
Nadia Michael

Publicity
Kim Nash
Noelle Holten
Jess Readett
Sarah Hardy

Rights and contracts
Peta Nightingale
Richard King
Saidah Graham